COLD

OUT OF THE BOX
Book 24

Robert J. Crane

COLD
Out of the Box, Book 24

Robert J. Crane

1st Edition

Prologue

It wasn't going to be easy to kill the Governor of Louisiana, but Brianna Glover was damned sure going to get it done.

How? Well, that was the trick, wasn't it? A simple bullet might do it, but making it simple wasn't necessarily in her best interest. It boiled down to a few choices, which she coldly assessed. Handgun or shotgun, up close?

Tough. Bodyguards loomed, always, around Governor Ivan Warrington, Louisiana State Police officers sworn to protect him. Could she knock them aside before someone drew a gun and blasted her? Maybe. But maybe not, and Brianna wasn't much for taking chances. Not for this.

Distance was her friend, she decided, viewing the objective as dispassionately as possible. It was a job to be done, and done as swiftly as could be reasonably accomplished. Planning was required, she decided, and once that was settled, the plan commenced in earnest.

The gun would be a rifle. That gave her distance, and less worry about bodyguards interfering.

A high-caliber weapon, too, to allow for a greater distance. Practice would be her aid—relentless, drilling practice, taking the skills she'd learned in her youth and applying them to shooting. It was perfect, right up her alley.

She finally settled on a .50 BMG round as her optimal choice for this shot. It would kick back on her shoulder like a pissed-off mule, but snipers were hitting targets with them in Afghanistan and Iraq from miles away.

That was, she decided, too cold even for her purposes. She'd do it closer than miles, in New Orleans, with the backdrop of the city to help hide her, and the crowds to blend into so she could escape once it was done. Not the capital, Baton Rouge, where Warrington lived, where he spent most of his time. She'd do it away from "home," as it were. Let him die off his own turf.

So she had decided it—New Orleans. With a rifle. At a distance of a little over a third of a mile.

Beyond the bodyguards. Past the crowds.

With one eye pressed to her scope, Brianna Glover would watch Ivan Warrington die.

*

On the governor's online calendar it listed the event in simple terms: Canal Street Ferry Rededication. October 26th, 9:00 AM.

In the local press it was covered with somewhat more glowing terms: GOVERNOR WARRINGTON TO REDEDICATE ALGIERS FERRY; PRICE DROP BACK TO FREE IN MOVE TO AID RESIDENTS.

That was the place, that was the time. Taking a room in a hotel tower a third of a mile away on Canal Street, Brianna started to prepare. She could have picked a closer tower, a closer building. Harrah's maybe.

She didn't need a closer building.

A third of a mile. Nineteen hundred or so feet as she'd calculated it—as the crow flew, anyway. She was on the fortieth floor, which added a third dimension of measurement to the calculation.

No matter. A hundred rounds a day, standard .50 BMG, for the weeks leading up to the big event. Then, in the week before, she changed it up, switching to her specially prepared rounds. They worked perfectly, adding a little signature to her plan. Was it, strictly speaking, necessary?

Perhaps not, she assessed again, with a dispassionate eye. But it would add a twist that would plague the investigators after the fact, and she liked that idea for more reasons than one.

So she practiced until the big day, and slept barely a wink in her hotel bed, rising at 5 AM, four hours before it would happen.

There were things that needed to be done, after all. She'd slept poorly, mind focused on the events ahead. Already planning.

First, she hung the DO NOT DISTURB sign on her hotel room door. It wouldn't do to have her in the middle of preparations—at any level—and have a maid come walking in.

She assembled the rifle from its component pieces by the soft glow of the desk lamp. She'd broken it down and put it together a thousand times in practice, it felt like. In reality it was probably a couple hundred; every day when she started her practice out at the old plantation she'd assemble it. When done, she'd break it down again. Every time, for months and weeks and however long it had taken to plan.

It wasn't difficult now. She only broke it down so that it didn't look suspicious in her golf bag, wasn't obviously a gun, and hid below the top level of the bag, buried among the three woods and nine irons placed in there for cover.

When it was fully assembled, she stuck it back in the golf bag, covering the barrel with a golf club cover. It didn't look quite right, but it didn't need to. It just needed to pass in case some overly ambitious maid decided to clean her room while she was gone to get breakfast.

The Ruby Slipper was a brunch and breakfast place just down Magazine Street. Brianna tried not to find dark amusement in the name of the street, and mostly succeeded. She bypassed the more complex gastronomical experiments on the menu in favor of a basic southern breakfast of eggs, grits, bacon and a biscuit. She ate about half of it, then went back to her hotel room.

When she stepped inside, all was as she'd left it. It was almost eight o'clock, an hour to showtime, and now she checked everything once more.

It was all ready.

The cooler at her feet had drawn an amused look from a bellboy who'd wanted to carry her things for her. She hadn't smiled as she'd said no, and he'd made a comment about her wanting to BYOB for the LSU game. Brianna just nodded. She was wearing a wig, and trying not to draw much attention. That'd be important to her getaway.

She'd booked several rooms in the hotel, and had an entire suitcase dedicated to changes of clothing, wigs, identity, things to make it possible for her to check in as many times as necessary to make sure she ended up with a room that had a perfect angle for the shot.

It only took the one, fortunately. Luck broke in her favor, as though destiny itself were handing her this opportunity.

She used a spotting scope next to her rifle's position to acquire the target. The crowds bustled before the ferry terminal—reporters, spectators, politicians who'd been involved in the legislation to re-open the ferry for free. They milled and buzzed, soundlessly, before the terminal, as she watched through her scope.

There he was, right on time.

Always right on time.

He came out of the ferry terminal, had been brought in from a rear entrance. She'd done a little legwork to decide how he'd get there this morning, and it looked like she'd guessed right. Louisiana State Police surrounded him, his bald head shining under the early morning sun.

It took every ounce of her self-control not to take the shot now. She was glad she was at this distance. She wouldn't have to hear a dull word of it this way.

Brianna pressed her finger against the room window, concentrating. A thick block of frost formed over the glass from her palm, and she held it there for a moment, bonding it around her hand, a solid piece of ice. With her other hand she formed a nail of ice, precise, controlled, to a tiny point, smaller than the needle on a record player. She applied it to the window in an ovoid pattern, making sure she cut enough room for the scope. Didn't need her shot being skewed by looking through the pane.

Once she'd gently cut into the window, she pulled the cut piece of glass, now bonded to her hand by a thick piece of ice, and dissolved the ice, casting it aside. It left her a foot-high ovoid cut out of the window to slide her scope and gun out.

Perfect.

She didn't slide the gun out just yet, though. That was the last thing she'd do when she was ready, just in case someone saw. A hole in the window on the 40th floor was a barely noticeable thing. A gun sticking out tended to attract more attention.

She focused in with the spotting scope. At this distance, using her metahuman sight along with the magnifying lenses, she could almost see the hairs between Warrington's eyebrows. Subtle, fine things, but they were there. She blinked a couple times to lubricate her eyes, then put aside the binoculars as he stopped his glad-handing and took his place behind the podium.

It was time.

She brought the rifle up, but didn't thrust it out the window. The barrel stopped about an inch short of the glass, and here it would rest, she decided, finding her natural, comfortable position. The stock was against her shoulder, eye just off the scope. She found her target through it, letting the light breeze blow through and gauging the direction.

Out of the west, less than five miles per hour. A nice tailwind for the bullet. She adjusted the scope almost without thinking. She'd been prepared for worse.

Drawing down, Brianna let out her breath. She didn't draw another.

Instead, she opened her eyes, finding her target through her scope.

With a careful hand, not losing her target, she reached into the cooler at the side of her desk and pulled out the bullet.

This was going to send a message.

Sliding it into the rifle, she closed the bolt, taking in one last breath…

Then let it go.

She opened her eyes again.

There he was.

Behind the podium.

Mouth open to speak.

To lie.

The safety clicked off with the ease of a simple snap.

She placed the crossed lines of the sight over his face—his smug, ugly face—

And stroked the trigger.

The crack of the shot was like a bomb had gone off in the room.

She'd forgotten her hearing protection—the earplugs, the muffs.

It felt as though she'd held her head underwater, the street sounds that had been so obvious a moment before—forty stories below—now gone as surely as if the world outside had died. As if all the cars had stopped. As if that second line band in the distance had quit playing.

Maybe they had. She wouldn't have heard it if they did, though, because her ears were ringing now, a loud, angry squeal that was going continuously in her head.

She moved to her binoculars, trying to shake off the painful feeling. She had to look. Had to confirm the kill.

Brianna looked through the lenses, trying to ignore the pain that the ringing was causing. She collected her thoughts, stared through the binoculars, saw—

Where the hell was he?

She looked again. He should have been crumpled behind the podium. There should have been swarms of people converging on him, there should have been *blood*—

There was no blood.

No sign of *him*.

Where the hell had he gone?

She stared, but only for another moment. Either she'd gotten him and they'd dragged him away. Or—

Brianna had missed.

"Impossible," she breathed. She'd practiced, trained, for—so long. This was her life, shooting.

She shook it off, head still ringing. There was a timetable to keep to—things that had to happen *now*.

Calmly, she packed away the rifle in the golf bag, throwing in the spotting scope, the last few things she hadn't packed before the shot—

How could she have missed?

—away in the suitcase, and rolled out the door less than two minutes after she'd fired—

She couldn't have missed. Couldn't have.

—wearing the disguise she'd had on when she'd checked in. Before the first police car rolled up outside, Brianna Glover was slipping out the back of the hotel and into the parking garage in the alley behind it. She almost bumped into a small Chinese lady as she passed, she was so lost in her own thoughts.

"Sorry," she muttered, turning her head and hustling to her car. She needed to move. She'd be across Pontchartrain shortly, out to Slidell before they even got the investigation rolling. She'd ditch this car and disguise where no one would ever find either of them.

Then she'd settle back to watch the news, because she had to have hit him.

But as she clutched the steering wheel and turned south onto Magazine, the first stirring of doubt crept into her mind.

What if she'd missed?

Well…

"I'll just have to shoot him again," she said to the empty car as she turned onto the crowded avenue. "And next time…I won't miss."

1.

Sienna

"When you said, 'It's good to be back,'" Dr. Charmaine Kashani said, looking down at her notepad, her jet-black hair smoothed over the heavy shoulder pads under her suit, her dark skin a perfect contrast to the beige walls behind her, "how did that make you feel?" She shifted her deep brown eyes up to look right into mine, furrowing her brow slightly in concern.

"Just absolutely effing grand," I said, blowing air between my lips soundlessly before letting loose my reply. "The way one should feel when being basically blackmailed into a deal involving working for the government in order to stay out of jail." My fingers tapped a steady rhythm against the soft black cotton of my dress pants. I tugged at the collar of my suit jacket, which made me feel like I was going to spontaneously combust from the heaviness and the heat it kept in. It also kept the gun on my hip hidden from the public, which was probably a plus given my reputation for killing people.

"I get the feeling you are not being sincere," Dr. Kashani said, pursing her own lips in concern, either faux or real. It was hard to get a pulse on her.

"I'm probably not," I said. "Let's just plan on that. Every word I say is a lie."

She tilted her head and barely smiled. "What is your name?"

"Charles 'The Hammer' Martel."

"Well, you probably got the middle part right, at least," she said, sighing and looking back down at her pad. "I can understand you might not want to participate in these sessions—"

"No, I'm so excited to be here. Next week I'll bring brownies, I swear. Love these dish sessions. They feel kinda one-way, though, with the dishing."

"Ms. Nealon," Dr. Kashani said, putting a *very serious* look on, "surely you must realize that the FBI cannot employ you without being certain of your psychological stability."

"Given that a few months ago I took on an entire FBI task force composed of criminal metahumans, I'm fairly certain that is not true."

She brought the pen up to the corner of her mouth. "How did that encounter make you feel?"

I just blinked at her for a second. "Wonderful," I lied, not even bothering to hide it. "I felt just…so great, knowing my country wanted me dead. It was like an orgasm, but with more people involved than usual."

"You can't shock me," Dr. Kashani said, shaking her head almost sadly, a little smile on her lips. "I've examined serial killers, Ms. Nealon—"

"Amateurs compared to me, amirite?"

Dr. Kashani straightened in her chair. "In what way?"

"Body count, at least," I said.

"Is that something you take pride in?" Dr. Kashani asked, leaning forward. Credit to her—most people tend to lean back when they contemplate how many people I've killed.

"Way to box me in shamefully, Doc," I said, sitting back on the couch. It wasn't as comfy as the ones I conjured in my head for my ongoing sessions with Dr. Zollers. She lacked his more affable manner, too, as she tried to drill into my psyche by trying to put me at ease. "If I answer, 'Yes!' then I'm pretty sick, and if I answer, 'No', you take it as me hiding it, right?"

"The mere fact you brought it up suggests you're not hiding it," Dr. Kashani said, shrugging slightly. "Whether you're using it to deflect from other, less comfortable topics, well, that's a more interesting question, at least to me."

"Nice," I said, and offered nothing more.

"Why don't we talk about something a little less controversial?" Dr. Kashani asked.

"Politics?"

"Hardly." She crossed one leg over the other, her white pants flawless. "You mentioned that you feel 'blackmailed' into taking this job—"

"Because I was, quite literally, blackmailed into taking this job."

"Perhaps you might explain that to me."

I stared into her eyes. There was a lack of judgment there that most people might have really desired to see in a therapist. Hell, for all I knew, she wasn't judging me at all. Maybe she was totally cool with everything I'd ever done in my entire life, even if I laid it all out in front of her. But I wasn't likely to forget she worked for the FBI, not me, and that made this a hurdle I was crossing, not a chance to get long-buried secrets off my chest.

"Sure," I said, because why hold back? "It goes like this—the FBI Director said I should take the job or else, and I took the 'or else' to mean bad things would happen either to me or the people I love. Admittedly I've only been working here a few weeks, and my quickie version of the FBI academy at Quantico wasn't exactly complete, but based on my limited knowledge of the law, that's blackmail."

She stirred at the end of this, nodding. "It certainly sounds coercive. What do you plan to do about it?"

I shrugged again. "I plan to do the job."

"And that's it?" she asked, peering at me. She had one arm on her knee, and looked like she might just fall out of her seat. "You—the girl who just brought up your prodigious body count in a therapy session without prompting. You are just going to take this 'blackmail' lying down?"

I forced a smile. It wasn't hard. "See, here's the thing about me, Doc—you ever heard the story of Brer Rabbit and the briar patch?"

"I'm not familiar with that one."

"Well, let me give you the Cliff's Notes version and leave out all the racist overtones," I said. "Brer Rabbit gets captured by his mortal enemies, Brer Fox and Brer Bear, and they're trying to decide how best to kill him. And Brer Rabbit, not wanting to be killed, decides to employ a little reverse psychology. So, for every torture they float as a possibility for inflicting on him he says, basically, 'Go ahead and do that, just, whatever you do, don't throw me in that briar patch over there!'"

"I think I see where this is going."

"It's not terribly sophisticated," I said, "but the point is made—eventually Brer Bear and Brer Fox, neither of them the sharpest knives in the drawer, give in to their cruel nature and inflict upon Brer Rabbit the punishment that he seems to least want. Of course, he gives no actual damns about being thrown in the briar patch; it's like home for him."

"How very illustrative," Dr. Kashani said, nodding along. Her eyes met mine. "But I must ask—how does this metaphor tie to your current situation?"

My phone buzzed in my jacket pocket and I pulled it so fast that Dr. Kashani blinked at the speed at which it was in my hand. For her it was probably like it had just appeared.

A message glowed on the screen: NYPD Reports Metahuman Incident at Bentsen Bank, 50th and 8th.

"Isn't it obvious?" I made the phone disappear into my pocket with the same speed and was on my feet just as fast. "Sorry, Doc. Duty calls." I patted the pistol riding my hip as I smoothed my jacket back in place to cover it.

"Just so I understand you," Dr. Kashani said, calling out just as I reached the door. "Are you saying that this job, to you—it is your…'briar patch'?"

I smiled. "I'm going after criminals with the full sanction of the law, Doc." I drummed my hand against the door frame, once, and disappeared through. The hunt was on. "Where the hell else do you think I'd rather be?"

2.

Olivia Brackett

I could think of a lot of places I'd rather be than Minnesota in the late fall. Any one of a number of Caribbean islands came to mind (though I'd never been), maybe Southern California—even my native Florida, though there were some unpleasant memories associated with that one.

"What do you think they're talking about?" Tracy Brisco, his dark hair long around the sides but thin at the top, hung over the cubicle wall between us, looking down at me. I'd been working here first, but when he'd come along, malingering after Reed had brought him down from his prison in the sky, he'd settled into the cubicle next to mine for…some reason.

The muscles in my neck were tense, tautness flowing like an unbroken stream down my back, as though someone had knotted every one of them. I sat in my chair, trying to face my computer, parsing through a crime report from Nevada that had a couple funny things about it. I didn't dare look at Tracy. "No idea."

As far as replies went to his incessant inquiries, that was one of my longer ones.

"Who's the new lady, y'think?" Tracy asked.

I kept my head down, looking over a crime scene photo of a smashed-up convenience store. "I don't know."

Don't look, don't look. Don't feed him attention. I didn't know, anyway. Reed was in with some woman with red hair that had been dyed to hold back the grey, I suspected. Miranda was in there, too, and they'd been talking. No one was near his office door or they'd have been able to hear every word, given that we were all metahumans here.

"I don't like this," Tracy said. His attention was on the meeting in Reed's office. "The boss seems tense."

I gave him a sidelong look. He could notice that Reed seemed tense, but not notice that I'd been avoiding and stonewalling him every day for the last ten months? "You don't say."

"Have you noticed?" He stretched his large frame and stood, pretending to stretch against his cubicle wall but taking care not to rip it down with his meta strength. "Something's up."

I shook off his observation. This crime report looked like a meta to me, and I grabbed a pen out of the coffee-cup-turned-pen-holder on my desk to put that thought in writing. Whatever was going on with the boss was above my pay grade. My job was to stop metahumans from committing crimes, not monitor Reed's meeting schedule. "Whatever," I said under my breath, putting down the first words of my summary of findings.

"Why don't you just type that up in an email?" Tracy asked. He'd turned his overlarge head back to me and was hanging over the cubicle wall.

I gave an involuntary shudder. A lump rose in my throat, and my pulse quickened.

"Because I don't want to," I said, trying not to look up at him. Focus on what you're writing. Keep your breathing level easy.

My hand shook.

"He'll reply to an email faster than—" Tracy started.

The pen accidentally shot out of my fingers and launched right at Tracy's face. I watched it go with surprise as it blasted off like a missile, but lacking the fiery contrail. Propelled by my meta powers of momentum, it flew unerringly at his chest—

Where it lost all speed just an inch from his skin, barely tapping against his right pec, not even hard enough to click the retractable ball point. It fell and he caught it, offering it back to me. "That just keeps happening, huh?"

With you around, yes, I thought, heart hammering in my ears like a frenetic drum beat. I stared at the pen, extended in his fingers. He had dirt under his fingernails, which reminded me of—

Oh, God.

My breath.

I couldn't catch—

Thunder in my ears.

My chair shot from beneath me and crashed into the cubicle wall behind me. I ripped the yellow paper I'd been writing on from my pad. My note was unfinished: "Convenience store robbery in Paradise, Nevada"—and that was it.

"Hey, are you okay?" Tracy asked, still holding my pen out to me.

I waved a hand at him without looking and half-staggered my way to Reed's office, the yellow page crumpled in my fist.

With every step I took away from him, my heartbeat seemed to subside.

Every breath got easier.

By the time I'd reached Reed's office door, I felt almost—almost—in control of myself again.

I knocked carefully, breathing slowly. No need to risk triggering my powers and accidentally wrecking his door.

Again, I mean. Last time I'd accidentally crashed it closed so hard it launched the glass out of the window like a shotgun blast of glittering shards.

"Come in," Reed said, peering at me from behind his desk. Miranda and the red-headed lady were still sitting, and I opened the door to find all three of them staring at me.

"Sorry to interrupt," I said, my composure mostly returned. The moments like that, where I completely fell apart thanks to Tracy, had been blessedly few, but…

They seemed to be getting worse.

"It's fine," Reed said. He was propped back in his chair, lounging. He extended a hand to indicate the red-haired woman. Now that I was closer to her, I could see faint wrinkles around the edges of her eyes and mouth that suggested middle age. "Olivia Brackett, this is Ariadne Fraser.

Ariadne is…an old friend."

"Nice to meet you," I said as she stood to offer me her hand.

"Forgive me for not shaking. I have momentum powers, and I wouldn't want your hand to come shooting back at you."

"Or your entire body to go launching past Olivia at a hundred miles an hour," Reed said with a faint smile. "Which is how I met her." He flicked his gaze to me, and there was a lot of amusement in his eyes. "Jogging, wasn't it?"

"Yeah," I said, and suddenly I felt like my voice was scratchy, and my face had to be tomato red, from the heat in my cheeks. "Accident."

"Oh, well," Ariadne said, returning to her seat with a tight smile. "No, I wouldn't want that. Nice to meet you, though, Olivia."

"What's up?" Reed asked, attention back on me.

"Meta incident," I said, holding up the paper. "Vegas area. Trashed convenience store. Happened fast, according to the clerk. Not a normal human level of destruction."

"Why is it always the convenience stores?" Miranda asked, furrowing her brow as she looked up at me.

"Target of ease and convenience, if you'll pardon the pun," Reed said. "People see them as places that have cash, and they're small, one clerk usually, so it's easy to control as a scene. Try to imagine robbing a grocery store with its twenty lanes and all that real estate in the back of the store where people could be hiding. Convenience stores are small. Fewer places to hide, ambush you. Lower risk, lower reward. If you want to step up to more complexity, then there's banks. Not huge places, usually, but more money."

"Thanks for that fantastic insight into the criminal mind," Miranda said, making a clicking noise that reminded me of a gun chambering a round. "I always wondered about that."

"Crooks are usually not that bright on an intellectual level," Reed said, "but some criminals have a sort of preternatural sense about the cost-benefit analysis of their crimes. They follow the money and the ease, which produces mostly predictable crimes—and crime scenes."

"Well, here's one," I said, trying to draw the attention back to me. "What do you make of the vandalism?"

"Without seeing it? Nothing," Reed said, pulling his feet down off his desk to sit up. "Could just be fun for this crook. Or a genuine statement of rage. I'll take a look at the scene photos once this is over." He pointed a wavering finger between Ariadne and Miranda.

"Do you mind if I go on this one?" I asked, feeling a chafing urge to get the hell out of the office. I glanced back through the window and caught Tracy watching me. I suppressed a shudder and anchored my eyes back to Reed.

Reed's eyebrows had climbed a little bit up toward his hairline. He was wearing a ponytail today. When his face broke from the deep thought, he did a full-body shrug. "Sure. If you want. Book a flight. Commercial, though, no private plane. I'll see about sending someone from our West Coast groups to meet up with you."

"Why not Greg Vansen?" I asked. No private plane? That was new. But I'd worked with Greg a couple times. He was distant, professional, and damned useful, with his ability to shrink, grow, and carry just about everything you could need on his person.

"He's not officially on our payroll," Reed said, shifting uncomfortably in his chair, "and I don't think we'll be using his services anytime in the near future." He pursed his lips, then licked them. "Olivia…we're going to be moving into a period of…there's no easy way to say this…" He looked me right in the eyes. "We're tightening the belt."

"Oh," I said, blinking. That explained the lack of a private plane. "Okay."

"Hopefully it'll be temporary," Reed said. He blinked a couple times, glanced at Miranda, who shook her head. "What? I said 'hopefully.' We don't know yet." He centered his gaze back on me. "That's what Ariadne is here for."

"I'm sorry…are we…broke?" I asked, trying to get my head around what he'd just said.

"No, no, no," he said, shaking his head. "We're not…" There seemed a wrestling cavalcade of emotion warring its way across his face. "Well…we're not…yet."

"If you could keep this discussion to yourself," Miranda said, a little tightly, and with a sideways glare at Reed before she turned a forced smiled upon me, "that would be quite helpful as we go through this process. Ariadne is an outside auditor, and she's going to help us identify ways to make things flow a little more smoothly in the business side of this agency."

"Oh. Well. Okay," I said, nodding along. I caught a distinct hint of relief from Reed as I did so. "Can I ask who you're going to send along with me? From the West Coast group?"

"Who do you want to go with you?" Reed asked, and there was a hint of hesitation in how he asked it. I caught another suppressed glare from Miranda and wondered what prompted that. Their whole discussion seemed to be about money. Did that mean certain members of our group were paid lots more than others?

"Uhm…I don't know any of them that well, I guess." I tried to think about who worked the West Coast and the only two that came to mind were Kat Forrest and Veronika Acheron, neither of whom I had much experience with. Kat was famous but I'd never even bothered to watch her show. Veronika, I knew, but we weren't exactly friends.

Reed looked at Miranda. "Who's cheaper, Kat or Veronika?"

"Veronika is expensive," Miranda said under her breath. "She's one of the highest paid players on the roster."

I blinked at that. "Wait…you pay people different than—"

"Based on experience, yes," Reed said, looking deeply uncomfortable. "When you started with us—"

"Entry-level, yeah," I said, trying to stop him before he said something about how I was a babe in the woods before I'd joined them. And probably still. My cheeks heated up. "Makes total sense."

"Go ahead and book your flight," Reed said, forcing a smile of his own. "I'll get somebody out there with you."

"Okay," I said, and stood. I looked at Ariadne and remembered my manners. "It was nice to meet you."

"Nice to meet you, too," she said, with a very pleasant if subdued smile of her own.

"Oh, and Olivia?" Reed asked as I reached the door. "Try to keep the collateral damage to a minimum on this one?" He wore a slightly beseeching look. "Unless you can convince the Vegas authorities to take you on, I mean. Or Nevada state."

He gave it a moment's thought, eyes looking toward the ceiling. "Actually, I might just call ahead to Nevada and see if I can arrange that. I know some people in their state law enforcement apparatus that we've worked with in the past, and it'd be nice to arrange a payday for this one in advance."

"Whatever you say." I closed the door as quietly behind me as I could and headed back to my computer.

Tracy was waiting when I reached my cubicle, hanging over the edge, looking at me with anticipation. "How'd it go?"

I woke my computer with a brush of the mouse, my heart hammering in my ears. Was it from my conversation with Reed—and the revelations therein—or was it—

"Fine," I said, ignoring that thunder running through my veins as I steered my cursor to the navigation bar and typed in a travel website we used to book tickets.

Tracy kept hanging over the cubicle wall as I typed. "Vegas, huh? I'm jealous."

"I bet," I said, keeping my eyes on the screen, the tapping of my fingers against the keyboard speeding up into a maddened hammering as I tried to finish so I could get out of here, out of this place—

Away from *him*.

"Might be hot there," Tracy said, leaning casually over the edge of the cubicle. "You should pack accordingly. Maybe some swimwear? Get a little lounge time at the pool? Or," he snorted, "you could just wear a bikini down the street. You know you have the body for it."

Bile rose up in the back of my throat and I had to stop for a moment.

Tracy's guffaws were like the cawing of crows in my ear, sounds of a carrion bird circling the carcass that was me. I tried not to hear him, tried not to think about what he was saying.

I clicked when I saw the ACCEPT button had loaded, my tickets a step from being booked.

"Wish I was going with you," Tracy said as I felt my phone buzz with the confirmation email. I glanced at the screen to be sure, then stood, the rattle of my chair's flimsy wheels clacking like a train about to jump the tracks. I could smell fresh, peaty earth, even though there was none around. We were in an office, after all, not a swamp, like—

My chair shot from behind me, launching sideways at Tracy. He evinced only a moment of shock and caught it midair with a slight fumble. He stared at it, the thing's momentum killed inches from his body, because that was his power—counterbalancing my own.

Killing everything around me, stopping every move I could make, holding me still.

"Have a safe trip," he said, waving my chair as he leered at me. "Try not to break anything too valuable." He put it back on the ground and gave it a solid slide back into position under my desk. "Or they'll start calling you 'Olivia Wreck-it' around here, too."

That name.

I felt cold chills break across my back as I walked through the short tunnel out of the bullpen into the reception area.

'Olivia Wreck-it.'

That had been what Tracy and the others had called me back home. Back when—

"Going out?" Casey, the receptionist, asked, barely looking up from her magazine.

"On a mission," I said, slowing as I passed her desk.

"Oh, cool. Where?" She looked up from the pages of her article about—well, whatever.

"Vegas," I said.

"Cool," she said seriously. "Don't lose."

I stared at her, probably blankly.

"Money, you know?" She stared at me since I clearly wasn't getting it. "Gambling?"

"Right," I said, my heartbeat subsiding. I forced a weak laugh. "Thanks." I took a deep breath, and found I actually meant it. "Thank you."

"For what?" Casey asked, her thinly penciled eyebrows making a light V.

"Nothing," I said, trying to smile but failing, and I went for the door, just eager to get out of that damned, confining hell for a short while before I'd be forced—inevitably—to face Tracy again.

3.

Sienna

"Slay Queen!" someone shouted as I stepped out of Dr. Kashini's office onto West 72nd Street. Manhattan was alive around me, cars honking from the logjam backing up toward Central Park, baking in the afternoon sun as they waited their turn to get the hell off this backed-up road onto—presumably—another backed-up road. At least that had been my experience in the month or so I'd lived in New York City.

Since the FBI had pushed me to move to New York City.

I ignored the call of "Slay Queen!" which was immediately taken up by a few more millennials walking down the street. It was a weird reaction, but one I was getting pretty familiar with the longer I lived here. I suppressed the eyeroll tendency, gave a vague nod in the direction of the shouts, and checked my phone for the status of my Uber. It was two streets and five minutes away.

"Damn," I muttered, and broke into a run, meta-speed. There were times when I really missed flying. And also times when I wished I had *Spider-Man* powers, or at least his web-shooters. This was one of them. The lack of uniformity to building heights meant that even if I scaled one and tried to leap rooftop to rooftop, I'd inevitably run into trouble within a block or two.

So, I ran down the sidewalk at a hard sprint, shouting, "S'cuse me!" and "Move!" amid shout-backs of "Slay Queen!"

and a real, constant effort not to smack the people who shouted that at me.

I met my Uber at the corner of 71st and Amsterdam, and he looked surprised when I jumped into the back seat, slowing down out of my meta speed-blur just enough to avoid crashing into his Mazda or ripping his door off as I leapt in.

"Whoa!" he said, looking up from his phone, mounted on the dash, where he'd apparently been tracking my high-speed move to intercept him as he sat at a traffic light. He was a black dude, about forty-five, fifty, and he had very slight wrinkles around his eyes, and a full series of dreadlocks. He glanced at the phone, then back at me, eyes lighting up in recognition. "Slay Queen!" he shouted with great pleasure.

"Gurk," I said, making the sound deep in my throat. "Let's go." I waved at the light, which had just turned green.

"Yaaaaaassss, Slay Queen," he said, and thumped the accelerator, lurching us along as a cavalcade of horns sounded behind us at his refusal to leave the starting block after 0.3 seconds of the light turning green. Man, people in New York City were in a hurry. "Where you going today?"

I just stared at him, then lifted my phone.

He laughed. "Sorry. Drove cab for twenty years before I switched over to this. Old habits, you know?" He had a Caribbean accent.

I thought about my own old habit of killing people who annoyed me, and softened a little bit. "Yeah. I do."

"What are you doing in New York, Slay Queen?"

I sighed, deciding to not bother addressing my nickname, and how much it irked me. "Work." I flashed the FBI badge that hung on my belt. "I'm stationed in Midtown."

"That's fantastic." He looked at me in the mirror. "Protecting us all from the bad guys, yah?"

"Something like that," I said, and checked my phone. Five minutes since I'd gotten the initial text. I flipped to the map app. 22 blocks away. "You said you were a cabbie for twenty years. How long is it going to take to get there?"

"This time of day? By car?" He thought about it a second. "Twenty minutes, at least."

"And on foot?"

"Fifteen minutes running." He grinned. "For us normal folk, anyway."

"Damn," I said. "I gotta run it." His brow furrowed. "Like you said—bad guys. Doing bad stuff."

"Go get 'em—SLAY QUEEN!" He shouted the last part as I jumped out the back of his car after triggering the payment button and leaving him a tip. I pocketed my phone and shot past a woman in a pantsuit who let out a scream of surprise as I broke into meta speed.

"I really wish people wouldn't call me that," I said, almost under my breath, as I leapt over 70th and crossed onto Broadway, horns sounding either in surprise at my move or in annoyance at someone beneath me. I cleared the street without any trouble, nearly crashing into a couple pedestrians but veering off at the last second.

I caught a whiff of a bakery or something as I pounded south on Broadway. A few leaves drifted down as I passed under the trees growing out of the sidewalk planters, my momentum ripping them clear of where they had dangled, nearly ready to fall, on the branches above.

"Whoa!" a guy shouted as I blasted by, missing him by inches. He shouted some obscenity at me, and I buried the urge to turn back and bury him. I leapt the next street, and the one after, blurring past pedestrians at a flat sprint, and much faster than the logjammed traffic to my left.

I had things to do, the day to save. Someone swore at me as I nearly knocked him over with the blast of wind that followed in my wake.

I didn't have time to smash some dude's nose up into his brain pan just because he got rude with me—no matter how much I might want to.

I leapt another intersection, feet pinwheeling, car horns blaring, and did a pinpoint landing atop the street light at the corner, then bounced off the facade of the building to my right to extend my jump before coming down thirty, forty feet ahead.

I pulled up my phone, keeping one eye on the pedestrians, the wisest of whom were throwing themselves out of my way as I shot down the sidewalk at the speed of a heedless, fearless moped (about thirty, maybe forty miles an hour), and the dumbest of whom were, well…

They were New Yorkers. The dumbest of them had their headphones in and were looking at their phones. Twelve of them per block nearly died as I blew past them, my approach barely registering until I'd nearly knocked them over just by virtue of passing close as I threaded between them on my way up the sidewalk.

I hooked around, following the roundabout at Columbus Circle. I slapped a light post with my hand, causing it to ring like a bell. Part of my move was simple momentum control; the other was an attempt to get the jaded, sleeping denizens of New York to wake the hell up and realize that the SLAY QUEEN (DAMMIT) was coming their way like a storm. I shot down 8th Avenue amid a flurry of shouts and honking.

Another few blocks and I could see the bank at the corner of 50th as I leapt the last intersection. NYPD cruisers were there in force, lights flashing, and the crowds surged in size as I drew closer, people gawking, pushed up against the police cordon.

"Move, people," I said, shoving my way through as gracefully as one could shove through a New York crowd. "Come on, come on," I said, losing patience as nobody moved, nobody looked. I was just another New Yorker, trying to get through.

There felt like a hum of bodies around me, so many heartbeats in close proximity, it was like my meta hearing started to pick them up as…well, a hum. I could smell them, too, this potpourri of human scents, feel them as I shoved past, being probably a little less gentle than I would have preferred.

"Slay Queen coming through!" a young Latino guy howled, grinning at me as he picked me out of the crowd. I shot him a look, one that was laced with irritation and appreciation, probably in about equal measure since I was still unsure what the hell to do with that particular sobriquet.

The crowd parted, though. I guess no one wanted to be slayed.

I ignored the murmurs and took advantage of the situation,

slipping through the aisle they made for me and ducking under the police tape as the NYPD officer manning the blockade nodded at me. "Lieutenant Church is in charge of the scene, ma'am." He pointed to a lady in a waist-length coat behind him, lingering behind a police cruiser that was parked as a barricade in front of the bank.

"Got it," I said, and plunged on toward Lieutenant Church. She was tall, a shade under six feet, ebon-skinned, and when I came up to her, she immediately looked down on my 5' 4" height with a raised eyebrow.

"Ms. Nealon," she said.

"What's the situation?" I asked, flashing my FBI credentials.

"Bank heist," she said curtly. "We've got eyes on two suspects, both wearing face masks. Guard pulled the silent alarm, and we set up a perimeter before they could alight."

"'Alight'?" I asked, frowning.

She ignored my questioning of her word power vocabulary and went on. "They have hostages."

I nodded. "Meta powers?"

She blinked, and her gaze cooled when it steadied on me. "I'm not sure."

I stared at her; she stared back. "Uh huh." I shook my head. "All right. I'll clean this up for you."

"Thank you. Please be careful," she said.

I looked over the facade of the bank as I felt a slight tick of annoyance in the back of my head. I was new here, but I already knew that 'I'm not sure' was code for 'These aren't meta criminals, but we don't want to send in a SWAT team when we can use a superhero to end this standoff.' The NYPD was well aware I was in New York, and that I was perfectly willing to come running when they called, so it made sense they'd call as often as they could. "Curse me and my caring nature," I muttered as I looked over the building and found it lacking. "Entry points?"

"Front door, back door," she said. "Back door is wired. Bomb squad is twenty minutes out." I snapped a look at her and she shrugged, almost apologetically. "Traffic."

"New York," I muttered. "Okay." I looked up; it was about a four-story, five-story building, mid-century. Did they have central air and heat back then?

Only one way to find out.

I took off toward the corner of the building at a jog. The brick work had a rough, grey, protruding look to it.

"Do you need any help?" Church called after me.

"When shit starts to go down, clear your snipers to fire if they get a shot," I said.

"Those are not our current rules of engagement," she said. "We are to wait for—"

"Thanks for being useless," I said, slipping my fingers between the bricks. Yep, there was a recess of a half-inch between bricks, the mortar buried deep in the cracks and providing me enough space to stick my fingers between them. "I'll go solve your bank problem for you all by my lonesome, then." I muttered the last bit as I started to climb the facade.

The crowd started chanting as I climbed, reaching a hell of a crescendo about the time I got to the fourth floor. "Slay Queen! Slay Queen! Slay Queen!"

"Well," I said as I reached the roof and rolled over the edge, "I guess I could have a worse nickname." But I was hard-pressed to think of one as I started to look for my entry point.

4.

Queen's *Don't Stop Me Now* was playing in my head as I slid down inside a metal duct, trying to go slow and apply pressure lightly so as not to cause the steel encircling me to creak. It was tricky business, one that required excellent hearing and good reaction speed, because the moment the metal began to yield and produce noise, I had to adjust so I didn't give away the game.

As it turned out, this building had, indeed, been a beneficiary of the technology of central heat—and air conditioning. Thanks to that, I now I found myself on the first floor, enjoying just about the tightest squeeze of my hips since the last time I'd seen my boyfriend, Harry. Apparently, these air vents were not meant for girls with a little extra width.

Still, I was making it. I'd reached nearly the end of the vertical shaft, and now I was peering into the lateral darkness of the first floor's overhead vents. This was my exit, but from here it was going to get a lot more difficult. I needed to be extra quiet, and also not put too much weight on the metal below me, not only because it would creak, but because it might not support my weight. To end this long crawl by spilling out headfirst onto the bank floor would be embarrassing and potentially fatal. How much would it suck for the Slay Queen to go out that way?

A lot. It would suck a lot.

I crawled into the horizontal vent, elbows pressing against the sides. It was a hell of a workout keeping my body in perfect alignment. Core strength was important, and it made me realize that I would hate yoga if I ever tried it, not only because that level of muscle control came as naturally to me as breathing, but also because it would be even more boring than crawling the length of a metal tunnel without anything to look at but the darkness.

A voice wafted up to me from somewhere ahead. "What's going on out there, man?" I could see a thin shaft of light feeding into the vent. Ah-ha. The first air exchange on this floor.

I crawled up to it slowly, trying to make sure that my shining face wouldn't appear against the dark venting, giving away that I was sneaking in here.

As I got closer, I got a fuller view of the snaking line up to the teller counter. I was almost directly overlooking the table where people endorsed their checks before joining the forever march to get some customer service. The hostages were all sat down between the line posts, velvet rope separating them from the crooks, who were malingering about. There were three that I could see, and not one of them looked calm, though they were all wearing masks. Their body language hinted at extreme levels of agitation—pacing, twitching, raised voices. Hell, the voices themselves told me a lot about their state of mind.

"How are we gonna get out of here, Todd?" one of them asked the other, presumably the ringleader of this carnival of idiots.

"I don't know," Todd said, and he sounded like he was close to fainting.

The three I could see were all carrying AR-15-style rifles. Common as dirt these days, and tough to tell the model from this distance, though they didn't look particularly fancy. They all shot 5.56 NATO or .223 caliber bullets, and looked like they were loaded with 30-round mags. Damn.

Shuffling along the metal shaft, I barely dared to breathe, thinking how little fun it'd be to have them ventilate the duct while I was shimmying through it. That professional reputation that I'd worked so hard to build, all gone in an instant and a hail of gunfire.

Plus, I'd be dead. That'd be bad.

Ahead, I saw another vent and detoured around it as much as I could. In the distance, it looked like the ducting came to an end, this exchange feeding out over one final vent, this one in the bottom of the duct rather than the side like the previous two. When I reached it, I peered down into the darkened room below. Using my metahuman eyesight, I could tell there was a toilet and a sink, shadowy outlines showing through from the faint light coming in from beneath the door. Looked like it opened right out into the bank lobby where all the action was.

Perfect.

I fiddled with the vent until it popped loose, then slid it aside and dropped down, quiet as a mouse. I locked the door and took the opportunity to use the restroom, because it felt like an important thing to do before all hell broke loose. I could hear Todd and the rest of his moron gang talking out in the lobby as I did so; seemed the bathroom door wasn't all that insulated.

Even better.

Once done, I sighed, as loud as I could.

"What was that?" someone asked, muffled, out in the lobby.

I flushed the toilet and flipped on the light, locking the door as I did so. Then I went about the business of washing my hands, because hygiene is super important. I did it quick, but left the water running.

Footsteps stopped outside the door and someone hammered on it.

"Occupado!" I said, as chipper as I could. Now that my hands were dry, I drew my brand-new government-issue Glock 17 from my hip and put it down at my side as I pretended to keep washing my hands. I let my hair fall in front of my eyes. Not so much that I couldn't see, but enough to hide my famous face from immediate exposure.

The door rattled against its hinges as someone tried to kick it down and failed due to their weakness.

"Hey, man, I said the bathroom is occupied," I shouted. "Wait your turn, hold your horses—or maybe stop holding your horses, depending on where you're holding them, because you seem just a little too excited—"

The door rocked on its hinges again, and I kept watch in the mirror, aiming the Glock blind through my armpit, barrel pushed against the back of my jacket. I'd prefer not to shoot over my shoulder, blind, but I could do it if necessary.

I had a better plan for how this would go, but trying to rely on the calm action of a criminal who was now trying to kick in a bathroom door…

Well, I was going to cover my bases no matter what, and if he came in here intending to drill me, he'd get drilled first, plan be damned.

The door rattled again, and I started to wonder if I'd have to unlock it for him, but the fourth time he managed to bust it open, to my relief probably as much as his.

"What the hell are you doing?" he asked, voice all tuned up from his exertions, but pride maybe a little restored now that he'd broken down the door. He sounded angry either way, but imagine how pissed he'd have been if I'd actually had to unlock it for him.

"It's a bathroom," I said, pretending to run my hands under the water again, not even looking up to dignify his stupid-ass question with my attention. "So, clearly, I'm having a barbecue. The suckling pig will be ready in about twelve hours, though, because it's a slow roast—"

I was watching his trigger finger for movement in the mirror through the strands of hair over my eyes. No action there, though; his face was ruddy and getting darker by the moment as he responded to my smartassery. He wore his AR with a strap across his body, but he clearly didn't know what he was doing with it. The safety was still on.

Apparently satisfied that the little smartass girl in front of him wasn't a threat, he let his AR hang in his right hand, which is no damned way to control that sort of weapon. A pro could have done some magic with it one-handed. This guy? He'd be lucky if he managed to keep from shooting his own feet.

Rolling my eyes as he put a hand on my shoulder, I slapped my hand on his and yanked him as I whirled around, pulling up my Glock as I pirouetted. He was so off balance that he spun, and I grabbed the unsecured barrel of his AR, bringing it across his neck as I kicked his feet from beneath him. I put my Glock against his temple and whispered, "Shhhh." Then I rested my chin against his trapezius and said, "Hi, I'm Sienna. What's your name?"

It took him a second to work out the answer. "Collin."

"Let me spell something out for you, Collin, because you strike me as an idiot—your goose is cooked," I said, watching the half of his face I could see for a reaction while also keeping an eye on the bathroom door. No sign of bad guys beyond, but they'd surely arrive soon to see what was going on with Collin.

"You might have gotten me," Collin said, struggling to speak over the AR-15 pushing against his Adam's apple, "but Todd and Markos aren't going to go down that easily."

"You know who I am?" I tapped the barrel of the Glock against the side of his head and he flinched, because it wasn't a gentle tap. His back was pressed against me, and it might have been nice if I wasn't holding him against me while slightly choking him. With a gun at his head.

"Yeah," he finally said.

"After all the people I've killed, do you think your friends really worry me?" I asked, still keeping an eye on the lobby.

"They should," Collin said, and now he just seemed like he was bragging. "My boys are stone cold, hard mothaf—"

I took a step back and Collin dropped, deprived of me to hold him up. He choked, AR at his windpipe and struggling to get his feet back beneath him. My back was against the sink, and suddenly I regretted being so incautious about splashing water, because some of the residual I'd left on the counter soaked through the back of my jacket in seconds, chilling my ass.

"Let's try this again," I said, stepping forward so he could stand. I tightened my grip on the AR, and I could tell he was trying to fight it with the hand he had on the weapon's grip, but failing against my superior strength. "Your 'boys' are just that—boys. And probably chickenshits, and useless, if they're as bad with one of these things as you are." I waggled the AR barrel against his voice box and he made a gagging noise. "I, on the other hand, am a stone cold, hard motha—well, not what you were going to say, but you get the idea. The sentiment is the same, because I'm gonna make your mommas cry."

Collin tried to struggle against the AR barrel at his throat and failed, dismally. "You think you're so badass. You know what it takes to kill you?"

"No," I said, "I only know all the things people have tried to kill me with—and failed. Speaking of." I thumped him in the side of the head again and pushed the Glock barrel forward, covering the lobby in front of me as I used Collin as a shield. I slowly brought the gun around, making sure that Collin had to hold the AR off his throat with both hands lest he choke. I used his body as a defensive shield as I found my targets, both peering over the bank counter with their ARs pointed. "Hey, bitches."

"The hell is she doing here?" one of them—not Todd—asked.

"Todd," I said, looking at the other, "you're clearly the brains of this operation." I watched Todd's eyes widen as he realized I'd called him by name, and I smiled a little inside at discomfiting him. "Explain to him what I'm doing here."

"She's here to kill us, man," Todd said with a dawning horror.

"Yeah, I'm here to—"

Wait.

What?

"No, I'm not—" I started to say.

But it was too late.

The idiots—the absolute idiots—were already swinging their guns around to take aim. Rifles versus my Glock, maybe ten paces between us. They had the cover of a counter, I had the cover of Collin's body.

Shit.

Gunfire exploded through the bank as they opened up on me with everything they had.

5.

Olivia

"Fear of flying?" asked the solicitous, slightly rat-faced man in the business suit sitting next to me.

I gave him a glance and that was all, looking away after the bare minimum half-second of eye contact I felt like I could get away with. "Not really," I mumbled.

"You sure?" He cocked his head, trying to look me in the eyes, and I shifted in my seat—which was in the middle, sandwiching me between him and a lady who had her laptop out and was typing away as we awaited takeoff.

Maybe I just don't like you, I thought but didn't say. Instead I shook my head. Confining places, like being sandwiched between two people like this? They made me feel anxious, like someone had put a set of electric beaters in my innards and started them running.

"Hm," he said, looking at me for a few seconds more before turning to look down at his lap. He had a satchel and opened it up, removing a tablet and a pair of earphones. I let out a low sigh of relief that he'd finally decided to leave me alone. It had felt like forever, though the whole exchange had only taken thirty seconds.

I took a deep breath in through my nose and let it out through my mouth. I repeated that exercise as the flight attendant went through the steps before takeoff, the safety briefing, and finally, the lady next to me in the aisle seat put her computer away and closed her eyes. She didn't seem to notice the bumping as we took off.

There was a certain tension in my head already as we lifted off. I tried not to think about Tracy, or anything else that might make it worse—like Tracy—as I put my head back and imitated the woman next to me, closing my eyes and at least pretending to sleep.

"Something to drink?" one of the flight attendants asked, jarring me out of a light doze. She thrust a hand at me—

The pretzel bag she was holding crossed a little too close to the proximity field surrounding my body and launched out of her fingers like it had been blasted from a slingshot. It hit the guy next to me, engrossed in his movie, in the cheek.

"Ow!" He slapped his face, a great, stinging red welt already showing on his skin. "What the hell?"

I looked at him with wide eyes. "Oh, wow. Uhm."

"I am so sorry, sir," the flight attendant said, flushing bright red. "I don't know how that happened."

He picked up the pretzels, which had rebounded off his cheek to land in his lap, staring at the bag as though it were conspiring against him. "It's fine." He opened and closed his mouth experimentally, and I wondered how hard it had hit him. He popped the bag open and a puff of crushed pretzel powder bloomed out, stirring him into a coughing fit. "How…?"

"Here," the flight attendant said, reaching over me to hand him another bag, so apologetically. "Would you like something to drink?"

"Diet Coke," the man said, taking the offered pretzels.

The flight attendant fussed about the cart, hurriedly pouring him a drink, forgetting all about me. "Here you go," she said, trying to carefully lean past me to hand it to him.

I felt that little twist inside me again as she leaned a little too close. Her hand passed my face, only inches away—

The Diet Coke launched from her fingertips as if she'd thrown it, and he turned just in time to catch it head-on. It splattered, almost slow-mo, ice bouncing off his nose and eyelids, his lips puckered in displeasure as it splashed all over him. "What the f—"

"I am so sorry, sir," the flight attendant said, now flustered almost beyond coherence.

I was caught somewhere between a nervous twitter and mortification, but somehow, I managed to say nothing. I might have let out a little squeak, though.

"Napkins," he said, brown liquid just dripping down his face, spluttering his words as he tried to blink cola out of his eyes. His lap was filled with ice and Coke, and the bulkhead and window behind him was drenched. How had a small cupful of Diet Coke made that much of a mess?

The flight attendant, apparently trying to redeem herself for her last two errors, lunged at the cart, coming up with a handful of napkins a moment later. She turned to thrust them at him, once again crossing my body—

I swear I didn't mean to do it. It just happened.

The napkins flew out of her hand as though caught by a hundred-mile-an-hour gust. The dripping man disappeared behind them as they papered over him. A few strays fluttered around him like oversized confetti.

I put my hands over my mouth to suppress whatever came out. My eyes must have been as big as pie plates.

"I am so, so, sorry, sir," the flight attendant said, almost miming my reaction exactly. Her hands were over her mouth, too, and boy, did she look red.

The man, for his part, was completely covered by the napkins, and serene, as though he'd somehow died under them. When he finally spoke, it was muffled, a tone of surrender. "Just leave me alone."

The flight attendant looked like she wanted to say something to that, but no, she didn't dare, so she turned her attention to me. Still several shades of scarlet, she managed to stammer out, "Would you like some—"

"I'm fine, thanks," I said, waving her off as I tried to regain my composure. The lady in the aisle seat between us, who had woken up sometime between the first barrage of pretzels and the final papering, shook her head before the attendant even had a chance to say anything to her.

Dejected, the flight attendant popped the brakes on her cart and rolled it on, awfully quickly if I wasn't imagining it.

"Hey, slow down," the attendant on the other side of the cart said. Nope, wasn't imagining it.

"I am never going to fly this airline again," the man said. He was still covered in napkins, and Diet Coke had leaked through, the paper absorbing them as he reached up and mopped his brow. An eye appeared as he cleared a few of them off into a pile on his tray table. He tossed the napkins disgustedly. "I think she did that on purpose."

I nodded seriously, not daring to show anything I was thinking. I snatched up the in-flight magazine from the seat pocket in front of me and started reading an article about Bora Bora, which sounded like a better place to be right now than where I was, sitting next to some poor man who I'd just bombarded with pretzels, cola and napkins in turn. There was a pulsing beat of guilt running through my mind; I tried my best to ignore it.

The rest of the flight passed in unsurprising silence, and I read the magazine cover to cover. The touchdown was little more than a bump, the taxiing only took a few moments, and soon enough we were at the gate. The man next to me had crammed his napkins down in his airsickness bag and they sat on his lap, awaiting a pickup that had never come. The flight attendant had never returned to our row to collect them, or anything else from him, and his face was still red, and he looked like he was really simmering by now.

As soon as the fasten seatbelt sign went off, I sprang out of my seat and grabbed my bag, ready to get the hell off this plane before I caused any more trouble. Soon I'd be far, far from this humiliating scene, and no one would have to know what I'd done.

"Hey," the guy next to me said, and I turned just in time to see him reaching out to tap me on the shoulder.

"No, don't—" I started to say.

Too late.

His hand entered my personal bubble just as the rising tide of my panic at seeing him reaching out for me hit a spike. His hand shot back as though he'd just been burned, my momentum powers launching the back of his hand squarely into his nose, which crumpled and squirted blood onto his already sodden shirt.

He fell back into his seat, eyes squinting as though he were about to cry. "What the hell?"

I didn't even bother to say anything. The aisle in front of me had cleared, and the woman next to me was already hurrying out. I took one last look at him staring at me accusingly, as though I'd set fire to his crotch and doused him in gasoline, and shrugged, my face as red as though it were on fire.

Then I bailed out, hurrying up the clear aisle and not daring to look back. "Thanks for flying with us," a peppy attendant said—clearly not the one whose day I'd ruined.

"You're welcome," I said, bustling into the jet bridge before anyone else could say anything to me. Because what else could you say after something like that?

6.

Sienna

Gunfire rattled through my body like a hundred miniature seismic shocks. Sixty rounds of .223 went off at 155 decibels per round, sustained, which was roughly the volume of a jet engine taking off. Except penned into a concrete and glass bank.

That lobby rattled around me like an angry thunder god in my eardrums. I dragged Collin out of the door frame at the first shot, pushing him to the ground and plopping down on top of him, less to spare myself the impact of hitting the floor hard and more to save his life.

Probably. I mean, it didn't hurt that I spared myself from busting an elbow.

"Aughhhhhh!" Collin's scream was drowned under the staccato rip of bullets. Pieces of drywall and chips of wood showered us—well, mostly me, since I was atop him, my Glock pressed to the side of his head. He was so nonplussed I doubted he noticed the cool metal against his temple.

A sting at the top of my scalp made me squint my eyes and suck in a breath to try and subdue the pain. It was minor, but present, a little trickle of blood starting under my hair where shrapnel had punctured my skin. Todd and Not-Todd were at the stage of firing where their muzzles had climbed well above head level, their shots no longer a danger to me, Collin, or anyone on this floor.

I didn't hear the click when the first magazine ran dry, nor the second. In fact, I barely noticed that they'd stopped shooting, my hearing was so jacked up. A quick look up confirmed that, indeed, the ceiling above the bathroom door was completely shredded, the ceiling tiles missing massive chunks, the silvery ducting I'd come in through riddled with black, shadowy bullet holes.

"I'm…I think I'm shot," Collin said, a little muffled beneath my hearing damage. He writhed beneath me.

"No, you're not," I said, taking a quick assessment of my own body to make sure I hadn't taken a ricochet in the fracas. I listened for sounds of Todd and Not-Todd reloading, but I couldn't hear much beyond a prodigious ringing in my ears and a couple of whines from the hostages in the lobby. Whom I'd forgotten in all the excitement. Luckily, the shooting had been directed in almost the opposite direction from them. Hopefully none of the rounds over-penetrated through the walls into other buildings, though it seemed likely that the NYPD had evacuated the area inside the cordon.

"I've been shot by a high-powered rifle!" Collin said, touching his ears as he let out a soft moan.

I lifted myself off him and took a peek for myself, pushing my weight to my knees so I could straddle his back, and running my free hand over his torso and side. I found the "high-powered rifle" wound pretty quickly—it was a scratch on his right bicep from a stray splinter. "You've been grazed by a wood chip."

Collin stopped squirming. "Really?"

"Yes, really, you loser," I said. "And as an aside, if you don't want to get shot, maybe look into a different occupation than criminality, because it really raises your odds of catching lead. Moron." I grabbed him by the scruff of his neck and dragged him to his feet. "Todd, Not-Todd—" I raised my voice so they could hopefully hear me "—we need to talk, and quick, because the SWAT team is going to kick down that door in about ten seconds thanks to your dumbass antics."

"What?" Not-Todd asked, at the top of his lungs.

"I said if you don't listen to me, you're going to die." I shoved Collin at the wrecked door frame and raised my voice so they could have heard me out on the street. "The cops are going to bust down the door in seconds, so unless you want to be dead in the next sixty clock-ticks, throw out your weapons and put your hands behind your heads!"

"You'll just kill us anyway!" Todd shouted back. Maybe he wasn't the brains of the operation after all.

"I don't kill unarmed men, Todd," I said, hanging back behind Collin in case they'd reloaded. "But I'm coming out this door using your friend for cover in about five seconds, because I want this mess finished before the SWAT team comes in. If you're still holding a gun, I'll end you myself. If you're not, we can put an end to this peacefully, without the need for anyone's brains to leave their skulls."

"She's going to kill us when we put down our guns, man," Todd said over the ringing in my ears.

"No, I won't," I called back. "I work for the FBI. Do you know how much trouble we get in for shooting unarmed people? The paperwork alone takes days." I thought the better of my joke a moment after it left my mouth, but I'd never been particularly good at putting aside sarcasm, even when keeping it up might bite me in the ass. "Look, I could have drilled you both between the eyes before you even raised your guns. Instead, I let you shoot off sixty rounds of .223 inside a New York City bank. Does that sound like the action of someone who's trying to kill you?"

"No," Not-Todd answered a moment later, "that kinda sounds like something a nutcase would do, letting us shoot all around innocent people in a crowded place."

I let out a slow breath that no one but Collin could have heard. And he didn't, because he was probably near-deaf at this point. Might have felt it on his neck, though. "Yeah. When you say it like that, it does make me look a little bad. But you're still alive, and not shot through the head by me, so…maybe let's keep that winning trend alive? Along with you?"

"I'm throwing out my gun!" Not-Todd said, and a moment later an AR-15 clattered to the floor in front of me.

"Man, what are you doing?" Todd sounded a step away from panic.

"Declaring my body a bullet-free zone," Not-Todd said.

"Lace your hands behind your head, come out from behind the counter, get to your knees and cross your legs," I said.

"Way ahead of you," Not-Todd said, and I could tell by his voice that he'd already moved.

"Not your first rodeo, I see." I pushed Collin down to his knees, and he didn't resist. "Todd…time's almost up. Which is it going to be? Jail or the morgue?"

There was a long pause.

"Todd?" I called back.

"I'm thinking about it!" Todd called back, voice strained.

"Let us reason together, Todd—do you think you're going to be able to escape?" I asked, slipping cuffs around Collin's wrists. He let out a little moan of pain.

The answer came back after a couple seconds: "Maybe."

"How?" I tried to avoid scoffing. "They've got the back door blocked. They're out on the street. You are surrounded, dude. What are you going to do? Shoot your way out?"

No answer. Maybe he was thinking it over.

"You come out shooting, they're not going to be nice like me," I said. "They're going to shoot back with snipers you won't even see. They will paint the building's facade with your brains, and they won't even care. A dangerous criminal gets shot down in the streets? Talk about a dog-bites-man story. Tomorrow, no one but your momma will even know you died."

"And two days from now, she'll forget you," Not-Todd chimed in from where he was kneeling with his hands behind his head.

"Shut up, Steve!" Todd said.

"Come on, man, you know your mom is all about the gin. She'll be so drunk you'll be lucky if it gets through."

"Todd," I said, trying to work around Not-Todd's—I mean Steve's—unhelpful efforts to help me. "It doesn't have to end here. Not like this. You could have a lot of years in front of you. Good years. You know, after some time spent incarcerated, but still…good years. It doesn't have to happen like this. You don't think you're going to get away…do you?"

"No," Todd said, and now his voice had broken. He'd broken. The AR clattered out in front of me, and I rose, leaning out from behind the shattered wall with my Glock as Todd, hands behind his head, paraded out from behind the counter.

I dragged Collin out of the bathroom, leaving a trail in the drywall dust and wreckage where he swiffered the debris clean with his body as I put him down at Steve's feet. "Everybody okay over there?" I asked, surveying the hostages. They were huddled, some whimpering a little, but a quick round of nods reassured me that I'd successfully drawn all the ire—and the fire—of the three amigos, which meant no innocents had caught a bullet.

Yay, me.

"Scene clear!" I shouted, and waited for the door to come crashing in. It crashed in seconds later, and I waved for the hostages to go, and they did, leaving me with the three robbers as I waited for SWAT to come in. "Clear," I muttered, mostly for the benefit of myself, as I eyed the chewed-up ceiling and the spent bullet casings that littered the floor of the bank lobby like broken glass.

7.

"You know, it's not everyone I'd keep SWAT back for when I hear a bunch of rifles going off like fireworks on the fourth of July," NYPD Captain Allyn Welch said as I worked my jaw, trying to pop my ears to eliminate the ringing. "But you, you're special."

"Yay for me being special," I said, as one of my ears popped, the tinnitus departing as my metahuman healing ability cured that eardrum first. "Excuse me while I celebrate your pronouncement by eating some paste."

He let out a small guffaw. "Have I told you how much I missed you while you were on the other side of the law, Nealon? Because it's good to have you back in New York and not causing criminal havoc."

I gave him a raised eyebrow. "Yes, I can tell how much you love, miss and appreciate me by how often you dump your non-meta garbage on me."

"Hey, I never said *love*." He warily eyed the ceiling of the bank where the idiots had unloaded their ARs. "Though I'd move closer to that sentiment if you could keep the bad guys from unloading a metric ton of lead into my crime scenes. Somebody could have died."

"Yeah, but nobody did," I said. "And I worked very hard at that, I'll have you know."

He let out a begrudging grunt. "Yeah, I can tell by the lack of corpses. Don't think I don't appreciate that, but if we could strive for less chaos—"

"One thing at a time, champ," I said, turning my attention to the tinted window that looked out on the street. "I'm not a miracle worker, and I think we should all just be impressed with the progress I've made on not killing people. I feel like I deserve some positive reinforcement for that. Maybe a gift card to Quality Meats up on 58th, or a day off or something, I dunno."

"Were it within my power to grant both, know that I would," Welch said, miming a bow. "Unfortunately, my discretionary fund from the NYPD is—lemme check here—oh, right, zero dollars. And also, someone has to pay for this." He pointed at the ceiling.

"Insurance should cover it since I didn't do it myself," I said with a light shrug. "I employed a very light touch here, destruction-wise. To the tune of nothing. Again, be amazed."

"Oh, I am. Also, grateful."

"Glad someone is." My phone buzzed and I slid it out of my pocket. "Speaking of." I chucked a thumb at the door. "Gotta get back to the office. We cool here?"

"Yeah, I think it's under control," he said, and turned to look at the police cruisers out front, filled as they were with Todd and Steve. Collin had been taken to the emergency room already for his splinter. I expected they'd get him a band-aid and send his ass to jail. "And I know where to send the paperwork."

"Awesome," I said, glancing again at the text message waiting for me. "Because this doesn't look like it can wait."

"How's it feel having a boss again, Nealon?" he called after me, right as I was about to head out the door.

"How's it feel having a barbed wire enema, Welch?" I asked, shooting him my best sardonic look. He chuckled and mock-saluted, and I headed out onto the New York sidewalk, my Uber already on its way to carry me back to Midtown—and the FBI's brand-new office of Metahuman Law Enforcement.

8.

I walked into the FBI's office of Metahuman Law Enforcement like I owned the place, even though the boss's glass door did not say "Sienna Nealon," but rather, "Willis Shaw." Located in midtown Manhattan, it was kind of a hole in the wall, presumably because the General Services Administration of the US government didn't have anything opulent and amazing for us, and also probably because Congress was at war with President Richard Gondry, and this division was his brainchild.

If Gondry could be classified as having a brain. Seriously, for a former college professor, he was pretty dense in a lot of ways. Now that I'd finally met him, I understood why Harmon had written him off.

"Nealon," Willis Shaw called from the door of his office. Shaw was a black man in his fifties, a little overweight, belly hanging just a bit over his belt, which still had a gun on it, unlike my last FBI boss. Shaw had worked his way up to SAIC (Special Agent in Charge) of the Memphis office before receiving this "promotion."

"Bossy," I said, closing the door with care behind me. No point in blowing a hole in the budget we already didn't have.

Shaw did not look amused, but then, nothing about this assignment seemed amusing to him, I guessed. "Did you let the NYPD use you again?"

I shrugged. "The NYPD, the FBI, the Johns on the local corner—being used is being used; what do I care who does it? Besides, the NYPD is so much gentler than you guys. Not as gentle as the Johns, though. It's like they're afraid of something."

Shaw tightened up a little there. A nervous titter of laughter escaped from one of the cubicles off to the side of our minimal bullpen. I caught a glimpse of Kerry Hilton, one of our agents, looking down hurriedly. Hilton was all right. For an FBI agent.

"You let them, the NYPD will have you working the corners for the rest of your life," Shaw said, putting his hands on his broad hips.

"If I let them, why do you care?" I asked, for about the millionth time. Not because I didn't know the answer, but because I felt like if I passed a little hell in Shaw's direction, maybe he'd pass it up the chain to where it really belonged.

"Because it's not our jurisdiction, Nealon," he said, ticking off the points on his fingers; "because it's a liability every time you get involved in one of these fracases; because one day you're going to screw up and people are going to get killed—"

"Or maybe I'll keep someone from getting killed…?"

"That's not something we get credit for," Shaw said, his face closing down, the last flicker of neutrality dying as he switched over to pure irritation. "We get the shit, not the joy—you understand that, right?"

"All of the blame, none of the credit," I said. "I am familiar with that arrangement, having been a recipient of its largesse for much of my working life, yes."

"Keep the blame out of my fledgling office, then," Shaw said, and opened his door wider, beckoning me in. "Now come on. We have real work."

"'Real work'?" I slapped my hands to my face. "Amazing! I never get real work. What is it this time? A floor in need of mopping? A shower in need of re-grouting? Do I get to be a truck driver today?"

"I thought you were a hooker," came a voice from behind one of the cubicles. Xavier Holloway. Or as I call him, "Il Douche."

"I'm just doing what your momma taught me, Holloway," I called over at him as I crossed to Shaw's office.

"Nice one," Holloway said, his face darkened like a cloud.

He was mid-forties, steely-eyed, dark hair, probably good-looking if he wasn't such a prick. That soured his appearance. "She was a secretary."

"So, she took a lot of dick-take-tion is what you're saying?" I offered as I passed into Shaw's office.

Shaw slammed the door before Holloway could reply. I couldn't see him through the frosted glass, but I did say, loud enough it surely bled through, "That guy is a Grade-A asshole."

"He's a damned amateur at it compared to you, Nealon," Shaw said, planting his ass in the chair and nearly upending it because he was clearly a little aggravated at me. "Because you are a USDA Prime-Certified asshole."

I sat in the seat across from him without being asked. We were in a familiar pattern of antagonism by now; no point in remaining standing out of misplaced politeness. "Sorry you got stuck with asshole inspection duty. Maybe you can parlay that into a second career as a proctologist after you retire from government service?"

"Dicks and assholes," Shaw said, shaking his head. "Got a call from New Orleans."

I kept a straight face, but only barely. "About dicks and assholes? Must have been a hell of a call. Was there a lot of heavy breathing…?"

"What did I do in my entire career to deserve this…?" Shaw looked at the ceiling. No answer was forthcoming, which made sense, because ceiling tiles couldn't talk.

"I don't think anyone in this office did anything to 'deserve' being stuck here," I said. "Except maybe me. But I can't just take it lying down, so…lucky you, you get a fractional amount of the firehose of annoyance I'm letting off. Tough deal. But you seem like a tough guy, so…"

"If you don't like it here, why not quit?" Shaw asked, so seriously, looking me right in the eye.

"Can't."

"Bull," he said. "This is a volunteer organization, Nealon."

"I was 'voluntold.' Talk to Chalke about it."

That turned his face to stone. "The Director isn't taking my calls at present. And besides, the last thing I need on this detail is a burning, raging—"

"I'm cool as a cucumber sandwich, thanks. Which are gross, by the way. Not sure where the Brits got the idea that cucumbers were a vegetable you could build a sandwich around."

Shaw put his face into his hand. "You know why I'm upset with you?"

I feigned thinking it over. "Because you've become a bureaucrat, and bureaucrats are always thinking about how to kick up the minimal amount of fuss so that they can keep coasting…?"

That lit a fire in his eyes. "I ain't no bureaucrat."

I nodded. "Yeah. I crossed the line on that one. I'm sorry."

He blinked, head cocked. "You mean it?"

I shrugged. "Sure. I'm trying to be a general asshole, not a total one."

He made a face. "You're falling short in all regards."

"Well, geez, I'm not perfect."

He looked displeased bordering on disgusted, lips puckered out, then grabbed a slip of paper off his desk. "We've got a live one. And it's big."

"Ooh," I said, perking up. "New Orleans? I don't think I've been there before."

"Well, don't get too excited. It's not a paid vacation."

"Speak for yourself. I'm gonna paint the Big Sleazy red on the government's dime, and the only one who could stop me would have to be a bureaucrat."

His eyes narrowed. "Failing. In all regards."

"Sorry."

"Someone tried to assassinate the governor of Louisiana," Shaw said, holding up the piece of paper. As he waved it, I could read a few bullet points:

-Governor Ivan Warrington

-Hotel Fantaisie

-Metahuman suspect

-Ice?

"Ice?" I asked.

He glanced at the paper. "You can read that? My tiny scrawl? All the way over there?"

"Meta eyesight," I said, tapping my temple. "I could have read it up on 50th.. Save me an Uber next time."

"Felt like I needed to get you out of the NYPD's thrall. Who knows what they'd have you doing next, Supergirl Nancy Drew?"

"I feel I should warn you since we haven't had much of this kind of business roll through here," I said, very seriously, "I'm not much of an investigator, so I'm not sure the Nancy Drew title works."

"That's fine," Shaw said, and here a spark of amusement lit up his eyes. "Holloway's going with you. He's experienced."

"At being a giant jagoff, yes," I said. "You're really tying all your a-hole problems together and throwing them out the window in a bundle today, aren't you?"

Shaw smiled. "Yes. Yes, I am. It's going to be a beautiful week, I think."

"Why not send Hilton? She's…"

"Almost in love with you?"

"Pretty sure it's just a little crush."

"This is a serious one," Shaw said. "I need someone who's willing to check your freewheeling self until you start going by the book. Which I'm not hopeful about."

"My mom made me read a lot when I was a kid. I've lost my appetite for books, and going by them." I leaned forward. "But where the rubber meets the road…I'll get the job done."

"I hope so." He waved the paper at me. "Your flight is already booked. Leaves out of JFK in two hours."

"I really prefer to call it by its hipster name, Idlewild," I said, rising. "Anything else I need to know?" I took the note.

Shaw shrugged lackadaisically. "Stop the assassin?"

"That was implied," I said, glancing again at the paper. "They used ice?"

"An ice bullet," he said. "Did it from two thousand feet."

"The ice bullet is intriguing," I said. "The distance, less so. That's about 550-600 meters. A Canadian sniper made a kill from over 3,500 meters a couple years ago in Iraq. Missing makes it even less spectacular."

"It was a near miss, apparently," Shaw said. "The governor was delivering a speech and stepped aside for a second to grab a missing index card from his chief of staff. Bullet whizzed past his elbow, buried itself in the ground. By the time they extracted it, it had melted to a nub." He held his thumb and forefinger millimeters apart. "No forensics to speak of."

I frowned. "I could be wrong, but I think I heard once that it's physically impossible to make a bullet out of ice."

"It's supposed to be," Shaw said. "By conventional means. Frozen water is too brittle to resist the explosive forces applied to a bullet. Whatever was done to this particular bullet, it held up remarkably, impossibly well given it was shot out of a gun after being exposed to the extreme heat produced in the firing. Ergo..."

"The working thesis is a meta made it with ice powers," I said, glancing at the paper, even though it offered no new information.

"Bingo."

"All right, well, I'm on it," I said, heading for the door.

"I feel very reassured knowing that," Shaw called after me. "My bureaucratic heart can rest easy knowing that the loosest cannon I've ever worked with is on the case. It's so fortunate that the stakes are very low, too. Just a nice, easy assassination of a US governor to cope with." He dropped the sarcasm and went serious. "Make sure you stop this crazy before they actually succeed?"

"I'll do my best," I called back, heading for the door. I glanced over at Holloway's cube. He was already gone. Shaw must have told him about the assignment before I even arrived, and he cleared out before I could pigeonhole him about our game plan.

"I'll sleep real easy at night knowing you'll do 'your best,'" Shaw said. He was standing at his door, arms folded, sour again. Who could blame him? I was carrying the reputation with his department with me, after all. Maybe not something a bureaucrat would care about, but a career FBI agent who prided himself on getting the job done...

"You should," I said, looking back at him seriously. "Because my best always gets it done. Always. Take that one to the bank. Just not the one at 50th and 8th." I winked. And off I went, to pack and catch my flight and kick ass.

9.

Olivia

"Hey there, honey bunches," Veronika Acheron said as I made it into the baggage claim. I wasn't too surprised to see her here, though I'd yet to check my cell phone in the retreat from the plane to see if Reed had sent me an update. Flipping it off airplane mode yielded two texts from the boss—one confirming the Las Vegas Metro PD and state of Nevada were cool with hiring us for this job, the other confirming he had sent Veronika to meet me.

"Hi," I said, a little tautly. Hopefully working with her wouldn't be a tragic mismatch on Reed's part.

Veronika sidled over, her flawless suit complete with a skirt and black panty hose moving with her sway. She planted an arm around my shoulders and squeezed gently. "Don't worry, kiddo. I'm not holding a grudge for that Orlando thing. Much." And she let go, heading off toward the baggage carousels.

I followed after, a little tentatively. Was she serious or kidding? I didn't know her well enough to tell.

"I never meant for you to get hurt there," I said. I'd worked with Veronika a few times since then on bigger stuff, as part of a team—the Scotland trip, the Revelen, uh…sojourn? But in all that time, I'd never worked with her one on one.

"I'm sure you didn't," Veronika said, paying more attention to the luggage carousel in front of her, the sign proclaiming that it was delivering from Flight 3847, from San Francisco, than she was to me.

My phone buzzed. It was an address, and I realized it was the one for the convenience store that had been robbed, the one I'd looked into that had kicked this whole thing off. Reed had texted it to me. Had he thought I was too dumb to remember to take down the address before I caught my flight?

That lovely seed of doubt firmly planted in my mind, I moved off to collect my luggage at my own carousel. I saw the soaked guy from the plane across the way, and he shot me a dirty look but kept his distance. I just stared down at my phone and pretended not to see him.

When my bag showed up, I grabbed it, nearly launching out of my hand just before I picked it up. Once it was on the ground, I deployed the handle and started to reach for it—

"Lemme save you the trouble of accidentally sending that across the room, huh?" Veronika swept in and caught it, pulling it along behind her next to her bag. She headed for the taxi line.

I stared at her receding back—and my luggage—and hurried after. "You don't have to do that."

"Yeah, but I doubt Reed wants to pay for a new luggage carousel or replacement for the glass windows here, so..." She shrugged and kept wheeling.

"I don't break stuff like that...all the time," I said, blushing and giving up my protest about halfway through.

"Oh, but sweetcheeks, you do," Veronika said. "Don't make me count 'em for you, because your property damage is really through the roof. Or rather through the wall, usually."

"I don't...I mean..." I felt my face burn, but I kept following her out to the taxis.

We got in, the cabbie loaded our luggage and we were off. Veronika stayed silent, her heavy black glasses down over her eyes, Vegas sunshine reflecting off of them. She scanned her phone like I wasn't even there, and I pretended to do the same while I worried about two different things—whether Veronika had actually forgiven me for our run-in in Florida, and whether Reed was worrying I might destroy everything on this case. I didn't know which of those bothered me more, but they both were working on my nerves from different directions—the Veronika thing because she was inches away from me, the Reed thing a little more distantly but just as importantly, because he was my boss.

"Have you considered taking up blogging?" Veronika asked, looking up at me from behind those dark glasses. "I feel like you'd do well on Tumblr. You could look at cats, and reblog cat pictures that you liked. Maybe some videos, too."

"I…why do you say that?" I asked.

"Because you strike me as a person who needs that sort of soothing hobby in her life," Veronika said, looking at her phone. "I mean, I don't come to the office that much, but you're always there when I do. Like a gym rat in the locker room. And I think it's because you don't have anywhere else to go or anything else to do. So…Tumblr."

"I have…I mean, I could…" I did a little stuttering trying to come up with an answer to that. "I've been in Minneapolis less than a year. I don't really know anyone but my co-workers, so…"

"That's a good excuse." Veronika nodded along. "It even sounds reasonable, to the uninitiated."

"'Uninitiated'…?"

"I've been an excuse maker my whole life." Veronika was nodding along like she heard music. "Especially for my antisocial tendencies. See my thing? It's books. Coping mechanism. Whatever you want to call it. I'd rather be home reading. I have a huge…library." She smirked, and I got the feeling she was trying to put out a double entendre but swerved at the last second. I pretended not to get it, keeping my face stiff in concentration. "Anyway, I know what I want, and it's mostly to be left alone. Not always, but a lot. No bones about it, I just come out and say it, now. For years, I used excuses. And that's what you're doing. 'I don't have friends because I just moved to town a year ago.'" She leaned over and started to pat me on the knee but thought the better of it and pulled her hand back. "No, sweetie. You don't have friends because you are terrified of people the way I'm terrified of crying in public." She sat back in her seat, looking back out the front window.

"That's not...I'm not..." I spluttered. "I'm not terrified of people."

She just nodded.

"Here we are," the cabbie said, and suddenly I had a mortifying thought—he'd been listening to our whole conversation.

I wanted to crawl under the rear axle of the minivan and let him drive over me, but unfortunately that'd probably just result in me accidentally shooting his vehicle into low Earth orbit. Instead I blushed and bailed out the side door as Veronika went out the other.

"Keep the meter running and wait for us here," she said, pure command, no question. The cabbie nodded, but she was already off. He'd apparently gotten out to retrieve our luggage, but he halted and made a little salute to her, like they'd both joined the army.

That had been easy. If I'd been in charge of this, I'd have let him unload everything and tried to keep my luggage by my side as I examined a crime scene.

"You need some self-confidence, sweet cheeks," Veronika called as I trailed her, hurrying along.

We were in the parking lot of a sun-drenched convenience store, asphalt glaring as it reflected the desert heat at us. A couple Las Vegas cop cars were parked out front, officers just hanging by their vehicles, talking. They spared a glance at us as we approached, but neither said anything.

I felt a little sticky before I even made it halfway to the doors, a tiny trickle of sweat trying to work its way out at the small of my back and my armpits, which I squeezed tighter self-consciously to trap any escaping drops before they wetted my shirt.

Veronika tossed a look over her shoulder. "You'd move a little faster and smoother if you'd pull that giant metal pole out of your rectum before trying to walk." She cackled and kept going. I followed behind, mortified, as I caught a chuckle out of both the waiting LVPD officers.

She really did not give a single care about anything. I brushed a stray blond hair out of my eyes as I squinted against the horrifyingly bright desert sun and trailed a few more steps behind her as the convenience store doors swooshed open for her.

"I don't have a pole up my…anywhere," I muttered as she walked inside. A cool blast of air pushed that stray hair I'd just moved aside back over my eyes.

"Clearly for way too long," Veronika said as the doors swooshed closed behind her.

I almost walked right into the doors and stopped just in time to prevent my nose from colliding with the glass. "What the…?" I asked the doors.

Veronika waved a hand inside and the doors opened again. I slid inside as soon as they did, eyeing them as if they were possessed by a devil. She just lifted her sunglasses and rolled her eyes. "If that's not the perfect metaphor for your near-non-existence in the eyes of the entire world, I don't know what is. Come on." And off she went, toward a plainclothes officer standing by what had once been a soda fountain.

I took a look around the convenience store. I'd seen the crime scene photos the LVPD had put online, but it really didn't do this place justice. There were four or five long rows of shelves and every one of them had been overturned. Every single glass fridge and freezer case had been busted open, glass littering the floor like tiny diamonds, spreading from the back walls of the store all the way to the front. My shoes found them as I walked, a satisfying crunch issuing with my every step.

"Somebody had fun up in here," Veronika said, nonchalantly, as she walked up to the plainclothes detective.

The detective turned around, and I realize for the first time it was a she. Mid-thirties, a little stocky, she had her hair cropped tight around her head and was wearing a shirt and tie along with dress pants and shoes. I didn't quite know what to make of her attire so I didn't say anything. Her hand rested just above the pistol that rode on her waist, as though she were looking for an excuse to draw it. I didn't want to be that excuse.

"You must be Detective Norton," Veronika said.

"You must be Veronika Acheron," Norton said, looking Veronika up and down only once.

"This is my barnacle, Olivia Brackett," Veronika said, nodding to me. "Shhh. Don't talk, Brackett. Just listen."

"I…excuse me?" I looked at her as though she'd swung a punch at me. No, wait, if she'd done that, she'd have ended up bouncing off in the opposite direction. I looked at her as though she'd connected a punch on me, because that was a hell of a thing to say in front of a Las Vegas police detective.

"Shhh," Veronika said again. "Tell us something good, Norton."

"Not much good to be had here," Norton said, looking the place over casually. "What you see is what you get. Nothing on the surveillance cameras; clerk thought he had a poltergeist when stuff started blowing up and breaking and falling over. We were going to write it off as vandalism and an inside job until we saw the footage—which backs up the clerk's story."

"How much damage?" I asked, looking the place over. The only thing that wasn't trashed were the front windows, and I wondered why.

"Why? You looking to make it a competition with the crook? See who can cause the most property damage?" Veronika asked.

I couldn't form an answer to that, and Veronika laughed as Norton moved on.

"Place is a total loss," Norton said. "Doubt insurance will cover it, either."

Veronika nodded. "Acts of gods."

Norton clicked her tongue. "Yep. Sure looks meta to us. No motive. No suspects. No one harmed, on the plus side. We were about done with this one until we got your call. Not a lot more we can do, not for this kind of crime, y'know? Homicides and whatnot get precedence, and combing through this place for forensics when there wasn't even a gun used?" She just shook her head.

"All right, we'll take it from here," Veronika said, staring very intently at Detective Norton. "If we come up with anything, should I just call you directly?"

Norton looked right back at her, a little cool, then blushed. "Here's my card." She handed it to Veronika.

"Excellent," Veronika said, taking it and putting her body

between me and Norton as she did so. It felt like something else happened there, but I couldn't see it. "I'll be in touch."

"Sounds good," Norton said, and off she went, out the door, with a look thrown back at Veronika. I was completely ignored.

"Nice to meet you," I said, adding the appropriate amount of sarcasm, once the doors had slipped closed for her.

"If you had any balls, Brackett, you'd have said that before she walked out," Veronika said, looking at Norton's card before pocketing it.

I worked my jaw up and down for a second before saying, "Sorry."

Veronika shot me a hell of a look. "What the hell? Don't apologize. You have no testicles, and be proud, because it means you can use your brain. Stop it with this meek mouse shit, though. Say it, next time." She shook her head. "Now…let's go." And she went for the door, too.

"Wait, don't we need to look around first?" I asked, my feet suddenly frozen to the floor. "Check out the scene?"

She just shook her head, but didn't stop. "What do you see here, Brackett?"

I glanced around once. "Destruction…?"

"And…?"

"I dunno. Looks like a whirling dervish went through here." I felt a chuckle come on. "Or a Tasmanian dev—"

"Close enough, yeah," she said, and paused as the doors slid open and heat wafted in on the rays of the desert sun. "Chaos, destruction, nothing on camera." She stared at me through those black glasses as though I were missing something obvious. "Speedster."

I blinked. "Speedster…?"

She nodded, smiled, and then headed out. I followed behind, and the doors swooped shut once again, and I missed colliding with them by an inch.

"Damn," I muttered, waved a hand by the sensor up top, and they opened again. I hurried out into the heat to catch Veronika before she left without me.

10.

Sienna

"Thanks, I got this," I said as I shut my Uber driver's door. She waved, almost bursting in her seat, and popped her Prius's back hatch as I wandered around to get my bag. After I'd pulled it out, she shouted something practically unintelligible at me and I shut the hatch for her.

It had been a weird ride. She'd picked me up at my broom closet of a loft in midtown, and spent the first five minutes screaming in excitement at recognizing me, top of the lungs, "SLAY QUEEEEEEEEN!" about half the way to the midtown tunnel. After that it had been a steady babble of her entire bio, which I'd taken in with nodding and a blank stare, thankful I'd remembered my tinted sunglasses so I could look out the windshield while she assumed I was watching her every strange, emotive gyration. She'd talked the whole way to JFK International Airport, pausing only to send and receive a few texts "to her mom," she said.

It was only as I was about to walk through the doors into the Departures terminal that I realized she was stone-cold lying to me.

"Sienna," a male voice called from beside the doors. I found myself looking at a middle-aged dude with glasses that were bordering on horn-rimmed, which had come dangerously close to coming into style now that hipsters tried to make up for the lack of attention their parents paid them in childhood by having massive frames that could probably be seen from space.

"Oh, for crying out loud," I mumbled as I rolled my suitcase onward, through the doors. I knew him on sight.

"Hey, can I have a word?" he asked, following after me, a pad of paper in his hand as opposed to a cell phone. Most reporters I met were usually filming me the entire time. Clearly, he was a classicist.

"Sure," I said, not stopping as I entered the cavernous, open-air space and started seeking out my check-in desk. "How about 'garbanzo'?"

"Garbanzo?" he asked, clearly not getting it. "Like the bean?"

"Yes, like the bean," I said, finding my check-in desk but pausing, just for a second. "It's a good word, 'garbanzo', and now it's all yours, champ. Not like anyone else is using it."

"It's a real shame garbanzo beans have fallen out of favor." He picked up his pace to bring himself even with me, then took a breath like he'd had to really exert himself to do it. He probably had; he didn't look to be in peak shape, and I was faster than…well, almost everybody. "But that's not the word I'm looking for, and I think you know that."

"Look, Mike," I said, and his eyebrows shot up in surprise. "Yeah, I know who you are. Mike Darnell, formerly of the New York Times, now with flashfunk.net—"

"Flashforce."

"I'm not saying that, because to utter the name of that frivolous website is to give it free advertising that it not only doesn't deserve, but also lends credence to a place that has worked so very, very hard over the last few years to destroy its reputation of being the number one funny cat gif site on the internet. And also, me."

Mike suppressed a smile. "Look…everything you're saying is fair. Especially about the cat gifs. We should definitely go back to doing more of them. But at this point, I'm part of the serious, investigative news portion of the publication—"

"Do you hear yourself? Next thing you'll be telling me Buzzfeed has a serious news division."

Mike looked torn. "They do. Sort of. Sometimes. But that's

not the point—"

"The point is you're a serious guy who works on serious stories for a cat gif website," I said, keeping my eyes on the check-in line I was headed for. It wasn't too busy, yet, but if I saw a swell of people headed that way, I was going to pick up my suitcase and sprint to beat them into the line.

This time he managed to subdue his surprise. "If you know who I am on sight, then is it a stretch to imagine you've read my stories? About you?"

"You mean the only ones on flashfunk-dot-suck that weren't incredibly vicious hatchet jobs about me? Pre-Revelen, I mean." I raised an eyebrow and finally looked right at him. "Since Revelen, I practically have to pry your website's collective tongue off my lady parts. And, no, I haven't read any of your work, but my mom posts the links on my Facebook wall."

He paused, thinking as he watched me, evaluating my deadpan delivery before finally pronouncing, "Your mom is dead."

"See, this is why you're the best investigative reporter on flashfunk's staff, because you actually know that," I said. "Most of the ad pumping, slideshow-creating chair jockeys you work with have probably authored a piece at one time or another offering up such excellent options as Cruella de Vil and the Evil Queen as possible moms for me."

He cringed, ever so slightly. "I did see that one, and I'm sorry. Genuinely. I'm just a reporter and not an editor, but I wouldn't have run that piece."

"Look at you, the unsung hero of my life. Just don't expect me to start singing your praises now; I left my lute back at my shoebox of an apartment."

He launched right into the interview. "How's Manhattan treating you?"

"Like a toddler treats a diaper," I said, folding my arms in front of me.

His eyes bored into mine. "You don't like interviews."

"Not since that one I tried with Gail Roth, no," I said, smirking a little. "And on the advice of the FBI general counsel, whose judgment I defer to, I do not presently accept interview requests."

"You know what your problem was during all that mess you went through the last couple years, Nealon?"

"That the entire US government turned on me and tried to hunt me down?"

He smiled, just a little. "Yes, that was, indeed, your biggest problem. But just behind that was the fact that your story about how you didn't do any of the things you were accused of never made it out. At least until that video of the Eden Prairie event hit the web and went viral." He sidled one step closer, and I eyed him like any other threat. He didn't back off, and I didn't feel threatened, which is why his spine stayed intact and within his body. "Wouldn't it have been useful to have just one reporter in your Rolodex you could have called to set things straight? Someone who would have listened? Who would have looked into your story?"

I blinked a couple times. "Wow. This is the first time I've had a reporter admit that the news media didn't bother doing their jobs because they didn't like me."

"That's not what I said."

"No, it was implied, and I heard it loud and clear because I knew it as I lived it," I said. "You don't think I figured it out after two years? Almost the entire establishment media had people camped out on my office lawn, and that meant everybody in your little priestly caste of 'truth-defending crusaders' had a friend or a friend-of-a-friend there when things went down. That's a lot of people that caught up in that criminal meta's feral power, a lot of very *connected* people who suddenly had a compelling reason to hate the hell out of me. Couple that with a well-admired White House producing a toxic cloud of talking points about how evil I was, and you guys just went right to sleep for that story." I chuckled ruefully. "It must have been like a bomb going off in your offices when that video broke and you realized how wrong you'd been about me."

Credit to Darnell, he gave a nod and a shrug, no sign of contrition. "I tried to warn them. I wrote a dozen stories that argued the opposite of the conventional wisdom that was circulating. It went hard against the narrative, and like you said, everybody in my field had at least one friend who nearly died in Eden Prairie. That might have tilted the coverage against you somewhat. But again—wouldn't it be nice to have an outlet you could go to in order to set the story straight when we get it wrong?"

"And that's you, guy who didn't manage to get a story published defending me when I needed it?" I mimed a shrug. "If you couldn't do it last time the mob turned against me, what good are you going to be next time it happens?"

"Look, I didn't get anything through the editor last time, but I didn't write anything intentionally hostile, either," he said, turning real serious. "I'm a facts-first guy. I'll call it down the middle; you've done some really bad things in your time, things I consider to be very objectionable. You've been pardoned on most of them, but the fact remains—you've committed murder."

"And might again, very soon, if you keep leaning closer to me while wearing that cologne."

He smiled, then backed off a little. "I've heard meta senses are highly attuned."

"This isn't anything to do with them being highly attuned. Drakkar Noir just smells like ass water to me."

He chuckled. "The point remains—you are not a nice person."

"I'm perfectly nice; I just don't like your cologne. People love me." Someone shouted, "SLAY QUEEN!" from somewhere behind me and I chucked a thumb in that direction without looking. "See?"

"They love you for now," he said, taking another step back and peeling a card out of his pocket and offering it to me. "But you have this tendency to make a mess every now and again—"

"Geez, you wreck the Javits Center one time and all of New York suddenly thinks you're trouble."

"—so I wouldn't be surprised to see this hero worship fade," he said, nodding at me. He offered the card again. "I won't promise you favorable coverage. But I won't slant things against you just because everyone else starts to hate you again, either. I try to be fair in my stories, and base them on the facts."

"Keep your card," I said. "If I want to get ahold of you, I'll pull your contact info off flashfunkadelic-dot-douchery."

He just shook his head, still smiling, as he put his card away. "Sure you will."

"Oh, and by the way," I said, turning to leave him, "you might want to tell your Uber-driving source not to text and drive next time."

His eyes sparkled. "I'm sure I don't know what you're talking about—and I'd never reveal a source."

"I bet," I said, heading over to the line and getting in, snaking my way around the pylons until I reached the front. Holloway was there waiting, next in line, and I slowed as much as I possibly could, pretending to check my cell phone for nonexistent messages as I walked the last ten or so feet to him.

"Who was that?" Holloway asked, his suspicious eyes on Darnell, who was already on his way out the door. The old school reporter flagged down a yellow cab and hopped in, disappearing as it accelerated out of sight.

I looked up from my phone, right into Holloway's eyes, and tried my best imitation of shock. "You don't even recognize your own father? How unsurprising." And I went back to looking at my phone.

The attendant at the counter called, "Next!" and Holloway left me behind without another word. Hopefully I could avoid him at the security checkpoint, at the gate, maybe even on the plane.

Otherwise, the flight to New Orleans was really going to suck.

11.

Brianna Glover

How did I miss?

The question echoed in Brianna's mind, over and over, the quiet of her safe house outside Baton Rouge echoing around her. It hung like a pall, a funereal feel except the funeral wasn't happening—yet.

She'd set everything up perfectly. Practiced until she was flawless. Lined up her shot…

And missed, somehow. Governor Ivan Warrington was still alive.

Brianna rubbed her fingers against her palm. The sparkle of ice appeared in the darkness, forming a snowball out of the air's humidity. She tossed it up, felt the wet smack as it came back down. Hardened it there, solidified the water vapor into a crystalline structure, threw it up again.

It came down hard on her palm, solid now. Not a snowball anymore, it was a block of ice the size of a softball. Brianna had been good at softball, once upon a time. Long, long ago—or so it felt—before she'd honed in on a sport she liked better.

She bolted up out of bed as the ice came down. She caught it flawlessly, thoughtlessly as she rose, striding across the darkened room to her laptop in the kitchenette.

This safe house didn't feel safe now that she'd failed. She'd left little sign behind in her flight from New Orleans, but perhaps enough. She'd need to move again. She had a backup, and a backup to the backup. The plan was never to get caught, after all, and she'd certainly worked hard at making sure that she wouldn't—unless she wanted to.

She didn't want to. Not until the thing was done, and preferably not even then.

A touch of her finger against a button on the keyboard woke the laptop, and she lifted the screen from where it had been folded nearly closed. It made a tone, then came alive, no password necessary. She tapped the keys quickly as she activated the Virtual Private Network, then a private browser window, selecting the Governor's event schedule from the bookmarks—

NO EVENTS SCHEDULED.

Brianna leaned back and nearly fell off the stool, forgetting it didn't have a back. She caught herself in time.

He'd cancelled all his events?

Of course he had.

She squeezed her hand closed on the ice ball, and heard a crack.

Blinking, she looked down. It was shattered in her palm, broken into six, seven, eight pieces, perhaps. She didn't count because she didn't care, but it was an interesting metaphor for what she was going to do to Ivan Warrington.

"Cancelled," she muttered, looking at the screen. Well, that wouldn't last. Warrington was a glory hog; he'd show his face again in public before too long. Something quiet, probably, something low-key, but he'd be out there, collecting his kudos. He wouldn't be able to stay away.

And when he did, she'd be waiting, and looking through the scope at him. But this time she wouldn't miss.

12.

Sienna

The New Orleans airport reminded me of one I'd been to in Virginia Beach once upon a time—very old school, an almost sixties or seventies style of architecture but with updates to bring it a little closer to the modern world. I had no idea when it had actually been built, but that few-windows, utilitarian vibe hung off the place.

I strolled through to the baggage claim as I perused my messages. Only one text had come in while I'd been in flight, and it was from Shaw, directing me to meet up with a local FBI agent named Burkitt down at the baggage claim. Whoever he or she was, it seemed like Burkitt was going to be our chauffeur, at least for now.

Holloway had, to my extreme joy, been booked a good ten rows away from me on the flight, owing either to the last-minute nature of the booking, Shaw being wise enough to know we shouldn't be seated next to each other, or the universe in general looking out for me. Whichever it was, I was thankful, because it meant I didn't have to interact with him until after I'd retrieved my bag from the claim and he was still standing around waiting for his.

I checked my emails, even the spam folder, waiting for Holloway to get his damned bag, but the carousel ran dry and he was still waiting around, staring at the ramp where the luggage dumped out like he had heat vision and could see his suitcase waiting just beyond it. The carousel had stopped, and I was out of the things to do on my phone other than browse the comment sections of internet sites, so I decided to skip getting hostile to total strangers who might or might not deserve it and bring it right to bear on Holloway, who definitely deserved it.

"What's the hold-up?" I asked, stopping about twenty feet from him. "Did the TSA deem your fifteen-inch 'marital aide' to be too much like a weapon to allow it on board? Should have gone with a less threatening model than the Dev-ass-tator—"

"You think you're so damned funny," Holloway said, not looking up.

To his bad luck, two ladies standing close by cut up into a wicked case of the giggles at my sick burn, looking up at him with mouths covered to suppress their laughs.

"Lots of people think I'm funny," I said, giving them a nod. "If this FBI gig doesn't work out, I might give stand-up comedy a try."

"Try it elsewhere," Holloway said, still glaring at the door to the carousel, probably willing it to open and dump out his stuff. "I don't like you, you don't like me—there's no reason for us to trip all over each other on this jaunt. You keep your distance, I'll do the same, we'll both be happier for it."

"That may be the smartest thing I've ever heard come out of your mouth, Holloway," I said, giving him a mocking salute. "Good show, old chap. I'll go find the car. You meet up with us once you get your dildo collected."

And off I went, very sure he'd transferred his lead-melting look to my back the moment I turned it. Holloway was the kind of guy who would have done it to my face if I'd been turned toward him; it was his bad luck I was too quick to catch his glare before leaving him in the dust.

"I know who you are," a suited agent said as I walked up to a black SUV in the NO PARKING zone outside the baggage claim.

"The feeling is not mutual," I said, looking him up and down once. Thin, looked like a runner, bald head, same black glasses as mine. His suit was grey, though, and pinstriped. "What's your name?"

"Burkitt," he said, and held out his hand to take my bag.

"I got it," I said, nodding at the car as he hit the button to pop the rear hatch.

"Where's your partner?" Burkitt asked as I threw my bag in.

"I don't have one of those," I said, settling the suitcase as much as I could. "I've got a remora, a seething little pissant who follows me around attached to my belly, sucking the life blood out of me while watching my every move."

Burkitt's eyebrows moved, causing his sunglasses to nearly fall off his nose. "Oh?"

"Yeah," I said, taking the passenger side as Holloway appeared at the baggage claim door. I couldn't fully see his expression, but I caught enough of it to watch it change from pissed to pissed-er (a word I just made it up) as he watched me resign him to the back seat. "It's a new thing the New York office is trying. Remora are cheaper than full-fledged agents, I guess."

"I've got longer legs than you," Holloway said, a little snappishly, as he reached us.

"I've got a punch strong enough to break through concrete," I said evenly.

"You threatening me?" Holloway turned beet red behind those sunglasses.

"I thought we were making random observations about ourselves," I said. "Otherwise why would I care that your legs are longer than mine?"

"Because you should sit in the back seat," Holloway said, fuming. "Shorty."

"And you should not be a throbbing, pulsating member," I said, "but here we are, me in the front seat and you being a giant dick. Alas, fate is cruel to do such things to us."

"Uh...I could sit in the back," Burkitt offered, a little feebly.

"You're driving," I said. "Holloway doesn't know his ass from a hole in the ground. There's no chance I'm trusting him to navigate New Orleans during rush hour."

Holloway went redder, if such a thing was possible. "Sure, I'll drive," he said, shooting me a mean smile.

"No, you won't," I said, looking at my fingernails.

He stared at me from behind those black sunglasses. "Why not?"

"Because I have this precognitive sense that something terrible would happen if you did," I said, putting my hand to my forehead. "Yes, yes, I'm seeing it now. If you drive, we'll get into a hundred-mile-an-hour collision that only one of us will survive," I said. "And it's not going to be you."

"Good God," Burkitt whispered.

"You heard that, didn't you?" Holloway's shade had now increased to the point that it looked like someone had poured tomato juice over his face.

"I hope so," I said, looking innocently at Burkitt. "You're not deaf, are you? You use your hearing protection at the range, right?"

"Hey, I don't know what's going on here, but I don't want to get in the middle of it—" Burkitt started to say.

"It's a simple power struggle, Burkitt," I said, looking back at Holloway. "See, Remora here wants to run the show—and run me. The problem he's up against is I don't get run by assclown tough guys. I kill them. I just want him to back off, but his pride can't handle that, so he's gotta keep ramping up the antagonism." I glanced at Burkitt. "You know what the problem is with a power struggle?"

Burkitt looked like he didn't want to bite, but he finally answered. "What?"

I pushed my glasses down my nose so I could stare straight at Holloway. "That shit only works if you have a prayer in hell of overpowering the person you're playing against." I didn't blink, just stared him down.

Holloway stared back—for another minute, and that was all. "Fine," he said, breaking off eye contact. "You want to win this pissing contest? You win. Cover yourself in piss."

"Why does it not surprise me that you don't understand the difference between piss and glory? Get in the back," I said, and he did, taking his sweet time to do so after stowing his gear. I watched him in the rearview the whole time to make sure he didn't pull his gun on me. So much glory.

I kept that eye on him the whole ride, realizing that next time I was going to pretend to be charitable and take the back seat myself. Really, though, my neck was just starting to get a crick in it from worrying he might frag me while he had a chance.

13.

Olivia

"If there really was a guy named Troy McClure," Veronika said as the cab bumped along Las Vegas Blvd, "and he'd really done a motivational film at one point called, *'Get Confident, Stupid!'*, I have to say, it'd basically be perfect for you to watch. Pick up some tips, maybe."

I blinked, trying to take in all of what Veronika had just said and coming up short on knowing who Troy McClure was—or wasn't, based on the first part of what she'd said. "Why would I need a movie like that?"

"Because you need confidence like I need to give Detective Norton a call later," Veronika said. When she caught my puzzled look she just smirked. "You know what I mean?"

"No," I said, sure I didn't want to know, either.

"I'll explain it to you when you're all grown up," she said. "You know, after you get that self-confidence problem solved. Not that it'd do you much good, since I can tell you play for the other team. Seriously, though, you should avoid dating until you get it ironed out, because any man who dates you is going to end up running over you and triggering some serious passive-aggressiveness explosions."

"I think we should stick to the case at hand," I said, feeling my face threaten to spontaneously combust, and not from the desert heat. "Maybe go over the particulars—"

"Okay," Veronika said, a dusty vacant lot bouncing by to our left. "There's a speedster in Vegas who tore up a convenience store. There're your particulars. Now let's get back to talking about why you think you suck."

I blanched. "I do not…suck."

"Not what I said," Veronika said. "I said 'why you *think* you suck.' Big difference. I don't think you suck at all. I think you have some serious self-loathing stuff going on there, though. Some twisted knots right in the middle of you."

"Thanks for the psychoanalysis," I said. "Heavy on the *psycho*."

"Pfft." Veronika dismissed me with a wave. "I'm the least psycho person you could meet. Here we are."

The cab pulled to a stop outside a hotel with a serious Italian influence. They had orange tiles on the roof of the square, European variety, and the stucco was all a desert sand color. My eyes slid over the sign out front: it was called the *Toscano Palace*.

Air conditioners graced the windows. In the distance, to my left, past the empty lot, the Strip sat baking in the midday sun. Veronika looked at it, then the Toscano Palace, then back again. "What the hell is this?"

I glanced at the Toscano Palace. "A motel?"

"Rhetorical question, Brackett," Veronika said. "Why are we staying in this pile?"

"Reed said something about, uh, tightening the belt before I left," I said.

Veronika slid back her cotton jacket to reveal a tight, form-fitting skirt that hugged her lean hips. "Do I look like I need to tighten my belt?" She glanced down, and must have realized she wasn't actually wearing one. "If I had a belt?"

I shrugged. "It is what—"

Veronika wore a pained expression. "Don't ever say that in my presence again. I am not staying here. Come on."

"But—Reed paid for our rooms here," I said.

She rolled her eyes. "He didn't pay for it personally, and he's not going to be personally offended if you don't stay here. I'm going to use my own money to check into a place a little more befitting my status as a metahuman superstar of law enforcement." She flounced her way back toward the cab, flagging him down just as he started to move. She paused before putting her suitcase in the back. "You coming?"

I thought about it. Going somewhere fancy with Veronika and paying for it out of my own pocket? Or staying in the place work had paid for—without Veronika.

"Come on, Shygal, what are you waiting for?" She smirked. "Can't afford the upscale life? Because I think I'm going to the Venetian, which is an actual Italian-style palazzo. You in or out?"

"I can't afford that," I said, shaking my head. I probably could; Reed had been paying me well for over a year now, but I had a feeling I'd see the prices and almost die, because the reality of my "success" had not set in, not remotely.

Besides, Reed's talks about cutting expenses gave me a little nervous quiver in my belly. What if I found myself doing secretarial work again in the near future? Then this past year—and my increased salary—would be a distant memory before I knew it, leaving me only with what I'd been able to save. Which was a lot to me, but hardly enough to retire on.

Plus...I'd have to go with Veronika.

"Live boldly, and for the now," Veronika said, holding the cab's door open. "C'mon, kiddo. Let's go live the Vegas high life."

I looked down and shook my head. "No, thank you."

"You know, the meek aren't going to inherit a damned thing," Veronika said, slipping into the cab. "Because the earth is going to be used up before you get it. Last chance to live a life without regrets."

Of all the things I'd missed out on in my life, I didn't think I was going to regret this. "No, thanks," I said.

"Kiddo, you should really work on not adding to your personal pile of regrets," she said, slamming the door and rolling the window down. With a little wave through the window, her dark glasses reflecting the image of the Toscano Palace, off she went, rolling back down the street the way she'd come.

I offered a feeble wave of my own as she cruised out of sight, then let out a little sigh once she was gone. "Whew," I said under my breath, "peace at last."

14.

Sienna

The twenty minutes or so from the New Orleans Airport into the city was passed in a fairly pleasurable manner, except for my constant watching of Holloway in the mirror for a gun in my back. Burkitt turned out to be a fairly decent conversationalist, and though not a local, he'd been stationed here long enough he knew his way around pretty well.

There were about ten New Orleans PD cars still sitting in the fire lane beside Hotel Fantaisie, the tower where the shooting had been staged. Next door I saw another building being worked on, a tower under construction at least half the size of Hotel Fantaisie's fifty or so stories. The construction crane disappeared under Hotel Fantaisie's portico as we pulled up.

I popped out and waved over one of the local officers, not even bothering to flash my badge. He came over dutifully, maybe even a little excited. "How's it going?" I asked.

"Better now," he said, oozing admiration. His gold name badge read 'Brook.' "You here to solve this thing, Slay—"

"Just call me Sienna," I said, heading after Holloway toward the massive revolving door into the hotel lobby. Burkitt, apparently, had decided to wait with the car.

The lobby was huge, a theater-sized screen against one wall of the lobby bar. There was seating radiating out from that, a coffee shop tucked into a quiet corner, and one entire wall was taken up by a long check-in desk that had about thirty or forty stations.

A local cop pointed the way to the elevators, over in the far corner, to Holloway, so I just followed him. The place was pretty quiet, only a minimal line for check-ins, a pleasant hum in the air along with the smell of coffee and—distantly—alcohol. I tried to ignore the latter as I trailed Holloway into the elevator.

My ears popped several times as the elevator raced up, a lot faster than I was used to. We arrived at the 40th floor without saying a word to each other, and I gestured to let Holloway know he should get out.

It wasn't hard to find the room in question. New Orleans cops waved us in the right direction, and off we walked, Holloway once again in the lead, the occasional muttered, "Slay Queen," making its way to me. I tried to smile at anyone I heard it from, but it was getting thrown around a lot. As far as superhero names went, it beat the hell out of 'Gravity.' I was pushing Reed to adopt the moniker 'Hurricane,' but he wasn't going for it. Yet.

Hurricane and Slay Queen. It had a good ring to it, I thought. Too bad mine was just a stupid internet meme that would probably last until Tuesday before it faded away.

The crime scene's door was open, and a detective was standing at it, waiting. He was the very model of a cop show detective, in his fifties, had the associated gravitas, and a face that suggested he'd spent more time scowling at perps than smiling at his kids or wife—if he even had them anymore. I noticed when he raised his hand to point at something inside the room, his left ring finger was bare. Divorce, I would have bet. I felt like I saw that a lot from cops of his approximate rank and age.

He acknowledged us when we got close, though I would have bet he got word of our arrival radioed to him by Brook or one of his fellows before we'd even left the lobby. "Parsons," he said, extending his hand to Holloway, "NOPD."

"Holloway," my "partner" said, pumping Parsons' hand once.

"Hello," I said, trying to sound a little gruff, taking his hand lightly and giving it one good shake. "I'm Johnny Cash."

Parsons chuckled and motioned us to follow. "Through here."

The hotel room wasn't particularly impressive for such a fancy hotel. It had a low ceiling, only about eight feet or so, but the windows spanned the whole wall. A circle of glass had been cut out of the middle of it. I gauged it at probably a foot in diameter.

"Glad you came here first, though there's not much to see," Parsons said, looking over the place like it was his own personal fiefdom. "Assassin took the glass with them. No fingerprints on anything, like their hand oil didn't exist."

"Chance for DNA?" I asked.

"Yeah," Parsons said, "maybe. But we'll get theirs and that of every other person who's stayed in this room for the last six months, plus from the cleaning staff."

I'd had some basic forensic courses at Quantico during my crash course month, and that jibed with what I'd learned. "Powder residue?" I asked.

"Not sure yet," Parsons said. "We're removing the window and taking it in, which means we'll get residue from the outside, but it doesn't look like she left any prints behind on the inside."

"You're sure it's a she?" Holloway asked.

"We have surveillance film of her," Parsons said with a nod. "About 5 foot 6, medium build, lean, but she's got some curves, so…" He shrugged. "Yeah, we're pretty sure."

"Hmm," Holloway said. "Not a typical MO for a woman. Using a sniper rifle, I mean. She's a frosty bitch. Literally, if that bullet was made by her."

"Not a lot else to see here," Parsons said, nodding at the bed, which had been stripped. "She took her bedding with her in her suitcase. Same with the towels—"

"Man, they are going to ding her credit card for all sorts of incidentals," I said, then looked at him. "Speaking of—"

Parsons just shook his head. "Credit card was in the name of 'Betty Page.' Address is here in New Orleans, but it's total bunk, just like the name. No one's heard of a Betty Page on that street." Parsons blinked. "Not this Betty Page, anyway."

"It's been a long time since Bettie Page's heyday; they could maybe be forgiven for not having heard of the other one, either," I said, looking over the room. "This really is a dry hole, isn't it?" I walked over to window, looking down, trying to get a sense of where she'd been shooting.

I found it pretty quick, and it was a long ways off. "Oof," I said, peering down. It was a pretty good shot she'd made, even accounting for the miss. I'd done a little sniping practice in my time and I probably would have struggled to make this shot. In sniping you dealt with factors like windage and bullet drop that I'd never learned to account for. If she'd actually hit it, at this distance, it'd suggest she was pretty good. And by the account I'd heard, she'd have made it if not for a last-second movement by the governor.

That made our assassin very, very dangerous.

Holloway eased up at my shoulder. I cursed myself for losing track of him while I was looking over the scene. He could have taken a shot at me and I wouldn't have realized it until my brains came exploding out my forehead. I eyed him sideways, but he didn't seem hostile—for now. "Decent shooting except for the miss," he said.

"Mmmhmm," I said, making way for him to move up to the hole in the glass and line it up for himself.

He did, and grunted with what I think was grudging respect.

"You ever make a shot like that?" I asked. "In Afghanistan?"

He bristled. "How'd you know?"

"You answer requests by saying, 'Copy that,'" I said. "Army?"

He nodded. "Airborne. Most amateurs would struggle with it, but it's hardly impossible."

"Metahuman powers give you a boost," I said, looking down, down, way down—over the Harrah's Casino between us and the nondescript, government-style building by the shoreline. New Orleans had a definite feel to it, very different from any other city I could recall being in, at least in the US. It almost had a more European vibe in a way, in regard to the older buildings here. "They make it easier to steady your hand, give you more precise muscle control."

He nodded along. "I've heard that. The right rifle makes it easier, too. Could you make this shot?"

I shook my head. "Not reliably, I don't think. But I'm more practiced with small arms and shooting out to a hundred, two hundred yards. I trained for combat, not this sort of distance killing."

"Distance from target suggests dispassion," Holloway said. "A desire to maintain that space, give herself room to maneuver, escape. It's a professional job, not a personal one where she wants to get up close and see him suffer."

I shook my head. "That's dime store psychology. I don't think we can assume anything."

"Just a working guess to start from," Holloway said. "I'm pegging this as a professional assassination. A political hit with a reason behind it." He looked over at me. "You disagree?"

"I neither agree nor disagree," I said. "I'm not ruling anything out—yet. I want actual evidence before I rule out any motives."

He made a face. "Doesn't look like there is much evidence."

I looked down, below, at the scene that was waiting, far in the distance, where the governor had been when he'd been shot at. "No," I said, "it doesn't look like there's any at all."

15.

When we were done in the hotel, we headed down to the scene of the shooting. Wind blew off the Mississippi river, ruffling a banner strung across two posts declaring FERRY GRAND REOPENING. Crime scene techs in suits were combing over the area, which seemed like a waste of time to me, but gave the abandoned area the look of a post-apocalyptic biohazard outbreak zone.

The scene had been a hell of a lot less controlled, at least at the outset, what with a crowd of spectators trampling their way out of here after the shot was fired. The ground was upturned, trampled, what little grass there was having been annihilated in the exodus. It was mostly concrete, fortunately, though even that was tracked with mud.

"Bullet impact was over here," Detective Parsons said. He'd brought us down, and was pointing at a shattered piece of pavement just beyond the lectern. There was nothing there other than a little damp residue where the purported ice bullet must have shattered and melted.

"You get a sample of this?" I asked, already pretty positive I knew the answer.

"For whatever good it does," Parsons said. "Lab might be able to trace where it was made if the water has any distinctive local elements to it."

I nodded. "The type of meta that controls ice? They can make it out of thin air by freezing the moisture. I wouldn't expect they'd bother pouring a cup out of the tap, but you never know."

"What's the name for this type?" Holloway asked.

"Jotun, I think," I said, a little hesitantly. "The first of them I met was literally called Jotun by older metas, and he was known as *the* frost giant of Norse legend. Patient zero for this type, near as I could tell."

"You think they're related?" Holloway asked.

"I doubt it, but maybe," I said, shaking my head. As far as I knew, Old Bastard Winter didn't have any relatives, though my knowledge of him was hardly comprehensive.

"What happened to that guy?" Parsons asked. He sounded genuinely curious.

"Died during the war," I said, trying to close that particular topic of conversation. I caught a flicker in the way he looked at me after I answered, and I sighed. "I didn't kill him. It was the other guys." He relaxed a little, though I don't know why. It wasn't like I hadn't racked a prodigious body count regardless of whether I'd done in Winter.

"Well, that's worth a look, genealogy-wise," Holloway said, staring at the hole in the pavement like it held the secret of life.

"To rule things out, sure," I said. "But it's a lot more likely this assassin was bottle-born." Parsons sent me another curious look. "Product of the artificial serum that unlocks meta powers in normal humans who aren't born with them."

"What's the difference?" Parsons asked.

"Control, usually," I said. "If they manifested naturally, odds are this person has had these powers for quite some time. Probably survived the war either by sheer cunning or lying low. That makes it tougher on us than some fresh meta that got empowered last week and decided to take a shot at your governor. Being less experienced, they'd be more predisposed to making mistakes. Though, obviously, we're not seeing many of those—yet."

"Lends credence to the idea that this is a natural-born," Holloway said. "Someone who's been working with their powers a while, maybe as a professional assassin. Who knows how to shoot."

"You thinking military experience?" I asked.

He shook his head. "Unlikely, at least in the US. We're still pretty new to running women through the training programs. But…" He paused, frowning in thought. "She doesn't have to be US. Other militaries have been training women snipers for longer. The IDF, for instance."

"The Soviets did," I said. "Think I remember hearing a story about an NVA female sniper that made a pretty decent amount of trouble over there during the war."

"That was in Carlos Hathcock's book, right?" Holloway was watching me with interest.

"Yep," I said, moving on. I heard Holloway make a sound of grudging respect under his breath. Probably hadn't met many women who'd read that one.

A young woman's voice drew my attention. "Excuse me?" She was standing about fifty feet away, dressed in a serious suit, her tanned skin bright against the dark of the SUV she was next to. My first thought was that if you put a pencil down the back of her skirt when she was relaxed—if she was ever relaxed—it would immediately snap in half when she resumed her normal posture.

Yeah. She was a tightass. I could see that from twenty yards.

"My name is Jenna Corcoran," she said. "I'm Governor Warrington's chief of staff."

I nodded at her. Made sense; she'd gotten past the perimeter cops. "Your timing is good," I said, exchanging a look with Holloway. My hostilities with him seemed to have been put on hold for the moment, because even through our black sunglasses we were both clearly thinking the same thing: this was convenient. "That's just the man we need to talk to next."

She stepped all the way down out of the SUV and beckoned us with perfectly manicured nails. "The governor is nearby if you'd like to…" She gestured to the car.

I looked past her to where Burkitt was parked, still sitting there like our driver rather than a fellow agent. "You want to ride with her?"

"Probably need to ask her some questions," Holloway said, under his breath. "But she might respond better to a female touch."

"You saying you want to ride with her?" I caught the flare

of brief anger in his eyes before his lips tightened back to an even line. "I don't want to cram us both in that car. Looks like a bodyguard in the front. We'd put the squeeze on her unless there's a third-row seat to that thing." I could see a bench in the second row from where she was standing, partially obscuring the view of the rear.

"I'll ride with Burkitt," Holloway said. "Record with your phone in your pocket, and let me know if you get anything good."

"What's the law on that in Louisiana?" I asked as Holloway moved toward Burkitt's SUV.

"It's probably fine," he said with a smirk. "Why don't you find out after you give it a go?"

"Jerkoff," I said, heading for Jenna Corcoran's ride. Why was it always black SUVs with these government types? Just once I'd like to see an official like a governor show up in a silver sedan. But no, they seemed to reserve those for people at my level.

Jenna Corcoran held the door for me and I slipped past her, scooting over to the far side of the vehicle. She followed after, closing the door behind her. I was right; the driver and the dude in the passenger seat were both burly bodyguard types, probably Louisiana State Police, since they were charged with protecting the governor. She didn't bother to introduce us.

"This whole sequence of events has thrown our schedule planning into a tailspin," Corcoran said, already looking at her phone once she was in. She even buckled her seatbelt, something I'd noticed most people riding in the back of official cars didn't do for some reason, as though the car being official somehow made them immune to accidents.

"Oh?" I asked, and fiddled with my own phone. "I hope you don't mind, I have to record my conversations during an official investigation." I put an apologetic tone on it and matched my smile to the sentiment.

"What?" She stared blankly for a second, then said, "Oh. Of course."

"Before I meet with the governor, can you tell me if there's any pending legislation, any recent executive actions that would be a good reason someone might want him dead?" I asked, then shut the hell up and waited for the answer.

It was a long time coming.

"Not that I can think of," Corcoran said, her deep green eyes moving low and slow as she seemed to try to recall. "Most of what we've been working on since he took office two years ago have been things like reopening this—the Algiers Ferry—for free, like it used to be. Algiers is the fifteenth ward, one of the poorest neighborhoods in the entire US. It's across the Mississippi, and the bridges are a little ways off. People who work downtown but live in Algiers—well, this gives them a convenient way to cross to the Canal Street business district. Governor Warrington has committed to—"

"You can spare me the campaign speechifying," I said, holding in a yawn. "I'm not in his constituency, so you don't have to worry about me voting for him. Did that move—making the ferry free—piss anyone off?"

Corcoran half-shrugged. "Maybe? I don't know. It seems a stupid thing to kill someone over, but—"

"Politics in general is a stupid thing to get worked up over, but hey, here we are," I said with a shrug of my own. "Any other, more divisive issues?"

"Maybe?" She seemed to think about it. "He's done quite a bit given it's his first term. There was a school bill he signed, with money earmarked for infrastructure spending. We're trying to bring underperforming schools in poor urban and rural areas up to a higher level than they're currently at—"

"Okay, yeah, I get it, he's a virtuous hero of the downtrodden," I said, already exhausted by talking to her about his accomplishments. "Anything else?"

Corcoran blinked her surprise away. "Do...do you not care about the poor and—"

"Oh, screw you," I said. "Yes, I care about the poor and downtrodden. But I'm not here to discover the local hero that is Ivan Warrington, surely a god among men, and the most caring of us all." I stared her down and tried to keep most of the chill out of it. "I'm trying to figure out who's trying to kill him, and stop them. That's all. The less fluff and bullshit you feed me while puffing up your candidate, the less time I have to spend sifting through the chaff trying to find the wheat on why someone wants him dead."

"I never knew you were this uncaring," Corcoran huffed, turning toward the SUV window.

"Wow," one of the state troopers said into the quiet that followed. "You really are the Slay Queen. In every respect."

"I'm not here to make friends," I said. "Take me to the governor—and maybe we can get on about the real job—saving his life." We fell into silence as the SUV rolled through the crowded streets of New Orleans.

16.

Olivia

I took a deep, long breath as I sat on the hard mattress in the quiet motel room. The air had a smell, like long-ago stubbed out cigarettes, like stale air that hadn't been recirculated in a long time.

The motel was a hole in the wall.

But it was quiet, and peaceful, and there was no Veronika, and that—that was the best thing of all.

Outside the thick, navy curtain, a line of light shone at the edges, where the brightness outside the window tried—and succeeded—to break into the room at the margins. Motes of dust floated in those bars of light, disappearing where they reached the shadows the light did not touch.

"This morning I was in Minneapolis," I breathed, quietly, to myself. "This afternoon I'm in Las Vegas."

Sometimes, in these quiet moments, I had to repeat these things to myself because they still didn't seem real. Not for the girl who was raised in a prison commune run by a totalitarian control freak. I shuddered as I pictured the ramshackle houses buried in the thick brush of a Florida swamp.

I shuddered again when I remembered the man who ran it all with an iron hand—indeed, a hand that could control iron.

And Tracy, his son.

Bleh. I got my breathing back under control the way Dr. Zollers had taught me. I'd had an appointment with him scheduled for this afternoon but had to cancel when this came up. That was unfortunate, but we'd meet when I got back. Sometimes these things happened. I liked Zollers. He felt like more than a therapist—he made me feel like he was actually my friend.

I put my head back on the threadbare bed spread, felt the rough cloth against the nape of my neck like I was lying on sandpaper. It didn't bother me. Later I'd take a long, hot shower with the door closed, letting the water boil my skin, fog the mirror to the point where I wouldn't be able to see even my shadow in it. The quiet, the sound of the falling water, the heat coming into my lungs—

Those were my peaceful places, and ones I could create just about anywhere.

Somewhere in those thoughts I drifted off, and woke to a buzzing. My phone was rattling on the nightstand, casting light toward the ceiling in the otherwise dark. The beams that shone at the edges of the windows were gone, and I blinked awake, grabbing it and answering, sleepily, without checking the caller ID. "Hello?"

"Get dressed and meet me at Freemont Street," Veronika's voice came, taut and lacking its usual humor. "We just had another incident."

17.

Sienna

"This is not what I would have expected for a place a governor would hole up after almost being assassinated," I said, eyeing the place we pulled up to after a very short drive, which mostly seemed to circle us around the block. I would have shot a look at the two purported bodyguards in the front seat, but even if I were blind, I could have seen the palpable sense of guilt hanging on them, the feeling that they were committing career malpractice.

The blazing sign said, "Willie's Chicken Shack," in neon.

"The governor feels most comfortable around his constituents," Jenna Corcoran said stiffly. I couldn't help but think of her in relation to both of her names. She was stiff enough that she commanded that level of formality.

"Oooookay," I said, shaking my head. Popping out the door, I could see a crowd gathered inside the restaurant, which was buried inside a strip of shops along a commercial street, maybe Canal, though I couldn't see a street sign. I could see a tall, bald white dude in a suit holding court among a crowd of predominantly white folks through the glass front window. "I feel for you, guys, really I do," I said, addressing the bodyguards in the front seat.

They didn't need to say anything. I saw the subtle, almost invisible nods. They were dying on the inside, having their principal out in public after an assassination attempt.

I headed for the entry, Jenna Corcoran a few steps behind me as I crossed the sidewalk. "Why the hell would he come here?"

There was a serious bristling in Jenna Corcoran's voice as she responded. "Most people don't know this, but the capital of Louisiana is—"

"Baton Rouge," I said, and caught a funny look from her when I glanced back. "What? My mother used to quiz me on state capitals, probably in an effort to kill time and keep me entertained."

"Anyway, there's no governor's mansion or capital building or anything for him to fall back to here in New Orleans," she finished. "And we didn't want to risk the road trip or a flight with the assassin still at large."

"But you have police stations in New Orleans, yes?" I held open the door and let her pass first. Age before beauty, after all. "Other secure locations where you could bunker him? You know, other than a chicken joint mere blocks away from where someone tried to kill him?"

The smell of fried chicken hit my nostrils the moment I walked in and I felt a subtle drool reaction begin as I smacked my lips together. I glanced over at Warrington; an excessively tall man, his lack of hair felt somewhat unique among politicians. He had a broad grin on his perfectly tanned face, and he was glad-handing his way through the crowd, talking to someone who seemed a little cranky or maybe had just overdone it on the red beans and rice and was feeling the digestive effects.

"Don't you want to talk to him?" Jenna Corcoran asked as I paused, torn between going to Warrington and ordering some fried chicken.

"Ehhh, he seems fine," I said, and went for the chicken. In my defense, I hadn't eaten since before my appointment with Dr. Kashani this morning.

"His life is in danger," she said, following me toward the line.

"If he felt that strongly about it, you'd think he would have gone somewhere safe."

She wandered off as I approached the counter, trying to

make my decision. As it turned out, they had daiquiris, too, but I had to pass on those for reasons of sobriety. Also, my employer would probably frown on drinking on the job. But mostly because of sobriety, since to hell with what my employer thought.

I ordered a three-piece meal and was waiting for it when Holloway made it through the door. He looked pissed when he saw me standing there with my receipt, waiting for my order, but I just shrugged. He made his way over, steaming, past the now-forming line, and when he got to me, he looked at Warrington, then at the receipt in my hand, and asked, "Well…did you get me anything?"

"Order 231," the clerk called, sliding my three-piece meal over to me.

I picked it up and looked into the bag before offering it to him. I probably didn't need this many calories, anyway. "You can have the chicken breast if you want, but if you touch the drumstick, I will rip your soul from your body without any warning or remorse."

Holloway looked at me evenly through his sunglasses for a long moment, then nodded. "That's fair."

We ate our chicken in silence as we watched Warrington work the crowd. He'd definitely noticed us, but didn't seem to be in much hurry to make his way over. "He acting like someone who was just nearly assassinated in your opinion?" Holloway said between bites.

The chicken was freaking great; I wasn't inclined to waste my mouth's valuable time answering him, but it was a good question. "No," I said, and went right back to eating.

Holloway eyed the menu behind as he gnawed the bone. "Shame we can't hit up the daiquiris."

I didn't react visibly, but I knew I'd pegged him on the hard-drinking thing. We can smell our own kind, you know. At ten thousand paces. I would have bet Holloway was a scotch guy.

Once we'd finished licking our fingers and killing time, we eventually had made our way to the bottom of the chicken, me more than him. He was eyeing my Cajun fries enviously, and finally asked, "You going to eat all those?"

I thought about it a second, and slid the rest across the table to him. "It took me a while to take off those extra pounds I was carrying. Better these go on your hips than mine."

Holloway didn't seem to care about his hips based on how hard he took down the Cajun fries. I kept the biscuit for myself, though, and nibbled it while he annihilated the potatoes. Once that was done, we were out of excuses for approaching Warrington. Neither of us moved, though.

"We should probably go talk to him, shouldn't we?" I finally asked.

"You ever talk to a politician?" Holloway asked, leaned back in the booth, seemingly unimpressed.

I thought about Harmon, the last President, who'd spent a year in my head. "Once or twice," I said.

"So, you know why I'm not rushing over there."

I nodded. "I got the speechifying from Jenna Corcoran on the way over. I could just about go the rest of my life without hearing her extolling the virtues of…well, him."

Holloway chuckled under his breath. "I hear that." Then he got serious again, all traces of amusement wiped from his face. "All right, let's get this over with."

We stood, making our way over to Warrington, who seemed to take no notice of us, but started to subtly detach from the crowd as if he sensed our approach. That sent a couple warning bells to ringing in my head, but I was hard-pressed to know if he was simply crowd-aware and human, as some people were, or possessed some sort of metahuman, preternatural sense like Harmon had. Having known Harmon so well felt like it might color my assessment, though, so I filed away those suspicions, at least for now.

"Thank you—thank you so much." Warrington pumped his last hand as he detached from the crowd and turned to face us with a smile that seemed warm and genuine. "Hey, how y'all doing?"

"I left behind 45 degrees and cloudy for 75 and sunny, so I'm fine, thanks for asking," I said, trying not to sound at all impressed. Though I was, minimally. Warrington oozed charisma, and with his eyes on me, I felt strangely like someone had shone a warm light on me.

Warrington smiled even more brightly. "It's a pleasure to

meet you, Ms. Nealon." He turned his spotlight-gaze on Holloway. "You must be Agent Holloway." He stuck out his hand and they shook, firmly. I realized he hadn't offered me the same, and mentally chalked another point in Warrington's column; I hated physical contact with strangers, and I had a feeling he knew that, either from sensing it or doing a little research on me.

"Pleasure to meet you, Governor," Holloway said, with a lot more enthusiasm than he'd mustered in our conversation about politicians a minute ago.

"Well, weather aside, I'm sorry y'all had to get called in on this," Warrington said, a perfect picture of Southern genteel manners, and it seemed sincere—as though he were actually embarrassed that someone had the temerity to ruin our day by trying to assassinate him. "I'm sure you have plenty enough to be getting along with back home."

New York wasn't home, but I didn't feel the need to share that with him. "We go where we need to," I said, trying to keep it formal.

"I think talking to me is going to be a waste of your time, but I'll answer whatever you'd like," he said, extending his long arm toward the booth we'd just left. "I am at your disposal."

"We won't take up too much of your time," Holloway said.

I blinked beneath my glasses. That was a neat trick; Warrington had just offered us as much time as we wanted or needed and Holloway had immediately demurred and said we wouldn't do that. I couldn't decide whether Holloway had been prompted to reassure him because he was in a position of power, or Holloway was just generally polite to people who weren't me.

"I think we've got a basic statement of events from the NOPD and Louisiana State Police," I said, "but maybe you can fill us in real quick on what happened. From your perspective."

"I was about to give a speech," he said, smiling, "reopening the Algiers Ferry at the low, low price of zero dollars per ride, and I remembered I'd forgotten one of my cards. And by remembered, I mean flipped the card before it and realized there was a major gap in what I was about to say. So, I stepped over to Ms. Corcoran to get that card and something whizzed by like an angry hornet about two inches from my head." He made a face. "Took me a second to realize what it was, and by the time I heard the shot, the troopers over there were hustling me out of there and to the car."

"Can you think of any reason someone would want to kill you?" I asked, mentally trying to find any inconsistency between what Warrington had said and the story I'd heard from Shaw back in New York or Detective Parsons's version of events. I couldn't think of any, though I'd read the witness statement later just to be sure. Any inconsistencies might hint at Warrington lying, which wouldn't exactly be shocking coming from a politician. After all, it was possible he'd staged the attempt for sympathy or something.

"Was there any reason for someone to go and kill Abraham Lincoln or JFK or Martin Luther King, Jr.?" Warrington's smile didn't waver a bit.

"Sure," I said, ticking them off on my fingers. "Anger over losing the Civil War, craziness and Communism, and racism, respectively."

Holloway raised an eyebrow, looking at me out of my peripheral vision. "You're going to put Lee Harvey Oswald onto Communism?"

"He defected to the Soviet Union and then Cuba," I said, not breaking off from watching Warrington, who never stopped smiling in the midst of all that. It looked natural, too. "To dismiss that as any kind of a factor seems a little strange, given that we were in the depths of the Cold War and it was an epic struggle that he'd already declared his loyalties on—twice. But notice I also said he was crazy."

"I did notice that," Warrington said smoothly. "Very charitable, I thought." He paused, steepling his fingers before him. "I can't think of anything I've done that would warrant that level of hostility, but I suppose, as you just ably pointed out, crazy could be a motive."

"Crazy is a motive less of the time than you'd think," I said. "But I do find it interesting you compared yourself to those three—all of whom died—rather than, say, Gerald R. Ford,

Ronald Reagan or John Paul II. You know, ones who lived. Like you think of yourself as a martyr."

Warrington's smile never missed a beat. "I prefer to think of myself as a visionary, someone who could help change things for the better. You know how I got my start?"

I shrugged. "I assumed that, like all politicians, you started out sponging and sucking off whoever would pay for it at the roughest corner in town."

"Ooh, that cynicism." He kept smiling, but Holloway looked like he was about explode in my peripheral vision. Yeah, I was still keeping a watchful eye on him. "Ms. Nealon, I must say—you do me wrong, there. I started out as a Metropolitan Council Member in Baton Rouge. One of the youngest ever elected to that office—"

"You started whoring early, then."

Holloway dropped another shade of red, started to grab my arm, but apparently thought the better of it. "This is the governor of Louisiana you're talking to. I know you don't have an ounce of respect for anyone on the damned planet—"

"I have plenty of respect for lots of people on the planet," I said, still looking at both of them from behind my shades, "just not anyone at this table."

Holloway fell silent, but looked like he was about to launch off like a nuclear missile. Almost exactly, in fact, I can say, having seen several of them launch.

Warrington just chuckled like I hadn't called him the cheapest whore in whoretown. "That's a common enough misperception about politics and politicians, and I don't blame you a bit for thinking it. I'm guessing you haven't a lot of dealings with…well, us."

"I lived with one for a while," I said, and Holloway's frown deepened. I did not elaborate, for obvious reasons.

"Oh, so it's personal, is it?" Warrington's chuckle deepened. "Can't blame you for that, either, but I wish you'd drop that practiced cynicism you wear like a suit of armor and really look at what we—meaning my administration—are trying to do down here. Louisiana currently ranks 46th in education across the entire US. I mean to bring us up—modest goals, at first, but I want to create a workforce for the 21st century that attracts the best companies—tech, manufacturing, hell, even Silicon Valley startups if I can—to come on down here and hire Lousianans. Education's key to that, which is why the bill I signed last year provides more money for schools in underprivileged areas, including rural as well as urban—"

"Ughhhhhhhh," I said, making a deep, guttural sound as I threw my head back. "You and Corcoran have this curious disease where you think I give a damn about your political accomplishments. Knock it off, please. You're not campaigning with me. Or Holloway, probably, though who knows where he's from."

"Ohio," Holloway muttered.

"That explains a lot," I said. "If you want to help us—and by extension, save your own life—tell me why someone would want to kill you over that education bill."

"I don't understand why anyone would." Warrington smirked his way through the answer. "It provides—"

I thumped my head against the table. "Enough. With. The. Talking. Points. Bullshit!" I lifted it back up. "Did anyone oppose your inscribed-by-God-on-stone-tablets-before-being-handed-down-to-you-by-His-own-hand education bill?"

Warrington actually blinked, though his reaction to my feigned hysterics was much more muted than any normal person's—including the spectators in the chicken joint. "Of course," he said softly.

"Why?" I asked.

"I assume because they hate the poor and the disadvantaged—"

"Oh, for crying out loud." I slammed a fist against the table. "You know I'm a cynic, and you still come at me with this propaganda? Give me the real reasons, not the horse crap you say in the press to dismiss anyone who disagrees with you."

"Okay, okay." Warrington motioned me to quiet down, then looked behind him, waved at a constituent being gently moved back by a bodyguard, then lowered his voice to a level where even Holloway probably couldn't hear it. "It blew up the state budget." He cleared his throat, then spoke again, maybe even lower. "By a lot."

"Thank you," I said. "And what did you cut to pay for it?"

"Stuff." Warrington let out a chuckle. Holloway was leaning in hard, trying to catch what he was saying, though how much luck he was having, I couldn't be sure. The governor was talking extremely low—not meta-low, which would have told me something interesting about him, confirming that latent suspicion worming its way around the back of my mind—but exceedingly quietly given the background noise in Willie's. "And more stuff."

"Nice," I said. "Mind having Ms. Corcoran give me a line-item on that? For our big brains back in Washington to look over?"

"Sure," he said, and motioned Jenna Corcoran over. "Would you mind emailing Ms. Nealon a link to the state budget and—" he looked around again, beckoning her closer before whispering, "—and giving her a detailed look at what we, uh, moved around, to pay for the education bill."

Corcoran stiffened, but nodded, giving me a very pointed look. "Right away."

"Thank you." Warrington smiled at her. "Anything else, Ms. Nealon?"

"If you had to steelman an argument against your own education bill," I said, looking him right in the eyes, "how would you do it?"

"'Steelman'?" Holloway piped up. "What does that even mean?"

"It's the opposite of a strawman argument," I said. "It's when you take a position against your own and argue it with full force. In this case, I'm asking the governor if he can play devil's advocate and say why his opponents might have voted against his beloved, holy, on-a-mission-from-heaven bill so I can see why—other than because they hate all the poor people, ever—they might have been against it."

"I told you, budgetary reasons," Warrington said. "Everyone's against pork barrel spending, until theirs gets blown out in the budgetary process. Because then what are you going to tell your constituents you've done for them come re-election time? We have a house and senate mid-term going on right now." He chuckled. "Ought to be a barn-burner, too." He stood, fastening his suit buttons as he did so. "Ms. Nealon—a pleasure.

Agent Holloway. Please feel free to contact me if you need anything else." He nodded, and off he went, state police bodyguards trailing behind as he walked out of Willie's.

"I'm normally not Miss Manners, by any means," Holloway said, apoplectic the moment Warrington was out the door, "but can you not be nice to anyone?"

"Yes," I said. "It depends on the audience. Like I told you, it was the people at the table that were the problem."

"Yeah, you're definitely not the problem." He gave me a light shove and I stood up, leaving the booth so he could get out. "I had a bad feeling about you from the beginning, Nealon, but this is just confirming everything Shaw and I thought about you—reckless, loose cannon—"

"My cannon is totally tied down," I said, "as you can tell by no one getting actually blasted yet."

"No one got blasted?" He threw a hand toward the door the governor had just walked out of. "What the hell do you call that?"

"A hard interview for an obvious liar," I said. "There's stuff he's not telling us."

Holloway put a hand on my shoulder, but must have seen the freezing glare I shot his hand even through my sunglasses, because he removed it immediately. "Of course there's stuff he's not telling us. He's a politician. Of course he's a liar. See above. But that doesn't give us license to go stomping on his feet. You may think you're invincible, but I'm not, and neither is my career. I get that you don't give a shit about being with the bureau long-term, but pissing off a power player like Warrington is a bad move. He's going to be in Washington in a few years, mark my words, and when he shows up, you don't want to be on his bad side if you're still in the agency." Holloway snorted. "Guessing you're not caring that far ahead, though."

"Nope," I said, and headed for the exit. As I started to reach for the door, an Asian lady with perfect, coal-black hair pulled into a tight ponytail beat me to it, holding it open for me as she slipped ahead.

"Sorry," she said, a little too brightly, her eyes on me. I gave her a quick once-over from behind my sunglasses. She was pretty, perfect skin, about my height, a lot thinner, had a look about her that screamed 'mom' from the ponytail down to the yoga pants.

I hesitated, and she brushed my hand as I passed. Something stiff popped into it, something like a business card, and I held onto it without evincing any reaction. I made my way onto the sidewalk, glancing back at her in the process. She bustled past me to a waiting minivan, not a thing in her hands now that she'd brush-passed (to use spy lingo) the card to me.

"Where the hell is Burkitt?" Holloway asked, scouring the street. Once he was looking away from me, I looked at the card in my hand.

It was for a massage parlor somewhere on Canal Street. A hand-written note told me to "Ask for Michelle."

Burkitt pulled to a stop in front of us, and I made it to the passenger door before Holloway could, earning me another glare and muttered curse. "Too slow, normie," I said, slipping in while he was grousing. I flashed the card to Burkitt while Holloway got in the back. "Ever heard of this place?"

I thought the FBI agent was going to choke on his own tongue, and he might have if his jaw hadn't dropped it out of swallowing range when he saw it. "Where'd you get that?"

"An Asian lady handed it to me as I was coming out of there," I said. "Why?"

He stared at the card. "Does that say…?"

"'Ask for Michelle,' yeah." I glanced back to see Holloway taking an interest in our conversation. "That significant?"

Burkitt cleared his throat, picking his jaw up off the floor mat. "I'd say so, yeah." He put the big SUV in gear, and the smooth roar of the engine suggested he'd accidentally goosed it a little much in his surprise, because he throttled back fast. "That's a front for the local Triads. You know, Chinese mafia. And Michelle?" He shook his head. "Probably Michelle Cheong." He swallowed, all serious. "She's the head of the local family."

"Curiouser and curiouser," I said, looking at the card and the hand-written note.

"Why is the local Triad queen trying to contact you while you're here to investigate an assassination attempt on the governor?" This came from Holloway, who sounded as confused about the whole thing as I was.

"I don't know," I said, pocketing the card. "But I guess there's only one way to find out."

18.

The sign above Michelle Cheong's Triad HQ just read "Massage Parlor," like it was the only one in the city. About a block from the hotel where the assassin had taken their shot and two or three blocks from where the governor had been speaking at the time, it wasn't entirely out of the realm of possibility that this Michelle Cheong had actual information to contribute to the investigation.

But the place had a slightly worn look, like a few of the businesses here on Canal Street did. Canal Street seemed to me like a cross between Fifth Avenue in New York and a local touristy, seedy district. The big brand names were clearly gussied up to be on par with their counterparts in other major cities. These places were polished, signs lit up in the twilight.

Then next to them would be some tourist trap shop selling New Orleans hats and Saints merchandise, looking like everything in the place had fallen off a truck yesterday, stuffed into shelves that might have been brought in remaindered from a K-Mart that had closed in the wake of Katrina.

"Just drop me here," I said as Burkitt brought us to a stop off the curb just outside the massage parlor.

Holloway started to get out with me but encountered difficulty with the child lock. "What the hell, Burkitt?"

"I have a three- and six-year-old," Burkitt said, getting out to open it since I was showing no sign of doing so.

"Stay here," I said, halting him. "If she wanted a crew, she'd have handed me the card in the open, or given it to you,

Holloway."

"You want to go into a Triad front without backup?" Holloway asked, like I'd just told him I was going to Mars without an oxygen tank. He finally shrugged. "Your funeral, I guess."

I looked the parlor over. It looked padded, with comfort-first versions of cots spread out inside with a dozen or so Chinese workers massaging the ankles and shoulders of customers that had come in off the street. A pitch man sat on a stool out front, saying, "You want a massage? 15 minutes, $20," to everyone that passed. A sign indicating longer massages for higher prices laid out the arrangement pretty clearly for anyone that either missed the hawker's pitch or wanted more than he advertised.

"The hell?" Holloway looked like he was ready to crawl between the front seats to join me. "You're actually going to get a massage, aren't you?"

"And accidentally take the soul of whoever got stuck working on me? Probably not," I said, closing the door. I heard him mutter something, muffled, through the vehicle's aluminum body about needing some work done on himself. I would have agreed and suggested he start with an enema to flush his head out of his ass, but didn't feel like making a scene by shouting it in the middle of Canal Street. "Wait for me," I told Burkitt again, and he nodded, slipping around the front of his vehicle to stand on the sidewalk.

The pitchman on the stool evinced no sign of recognizing me as I walked up, a rare surprise. "You want a massage?" he asked, sounding a little like he was delighted at having snagged another prospect.

"I'm here to see Michelle," I said, handing him the card. He took one look at it and started to pocket it. "Nuh uh," I said, and he handed it back. I put it back in my jacket, leaving it unfastened when I finished, my gun easily accessible for a draw. Holloway had been a little paranoid in my estimation, but he wasn't wrong; I was walking into the Triads' New Orleans front, and I was not going to do that like a lamb walking into a lion's den. Not that I was ever a lamb if I could avoid it.

The massage parlor had a nice, sandalwood incense scent, but the white paint on the walls was fading and matched the storefront for its lack of glory. Calling the parlor a hole in the wall would have been a disservice to holes in the wall, especially those hole-in-the-wall-type restaurants where you could find really good food and decent décor hidden behind a rough-looking facade.

But who knew—maybe this massage parlor held the keys to the body pain/chakra universe.

"Hiiiii," gushed the little Asian mom in the yoga pants, emerging from a door in the back of the parlor. She was wearing latex gloves and offered her hand, which I took, and she worked me, shaking my hand with more length and enthusiasm than it had ever been shook by anyone, ever. "I am so excited to see you here. I wasn't sure you'd accept my invitation."

"Well, what can I say?" I looked around the place. A few of the customers in the cots up front were taking notice. Others were apparently sleeping as their masseuses worked on them, or else they were feigning disinterest like pros. The masseuses were paying attention, though; I caught a lot of surreptitious looks as they plied their trade. "When you're new in town, you accept every invitation you get."

"I'm Michelle. Is this your first time to New Orleans?" She still had my hand, and it felt curiously warm through the latex. Part of me wanted to pull it back, but she was gently kneading the pad of muscle tissue between my thumb and my wrist and it felt *awesome.*

"Uh, yeah," I said as she tugged me toward a set of cots in the back of the shop.

"What do you think so far?" she asked, eyes bright and excited.

"It's…interesting," I said, trying to be diplomatic, possibly because she had my hand and also possibly because she'd started to work the middle of my hand and I never realized how much tension I carried in there. Who would have guessed the muscles I clenched so regularly to punch people would develop knots?

Michelle laughed. "That's a nice way to say it, but I've got another—New Orleans has history, and she wears it on her sleeve. Come on, lie back, let's get started."

"Huh, what?" She'd maneuvered me over to one of the beds and was gesturing for me to sit down.

"Come on. Complimentary; relax while we talk," she said, and gave me just a little guidance.

I plopped down on the cot, not really trying to fight it. It wasn't like I'd ever had a massage before. Most latex gloves didn't exactly protect from my powers. I glanced at Michelle's hand and saw a double layer, a second glove jutting out from beneath the first at her wrist.

She caught me looking and grinned as she circled around to my feet and untied my boots. "Try to relax. And let me tell you about 'Nawlins.'"

"Uh—uhm—"

"Shhh," she said, pulling the boot off with care. "You've got your powers and your gun, and all I've got is latex gloves." She gestured to someone and I looked back. There was another masseuse there with a double layer of blue latex gloves. "Li Na is going to get the tension out of your shoulders while I work on your feet and calves."

And Li Na did. She had her hands on my shoulder in a hot second, a warm oil coating her gloves as she slipped her hands past my jacket collar and down into my blouse, hitting my trapezius muscles right where they were tightest. "Ahhh—I—ahhh—" Several other completely nonsensical mutterings dripped out of my mouth as I melted under the efforts of two Triad massage artists. And they were artists.

I'd been struck dumb by the local Triad leader. Not good for an FBI agent.

Michelle had both my boots off now, and my socks, and she'd discovered a knot in the arch of my foot and she was really going at it like it was her worst enemy and yet best friend. There was a gentility to the way she swept her finger back and forth over that taut line of muscle or ligament while cradling my foot that disarmed me. "Now, what was I saying? Oh, right—'Nawlins.'"

"Uh huh," I said, barely managing to not drool on myself. Li Na was discovering all the tension I'd piled into my shoulders while climbing that building earlier today and then crawling down the air vents. And it was a lot of tension.

"I've lived here for twenty years," Michelle said. "Seen all the charm. All the seedy stuff, too." Her grin was Cheshire-like, especially with my eyes partially closed as I drifted into a relaxed state. "I was here before Katrina and after. The city took a real hit there. Longstanding institutions washed away—Charity Hospital, for instance. Oh, not literally. But it closed after that and never opened up again. Did you see that big grey, boxy building when you came in?"

"Looked like it had been abandoned for like ten years?" I asked, trying to string words together in spite of the exquisite assault on my feet and shoulders. Li Na was now working the painful areas of my back—while I was lying on it. She had shoved her hands down the back of my shirt and was playing my muscles like a piano.

"It's been a little longer than that now," Michelle said wistfully. "But this city? She can take any hit. Come back stronger."

"You must really love it here," I muttered.

"I do," she said, finding a knot in the bottom of my foot that made me gasp as she worked the edges of it. "I started my career here, you know. Not just in New Orleans, but in this very shop. My father made me begin at the bottom. I lived with the workers, climbed my way up the ladder—"

"And now you're a yoga-pants-wearing mob boss?"

Michelle laughed, and it sounded positively delightful, like we were sitting around her upscale suburban home swapping mom secrets, like '27 Tips for Removing Stains' or 'How to Blow his Mind While Improving Your Pelvic Floor with Kegels.' Actually, those might have been rejected Cosmo articles. "Don't knock the yoga pants until you've tried them," she said once she'd finished chuckling. "As much heroing as you do, you should get a pair. They're close to spandex but not quite as shiny."

"You're the second person to suggest that. Never really gone for the spandex-clad hero look," I said. "Jeans, suit, whatever…I've got a professional creed or something to uphold."

"And steel-toed boots," she said.

"Hey, when I kick a man in the jimmy, I want him to really suffer for my art," I said, feeling like I was melting into the cot. Which was quite comfortable, come to think of it.

Michelle laughed again. "I can understand wanting a man to suffer."

"I bet you do. What's your preferred method—concrete shoes? Pliers? A blowtorch? Opera?"

"Don't knock opera until you've tried it, either," she said, switching feet and giving my heel a thorough kneading that made me let out a little grunt. "I'm a sucker for *Turandot. Nessun Dorma* gives me chills." She shuddered. "And makes my kids whine every time I play it while I drive them to school."

I peered out at her through slitted eyes. "Do you really drive a minivan? Because if not, my mental image of you is going to be totally ruined."

She smiled, a big, toothy grin. "Honda Odyssey."

I laughed, then stopped when Li Na hit a knot in my shoulder the size of Charity Hospital. "Okay, not that I'm not enjoying this, or your talk on New Orleans, but what's the real reason you had me come here?"

"My father had many different businesses," Michelle said, really sinking her fingers into the sole of my foot. It was like she had meta power and dexterity in her fingertips, but it wasn't. Li Na was working over my shoulders in the exact same manner, like her fingers were powerful wires, perfectly focused and directed to teasing out every knot in my musculature they could reach. "Do you know why I picked this one to work?"

"Because driving trucks laden with drugs had worse hours and would force you to subsist on gas station food, thus stretching the bounds of your yoga pants?"

"That's not a bad point," she said, "but no. Or mostly no, at least." She lowered her voice, breathing lightly as she hit another tension point in the bottom of my feet. "I like to help people relieve their woes. And you—you have so many woes. Your body is so tense that it's working against you."

"Yeah, well, I'd charge it as a co-conspirator, but it keeps getting me out of real trouble," I said. "Especially my fists."

Michelle barked a command softly but forcefully in Chinese, presumably, and suddenly Li Na had one of my hands in hers, working her way along my index finger starting at the tip. It felt great, of course. "You know what else is working against you?" Michelle asked.

"No, but I hope you're going to tell me, because if you don't, I feel like I'm going to be even more disappointed than a guy asking for a happy ending and finding out you don't serve that here."

"Everything's available…for a price," Michelle said, grinning through my darkened vision, my half-closed eyes.

I shuddered a little, and not from joy. "Let's just ride past that and pretend you didn't say it, and maybe you can tell me what you mean by 'working against me' instead."

"Sure, sure," Michelle said, "just a second." Another lady was standing next to her, dark-haired and dressed in very, very plain clothes—a cloth uniform-like top and pants that matched. She looked to be in her fifties and little slivers of grey hair were streaking through the black. They exchanged words in Chinese. Then the older lady walked out the door and turned right, heading west up Canal Street, disappearing with a last look back at me.

"Who's she?" I asked, watching her go.

"One of my many, many employees," Michelle said. "Now…where were we?" She prodded that tendon on the underside of my foot, and I grimaced because it hurt.

"Someone or something is working against me, you said."

"My, my, you have a keen grasp of focusing on your enemies and hobbles," Michelle said, running a finger solidly up my left Achilles tendon and against the meat of my calf, pushing my pants leg out of the way like it wasn't even there. It didn't appear to want to resist her any more than I did.

"You get people trying to kill you as often as I have, it becomes a survival mechanism," I said, moaning because now Li Na was hitting a real kink between my shoulder blades, her hands pancake-flat beneath my back yet still somehow effective.

"I can imagine," Michelle said. "You ask what works against

you here? Probably the same thing as in any city: natural enemies to what you represent." I opened my eyes, watching her face as she worked on my foot.

"What do I represent?" I asked.

"The law," she said, smiling slyly. "For example, someone in my world might see your arrival as a harbinger of trouble that could come their way—an unpleasant change to the status quo that heralds worse to come."

"So, like rats see water flooding into a sinking ship?" I stared at her.

She cocked her head at me, not missing a beat. "Rats tend to survive sinking ships a lot better than human beings do." She thudded the base of her hand against the meat of my left heel and I almost gasped. She seemed to smile, acknowledging my pain. "But no, I hardly see New Orleans as a sinking ship. The water she took on was years ago; now she's riding high again…especially if you listen to our new governor's assessment of the situation."

"Funny thing about that," I said. "I've never heard a politician give an honest dead reckoning of a situation in their own state unless they're trying to get elected to fix it, and then they usually err on the side of it being worse than it is."

"It's almost as if they're working in their own interests," Michelle said, adopting a sort of faux-scandalized tone. "Amazing, that."

"Which brings us around to the same question again," she said, considering something—my foot, what was on her mind—very carefully as she worked. "What incentive would someone in my position have to work with someone like you?" She looked me right in the eyes. "Let's say they knew…something…about what happened here today. Why would they want to stick out their neck and help someone like you? Someone who could bring a considerable amount of trouble on them?"

Michelle was a subtle person, the kind who invited a known superpowered person and federal agent into her massage parlor to soften them up before dropping something. I, on the other hand, was not subtle, and I had a strange feeling I was being tested here for exactly that. The conundrum seemed obvious—Michelle wanted to share something about the assassination, but she wanted some assurances that I wouldn't bring the hammer down on her or her criminal enterprise if she did. Quid pro quo.

It put me in a slightly tight spot, but not really. "My purview is metahumans committing crimes," I said. "Ordinary OC activities are out of my purview, and I don't tend to worry about them unless I stumble on something particularly egregious in the amount of pain it's causing, where leaving it alone would be a moral wrong."

"An interesting line to draw," Michelle said, giving me another slap on the bottom of the foot that seemed to signal she was wrapping up. "Very well." She pursed her lips. "One of my employees ran into a woman on her walk to work the other day. Just after the shot, and behind the Hotel Fantaisie."

"Oh?" I tried to nibble the bait, not go after it like a mechanical shark leaping open-mouthed toward Roy Scheider's sprinkled chum.

"Yes," Michelle said, doing a little cold-playing of the news herself. "A woman carrying a golf bag, pulling a suitcase…and wearing a wig." A small smile spread across her tight lips. "Might that be of interest?"

"Yes, it would," I said as Li Na seemed to finish up at my shoulders. "Where can I find this witness?"

Michelle's smile got just a touch wider as she peeled off her gloves one at a time. "Why, she just walked out the front door a minute ago. You know?" The smile turned into a grin, pure mischief. "The lady that I spoke to just now?"

"Crap," I said, popping to my feet in a single jump. Michelle leapt back as though expecting this, but Li Na almost caught a shoulder in her nose for being slow. "You could have stopped her." I looked down. "Hey—where the hell are my boots?"

"Hmmm," Michelle said, making a show of looking down, befuddled. "I don't know." She looked back up at me and smiled. "I'm sure we can find them—if we looked very hard for the next few minutes. But then you might not be able to catch…" She chucked a thumb over her shoulder, still smiling.

"You set me up," I said, glaring at her. "She got a cell phone?

So you could call her back?"

Michelle shook her head. "Lives at a boarding house I run for my employees in town, but she has a tendency to disappear elsewhere, especially when she doesn't have a shift for a few days." Her grin got really toothy. "Which she doesn't until…oh…three days from now, I think?" She waved me to the door. "Go try and catch her. I'm sure we'll find your shoes by the time you get back."

"Damn you—and thank you," I said, and bolted for the open door out onto Canal. The street was buzzing with activity, the afternoon rush in full swing.

Holloway and Burkitt were lounging on the SUV's hood and both snapped to attention the moment I burst out. "A Chinese woman, probably in her fifties, came out of here in the last three minutes or s—"

"That way," Holloway said, snapping up to point to the nearby street corner. "Down Bourbon."

I looked toward a narrow street, clogged and glutted with pedestrians surging in and out. "I finally get to visit Bourbon Street," I said, bolting for it. Traffic was high; no chance in hell they'd beat me taking the SUV. Not at this hour. "And it's for a foot chase where I'm barefoot." I could already feel the pavement skinning away at the soles of my feet as I burst into a metahuman-speed run. "So much for being the Big *Easy*."

19.

Olivia

My Uber dropped me at the end of Fremont Street and I was left staring down the strange, tunneled street in the fading desert light as the sun sank behind the buildings. Something was clearly going on, the LED display that roofed in the entire length of the street lit red, a bizarre tableau that made it look like hell had come to Vegas. It shed its light on the street below, which seemed to be almost abandoned. I half expected a tumbleweed to roll through any second.

The storefront windows to each of the four casinos that comprised the mass of Fremont Street had been shattered, sparkling glass reflecting the red shining down from above. Veronika stood at the crossroads of the four hotels, looking around as though something were going to happen at any moment. She was alone in this, whatever pedestrian traffic usually present at this time of day vanished like an ice cube on a Vegas sidewalk at midday.

"You should have stayed on the Strip with me," Veronika said as I approached, coming in at a jog.

I eyed the zipline that hung over us. It was abandoned, and I wondered what it must have felt like walking down this street and seeing people zip over you. I would have guessed anxious. Or at least *I* would have felt anxious to have people zipping over me. I'd be afraid they'd fall and clean my clock. Or bounce off, I guess. Fatally.

"What's going on here?" I asked. The cops looked like they had started to establish a perimeter on the west side.

"Shhhh." Veronika held a finger up to her lips. "Be vewwwy quiet."

I stared at her blankly. "Why?"

Her neck sagged as her face contorted to disbelief. "Are you joking? Or are you just a millennial?"

"No and yes," I said, trying to figure out what the hell she was talking about.

"You don't know Bugs Bunny?" she asked, still staring at me like I was an idiot.

"I had an…unconventional upbringing," I said, shaking my head. "Kinda cult-like. Not much contact with the outside world. Cloistered, you could say."

"Well, we're wabbit hunting, okay?" Veronika looked around slowly. "The speedster is tearing around here, ripping shit up like you wouldn't believe. They've evacuated the hotels and casinos, funneling people out the back. Now he's just going ape shit tearing everything apart for fun, I guess."

"Not stealing anything?" I asked. I still hadn't seen any movement yet, other than a few flickering signs and the overhead oscillation of the red-lit roof.

"Hell, he could have carried away half the casino vaults by now and the only way we'd know is if he zipped by waving a ton of bling and showering us in hundred-dollar bills like ultra-premium strippers," Veronika said, her hands starting to glow blue. "Actually, I wish he would do that."

I felt myself flush. "Wouldn't that, uh…degrade us?" She gave me another withering idiot look. "Uhm, or something?"

"If getting showered in dollars while keeping my clothes on is degrading, then I wish I could get degraded like that every day," Veronika said. "Every. Damned. Day."

Before I could piece together a reply to that, I heard something in the distance. "Did you—" I started to ask.

Veronika flicked a blast of plasma the size of a pencil eraser past my face and held her glowing finger to her lips to shush me. Her lips took on the burning, ultraviolet cerulean quality of her plasma powers for a moment before fading back to her customary crimson shade, and she cocked her head to the side, looking at one of the casinos.

"You should, uh, be careful doing that," I said, watching the little piece of plasma fade off into the distance. I didn't think she'd noticed, but it had caught my personal space bubble and been arrowed through the air to land somewhere near where I'd entered the Fremont Street corridor.

The doors to Binion's Gambling Hall were thrown open and something was moving inside, a clang and clamor rising within as a slot machine came crashing over. No coins came spilling out, to my surprise. Probably kept those locked up tight.

"Heads up, cutie-pie," Veronika said, and I did a double-take to make sure she was talking to me. She was.

I frowned and shook it off, my attention stolen by the blur of motion coming out of Binion's. It was hard to see, but it had a black tinge to it, the air rustling as cocktail napkins exploded out the front door of the place in a whirlwind, as though Reed himself were exiting with all the force of his winds with him.

"Hey, Professor Zoom!" Veronika called, waving at the blur with glowing blue hands like she was guiding in a jet aircraft. "Over here!" She put her head down, steadied her feet. "You are cleared for clashing. Also, you should really wear something reflective in that clothing. You know, since you're out jogging and all, and it's getting toward night."

A high-pitched titter echoed over Fremont Street, and the blur, which had held still for a quarter-second, long enough for me to see a shadow with a hoodie over its head, shot at Veronika, who had anchored her feet for this. She thrust out a hand, glowing with blue plasma, and I could feel the heat where I stood, ten feet away.

I watched as it happened, the speedster blurring in at 600, 700, 800 miles per hour? I didn't even know. I couldn't see anything but a blur of motion, then a sudden black human-shaped object popped into view next to her for a second and then—

Veronika went sailing into the front windows at the Golden Nugget, plasma trailing behind her until it snuffed out just before she disappeared through the twinkling glass.

"Uh oh," I said, looking at the black figure, who just sat

there, in a blurred state, as though shifting back and forth between their two feet so fast I couldn't quite get my eye to settle on them.

We were all alone now, not a cop in sight.

Gulp.

20.

Sienna

The Big Easy was so far being nothing of the sort; it was more like the Big Hard, especially on my tender bare feet as I sprinted around the corner onto Bourbon Street.

The faint scent of sewage tickled my nose, like there was an open main in the distance. Crowds swirled, cramming a street that looked like it had been made for horse-drawn buggies and never widened when the automobile came along. There was so much neon visible it felt like Vegas was nodding in admiration. An adult toy store beckoned from my left. Surely more fun than running barefoot along a crowded street. I ignored the call to adventure that it presented in favor of the task at hand.

Bars lined the street after that. Bars and restaurants. But mostly bar/restaurant combos. Yes, Bourbon Street was bars, bars, everywhere, and not a drop I could drink.

The steady thud and scrape of my every footfall made it plain to me that Michelle—damn her and, yes, thank her—had orchestrated this, every bit. She'd meant for me to get caught flatfooted, or rather, barefooted, and to have to run my ass off to catch the only damned witness I had for whatever scrap of info she might have.

Why did she do this?

Hell if I knew. Maybe it was as simple as a criminal needing to balance helping a cop with causing her a problem, too.

Maybe there was something more ominous coming, like a sudden explosion that would spray the street with glass, forcing me into a John-McClane-type situation that would bloody the hell out of my feet.

If that happened, my vow to avoid looking too deeply into her criminal enterprise? Null and void. I'd move down to New Orleans and tear her shit apart brick by brick, twisting every case the FBI handed me into being Michelle's responsibility somehow. It might be a bit of a stretch, but I could probably do it.

It took me about a hundred yards at a flat-out sprint before I realized that I didn't need a field of broken glass in order to turn my feet into a bloody, McClane-like mess. My skin, exposed to the natural skid and push of running, was doing that to itself just by virtue of my meta speed.

I should have known. There was a reason I went through boots like some people went through underwear. Every step started to hurt, and I blotted out the pain. I was really good at that.

"Slay Queen!" someone yelled. That I wasn't so good at blotting out, especially when the crowd took it up in a slow-moving chorus of surprise at my high-speed approach.

I was bolting down the middle of the street, which was crowded, people moving through in groups. I was sprinting my ass off, passing through another intersection so quickly I almost hit a slow-moving car. I leapt right over it instead, keeping an eye out for my target as I reached the apex of my leap—

Nope. There were a lot of jet-black heads bobbing in the crowd ahead. Bourbon Street wasn't exactly packed from curb to curb, sidewalk to building, but it was pretty damned busy. No cars were moving on it, at least not for a few blocks, and the one I saw was cruising really slow with the crowd, maybe five miles an hour or so.

The landing drew a grunt of pain as I skidded, crushing my little toe when I came down. I suppressed the scream and the profanity that might have drawn under normal, in-my-apartment-and-stubbing-my-toe circumstances, but it damned sure hurt. I couldn't quite hear the crack over the background noise of Bourbon Street, but it must have been there, subtle and quiet under a nearby shout of, "Slay Queen!" by a really inebriated jackass in a leather jacket.

"Hi," I said as someone stepped into my path and I detoured around them, skinning a layer off the sole of my foot as I pushed sideways.

"Whoa," some guy behind me said, loud enough that I heard him clearly. "Look at the bloody footprints. She's following a trail."

"No, I'm leaving one," I shouted behind me.

I kept sweeping the crowd, looking for black hair, black hair, black hair and a certain skin tone. I'd find a possibility, then look to the clothing, and it was an easy elimination nine times out of ten. Americans wear denim. Denim and yoga pants, and lots of it.

Not this lady. That was what had been distinctive about her—she was wearing cloth pants. It was a very different look. Maybe just old.

Bourbon Street was young people and tourists on vacation. Denim, denim, denim. Blue jeans, black jeans, black stretchy pants, clear and obvious in the waning twilight and neon shine.

"Ow, ow, ow." I hobbled to a stop, picking up first one foot, then the other as I checked myself for injury. I flicked a shard of glass out of the ball of my left foot. I'd felt it, but thought it was a really lodged-in pebble. Removing it caused a steady stream of red to well up and run down the side, following the course of gravity.

"Are you okay?" a guy with a deep Southern accent asked. He was wearing a purple hat that proclaimed him a fan of LSU.

"Nothing that a good face-punching of a certain Chinese mob-running yoga pants mom wouldn't fix," I said, checking the other foot quickly. It was lacking a layer of skin or five, oozing blood from a dozen capillaries.

There was nothing for it; I broke into a run again, zigzagging my way through the Bourbon Street crowds as gingerly as my feet allowed.

Black hair—nope. Black hair—there. Cloth pants? No.

Neon burned my retinas as I ran down the street, fighting to ignore the screeching, escalating pain in my feet. A horn honked behind me and I looked back to see Burkitt and Holloway in the SUV, probably five blocks behind me. The lights were flashing in the front windshield, but the crowds were not exactly parting for them. I could see Canal Street another five or so behind that.

I'd run ten blocks in less than a minute. No wonder my feet were shredded.

"Has anyone seen a Chinese grandma?" I shouted, trying to make myself heard over the occasional shout of—yes—"Slay Queen!" That was going to get old. Hell, it already was. "Yea tall?" I held up a hand a little bigger than myself. "Anybody? Bueller?"

"Hey, are you looking for that lady?" Some guy in a Saints jersey pointed at a woman next to him in a touristy Panama Jack shirt, a pair of mom jeans, and her hair in a tight bun.

She looked scandalized. "I'm Korean, jerk face!" She hauled off and slapped him across the shoulder.

"Ouch," I said as he clawed at his shoulder in misery. It looked like she hadn't held back. "Also, clearly no." I moved past them and she huffed off. "Anyone? Looking for a Chinese grandma-type, answers to the name of—hell, I don't know her name." I used an unsuspecting couple burly guys as a support, planting my hands on their shoulders and shoving off them to spare my poor, tender feet. It gave me a little boost, and a farther look down the street.

There wasn't a hell of a lot of hope that I could see. The next corner had—surprise—another bevy of bars, one of which was open air, pumping throbbing music out onto the street.

"Sonofa," I said as another honk sounded behind me, now only a block back. I'd slowed my pace and they'd picked it up, and Burkitt and Holloway were now right there. I was tempted to wait for them, but I pressed on, stumbling ahead, my feet now screaming at me with every single step. I'd ignored it before, but now the pain was so intense I couldn't ignore it any longer. I was limping, trying to walk on the less-sensitive, marginally less wrecked edges of my feet rather than plowing ahead at full speed and skinning them down into hamburger meat.

"Get out of the damned way, you idiots!" Holloway shouted, voice echoing over the idle chatter and loud music on Bourbon. "Can't you see the flashing lights?"

"Somebody must have got wrecked," a guy in front of me said, walking in a line with four or five of his buddies. They looked like the offense for one of the local college teams, but hell if I had enough blood flow left in my body to remember any of their names.

"Yeah," I said, causing him to look back. "It was your mom. Move out of the way so the ambulance can come get her, huh? Your rivals really had a good night with her. I mean, she had fun, too, but if you don't move out of the way so she can get treatment, she's never going to walk right again."

"What the—" he started to say, eyes flaring to hate as his buddies laughed. They hauled him out of the way before I had to, and I stumbled past as they held him back.

I stopped at the end of the next block, right in the middle of the street. My bloody footprints were almost puddling now, crimson coming out of me thick and heavy. I could hardly walk, I'd done such a damned number on myself. A wise person might have stopped before ripping their own feet to shreds, but I guess nobody ever called me wise.

They called me Slay Queen, duh. Because I pursued the target until the job was done.

But now it was starting to look like maybe I was the one who was done. One final stumbling leap and I still didn't see her. Nowhere in the crowd ahead, which seemed to thin the farther we meandered along Bourbon, did I find a Chinese grandma sticking out at me. She could have taken off at any one of a dozen or more cross streets. I didn't keep track of any of them, so stubbornly had I plunged ahead trying to find her on this one, singular track.

Probably because given the dozen cross-streets, and each one thereafter carrying its own cross-streets…the possibilities became infinite very quickly. Or at least near enough that I could never have tracked her down.

"Shit," I said as Burkitt honked again behind me, now only twenty feet back, cutting through the crowd as it split to give way to them. I rested my hands on my knees, trying to distribute my weight in a way that didn't make the bottoms of my feet scream pain at me. I didn't find one.

"Any luck?" Holloway shouted as Burkitt pulled up behind me. I had a hard time hearing him over the music blaring out of the bar to my left.

"Only the bad kind," I said, standing up straight, but only through great effort. "I haven't seen one damned Chinese grandma anywhere on this street. I don't think she's here."

"Oh, we're looking for a Chinese grandma?" Burkitt was now hanging his head out the window, too, talking to me. "Like that one?" He pointed toward the front of the bar.

And there she was.

She was standing out front, watching me carefully, oversized bag held in front of her like a shield. As soon as I saw her, she shuffled her way over, keeping the bag between her and me as though it might protect her from me kicking her into orbit. It wouldn't; only the pain in my feet and the knowledge that Michelle was wholly, entirely responsible for this would save her.

"I think you have been looking for me," she said, once she was close enough that a human could have heard her.

"Yes," I said. "I have." I glanced at the bar behind her. Blue light spilled out the front door and there was no front window, allowing the band playing inside to blare out onto the street. Must have been like a free sample to entice people to come in. Personally, I might have if they'd offered me a place to sit and rest my hamburger feet. "Have you been waiting here?"

She nodded, only once, and she didn't smile, which saved her from a kick right to the damned vaj, bag-shield be damned. "This is where Michelle told me to wait for you." No smile. At all. "Did she not tell you that this was where I would be?"

That was the only thing that saved her. But the next time I saw Michelle?

Well, those yoga pants were going to have the imprint of my foot in them for all eternity.

21.

Michelle wasn't at the massage parlor when we rolled back by with the grandma, whose name was Liu Min. I hobbled inside, the guy on the stool out front pausing to look at me as I dripped blood onto the sidewalk with every step. Didn't even ask if I wanted a foot massage for some reason; maybe he didn't think rubbing the exposed fascia would do much good.

One of the employees pointed to my boots sitting on a counter in the back, and I made sure to rub every bloody footprint into the low pile carpeting and leave streaks on the bare tile floor up front as I went. "Worst. Foot massage. Ever," I declared to the gasps and general shock of the customers on the cots in the front of the store as I dragged back past them.

"I called the office," Burkitt said as I climbed back in the back. He and Holloway were up front this time, both strangely quiet, which was possibly related to my bloody hamburger feet, though I wasn't entirely sure. "They're getting the local sketch artist to meet us there."

"Awesome," I said, dripping as much sarcasm as blood. "Then maybe we can run it through facial recognition and push it out to local news to see if we can get a match."

We fell into silence until we arrived at the local FBI office, a three-story, newish brick building a stone's throw from the shores of Lake Pontchartrain. It was about twenty minutes, I gauged, working through the silence of dusk falling on the city. The tall downtown fell away to more medium-sized buildings down to long gaps between the buildings, until finally we arrived at the FBI office. It was nestled away behind a head-high (to me) black iron fence that surrounded the parking lot.

Once we were inside, Burkitt took Liu Min back into a labyrinth of interrogation rooms while one of the locals showed me and my bloody feet to the women's locker room to shower. I didn't actually shower because most of my ensemble was still good enough to go along with, but I did spend about five minutes or so with my feet under the cold spray, watching crimson traces dissolve in the clear water, washing it down the drain.

When I came out, Holloway was waiting for me outside. He eyed my feet in vague disgust, then nodded in the direction that I assumed we should go, pushing off the wall he'd been leaning against and leading the way.

The FBI office wasn't as limited as our small branch in Midtown Manhattan, but it wasn't as labyrinthine as I imagined the Hoover building in DC was. It was a mid-sized office for a more mid-sized US city, neither huge nor small, and I guessed there were probably 30-50 agents housed here.

"She's working with the sketch artist now," Holloway managed as we walked along. He looked down at my feet again, which were covered with toilet paper as though I were a mummy. "Could be a while."

"She know anything else?" I asked.

He shrugged. "She bumped into the lady one time, on her way to work, for all of two seconds. If she knows more than she's telling, she's a hell of a liar."

"She works for the head of the Triads here in New Orleans," I said, "so I wouldn't rule out that she's a hell of a liar, especially given the trick that yoga-pants-wearing hell beast just pulled on me."

I half-expected Holloway to laugh at my pain, but he just shuddered. "I've got plantar fasciitis," he said, as though that explained anything. "I wouldn't have made it ten feet without my shoes, let alone half the length of Bourbon Street."

"Yeah, well, I guess that's what makes me special," I said. "Though apparently I could have walked and produced the same result."

He did a little half-shrug. "I'm not going to argue to make you feel better. Yeah, you got set up. But at least we got more than we started that little sojourn with. And you didn't know you were being baited."

"I had a feeling," I said, still limping my way along down the white-tile hallway. "She teed it up perfectly, though, put a time limit on me—'No, I don't have a way to contact her outside of work; no, she won't be back in for days'—I went hook, line and sinker for it, hard. And now I'm going to be walking like an Egyptian or whatever for at least the rest of the night."

He squinted at me. "Did you really just go with a Bangles song as your reference?"

"I don't know, it's what came to me," I said as we reached an open bullpen area. If there was any constant in my life it was that I was forever working in places that had bullpens. Something about the communal office effect seemed to be universal in law enforcement, which was where I spent my working life.

Burkitt was working at a cubicle, and rose when he saw us coming, doing a hard lean against a cubicle wall so that it bowed slightly from his weight. "Sketch artist is probably going to be a few hours. She's real thorough."

"It's 7:30," Holloway said, checking his old-school watch, the leather band snaking around his spray-tanned wrist. "I'm starving."

"Agreed," I said. "Willie's was good, but if I don't get something to eat soon, my feet are going to be the least bloody thing in my near proximity. Regenerating the soles of both my feet is going to burn a lot of calories."

Burkitt shrugged. "You've got time. Takeout and delivery options near here are just so-so. If you want, you could run out and get something. I've got your numbers, so if anything breaks loose before then, I can call you."

"You don't want anything?" I asked.

Burkitt patted his belly, which wasn't quite visible under his ballooning shirt until he put a hand against it. "I'm down fifteen pounds in the last couple months because I don't eat after 5 pm. It's a new diet I'm trying. Working so far."

"I'm on a diet where I need lots of red meat and scotch,"

Holloway said, clearly unimpressed. He glanced at me. "Steakhouse?"

"I'm in for the red meat, pass on the scotch," I said, "but yeah, let's do it." I knew he was a scotch guy. I could practically smell it coming out of his pores.

"I know a good one downtown," Burkitt said. "I'll text you the address." He fiddled with his phone for a second.

"Shall we?" Holloway asked, making an exaggerated motion toward the hall to the exit, as though I were a princess he was allowing to go first.

"After you," I said, and he didn't stand on ceremony. He went, and I followed a few paces behind, curious as to whether this dinner would go as fabulously as all the rest of my interactions with Holloway. If so, mine was not the only blood that would be shed this night.

22.

"You know what the problem is with 'your type' of jobs?" Holloway asked after he'd consumed about half his second scotch.

I just stared at him, not too surprised that in scotch-o veritas had revealed his true feelings about metahumans. It wasn't like he was the first lawman to consider anyone unlike him to be 'the other,' or that he might have some animus against me because I was different than him. My feet were still wrapped in toilet paper and uncomfortably crammed back in my boots so as not to ruin them, and I ignored the low mumble of pain from the nerves in my feet as I sipped from my water. "Gee, I can't think of a single thing wrong with 'my type' of jobs. There are definitely no adverse consequences at all."

Holloway laughed into his scotch, sloshing the liquid so that it almost slopped over the rim. We were sitting in an old-fashioned, wood-paneled steakhouse that reeked of mahogany or some other such rich scent. He'd drained his first round within a minute. The server reappeared with another a moment later, not even asking before bringing a refill. Holloway just had that look.

"Here's the thing about these jobs that I've learned in the last couple months," Holloway said, as though he were some kind of expert after just that much time spent. Like I hadn't been doing this for years. "It's worse than dealing with normal criminals."

"You don't say," I deadpanned. "I thought dealing with

people who can shoot flames out of their hands and control the very elements was bound to be so much easier than your ordinary, garden-variety crook."

"You're being an asshole, and I respect that, being one myself," he said, scotch back in hand, another quarter of it disappearing down his gullet. "Game recognizes game. But hear me out—your ordinary criminal, when they get cornered, they've got two avenues of recourse." He put the scotch down. "Surrender or pull a gun. Right?"

"Sure. Or do the hokey-pokey."

"Or that," Holloway said. "But one of your kind—well, the options are nearly limitless. They can still pull a gun—" he gestured to my hip, where my Glock imprinted against my jacket "—or pull from a possible gallery of powers that defies the damned imagination." He shook his head. "Like this assassin, for instance. If we catch up to her, what can she do?"

I thought about it a second. "Pull ice out of the air around her and throw it, shoot it. Freeze your skin, blood and bone if she lays a hand on you. Coat her skin in ice armor strong enough to resist bullets and punches—"

"See, that's some crazy shit right there," Holloway said. "These are things which should not be possible in the natural world. You don't see any animals with that ability."

I eyed his drink as he started to raise it up for another sip, which would probably end it. "You don't see animals with tumblers of scotch, either. Which is just another factor that separates us from them."

"It was a hard climb to the top of the food chain," Holloway agreed, "and it feels like there should be some benefits for us for getting there, you know? Which reminds me, we should expense this meal."

I'd seen the menu, and after three scotches—the third arrived again with nary a word said by the server as he dropped it at the table—I had my suspicions that any effort to expense this meal to the FBI was going to involve some element of fraud. The prices weren't utterly ridiculous, but neither were they anywhere near the per diem we were expected to adhere to as government employees on the job. I just shook my head and returned to the subject at hand rather than pursuing the topic of financial malfeasance on our part. "Metas may have more immediate danger to offer, but ever since this serum came along, it's a threat that's part of our world, and we're going to have to deal with it."

"But I don't have to like it," Holloway said. "Like crooks with guns. I don't like that, either. I deal with it, though." He made a motion of shooting with his finger. "But I wish they'd go away."

"Yeah, it's always a totally great thing when the state has an unchallenged monopoly on force," I said, nodding. "That never ends badly—except the hundred million people it killed last century."

"Oh, you're one of those," he said, snorting through his next drink. "Big surprise, you not liking authority."

"You love it, though, don't you?" I asked. "Maybe it's because I've had the boot put on me, but I start to get skeptical when someone tells me that my government can solve my problems."

"There's a chain of command," Holloway said. "That's how a civilized society works. We protect the people. That's why we have authority."

"Look, I don't inherently hate authority," I said. "I just don't trust it to avoid being corrupted. I tasted the consequences when a dangerous man turned that power against me, and it cost me two years of my life." More, if you counted this detour I was currently on. "I think my question to you would be—why do you trust it so much?"

"I came out of the military," Holloway said, straightening up in his seat as the server delivered a giant slab of meat to the table in front of him. He started cutting into it, and there wasn't even enough pink left to blush my cheeks, the savage. Overcooking his steak—another mark against him in my book. "You learn to obey the orders given, period."

"See, I've met military guys who came out with a different feel," I said. "Maybe they got the bad commanding officers or something, but they walked away with an inherent suspicion of authority, and the people who would tell you what to do."

"You can't have no rules," Holloway said around a big bite of overcooked meat. "That's chaos."

"Hey, I'm no anarchist," I said. "I'm all for rules and order—but there need to be limits on us, on what we can do if we're trying to keep that order. Otherwise you're kissing your freedom goodbye for that order, and you're basically living under tyranny." *And you came about an inch from it, if not for me*, I thought but did not say. The Harmon secret was going to be one that would probably die with me and my friends, since it resulted in the death of the last President of the United States.

"We protect these peons, okay?" Holloway pointed his fork in a rough circle around us at the other diners, and his voice carried. "They owe us. You think we overreach? I've been with the bureau fifteen years now, and I say screw you. You don't have any idea, Miss I-been-here-six-minutes."

"Technically I was with the bureau for five years and change before this. Albeit loosely."

"None of that counts in my book," Holloway said. "You ran your own show back then, you weren't really part of us. And when they tried to bring you in line, you bolted." He chewed a stubborn bite. Shouldn't have cooked it so hard, moron. "I know that's where you'd rather be right now. With your brother. Freelance law enforcement." He looked like he wanted to spit right there. Maybe from the overdone steak, I dunno. "Your loyalties were clear before. Seeing what you did to our agents in Revelen, though—"

I almost did a spit-take with my water. "'Agents'? That's what you call that criminal bunch of Suicide Squad wannabes?"

"They worked for us." He leaned in, gesticulating with his fork. "They were on our team."

"If they were five days out of prison when Chalke sent them after me, I'll eat your overdone, shoe-leather steak. Which is a crime again decency, by the way."

"Doesn't matter." Holloway's face was red—like my steak. But much, much less appetizing. "They were on our team." He sat back, dabbing at the corners of his mouth like he'd left crumbling pieces of burnt meat behind on his lips. "Like you are, now. I didn't like them, but they were part of the—"

"Tribe?" I asked, using my knife to very carefully cut off a beautiful piece of pure, red meat with a blackened edge. "They were of your tribe, so you're mad at me for whooping their asses when they tried to murder me?"

"They had the lawful authority of the Unites States government behind them," Holloway said. "Like you do, now. Hope you don't run into anyone who feels about you the way you did about them. Especially since you were in prison not that long ago."

"Not to go all Godwin's law on you," I said, cutting another even piece, "but the SS had the lawful authority of Germany behind them when they started rounding up undesirables. Same with any oppressive regime worldwide, whether it's Stalin's or Mao's or Robert Mugabe's. Lawful authority shouldn't impress you all on its own. And," I said, popping the steak into my mouth as Holloway's face went from red to purple at my vicious comparison, "I kinda expect the people we're after are not going to come quietly just because I say I'm with the FBI."

"Yeah, well," Holloway said, draining his third scotch, "I guess we see where each of us stands."

"Indeed, we do," I said. "You're standing in a place where you should have ordered the damned chicken instead of ruining a perfectly amazing cut of meat by scorching it to death like a Gavrikov. I mean, really—what's the point at that stage of burn? You could be eating cardboard and you wouldn't notice. Is that the reason for all that scotch?"

Holloway looked like he was going to blow up, but his phone rang before he could construct a response. He fumbled in his pockets for it, ultimately coming out with it and answering without even asking if he could take it—you know, in the name of politeness. "What, Burkitt?" he almost shouted.

I could hear Burkitt loud and clear on the other end. "The sketch is done and we're running it through the database. Get back here ASAP."

23.

Olivia

"Uh, hi," I said, not really sure what else to say. I was staring at the black, blurry figure, vibrating a few degrees off normal. I didn't know the science behind how they did that, but it seemed very much like they were internally spasming their muscles. I wondered—would their abs be sore from this tomorrow?

"Are you nervous?" the shadow asked, blurry. "You seem nervous."

"Ahhhh…" I stared at the blur. "Well, I have to admit—confronting blurry people destroying downtown Vegas is a new experience for me."

"I'm not destroying anything," the blur said, voice a strange kind of harmonic resonance akin to someone speaking through a tuning fork. I couldn't tell if they were male or female, only that they were human. Presumably. "I'm just making a little mischief."

I glanced around Fremont Street somewhat theatrically. "I think this qualifies as more than a 'little' mischief. Look at Binion's." I pointed. "That place is trashed. Like 'frat house on the morning after a kegger' trashed." I was not speaking from personal experience, having never attended college myself.

The blur zipped behind me, and I turned to watch them. They weren't making any aggressive moves toward me, which seemed strange after what they'd just done to Veronika. "Hm." The blur's voice went a touch higher, looking around, admiring their handiwork. "This…is nothing, though." They turned to look at me, and somewhere in the blur I caught a flash of dark eyes. "The convenience stores? Nothing. I could do more, you know."

"I'm sure you could," I said, glancing back to see if Veronika had picked herself up. I couldn't even see her, just the hole in the wall where she'd vanished. "The question is…do you want to?"

"Kinda," the blur said, looking right at me. "You're a cop, right?"

"Oh, no, I'm not, uh…exactly, no," I said, feeling a hot flush up my cheeks. "I'm more of a…contractor."

"You've got powers?" the blur asked. "Like her?" They pointed in the direction Veronika had flown.

"Yeah," I said. "I…yeah."

The blur zipped a couple steps more toward me. "What kind of powers?" There seemed to be a genuine curiosity behind the distorted voice. "Cool powers? Like your friend?"

"Veronika and I aren't really friends so much as co-workers," I said, feeling a twisty emotion in my belly like I desperately needed to correct that record lest this heinous criminal think…uh…whatever of me. Why did I care? I didn't know, but it seemed foolish in that moment. The thought occurred—in my life, how many times had I cared about someone's opinion when they were just as much a dipstick as this person?

Politeness, though. Manners. These thoughts kept me talking nicely.

"Uh huh, uh huh," the blur seemed to coo, harmonically. "What kind of powers do you have?"

"Oh…they're…nothing, really," I said, waving them off, fake laughing a little for social reasons, maybe? I didn't even know why I was doing what I was doing. I felt really hot, uncomfortably so.

"So, they're not exciting?" The blur let out a hiss of air. "Boring, then. Yeah. I'm bored. Okay, time to go."

The blur shot toward me.

"Wait—" I started to say as they zoomed from zero to a hundred miles per hour in a millisecond.

I didn't even get the full word out before the blur reached my personal bubble. It didn't occur to me until they'd launched into motion that, really, mine was sort of the perfect power to go against this particular villain. Because the moment they reached arm's length of me—

The speedster got caught in my personal bubble, their momentum magnified by a factor of ten, a factor of a hundred—

They orbited around me like they'd been trapped in my own personal gravity well, zipping past, and shot out of it into the air behind me. They shattered through the ceiling of Fremont Street and into the sky, a vague, "AHHHHHHHHHHHHH—" trailing after them.

I stood there in the silence for a moment after they'd gone, just staring up at the newly minted hole in the roof. A little tinkling glass forced me to spin around—

Veronika was pulling herself out of her hole in the wall, blood dripping out of her nose and a few other cuts on her skin. A bruise had already started to form on her forehead, but the look in her eyes was pure murder, both hands already glowing bright blue with searing hot plasma. "All right," she said, "where is that son of a bitch?"

I blinked at her a couple times, then pointed at the hole in the ceiling. "But…way past the roof at this point," I said. "Like…miles away, probably."

She slumped back onto her haunches, all that meanness and fight just gone out of her in a second. "Well, good," she said, the plasma burning off, her hands returning to normal. She mopped the blood trail under her nose, smearing it. "Because I think I need medical attention before we try for round two." And with that she keeled over backward, dead to the world.

24.

Sienna

"Sitrep," Holloway said, looking like he was going to keel over as we made our way back into the FBI bullpen. I'd driven as he'd grumbled something about me being an anarchist. I was amazed he was still upright after mainlining three scotches in twenty minutes or so, but he definitely wasn't functioning on a very high level.

"The sketch artist finished about a half hour ago," Burkitt said, smiling as we sauntered up to his cube, which was adorned with zero pictures of his kids, surprising me. Wasn't it federally mandated that if you had kids, you had to be eager to brag and show pictures without your single acquaintances even asking?

"Where's Liu Min?" I asked.

"We cut her loose once she was done," Burkitt said with a shrug. "Got an address and phone number where we can reach her if we have any other questions. She did have a cell phone, and said the manager of the massage parlor calls her on it all the time."

"But of course," I said. Next time I saw Michelle, she was going to find out what those yoga pants tasted like—all the way in the back of her throat.

"Here it is," Burkitt said, raising up a picture of a blonde woman with sunglasses on. It wasn't a great picture, thanks to the glasses being in the way, but it beat the hell out of the limited surveillance footage I'd seen because of one crucial factor:

Her hair was blonde. Yellow-blonde, not white-blond, a sunny color that was a marked contrast to the black wig she'd been wearing.

"Hello, Elsa," I said, looking at the photo, which was a photocopy of the original. There was already a stack of them on Burkitt's desk. I looked up. "Blonde-ish, winter powers—"

"I got it," Burkitt said, grinning. "My kids love that movie."

"My wife has the kids," Holloway said, a little more grouchily, shoving his way back into the conversation. "And all my money. We don't really talk, the ungrateful little shits."

"How utterly unsurprising," I said, turning my attention back to the sketch. "You said it's running now?"

"Yeah," Burkitt said. "It'd be a miracle if we got a hit before tomorrow, th—"

"Hey, Burkitt," a dark-skinned woman called from across the bullpen. "Your sketch got something."

"Do you believe in miracles?" I asked, deadpan.

"Not since 1980," Holloway hiccupped.

We made our way across the room to a smaller office off the main bullpen where a few computers sat. A tall, broad-shouldered guy was sitting at one of them, the printer next to it quietly humming as it spit something out. "Hey, Clemons," Burkitt said. "This is Holloway and Nealon from—"

"Yeah, I know," Clemons said, not looking up. "Your sketch turned up an interesting result." He picked up the paper the printer spit out and handed it over his shoulder to us. "Jane Doe from a missing persons case."

"So, our assassin decided to check out of civilized society before beginning her assassinating career," Holloway said, thumping into the doorway as he tried to keep upright. "What's 'interesting' about that?"

Clemons was the kind of guy whose eyebrows seemed to naturally rise in response to stimuli, which gave him a funny look as he peered at Holloway. "The interesting part? This is from a—a whaddya call it, where they make a model of a dead and decomposing body that they can't identify?"

Holloway shrugged. I didn't know, either, and apparently

neither did Burkitt.

"Well, it was one of those," Clemons said, flapping a strangely realistic photo image of a woman who looked a hell of a lot like our sketch. "Shown all over the news, based on a body that was found partially decomposed in Caernarvon Freshwater Diversion, Plaquemines Parish, in June of last year." He pulled up a grisly photo of a dead body floating in water from a crime scene file. "So…looks like your assassin bears an awfully close resemblance to a dead woman."

25.

"What the hell is going on here?" I asked, pacing around the small computer room. Holloway and Burkitt were standing, like me, and Clemons, the local geek—except he didn't look like a geek, really—was sitting in front of the computer, still tapping away like he had more to find.

"Murder, intrigue, desperation," Holloway managed to slur out, still suffering the effects of the three glasses of scotch he'd inhaled at dinner.

"Assassination, not murder," Burkitt said, arms folded in front of him. "Technically. And attempted, at that."

I rubbed my forehead. "My job is to pound superpowered criminals into a paste when they get out of line. Not run half-marathons in my bare feet along Bourbon Street or try to untangle mysteries about dead women rising from the grave to shoot the governor of Louisiana."

"Is there a metahuman power to rise from the dead?" Burkitt's face froze in a stricken look. "Is that a real thing?"

"Not as far as I know, and I'm actually related to the Greek god of the dead," I said, continuing my pacing as Burkitt relaxed about a half a millimeter. "But that doesn't mean there isn't one I don't know about." I considered, just for a moment, reaching out to old Hades and seeing what he had to say about the subject, but that'd be a pain in the ass, at least until bedtime, and at that point I already had another call I wanted to make.

"So, is this gal actually dead?" Holloway asked, looking at

my feet.

I had my boots back on, but I got the implication. "You think they found her corpse, dead from drowning, but she healed and came back to inflict furious vengeance on the parties who wronged her? Which maybe includes the governor?"

Holloway blinked. "Huh?"

I pointed at my boots. "You were looking at my feet. I figured you were thinking about how fast metahumans heal."

Holloway shook his head. "No, I'm just having trouble holding my head up at this point. Got real sleepy all the sudden."

"A gallon of scotch will do that to you," I said, rolling my eyes. Burkitt and Clemons averted theirs; I guessed squealing on a co-worker for drinking during an on-the-job dinner was part of that whole blue wall of silence thing. "But you raise an interesting point. Maybe she isn't dead. Maybe the coroner thought she was, from drowning, but once her lungs got clear enough to draw a breath, her body healed and she came back. Angrier, certainly, probably with some higher brain function reduced, but—"

"Wait, that can happen?" Burkitt asked. "I thought you said there was no metahuman resurrection power."

"I was thinking in a more classic, 'He arose!' sort of sense," I said. "There have been cases where a metahuman powerful enough was badly wounded or suffocated somehow and as soon as they got breath in their lungs and oxygen to their brain, they sprung back to life, fresh as a daisy. A rabid daisy, because of the higher brain functions being shut down so long, but still—a daisy."

"So, we have a dead body that may not be dead," Holloway said, rubbing his head as if the hangover had started to set in. "Here's another reason I hate this detail. Any other job, dead people stay dead."

"Not so," I said. "This isn't restricted to your current job. Metahumans are out there, now, and always have been, though more and more are coming out these days. Your issue is not with this job, it's with change in general. You dinosaur."

He flicked me a single-finger salute. "Fine, expert. What do we do now?"

"It seems to me," I said, "in my non-expert opinion, this so-called lead has left us with more questions than answers. Now we've got a possibly dead or maybe not dead girl—"

"Twins," Clemons said, tapping away.

I blinked as that one settled on the room.

"It's never twins," Holloway said with an air of barely contained impatience.

"It could be," Clemons said. "Identical twins."

"It's not twins, dammit," Holloway said.

"Is it not because it's *really* not," I said, "or because you don't want it to be?"

Holloway was holding his head, eyes closed, and did not answer.

"Anyway, I'd be remiss if I didn't point out that this could actually be a false positive," I said, looking again at the sketch. "We are going on a drawing composed by a woman who saw our suspect for all of five seconds, tops. It wouldn't be a stretch to say she could be wrong and this is officially a wild goose chase."

"Also, the result is of a decomposed body partially recomposed by an artist," Burkitt said, the voice of reason. "It could be off in the details, lending credence to the idea this lead is setting up a wild goose chase."

"Well, your goose took a shot at a governor, so she's certainly wild," Clemons said, and he looked up. "I'm into the autopsy file on the Jane Doe, if you have any questions."

"Holloway is wondering if the curtains match the carpet," I said, drawing such a hateful look from him that it made my night worthwhile. "Also, do we have a cause of death?"

"Cause of death is listed as drowning," Clemons said, and then he double-clicked the mouse so a way-expanded view of an overhead cadaver photo blew up on the screen, then turned away like he didn't want to look at it. "As for that other question…"

"Ew," I said. The body had clearly been in the water a while. "If she did come back from the dead, she'd sure have a lot to be pissed off about."

"Okay, I have a question about this," Burkitt said, looking

like he was really hesitant to even ask. "If she was this badly decomposed…I mean…how would a meta even come back from this?"

"Like this," I said, and pulled my right foot out of my boot, ripping off the toilet paper I'd mummified my foot with in the process.

Burkitt stared at my foot, eyes widening as he looked. "Half the sole of your foot has already grown back."

"Yeah, they do that," I said, pushing the toilet paper back in place as I stuffed my foot back into my boot. "As long as my brain gets oxygen, my body repairs itself." I paused, coming up with a list of qualifiers to that which I didn't want to list out right there. "Subject to some reasonable limitations."

"Do you grow a new arm or leg it gets chopped off?" Burkitt asked.

"Yes," I said. "And that's come very in handy on multiple occasions."

"Okay, question," Clemons said, now spun totally around in his chair to face me. "If you were decapitated—"

I raised an eyebrow. "You been reading Holloway's diary?" Holloway just rolled his eyes.

"—and they put your brain in a jar, would you be able to grow a new body?"

"That's a great question," I said, "and one I hope I never have to discover the answer to, for obvious reasons."

"As much fun as it is to think about ways to harm Nealon here," Holloway said, "can we get back to the dead body we're talking about? And just leave the various ways to kill this young lady for my diary entry later?" He raised his voice to slightly high and mocking, "'Dear Diary, Today I discovered that trying to bleed her to death via excessive road rash does not work. Next idea.'"

"Good point by Holloway," I said.

"About the diary?" Clemons asked.

"About us getting back on track," I said. "The diary is just mildly disconcerting. Let's play this two ways: one, our assassin is *not* the person in these autopsy photos. If that's the case, we're on the wrong track and at a dead end until something else breaks. However, if they are either the person in the photo or related—"

"Twins," Clemons muttered, drawing another pissed-off look from Holloway.

"—then we've got a break and we need to exploit it fully," I said. "And we need to figure out how the hell this ties to Warrington."

"Here's another head-scratcher," Burkitt said. "Why did this lady assassin make an ice bullet? I mean, she went through all this other trouble to maintain her anonymity—fake credit cards, cleaning up the room, picking up her brass and wearing gloves so there were no fingerprints—"

"She could just be a person that doesn't leave fingerprints," Holloway said, holding up a hand. "Some people just don't make the grease needed to generate them."

"Either way," Burkitt picked up, "she goes through all this trouble, then signs her work by making a bullet with powers."

"But were they her powers?" I asked. "Someone else could have made the bullet."

"My head hurts," Holloway said.

"Scotch," I muttered.

"It's way too complicated," Holloway said. "Too many questions."

"Seriously, though, Burkitt has a great point," I said. "Why bother with an ice bullet? A regular bullet would have done as well, though I guess this one didn't hold fingerprint evidence. Or ballistics."

"That gave us less to work on," Holloway said. "That's not nothing, in terms of a reason to do it."

"Maybe," I said. "Something about it doesn't sit right with me, but we'll puzzle it out later. Now, we've got something to do." I looked at Clemons. "Where's she buried?"

Clemons minimized the corpse photo window now that the question I hadn't really wanted answered had been kindasorta answered, if that wasn't seaweed. "Blackford Cemetery." He frowned. "Huh."

"That place is huge," Burkitt said. "Right out the interstate. We passed it on the way in from the airport."

"Hey, Burkitt," Clemons said, still frowning. "You ever heard of a Jane Doe getting buried at that cemetery?"

Burkitt paused halfway out the door, and then he started frowning. "No. Unidentified and unclaimed bodies usually get held for years at the coroner's office. Hell, I think they've still got corpses from Katrina there."

"Exactly," Clemons said, and shook his head. "No record here of who claimed the body or paid for a burial plot, but if I were on this investigation—"

"You'd ask whodunit?" I flashed a grin of my own to match his small smile and nod. "Adding it to the list for whoever we talk to when we get out there."

"It's pretty dark, you know," Holloway said, finally spurring himself into motion. "How likely is it we even get hold of anyone at this Blackford at this hour?"

"I don't know," I said. "See if you can find a contact for us there, Clemons?" He nodded, and we headed out.

"What's your genius plan if they tell us to come back during normal business hours tomorrow?" Holloway asked. I could hear the stumble in his step as he followed behind me by a few paces.

I didn't bother to turn as I answered. "That's what I've got you for, Holloway. I've got an activity planned for you to sweat your way back to sobriety." I didn't let him see me grin. "Say, Burkitt…you got a shovel in that car? Because we're going to need one."

26.

"I can't believe you bought me a shovel," Holloway said, sounding a little nonplussed from his place in the back seat, with two shovel heads draped over it next to him. The black Louisiana night was broken every few hundred feet by a light pole as we cruised down Interstate 10, a sign for Metairie passing us by as we rolled onward.

"I seriously need your help in excavating the corpse," I said, trying to keep a straight face. I wasn't watching him nearly as hawk-like now, mainly because I doubted in his present condition he could shoot straight enough to hit me at six inches, let alone whatever the spacing was between us. "What's the point of having a big, strong man around if he doesn't spare my sensitive lady self from the hard labor portions of the job?"

"You should have been in the military, Nealon," Holloway said, settling his head back and clipping one of the shovel heads as he did. He was so impaired he didn't even realize I'd set them that way to mess with him. I could easily have turned them around, far from where they would bonk him. "You'd love basic, and you'd make a hell of a drill sergeant."

"I've thought about it," I said, "and it did sound like fun in my warped, crazy sort of way. But following orders is a tough gig for me, especially on a long-term basis."

Burkitt caught that from his place at the wheel, even if Holloway was too blasted to put it together. "How's that work with you being in the FBI, then?"

"TBD," I said.

"What the hell does that mean?" Holloway asked.

"To be determined," Burkitt answered for me. "How long you been in now?"

"Three months or so," I said.

"I guess the honeymoon is over if you're thinking like that." Burkitt tried to put a little humor into it, but I caught his genuine question behind it. Most people didn't start a job thinking they'd be out soon, and certainly not this kind of job.

We pulled off and took a right at the next exit, and I could see the cemetery in question. It was sprawling, looked like it went on for miles, and a megachurch with a tall steeple made for a nice background to the scene. We pulled up into the parking lots and found a couple guys standing there, both black, both huddled against the fifty degree or so weather in windbreakers, one with grey hair and a slump, the other younger, thin and tall.

"Man on the phone told us we'd know you when you showed up," the grey-haired fellow said as I stepped out of the SUV. Burkitt had parked right by the curb. "Reckon I do know you." He extended a hand to me, first. "Ma'am. Sam Purvis. I'm the caretaker."

I shook it, carefully, and only for a few seconds. "Sam, nice to meet you. This is Holloway and Burkitt." I looked behind me; only Burkitt had made it out. "Well, that's Burkitt. Holloway we only let out when he's had his nap and juice box."

"Screw you, Nealon," Holloway said once Burkitt had let him out of the child-locked backseat.

"Don't go thinking I'm easy just because I'm a succubus, okay?" I kept my tone light. "That's a vicious stereotype probably started by those sluts in the Persephone community who are just jealous of the legend of my sexual prowess. So…I guess I mostly blame Kat for that one. Which is maybe unfair."

"This is Deandre," Sam said, brow furrowed like he was trying to either make sense of or ignore what I'd just said. He nodded at his sidekick, the younger guy.

"Hey, Deandre." I shook his hand, too.

"Slay Queen," he said, almost under his breath.

Holloway fixed him with an icy glare. "She hasn't killed anyone yet today, kid."

"That you know of," I said. "And the day ain't over." I turned back to Sam. "Did our guy on the phone tell you what this was about?"

Sam nodded slowly. "I didn't have to look it up. I remember that funeral."

I looked over the cemetery. There had to be ten thousand plots, maybe more, in this place. "You remember that specific funeral?" I blinked a couple times. "For that specific Jane Doe?"

Sam caught my implication. "Heh. I know, you're thinking, 'He's old; how does he remember that?' But I do, because of the specific circumstances around it. See, something not many folks know—we get a lot of rain around here—"

"I knew that," Burkitt said under his breath.

"—and when you try to bury a body when it's raining really hard," Sam went on, like he hadn't heard Burkitt (and maybe he hadn't), "well…you ever been to a funeral?"

"Too many," I said.

"You know how at the graveside, they leave the coffin on a lift and lower it down after a few words are said?" Sam asked.

"Fancy ceremony for a Jane Doe," Holloway said.

"Mmhmm," Sam said. "But you know how we do that, yeah?"

"Sure," I said. "Priest or preacher says nice things about the departed, some comforting words or a passage of scripture, and then—" I mimed pulling a lever "—down we go."

"Exactly," Sam said. "Well, her funeral, see, we'd dug the hole the night before, and it started raining 'round midnight or so. By the time the service gets done and the coffin gets out here, we've got a nice tent set up, but water's running in from all over, flooding into the grave. When we go to lower the coffin…it don't go down all the way." He was looking at me with almost glowing eyes. "Sat there about a foot from surface level."

Deandre nodded. "Now I remember that one."

"So, what do we do?" Sam went on, seemingly energized by

his story. "Well, we bring in the backhoe and we bury her under as much dirt as we can. Which ain't much as we shoulda been able to, if the grave hadn't flooded." He made a motion with his hand to somewhere in the darkness behind him. "So, yeah, I remember her funeral. Or at least afterward. And I got some good news for y'all, if you're going to use those shovels I saw in the back—you won't have to dig all that deep, I don't reckon. Because odds are good, she's real near the surface."

"Excellent," I said, "because I didn't get a full dinner in, and my colleague is very plastered and probably useless for this. You want to show us the way?"

"Follow me," Sam said, waving us on. He had a fluorescent lantern in his hand and turned it on, sending a white light radiating out in all directions around us. "It's thisaway."

I followed behind Sam as he started a slow walk into the graveyard, taking us past a black, wrought-iron fence that encircled the place. It looked vaguely gothic to me, and a little chill shuddered its way down the skin of my back in the cool night. The heat of the day had gone away without a trace.

"You say you remember the funeral," I said. "Do you remember if anyone was at it?"

Sam was quiet for a long moment as he weaved along, picking a path between the gravestones. "I know there were people there, that much I recall. Smallish crowd, as these things go. Ten or so, maybe. But I didn't know any of the mourners, if that's what you're asking."

Burkitt appeared behind me, shovels over his shoulder. "Do you know who paid for it?" He must have opened the hatchback and fetched them while I started after Sam, and caught us. "The burial plot and funeral?"

"No, but Deandre can go give our office lady a call," Sam said, nodding at him. "We'd have a record of that. The office is closed for the night, but it's all online now, so she oughta be able to look it up."

"Everything online," Holloway murmured, and his voice held the aura of bitching. "I tell you, I don't know what this world is coming to." He stumbled forward, passing me and catching Sam, and gave the caretaker a bump of the elbow—gently—to the shoulder. "You know what I mean, old timer."

Sam looked at him a little strangely. "Don't reckon I do. Putting it all online made my job a lot simpler. I hated the old paper logbooks. You know how many of those we lost in Katrina? Now I have one of these boys input it, and it's in the cloud in seconds. This place washes away, the records stay." He pulled out a smartphone. "I'd look it up for you myself from here, but this phone lacks the necessary capacity to properly load the page in its browser. Too much information, too little brainpower." Sam gave Holloway a little side eye that I was pretty sure my drunken partner missed, and he said, "Common problem going around, I imagine."

I stifled a hard laugh at Holloway receiving a sick burn from a graveyard caretaker. It was compounded by Holloway's dumbstruck face, like he couldn't quite wrap his head around what he'd just heard.

Burkitt's light chuckle finished quickly, right about the time Sam brought us to a stop. "Here we are," Sam said, and there was a green mound and a small gravestone right in front of it, an angel carved into the surface beneath a simple inscription.

I stared at it, trying to push away a foreboding feeling. The last time I could recall being in a graveyard like this was in the Necropolis in Edinburgh, Scotland. Good things had not happened there, and the grave I'd looked into had been intended for me.

"You might want these." Sam tossed me a pair of heavy gloves that had hung on his belt. "Probably a bit big for you."

"I'll make do," I said. Burkitt looked at Sam askance, but the older man shrugged; he only had one pair, and I was going to need them more, though I doubted Burkitt knew that—yet.

"Oh my," Sam said after about five seconds of watching me dig.

It didn't surprise me that this was the first time he'd seen a metahuman work. Seeing me do crazy shit on TV was a lot different than watching me dig up a grave in real life, and the sheer volume of dirt I moved in two and a half minutes had Sam almost gasping.

"Yeah, yeah," Holloway said, leaning against a nearby tree about two graves away, "she's fast and strong and super blah blah blah. Let's all be amazed and call her the Goddess of

Death."

"That seems like an upgrade from Slay Queen," I said, pitching a shovelful of dirt right at him. It hit him in the chest, exploding in a puff as he bounced off the tree in surprise and outrage. "Oops," I said mildly, having already delivered another five shovelfuls onto the pile I was carefully making.

"Why did you even buy a second shovel?" Burkitt asked, leaping clear of the grave as I started attacking the very ground he'd been standing on a moment before. I hadn't wanted to say it, but he'd really been holding up my progress, and if he'd waited another minute to take the hint, I'd have told him to move myself.

"To annoy Holloway by making him think I needed his help," I said, digging a square foot of dirt out, eliminating the small patch where Burkitt had been standing in about twenty seconds flat. Now the grave was down three or four feet and I'd only been at it three minutes.

"Up yours, Nealon," Holloway said, still trying to brush the dirt off himself.

"Don't be so butthurt, Holloway," I said, not missing a shoveling beat. "I can smell your hemorrhoid cream from here."

He was quiet for a second. "You can smell that?" he asked quietly.

"Ewwww," I said, pausing and making a face. "That's what that chemical smell you give off from your pants is? I thought maybe you had some sort of jock itch you were treating."

"Wait," Burkitt said, paused, shovel in hand, now towering a few feet above me at the edge of the excavated grave. "Can you smell people's butts from a distance? Like a dog?"

"I'm a real bad bitch," I said, keeping my head down. "And yeah, kinda. It all sort of fades into a background nasal symphony of—"

"Oh, Lord, thank you for passing me over for these powers," Sam said. "The last thing I need to be doing is smelling someone's butt at twenty yards. Especially Miss Maisie Grantham's."

"I don't know who that is and I feel all the better for it," I said. About ten seconds later my shovel made contact with something hard. I'd been carefully paring back the power of my digging the farther I'd gotten into the ground, making initial probing thrusts with the shovel and then, sure that the next six inches or so of dirt were clear, quickly scooping it out in a frenzy of metahuman speed.

"Pay dirt," Burkitt said, and Holloway staggered into view. He almost looked like he was going to pitch forward into the grave beside me, but Burkitt steadied him with the shovel's handle just in time. Holloway didn't even say thanks.

"Yeah, well, let's hope," I said, gently sweeping away the dirt from the surface of the coffin, first with the shovel head, then squatting down and doing it with my gloved hands. Sam was at the edge of the grave now, too, his fluorescent lantern providing a guiding light. I'd unearthed the top of it, and the cracks where it opened were pretty obvious, the bowing surface reminding me of the arena at the Minnesota State Fairgrounds. "Any tricks to opening it?"

Sam shrugged. "Not particularly." He peered into the grave. "Hm. That ain't one of our lower-priced models."

"You're saying this is a higher-priced coffin?" I asked, squatting on the bottom section, where, presumably, the feet would be. Sam just nodded. "Curiouser and curiouser." I lifted the front of my blouse over my nose, skeptical that would do much to help against the olfactory assault I was about to experience, assuming there was a corpse in here. "Doesn't look like anyone clawed out of it, that's for sure."

"You think there's a body still in there?" Burkitt asked, leaning over now.

"Why wouldn't there be?" Sam asked. His brow was deeply furrowed, eyes shining in the light.

"Long story," I said. "Let's find out for sure so we don't have to waste an explanation for Sam before we know." I braced myself, putting a hand on the side of the coffin, the seam where it opened. "One, two—"

I heaved the coffin open, and my shirt over my nose did *nothing* for the smell. Nothing. My eyes burned, it was so fierce and immediate, like years of rot had been waiting to escape given just a half a chance. There was a collective gasp above me and I knew that the rest of them must have caught the stench, too, like death and swamp water had mingled and come to rest here, forever, brewing in an ever more potent mixture.

Until now.

It took me a few seconds to regain my composure, to blot the burning tears out of my eyes and look into the coffin. Once I was done, I shut it, quickly, in hopes that the smell would go with it.

It didn't, not entirely, but it helped.

"I guess that answers that," Burkitt said. Holloway was gone from graveside, and I heard him heaving up his guts not too far away.

"Why would you have thought the body was missing?" Sam asked, dropping his own shirt from around his nose. His eyes looked clear.

"We thought she might have been a meta," I said, "and still alive."

"That was not a long story," Sam said. "You could have told me that in three seconds." He looked back down at the closed coffin and waved the air in front of him. "Well, now you know she's still in there. What next?"

I looked up at Burkitt, and he looked back at me. "We send this back to a coroner with a strong stomach for a second round of testing, I think." I put a hand on my hip. "And then…" Holloway was still retching, one hand on the tree he'd been leaning against not long ago. No ideas were forthcoming, and I saw no reason to sugarcoat it. "And then…hell if I know."

27.

"I want to believe this means something," I said, staring at a note that Deandre had handed us when he'd come back to the open grave, "but it just doesn't."

"I'm not sure it actually does mean anything," Burkitt said. He was standing over my shoulder, looking at it while a coroner's assistant was loading the coffin. A few Louisiana State Police were lingering around the graveyard near us, looking bored.

The note read, "Rouge Future, LLC," and that was it. Deandre's call had turned up no phone number, just an office address here in New Orleans and nothing else. "Well," I said, looking at it again, "at least we know who paid for this lady's funeral. In theory, at least."

"We should be able to look up the owners of the company," Burkitt said. "You want me to call it in to the office? Clemons is probably still working."

"Have at it," I said, handing him the note. I saw Sam standing by Holloway and headed that direction to intervene, if necessary.

As I approached, I heard Sam say, "Son, I know the whiskey is strong, but you just gotta tell it no."

"I'm fine, old man," Holloway was saying, but then he went to retching again.

"Stubborn fool," Sam said as Holloway bent over and heaved again. "Won't listen to anything or anyone."

"I'm not an alcoholic," Holloway said between gurgles and

spits.

"That's what I told myself for years," Sam said, looking at me sagely.

"Don't try to talk him out of drinking," I said, as Holloway launched into another round of heaving. "This is the most interesting thing that's come out of his mouth all day."

"Asshole," Holloway said, gasping for breath. He'd puked up everything his stomach had and was now trying desperately to get a breath in.

"Back atcha," I said. "Thanks for your help, Sam."

"Wish I could do more," Sam said, nodding as he took his cue and headed off.

"You need a couple shovels?" I asked. "I bought 'em and I don't need 'em anymore, now."

Sam shook his head and smiled. "You might want to hang onto them. This is Louisiana." And he started to walk off, ambling into the dark.

"What the hell does that mean?" Holloway asked, finally turned our way, face about as pale as mine usually was. "Some kind of a riddle?"

"Lots of secrets 'round here," Sam said, vanishing into the dark. "You might not be done digging."

"Huh," I said. "So, it kind of was a riddle." I thought about it a second. "And maybe also literal."

"What do we do now?" Holloway asked, seemingly done with his vomiting for the moment.

"Probably hit the hotel, call it a night," I said, looking at the dark skies above.

He nodded along. "That sounds good. I could use a shower."

"Yeah," I said, "wash off that vomit and hemorrhoid cream; you'll feel like a brand-new man."

Holloway's head sagged. "I don't even have words to express how much I hate working with you."

"Really?" I sunk a hand around his arm and helped him upright. "Because I am having just the grandest time babysitting your dumb ass, lemme tell you. Highlight of my career, right above saving the world those five or six times." I dragged him along, keeping him from tumbling over.

"Got a record on ownership of Rouge Future," Burkitt said as we returned to him. He eyed Holloway for a second before taking up the dumbass's other arm and helping me along back toward the parking lot. "Mitchell Werner. Clemons found a business number and gave 'em a call. They open at eight tomorrow."

"We should drop by and talk to them, then," I said, giving up and just slinging Holloway's arm over my shoulder. He'd stopped resisting, but I could tell by his breathing that he was still awake and listening. He'd apparently just given up on his gross motor functions and decided letting me carry him was easier. "Anything else Clemons came across?"

"Yeah, one thing," Burkitt said, taking up Holloway's other side. "He said the autopsy report—the original—wasn't entirely complete. Had some stuff missing. He flagged it, but the coroner that performed the autopsy was gone for the night. They said he'd call back first thing in the morning, and they'll fax over a copy if they can find it before then, but…" He shrugged. "I wouldn't expect much action on that this late at night."

"I was just telling Holloway we were probably done for the evening," I said. This graveyard was so big, and I was already tired of dragging the lunkhead along. "Which will give him a chance to sleep it off before having three more rounds of scotch for breakfast."

"I'm done, I swear," Holloway mumbled. "No mas."

"Sure you are," I said. "And I'm going to stop making fun of you for your ass cream and sparkling personality, too. Any minute now, really."

"So, uh…how'd you get stuck with this guy?" Burkitt asked me once we'd dumped Holloway in the back of the SUV and closed the door.

"I honestly don't know," I said, hand planted on the car door handle, ready to open it once we'd finished talking about the passenger inside. "I mean, I'd assumed I'd burned off all the shit karma I'd accumulated in my life during that whole 'running from the law' phase of my life, but no, apparently I have more to atone for." I shrugged. "Or my boss hates me." I pretended to think about it. "Yep. That's probably it. Also, I called Director Chalke the Assistant Undersecretary for Wanking, and she probably holds a grudge."

Burkitt's eyebrows almost reached orbit, they rose so fast. "Wow. That's gutsy."

"What can I say? I like to live on the edge."

We got in and he started it up. "Back to the hotel crime scene?" he asked.

"Yeah. They did offer us a free room, after all, and since Holloway paid for dinner on his company credit card, we probably ought to offset that. I don't think the scotch he ordered was cheap."

Burkitt settled into silence as he got us back on the freeway. As we passed the cemetery, the flashing police lights played a familiar red and blue visual melody. I'd certainly seen that particular display enough times to last a lifetime.

"Can I ask you something?" Burkitt asked, a little tentatively.

"We just exhumed a corpse together in the dead of night," I said. "If this isn't the time for bold questions, when the hell is?"

Burkitt chuckled. "You got chased by the agency for the last two years."

"That wasn't a question."

"Why would you come to work for us after all that?" Burkitt asked.

"Wow," I said. "Now *that* was a question. Good one, too. You probably know there was some pressure on me." I didn't look at him, but he was eyeing me as he drove. "My background—well, I might have been innocent of what they accused me of, but I'm not *innocent* innocent, y'know?"

"I didn't think I missed a hearing on awarding you sainthood."

"You have to be dead to be a saint," I said with an ironic smile, "and while I'm sure there are plenty of people who'd love for me to fulfill that condition…I'm no saint. Or saint-worthy, rather, even absent the death requirement. Though I do keep performing what you could consider miracles, I suppose."

Burkitt chuckled again. "I don't hear a reason in there anywhere. Not a good one, anyway."

"Maybe I didn't have a good reason to join," I said. "Maybe blackmail, compulsion, whatever you want to call it—maybe that's enough for now. That and knowing I'm doing something I should be doing anyway."

Burkitt just grunted. I didn't know whether to take that as him believing me or not.

I would have bet on not, though, if I had to. He didn't strike me as a sucker.

28.

Getting Holloway into the lobby and elevator was an adventure and chore all its own.

Burkitt dropped us under the hotel's portico and offered to help, but I'd demurred. Getting Holloway upstairs and into his room should be easy enough for a metahuman like me, right?

Wrong.

So wrong.

Sure, I dropped him off in a chair in the lobby while I handled check-in for both of us, and I got him picked up and into the elevator all right.

"Need a luggage rack?" the front desk clerk had asked me when she'd seen him.

"No," I'd replied. Our luggage was already in our rooms, according to what the manager had told us when we'd dropped off earlier. All I needed to do was get Holloway to his room, open the door with the card key, and drop him unceremoniously on the bed. Hell, maybe I could even heave him like a sack of potatoes into the room's entryway and be done with it. I had plans for this evening, after all, and they definitely didn't include spending any more time with this yutz than I had to.

I got him into the elevator still upright, and when the doors closed, I could see my reflection in the mirrored steel. The lines of my face were set hard, unamused, my RBF even more pronounced than usual, offset by a sheen of dirt that graced my features. My brow was a hard line and my lips matched it.

After a second, I noticed Holloway's eyes were open, and he was looking at me in the reflection. "You should…smile more," he slurred.

"You should drink less, Aaron Burr," I said, "and shut your damned fool mouth before it gets you slapped."

He chuckled and I could feel the vibrato through his arm and where his side pressed against me. The elevator dinged to herald our arrival at the floor, and I pulled him out, looking for guidance. Our rooms were 4505 and 4507, and the signage at the T intersection ahead told me they lay to the right. I went in that direction, watching the numbers descend from 4525 down and let out a small curse under my breath.

"You're funny," Holloway said, still mumbling.

"You're not," I said, making sure I had the two key cards in my hand. I didn't know which was which, but a quick try of each would do the trick. "Also, being this close to you? It's making the chemical smell of your ass cream burn my eyes."

To this he did not respond, and I continued onward as fast as I could. It was well past eleven at night, and he was not particularly heavy but awkward as hell to carry. I reached room 4507 first and stumbled to a stop. I tried the first key card, waving it over the magnetic plate. It gave me a little red light to indicate I had gotten it wrong.

Okay, fair enough. I flipped the key cards so the second was on top, ran it over the magnetic plate.

Red light.

"Sonofa…" Now what the hell was I supposed to do?

I sent an unrequited glare at my partner, who was purring softly, as though he'd either fallen asleep in my arms or was aiming to be petted. I doubted it was the latter, as his eyes were currently closed, but either way I wanted him off my shoulder as soon as possible. He wasn't that heavy, but I could still feel the circulation starting to cut off to my fingers on that side because of my awkward carrying position.

For a moment I was afraid it was going to turn into a physical comedy routine as I tried to balance him with one hand while fiddling with the key cards with the other. If it started to look like that, though, I was probably going to shove his ass out the window at the end of the hall and be done with it.

No, no. I took a deep breath. No more murder if possible. That was what I'd vowed to myself when I took this job. I was going to play by the rules, and that meant not taking the easy way out and shoving Captain Asscream out so he could enjoy the sensation of flight for a few seconds before his life came to an abrupt end.

I tried the first key card again, holding a different side down this time. Red light.

Then the second again, other side down.

Green light.

"Hallelujah," I muttered, bringing Holloway around to push him into the darkened room ahead of me. I looked around for the light switch and found it behind the door, Holloway's body blocking me from accessing it. "Crap."

Whatever, I could see in the half-light well enough. I dragged Holloway through the thin entry hall past the bathroom, his limp and insensate form offering little in the way of help or resistance. "Lightweight," I said as I finally—finally—reached the bed with him. "Maybe if you'd spread those scotches out over a few hours instead of chugging them you'd be upright and moving right now."

I plopped him down on the bed and he rattled the frame with his landing. I rose, so happy to finally be done with my physical labors for the night. With a quick throw, I frisbeed his key card onto his unmoving form. "Here. You might need this tomorrow. If you make it out of bed in the morning."

As I turned to go, something stopped me.

A hand. On my thigh.

"What the hell?" Fingers were softly wrapped around the outside of my leg, clamping lightly as one of them rubbed back and forth. I looked down and followed the fingers to the hand, the hand back down the offending arm, and the damned arm back to—

Holloway.

He was leering at me, eyes half-closed, from the bed, his hand on my leg.

"Okay," I said, my internal heat spiking into dangerous ranges, "lose the fingers or lose the hand."

"I'd like to lose 'em—in you," he said, and hooked his hand

around my leg with a yank.

I'd like to think that given my metahuman powers, my countless hours of training, fighting, preparation, battle, whatever—I'd have been ready for a drunken co-worker grabbing my leg in a darkened hotel room. That I could have been prepared for it, reacted effortlessly and easily, with a proportional response that satisfied the attack on my honor, but didn't cause acres of collateral damage.

But either he was stronger than he looked or I was tired from foiling a bank robbery, running Bourbon Street barefoot, digging up a grave and dragging his dumb ass all the way to here, because he pulled me off balance with almost no effort at all.

I fell down on him with a cry of surprise and he grunted in pleasure or pain. I hoped the latter.

He was all over me for a second in my surprise, wet lips on the side of my neck as I went through a cold splash of surprise that clawed down into my belly and turned hot. His hand found my breast and suddenly I was burning, my face flushed and my stomach churning with disgust.

"Get the fuck off me!" I slapped him in the groin with minimal power and heard him make a sound like a balloon pushing all its air out, squeaky and pained. Every muscle in his body clenched as he went defensive, and I fell off the bed and caught myself in a squat.

Flexing my legs, I came back to my feet with my hands up, defensive and ready. I found Holloway holding his crotch, still making that squeaky noise, like he was trying to get air back into lungs that had been permanently deflated.

"Why…did you…do that?" he managed to get out.

"Because you grabbed and groped me and tried to pull me onto the bed with you, dipshit," I said, backing away slowly. He didn't look to be in a great position to grab me now, but then again, he'd surprised me the first time, and I didn't intend to let it happen again.

"I thought maybe you might want to…you know…blow off some steam after a long day." He really labored to get the words out, sucking in breaths between gritted teeth.

"Asswipe, I have run miles and moved earth, and capped it

all off with carrying your dead drunk ass around New Orleans." I had nothing but a glare for him. "The only thing I want at this point is to sleep." I'd reached the hallway, but didn't dare turn tail and run, even though he was in no condition to follow me. No chance in hell was I letting my guard down around a potential threat now that it had manifested itself in such a way. "And be assured," I called back, though I could no longer see him, "even if I did want that, you'd be the last person I'd want it from at this point. Seriously, you'd be just behind Anthony Weiner and Harvey Weinstein on my list."

If he made a reply to that, I didn't hear it. I opened the door and got out into the hallway as quickly as possible, shutting the door behind me as though it would prevent him from pursuing.

Once I was out in the full light of the hallway, I paused, my breath coming in steady, heavy bursts. My pulse was in the redline, adrenaline spiked as it pumped through my veins. The world felt blurry around me, and I checked both sides of the hallway to be sure no one was out here, no other threats in proximity.

There weren't. I was alone.

I checked my hand; the other keycard was, miraculously, still there, clenched between my fingers. With a wary eye on Holloway's door, I moved over to mine haltingly, never daring to look away from his for fear it would burst open and disgorge the handsy monster that had just assailed me in a dark hotel room.

Once in my own room, I turned on the lights, found my suitcase, and pulled my doorstop alarm out. Ten bucks or so, a neat little purchase I'd made on Amazon as soon as I'd gotten my New York apartment, which lacked an alarm of its own. I flipped the on switch, tested it, and a siren's wail filled the air. That done, I dragged the desk chair over to the door and blocked it, then set the alarm up directly underneath the doorknob. If anyone tried to force open my door, it'd trigger the alarm and scream so loud it'd wake me, giving me a critical few seconds to engage.

Then I propped the chair under the knob as well, wedging it

in so if someone tried to come through the door, it'd be a lot harder for them.

Once I'd taken these precautions, I stepped back from the door slowly, a few halting steps at a time. I shoved the window's curtains and sheers closed and then pushed the desk squarely in front of it. That was the room's only other potential entry point, and I'd just blocked it to the best of my ability. Sure, it was unlikely anyone would attack me via that route, but having been a former flight-capable meta myself, I knew firsthand it was hardly impossible. Hopefully they'd come right in the middle, where they'd slam into the desk.

When all my preparations were finished, I sat down heavily on the bed. My heart was still thumping in my chest, and the stale, air-conditioned smell of the hotel room filled my nostrils. I looked at the door again, then the window, and ran through possible escape scenarios if there was a fire in the middle of the night.

Then I sat there, on the bed, fully dressed, facing the door, for quite a while before I was finally able to calm myself enough to lie down.

Even so, it was hours before I managed to get to sleep.

29.

Olivia

"This looks like the spot," I said to the officer who'd driven me out into the far edge of Las Vegas. They'd gotten a report about a meteor falling to the earth and impacting outside of town, and it hadn't taken their top brass long to put two and two together and figure out that probably was the supervillain I'd accidentally launched out of the roof of Fremont Street.

I stood on the edge of a small crater, no more than five feet by five feet, but with a clear, human-shaped impression plowed into the dirt. The blur had landed rather heavily, not a lot of roll or trail to the impact site. That suggested they'd gone largely up and down in a tight arc rather than a long, loose one that would have stretched the crater to be a lot longer in one direction.

Ouch, either way.

"How far away from Fremont Street are we?" I asked the cop, a patrolwoman named Dominguez who was about five foot nothing and looked grizzled as hell, like she'd been through the ringer a few times.

"Eight, ten miles maybe, as the crow flies," Dominguez said, not one to waste a lot of words. I'd figured that out about her very quickly on our ride over. "This is Spring Valley."

"And they just picked themselves up and dusted off and ran thataway," I said, looking at a trail of dust that went off to my left. "What's over there?" I pointed, because one of the Las

Vegas suburbs looked to stretch out a few miles in that direction.

"Summerlin South," Dominguez said. And that was it.

"Hookay," I said, and made my way over to the speedster's tracks. The sun was starting to sink below the horizon, and there wasn't a lot to go on, track-wise. I'd taken a very basic course on this when I'd joined up with the agency, at Reed's insistence, but other than a general direction the footprints were going, they didn't really leave me anything to work with. The combination of the speedster's fast tread with the blowback of dust that seemed to follow in their wake had erased most of the evidence that they'd even been here. "Looks like they survived the fall."

Dominguez just grunted.

A cool, dry desert wind blew out of the east, from somewhere beyond the purpling sky on the horizon. I looked down into the crater and something caught the glint of the last rays of the sun beyond the western horizon.

I scrambled down into the crater, feeling like I was climbing into a grave. Mine, maybe. At the bottom there was something small, smooth, about two inches across, buried in a thin layer of sand. I scooped it out and brushed it off; it was a card, a driver's license for the state of Nevada. Or a fragment of one, at least, since the front had been scuffed so bad, I couldn't see a picture or a first name. The last name was barely legible, though: Cruml. There might have once been more after the L, but it was gone now.

"You mind running this, see if you can get a match?" I said, handing the card up to Dominguez.

"Not a lot to run, here," she said, but went for her shoulder-mounted mic anyway, as she walked away from the crater like I wasn't even there.

I climbed out and started to brush myself off, then stopped. Actually, if I could just…

I waved a hand at myself, and my bubble activated, my clothes rustling. A cloud of dust blew out off me like I'd run a fan beneath my clothes, and when Dominguez turned around, I was coughing, waving a hand and blasting the dust off in small bursts. It had almost worked, my idea. "Any luck?"

I asked, coughing through the residual desert dust.

"They'll get back to us," Dominguez said. "Need a lift?"

"Yeah," I said. Veronika was going to be staying at the hospital for the night, anyway. She was fine, but they wanted to keep her for observation. I counted myself lucky I wasn't in the same boat. "Might as well head back to my hotel." I looked at the darkening horizon to the east. "Looks like we're done for the night anyway."

30.

Sienna

I woke to the buzzing of my phone, and a New Orleans number glowing on the screen. I answered it and managed to get out a croaked, "Hello?"

"Hey, it's Burkitt. How's it going?"

"Better than Holloway's morning, I hope." I yawned, brushing stray hairs out from in front of my eyes. "That's about all I've got for now."

Burkitt laughed on the other end. "I just dropped off my kids and I'm headed your way. Figured Holloway would be sleeping in and suffering, but that you'd be up by now. You a late-nighter?"

"Not really," I said, sitting up and massaging my face. "Dumbass decided last night that my kindhearted decision to deliver him to his bed intact and not dead meant I was super interested in letting him get with me, so that kind of screwed up my sleep schedule."

There was a long pause on the other end of the line, and I realized that maybe I shouldn't have said that. "Wow," Burkitt finally said. "That guy is a hazard. You should report him for…well, everything, actually."

"Maybe I will," I said, still trying to get awake. The other side of that was implied, too, because I was torn—*Maybe I won't.*

"Look, I was calling because I need to pick you up anyway

and one of my favorite breakfast places is right by your hotel," Burkitt said. "Figured I'd see if you wanted to go with me. I promise you no drinking or inappropriate behavior from me."

"You do seem like a lot more of a gentleman than that douchecanoe." My stomach rumbled, and I realized for the first time since, well, when I was up until all hours thinking about everything, ever, that I hadn't even finished dinner last night. I reached down and massaged my left foot and found a full and fresh layer of skin where last night there had been exposed muscle and fascia. "Hell yes. I'm starving."

"Good deal. I'll text you the address."

"I need a little time to get ready," I said, massaging the back of my neck. Had it been the slightly unconventional events leading up to bedtime or was I a little more stiff than usual? "I mean, I know I'm superpowered and all, but I'm still a girl and it's going to take me a little while."

"I'm married, so I kinda figured," Burkitt said with a laugh. "My wife told me to give you lots of advance warning, but I was balancing it with not wanting to wake you up too early. I'm about forty minutes out given the traffic, so you have some time."

"Sounds good. I'll just meet you there." I hung up and got to work.

I'm not much of a girly girl, but I had acquired minimum standards of appearance in the years since I'd first left my house. After starting at the FBI (this round), I'd taken those up another notch without even being asked. I'd finally caved to a very minimal use of makeup. After years of people seeing photos of me without it, I found a small amount of base makeup and a little eyeshadow went a long way.

Once I'd dressed and done all that, I moved the chair out of the way of the door, switched off the under-door alarm and removed it, tossing it in my suitcase with a thump. My holster went on my belt, and lemme tell you something—finding a pantsuit with belt loops big enough for a sturdy enough belt to securely hold a gun holster? Not the easiest game in town. Fortunately, I did all my shopping with this in mind.

These are the perils of being Sienna Nealon. You have to shop with violence in mind, always. Which was also the reason

I'd discovered early in my career that dresses really didn't work for me.

I looked out my peephole before I opened the door, and exited by looking down the hall in both directions first before walking out. I was normally a cautious person, but Holloway—damn his eyes, and his hands, and every other gropey part of him—really had me on edge. It occurred to me that a year or two prior, if this had happened, Holloway might have gotten a broken jaw or ended up dead for the shit he'd tried.

Clearly, I was learning, or maturing or something. I should have ruptured his testicles, though. That would have taken some of the starch out of his shorts.

I was still raging in my head as I rode the elevator to the lobby, the quiet whir of the machinery outside the box like a mechanical soothing device, as though it were trying to calm me down. It was hard to believe after all the crap I'd been through in my life that a drunken co-worker trying to molest me would have this much effect, but here we were.

My phone GPS informed me that the restaurant Burkitt had chosen was just across the way from the hotel. I exited onto a back alley that had a massive parking garage looming a few stories over me. This was, if I remembered correctly, the route our assassin had taken when she'd left. I eyed the parking garage, which had yellow crime scene tape strung like banners over all the entries and exits. CSI vans were still parked all over, probably making the parking situation around here even worse given that they'd completely blocked the ramp. I saw eight cars circle while I walked down the alley, and my adopted New Yorker heart felt a pang of pity for them. This was why I didn't bother driving in NYC. Also, I don't like driving.

The alley was a little dingy, opening up onto Magazine Street ahead. Magazine was long, stretching for what seemed like an infinite distance in either direction, off into the horizon as far as I could see. It was mostly older buildings, too, with a real sense of history. One of the buildings was some sort of plaster or concrete on the first floor and brick the subsequent three, with latticed windows placed every few feet. The next building over was a pinkish white style that I thought of as colonial, or classic New Orleans, like it was a manor house plopped right on the corner, complete with wrought-iron balconies draping the second, third and fourth stories.

Everything was like that—eclectic, some places with an older feel mixed with the occasional dash of newer ones. And balconies with wrought-iron railings seemed prominent. It had real charm, a classic sort of feel unique to this place.

The air held a little chill as I crossed Magazine Street to that pink building with the balconies and railings. It had a restaurant sign proclaiming it the Ruby Slipper. I confirmed the name was the one Burkitt had sent me via text. The place was humming when I came in, and to my surprise Burkitt was already sitting about five tables back from the hostess station. He waved when he saw me come in, his back to the wall.

"Hey," I said as I walked up. He rose to greet me, and I gave him a good once-over as I did so. He was what the spy community called a "grey man," someone who blended in so perfectly that they just disappeared, didn't stand out anywhere. He was perfect at it, really, and if I hadn't been looking for him, he'd have faded right into the background.

I sat across from him a little uneasily, and he picked up on it right away. "I've got your six," he said, faintly smiling. He must have seen me look over my shoulder, which I'd done to check the approaches to me from behind.

"Thanks," I said. He'd figured it out, probably because he was the same way I was. Lots of FBI and law enforcement types were; you don't sit with your back to the door if you can avoid it. It's a good way to get shot in the back of the head. By saying he 'had my six,' he meant he'd watch my back. It was nice gesture, but…

"What's good here?" I asked, giving the menu a glance. It was a double-sided, laminated card about as long as my arm. It was splashed with wild colors, hues of red and orange, and had items on it like Bananas Foster Pain Perdu French Toast, which set me to drooling just reading the name and description.

"Everything," Burkitt said, still wearing that sly smile. "So…you want to talk about the case?"

"Anything break in the night?" I asked, still looking at the menu.

"Other than Holloway's hopes of not going to bed alone?" Burkitt flushed as soon as he said. "Sorry. That was—"

"It was funny, actually," I said, chuckling under my breath. "Thanks for that."

He brightened a degree. "I have a dark sense of humor. I have the worst time going to funerals, because I have all these amusing riffs that I want to make, but know I shouldn't."

I looked up at him for a second. "Such as?"

He looked like I'd jabbed in the solar plexus with a stick, frozen in place, thinking. "Well, now you've called me out on it and nothing's coming to mind."

"Think about it and get back to me on it, then," I said, putting down my menu as the server approached. She greeted me without a flicker of recognition, had a harried look as though she had been overworked all her millennial life, and asked if we knew what we wanted. I ordered coffee and the French toast I'd had my eye on, and Burkitt did the same. He waited a good ten seconds after she'd cleared off before he spoke again.

"So…the case," he said, easing back to that topic. "There weren't any breaks during the night, no."

"I wish there had been," I said. "Holloway's fingers. Those should have broken during the night."

Burkitt chuckled. "That's a good one. And brings an interesting point—why didn't you shellack him? I mean, you could have—"

"I don't know if you know this," I said with great deadpan, "but after a two-year fight to the top, I just managed to get myself removed from the FBI's Most Wanted list and straight into a top position with the bureau. I figure assaulting one of their agents, my co-worker, no matter how richly deserved, would probably result in a negative performance review and possibly my return to fugitive status."

"You think breaking the hand of a guy who's groping you unasked is going to get you back in trouble?" Burkitt's face was completely devoid of anything, feelings-wise. I could not tell which way he leaned on this question.

"Or something," I said. "It's a vaguely defined fear on my

part, probably prompted by traumatic memories of my two years running." He still said nothing, so I felt compelled to elaborate. "It was not the best time of my life."

Burkitt looked down at the perfect white tablecloth for a second, then cleared his throat. "Do you know what my last job with the bureau was?"

"Afraid I don't," I said, forcing a smile. "I should get better at this whole 'detectiving' thing. If that's not a word, it should be, because 'detecting' is too ambiguous and ill-defined for what we do."

"I worked financial crimes," Burkitt said, looking me in the eye for a few seconds, then back to the table, where he proceeded to straighten up his bundle of silverware and napkin. "Three years in that job before I came to the New Orleans office, which was…a year and a half ago?" He thought about it a second. "I was working on one case most of the time I was there." Now he did look at me, straight in the eye. "Nadine Griffin."

A little chill ran through me. "Oh," was all I managed to say.

"We worked so long to build a case against her," Burkitt said. Now that he'd gotten it out, he wasn't looking down anymore, he was looking straight at me, and I felt a little like I was speared by his gaze. "Then our office gets bombed, and the US Attorney's office gets shattered, and suddenly our case is gone. Years of work and it's wiped clean in the course of a day."

I didn't say anything. I'd been in New York when that had happened. They'd called Nadine Griffin the Queen of Wall Street. She'd done a lot of dirty things in her time. Insider trading. Fraud. Corruption. But right at the top of the list for dirtiest things she'd done, as near as I could tell, was paying a fixer to destroy all the evidence against her via a two-pronged assault against the federal offices where all the evidence against her was held. For that, she'd hired my great-grandfather's later employees, Yvonne, AKA the Glass Blower, as well as ArcheGrey1819, who handled the cyberattack portion of the show.

"So, all this happens and suddenly we're screwed," Burkitt says, still keeping the eye pressure on me, but smiling now.

"Our whole case is gone. Physical evidence, digital evidence, everything. Down the drain, along with our field office. I was one of the last ones out."

"Lucky you."

"When Griffin's house burned down," Burkitt said, "and she went missing?" He chuckled, low and amused. "We thought maybe she made a break for it. I mean, she's still a person of interest even now, did you know that?"

"I did not," I whispered, a little hoarsely.

"Because you can't clear your name by destroying all the evidence, no matter what she thought," Burkitt said. "We were going to get her on something; the SAC had decided it after the shit she pulled. We were going to nail her on parking tickets if we had to. But then she goes missing for no apparent reason, and…" He shrugged. "I mean…we all had our suspicions, of course. Everyone 'knows,' at least as much as one can know without actually knowing…she didn't come to a happy end, did she?" He leaned forward. "Because it was killing me, like, literally killing me. I couldn't sleep at night thinking maybe she got away. Even now, two years later, I still wake up sometimes wondering if she's on a beach somewhere, living the high life."

I was sweating a little. Was it hot in here? I mean, it was Louisiana, but it was October and 70 degrees. But it felt hot. "I'm sure she got what was coming to her," I mumbled, looking away, away from his eyes.

Burkitt sat back and took a nice, relaxing breath. "I'm glad to hear you say that. Really, I am."

"Well, I'm not pleased that I felt compelled to say it." I did not look up.

"I'm not recording our conversation, Nealon," Burkitt said, looking around. "Hey." I looked up, and he was looking me right in the eyes. "I'm not. I just…needed some closure on that. You didn't admit anything, okay?"

"I have no idea what you're talking about," I said, but it was hollow and lies and bullshit and we both knew it.

Burkitt just grinned. "Of course not. Still…" He exhaled mightily. "I'm going to sleep so well tonight. You have no idea."

"Look, Burkitt," I said, trying to rally myself back to acting like a normal person, and not one guilty of murdering Nadine Griffin—which I actually was, since I'd dropped her, locked in her safe room, into Long Island Sound. "I don't know what you think of me—"

"I think you're a person who's so obsessed with justice that you get the job done," Burkitt said. "No matter what."

"I was," I said, and now I could look him in the eye. "That's exactly who I was. I started doing what I do to protect people. But you can't protect people if you can't provide some kind of retributive justice, some incentive for people who want to do bad things to not do them. The worst of us, well, they don't respond to that, and so I figured you have to take them off the board before they threaten innocent lives."

"Sure," Burkitt said. "We all—or almost all of us—acknowledge that's the case, when lives are on the line."

"Except…I wasn't just acting when lives were on the line," I said, trying to give myself a lot of space to deny, deny, deny in the event he actually was recording our conversation. "I did wrong. I broke the law. I embraced retribution over actually seeking justice. I used my badge, the shield of the law that I carried at the time, even when I was working privately for city and state police forces, to pursue people by any means necessary."

"I like that, personally," Burkitt said, leaning forward again. "You worked in the field long enough to know that sometimes, justice just doesn't get served by the system."

"I know," I said. "But let me tell you the other thing I learned over the last two years—it sucks when someone takes the system and uses it against you almost the exact same way you've been abusing it. I got depowered and strapped to a gurney and paraded in front of a show tribunal so banana republic that even the most power-mad, self-justifying dictator would have had to take a deep breath and go, 'Wow. That is a seriously corrupt system right there.' I got the full flavor of what happens when you put aside all the protections of the law to come after someone, throw out all the rules and toss the damned kitchen sink at them. And I hated it."

Burkitt sat back, looking a little impressed. "So, your time on the run made some kind of convert of you? As to the righteousness of the system? Which you admit was perverted against you?"

"In a way," I said. "I *want* to believe. That we can do good, that we can stop the bad guys without becoming them. That I don't need to go out there and be the furious hand of brutal justice that I, um, occasionally might have been in the past. I want to believe that now that there are actual laws governing metahuman behavior, we can police the right way."

Burkitt kind of smiled under the smoky gaze he kept on me. "Nadine Griffin wasn't a metahuman, and she got away with—literally—murder. We haven't been able to pin anything on her. Not that she's a huge priority at this point, being 'missing' as she is. But there's just nothing to go on."

"Maybe Nadine Griffin is the exception that proves the rule," I said, taking a deep breath. "Maybe she's the sacrifice we have to make to do things the right way. I lost my due process rights; they got trampled all to hell when someone weaponized the system against me and ditched all those protections that we're all supposed to have. That's what I was doing to people like, uhm, you know. People. Vague, undefined people who I will not admit to—"

Burkitt waved a hand. "Let's just assume for purposes of our conversation that you're talking about those people you were pardoned for back in the days before the truth about metas came out."

Thanks for the cover, I didn't say, but he could probably see the gratitude in my eyes. "That's exactly who I'm talking about," I said, and again, we both knew it was bullshit. "We have these rights for a reason. We have that whole 'let a thousand guilty men go free rather than imprison one innocent' idea for a purpose. I've been on the receiving end of drone surveillance and airstrikes, been shot at without warning by FBI agents, had the entire military and law enforcement apparatus of the US after me at various points, had Spec Ops guys try to bag and drag me in a foreign country—" Burkitt raised an eyebrow at that one. "Every single tentacle of the US government that could be used against me, they've used against me. A shadow justice system and courts. A particularly nonconforming prison. I could go on all day."

"And you think because of your experience," Burkitt said, "the heinous criminal scum you deal with don't deserve this kind of treatment?"

"Some might," I said. "But I want to believe in a system that affords them every chance—which I never got. I got railroaded for things I didn't do, and the system worked against me because it was stacked against me. Not because of evidence, but because the people in charge decided to do it that way. I don't like that. If they got me on evidence, okay. Fair and square, it's done." I sat back in my chair. "But they didn't. And it burned."

"Not many criminals would take their arrest with such magnanimity," Burkitt said, still smiling. "Most of them would feel the burn regardless."

"It doesn't matter how they take it," I said. "This isn't about them, not really. It's about us. It's about the eye of the government, which is not all that different from the Eye of Sauron, turning on someone who doesn't deserve it. Having been the recipient of the attention, the attacks, the injustice…that's not the way it should be. And it terrifies me that it just might fall on someone who truly, truly doesn't deserve it."

"That does happen sometimes," he said, looking down at the table.

"Then they deserve a chance," I said. "And that's why I'm here, now. Because I want the bad guys to face justice—but the right way. The way it wasn't done with me." Now it was my turn to look at the table. "Hell, that may be the only reason I actually agreed to take this job at all, in spite of the pressure. To prove to myself that it could be done the right way."

"Wow," Burkitt said after a few seconds of silence. "I think I actually feel inspired by that." He sat up a little straighter in his chair. "Like you just washed away some of the cynicism that's been clouding my eyes for the last couple years. Huh." He shifted, as though something uncomfortable had just happened between his ass and his seat. He put his hand in his jacket pocket and came out with his cell phone, staring at the screen for only a moment before he looked up, and before he even said anything, I knew breakfast was over.

"What is it?" I asked.

"The coroner must have woken up, finally, because the autopsy report came in," he said, holding up a hand to get the attention of the server as he stood. "We gotta go. Now."

31.

"Why do we have to go to the office to view an autopsy report?" I asked, following Burkitt to his cubicle. The FBI office was lit and seemed whiter today, the walls maybe catching some sunlight from the windows far in the distance, giving it a brighter hue than I'd noted last night. "Are corpse pictures classified or something?"

Burkitt chuckled under his breath. He carried a white Styrofoam takeout box, our food from breakfast that our server had oh-so-kindly put together for us as we paid and sprinted out. I'd devoured mine on the way, because no way in hell was I missing a meal when I had a perfectly open transit window from downtown to the office. (The Bananas Foster Pain Perdu French Toast was Amazeballs.) "No, but I have problems with the interface on my phone." He tossed his takeout next to the computer and slid off his jacket to reveal his dress shirt hanging over a wiry frame. "Lemme get logged in here and we'll see what we've got."

"Sounds good," I said, hovering behind him, not really sure what I was supposed to do while I waited. I pulled my phone out of my pocket and realized—hey, I should probably call that gropey jackass that traveled here with me and let him know there was a break in the case. So I did. "Hey, dipshit," I said once I'd made it to Holloway's voicemail. "We got the autopsy report. When you drag yourself out of bed and quaff down your twelve ibuprofen or whatever, get your lazy, sorry, drunken, unprofessional ass down to the field office." Then I hung up.

Burkitt didn't say a word, but I caught a few straying eyes over the cubicle walls.

"Here we go," Burkitt said, Windows 10 having finally booted up and allowed him in. He opened the report and we were immediately greeted with photos of the same dead body from the crime scene pics last night, except laid out on a metal slab and opened, chest to pelvis with the familiar Y-shaped incision that coroners used.

I looked at her with a jaded eye as Burkitt scanned the text. She had probably been pretty once, but whatever beauty there'd been had been washed away by the bayou and however long she'd spent in the water. Water was one of the most destructive elements on the planet, and could dissolve a human body to near nothingness if given long enough to work. I estimated she'd been left in the water for less than two days based on the decomposition, and then had a thought—how sad was my life that at twenty-six I'd developed a mental model for human decomposition based on water exposure?

"Huh," Burkitt said, and I leaned in next to him to read what he was looking over. I skimmed it and found the thing that had gotten his attention pretty quickly.

"Track marks," I said, shaking my head. "Not a meta, then."

"'Suggests heavy intravenous drug use,'" Burkitt said, reading aloud. "Why does that rule out her being a meta?"

"Meta healing eliminates track marks," I said. "Even the lowest-power meta wouldn't show more than three or four at a time, even for a heavy user."

"Interesting," Burkitt said. "Hey, did you get to the part—"

"Cause of death?" I had just hit it. "Yeah."

"She drowned?" Burkitt sat up a little straighter in his chair. "I don't get it."

I felt a little smile play across my lips. "Well, you see, when you get water in your lungs, you can't take in air—"

"Ha ha," Burkitt said. "I get the mechanics." He pointed at the screen. "This has her listed as a suicide."

I nodded. "Look at the tox screen." Did a little pointing of my own. "She was high as a kite when she went into the water. There's room for interpretation on that ruling."

He turned his head to frown at me. "Ohhhh. You mean—"

"Someone drugs her up—" I mimed shooting up into the forearm "—enough heroin to knock her out, then tosses her in the drink. Pretty much guarantees death, but it could look like a suicide." I thought about it for a second. "Hell, she could have taken it herself and they could have just tossed her in. If she was high enough, there'd be no signs of a struggle because she'd have been in la-la land, no fight in her."

"Maybe. I'll put together some questions for the experts," Burkitt said, "and forward the report to them." He tapped his chin. "I don't know about you, but after reading this, I don't feel any more enlightened."

"Nope," I said, checking the time on my phone, "it's just another firehose of non-specific clues in a case already awash with them. But it does rule one thing out—this is not our assassin, because we have this woman's corpse and she's definitely not meta. So, in terms of catching our bad gal…" I straightened my back and stood up. "We're back to square one, and unless there's some useful clue hiding in this field of endless questions…we have just about nothing."

32.

My phone started to buzz a few seconds after I'd made that dramatic pronouncement, and I looked down at it once I'd fished it out of my pocket, then felt my eyes widen in surprise.

FBI DIRECTOR CHALKE, the caller ID read, so I answered it. "What's up, bitch?" This was a woman who'd lightly threatened me into taking this job, and whom I'd called the Assistant Undersecretary of Wanking, so I felt no need to be formal with her.

There was a very slight pause on the other end of the line as Burkitt shot me a puzzled look, then shook it off. He clearly had no idea who I was talking to, or he'd have shit a brick right there.

"You really are a rebel, aren't you?" Chalke sounded like she'd taken my insult in stride.

"I like to march to the report of my own machine gun, yeah," I said. "So, again—what's up?"

"Your current case," she said, finally getting that I wanted to forgo pleasantries. "I'm watching your progress, or lack thereof."

"Yeah, it's a tough one," I said.

"Where are you at with it?" she asked. "The last thing I have is your verbal report to SAC Shaw from last night."

"Nothing much this morning," I said, lapsing into professionalism to deliver it bullet-quick. "Autopsy report just confirms that the dead body is not our meta assassin, assuming our assassin actually is meta and didn't have someone make the bullet for her. Either way, unless we get a new report back that the body we exhumed last night is different from the body they found and buried two years ago, we're either dealing with an unrelated lookalike or a twin, and either way, we have no ID and no leads, except checking into the outfit that paid for her burial. Which we will be doing in…" I glanced at my phone clock and found it was nearing nine AM. "Well, soon."

"Who paid for the burial?" Chalke asked. She sounded pretty focused, maybe a little strained.

"Some LLC out of Baton Rouge," I said. "Rouge Future, I think? They have an office here in New Orleans. We're heading for it in a few minutes. No answer at their office numbers last night, no returned call as yet this morning from the messages we left." I looked to Burkitt for confirmation. He had a furrowed brow, probably wondering how I'd gone from, "What's up, bitch?" to providing a case summary on this call. I made a mental note to step back before I told him who I was talking to, in fear the brick he would shit might crush my toes.

"Do you have your team back at the office looking into this company?" Chalke asked.

"Burkitt does," I said. "Nothing much came back, as I recall." He shook his head to confirm. "The registered agent or whatever—they're not known to us, no criminal record, blah blah blah."

Chalke was quiet for a second, then she spoke, very low. "I don't think I've ever taken a report from a field agent that included the phrase 'blah blah blah.'"

"I'm special. Obviously."

"Indeed," Chalke said. "Keep me apprised. The President has a particular interest in this case. I'm briefing him personally."

That prompted me to frown. "What? Why does he care about what happens in Louisiana?"

"Governor Warrington is a key ally of the President," Chalke said, and I could almost see her smarmy smile, even with a phone and thousands of miles between us. "President Gondry wants to make sure that nothing happens to him."

"It's why I'm here," I said, and the not-so-subtle click on the other end of the line told me that our conversation was over. "That and the local cuisine." This I said to Burkitt, who was still looking at me with undisguised curiosity.

"Who was that?" Burkitt asked.

"Director Chalke," I said, and watched him almost choke on his tongue. "How far away is this Rouge Future office?"

"Thirty minutes, this time of day." He shook his head, as if trying to escape the idea I'd just talked like that to our boss and head of the bureau. "It's in Metairie."

"We should probably get going, then," I said, checking the time again. "Since they're the only lead we have at this point." Hopefully, when we got there, that would change.

33.

"Son of a bitch," I said as Burkitt and I hit the parking lot, heading for the SUV to start our road trip. It was a little warm, sun beating down and the mercury rising toward 80. But that wasn't what prompted me to swear, not even as my shoes felt like they stuck to the asphalt and sweat seemed to form spontaneously on my skin from the sheer humidity.

The thing that got me swearing was the sight of Holloway stumbling his way toward us from the entry gate, dark sunglasses covering his eyes and his hand over the top of them, as if he couldn't block enough light without manually adding to the shades.

"Hey," Holloway said, trying to flag us down as I kept walking. "Hey, Nealon, wait up a second, will you?"

"Keep your hands where I can see 'em, Holloway," I said, not veering from my course. Burkitt snorted, eyeing Holloway but not changing direction to meet him, either. "I'd hate to have to drop you—oh, hell, who am I kidding? No, I wouldn't. Not at this point. But I doubt Shaw would understand, so…"

"Just hold up a second, will you?" Holloway broke into a jog to catch us. "I want to apologize."

That made me slow, but I was still keeping a close eye on him. After the crap he'd pulled last night, hell if I knew what he was going to do for an encore. Maybe he'd drill me with a bullet in the back right here and claim some outrageous thing like I'd threatened to kill him. Which I probably had, though I couldn't exactly recall. I'd certainly thought about it.

"I'm sorry," Holloway said, drawing even with me, hands held up to show me he was openhanded. Probably to avoid getting shot or beaten down or some similar fate. Which he totally deserved. "Truly, genuinely—I was out of line. And an ass."

I didn't stop walking, though I might have slowed a step. "You're just saying that because I'm scary as hell."

Though I couldn't see behind his sunglasses, I caught the motion of his head, and it strongly hinted at a roll of the eyes. "I've dealt with lots of scary people, Nealon. You're not even top five. I estimate I'd have to do something a lot worse before you'd really bring the hurt. Not that I'm going to." He waved those hands, still open-palmed. "Just trying to say—I'm not apologizing out of fear. I'm apologizing out of shame, because I was, to use one of your favored words, a total dipshit."

"Apology acknowledged," I said, and resumed my pace. The SUV was just ahead, and Burkitt already had the fob out, unlocking it.

"But not accepted?" Holloway kept a reasonable distance from me.

"You seem contrite," I said. "But let me ask you—you ever arrest anyone after they've done something horrible and had them all apologetic, weeping, 'I'm so sorry, I shouldn't have done that horrible thing'—murder, rape, bombing, whatever?"

Holloway didn't flinch, but he did slow a little. "Yeah."

"It's like that," I said. "Maybe you're sorry, maybe you're not. Talk is cheap. We'll see over time whether you mean it or not."

"I guess I couldn't ask for anything better," Holloway said, but he didn't seem happy about it. Good.

I stopped and veered for the back seat, beating him to the door before he could break for it. His eyebrows rose in surprise, but he didn't say a word, he just went for the passenger seat. "You don't want me at your back, do you?"

"Nope," I said, and we got in. The car ride was pure silence as we pulled out of the lot, and stayed like that all the way to our destination.

34.

Rouge Future, LLC was located in an unimpressive office building, the kind that Reed was probably seeking out to cut his costs. There was a proctologist's office next door, and it had a hand held up in a "high five" sign, which I thought was a little weird, but hey, marketing.

"What the hell?" Holloway muttered as we went by. Burkitt nodded subtly. I guess none of us got it.

The building smelled of plaster and construction, presumably because someone was doing a buildout somewhere inside. We stuck right to the business at hand, though, and found Rouge Future, LLC in Suite 120, behind a rough-looking wooden door that also had four other faux-brass placards on it. They read:

Coalition for Our Children's Future

Forward Louisiana

21st Century Bayou

Rouge Future, LLC

Werner Consulting

Louisiana Online Future

There were six more spaces below that for other nameplates to be slid in, and I touched the end of the one marked 21st Century Bayou. It slid out easily, and I frowned as I pushed it back into place. "This smell a little like a fly-by-night to you guys?"

"It does have a little of that aroma," Burkitt breathed as he opened the door and entered. Holloway caught it and held it open for me. I stared at him, he stared at me, shrugged, then held out his hand indicating I should go first. I did, but my face probably told him how I felt about it, and I heard him make an, "Oof," kind of noise under his breath. He probably wouldn't shoot me in the back on such a small opportunity, but you better believe I was listening for the sound of a gun leaving its holster, and my hand was right by mine as I walked.

The interior of the office smacked of luxury in a way that the rest of the place certainly didn't. The walls were nicely covered with a textured wallpaper and hung with pleasant scenes interspersed with photos of a tall, dark-haired man hobnobbing with what I presumed were scions of power: men in suits, women in pantsuits, the occasional tuxedo or formal dress thrown in, and backgrounds that spoke volumes about how connected this dude was. Which I imagined was the point of the entire display.

"Burkitt, you know any of these folks?" I nodded to the walls as we approached the front desk, which was presently unmanned. Kind of like how Holloway would be if he ever groped me again.

Credit to him, Burkitt was already looking. "I see Senator Urquhart, Congresswoman Gastan, Congressman Richard—yeah. These people are probably what you expect. Big deals. Not sure who the common thread guy is though."

"The common thread guy," came a voice from a door just behind the desk, "is Mitchell Werner." The man from the pictures appeared, sporting a dark beard and mustache combo, well-groomed. He was wearing a pink dress shirt with suit pants, no jacket or tie, and had a stainless steel coffee mug in hand. He was grinning like he'd been waiting all his life for this meeting. "That's me, in case it wasn't obvious."

"You think adding the beard is enough to make you anonymous?" I glanced at the photos, then back at him. "Because I think the shifty eyes and shit-eating grin give you away."

He laughed. "Fair enough. What brings the great Sienna Nealon to my humble door?"

"You don't check your answering service?" Holloway asked, still wearing his sunglasses. I bet his head was just ringing. He didn't even slide them down his nose to glare at Werner.

"Nope." Werner took a sip of coffee. "That's my secretary's job, and she called in sick this morning with, uh…" He grinned even wider, looking right at Holloway. "Well, with what you've got, I think. She called it the flu, but we've known each other long enough at this point…"

"We're here about a body you helped bury," I said, deciding to go at him in the most confrontational possible manner, see if I could rattle him out of his smug sweetness, which was a combo I found almost intolerable.

He laughed again, a short, sharp bark. "Beg pardon?" He didn't sound upset. More like he knew I was trying to rattle him and wasn't rising to the bait. A cool customer.

"A Jane Doe found in Plaquemines Parish a couple years ago," I said. "Down at the Caernarvon Spillway? Rouge Future helped pay for her funeral?"

"Ohhhh, sure," Werner said, motioning us forward. "Come on in, by the by. No point in just standing out here in the lobby. I've got chairs in my office." He disappeared inside without waiting for us to accept or decline.

I traded a look with Burkitt. He shrugged. Holloway offered no comment, so I just nodded and Burkitt led the way into Werner's office. Holloway trailed behind, but broke off as I entered the office. He headed on past it, deeper into the suite, presumably to nose around since we'd been asked in. I halted at the door so as not to give away the fact that Holloway was off doing his own thing. In fact, I did my best to fill the door frame, which is tough to do when you're 5' 4". But it would have been a lot harder for Holloway to hide my famous absence from Werner, so I just stood there and pretended to look at the secretary's desk just outside as though there were something absolutely fascinating anchoring me in place.

"What kind of work do you do here, Mr. Werner?" Burkitt asked, almost certainly aware of the game Holloway and I were playing. They taught it at Quantico, after all. You don't need a warrant if you're invited in.

"I do a few different things," Werner said, sinking into his chair and planting his mug on his desk like some sort of flag. I looked into his office, giving it a quick once-over. It was decorated in a similar style to the waiting room, with photos of him with powerful people, presumably mostly state and local and less national, since I recognized few of them. There were two I did recognize, though; one of him shaking hands with the late President Gerry Harmon and the other with him clasping the hand of then-VP, now-President Richard Gondry. I could tell by Gondry's hairstyle that it was before his accession to the throne.

"You know who I work for, right?" I tossed that into the room like a grenade, trying to get Werner to be forthcoming in a way I suspected was not natural for him.

"Sure," he said, coolly, from behind that same shit-eating smile. "And I'm happy to help the FBI any way I can. You wanted to know about the funeral we paid for? We did it as a public service thing. The Jane Doe in question? Got a lot of local media attention because they thought she might have washed down the spillway from near here." He tried to look me in the eye but was thwarted by my sunglasses. I got the feeling he was very practiced at looking people in the eyes and lying to them. "We figured…it would be a decent thing to do, picking up the tab so she didn't get thrown into some potter's field."

"That was, indeed, damned decent of you," I said, attributing no decency to him at all. "Did it get you any good press?"

He shrugged. "It wasn't for press. Like I said, public service."

"You have a few companies in this office," I said. "How many employees do you have?"

"Full-time?" Werner grinned. "Just me and my secretary. We employ quite a few consultants and some part-time—"

"What does Rouge Future do?" I asked, cutting him off because I didn't need to hear that particular line of bullshit to its conclusion.

"We're an LLC," Werner said, emphasizing that up front for some reason, "oriented toward trying to organize the Baton Rouge area for the bright future that it could be the recipient of, provided the right leadership initiatives."

"Wow, there sure were a lot of buzzwords and qualifiers in that word soup," I said, blowing air between my lips. "What about these other groups? 21st Century Louisiana Circle Jerk and Werner Consulting?"

His grin never wavered. "Well, 21st Century Bayou is a PAC—political action committee—designed around environmental issues that affect the bayous of Louisiana, and Werner Consulting is a strategic messaging firm oriented toward assisting candidates in crafting and honing their campaign communications and tactics."

"Politics," I said, not bothering to hide my sneer of disgust. "You're a political operative."

"Guilty as charged," he said, eyes flashing above that grin, probably not realizing just how poor his choice of words was. "Can I ask what this funeral we paid for has to do with—well, whatever you're here for? The attempt on Governor Warrington's life, I assume?"

"How did you know that was what I was here for?" I asked. It was hardly a stretch for him to have heard about my arrival and the purpose of my trip on the local news, but I wanted to see if he tried lying.

"That news spread in political circles like a good, dirty rumor," Werner said, eyes still sparkling. "*Everyone* knows why you're here, even people unconnected to local politics." Somehow, he simultaneously made the phrase "local politics" sound like it was the name of his god and made people unconnected to that sound like the lowest form of life, and without a lot of variance in tone. His facial expression moved quite a bit, though, ending in a sneer for a moment. "Interesting, interesting."

"What's interesting about an assassination attempt?" I asked. He didn't bother to answer, shrugging instead. I cocked my head at him. "If you had to speculate on a motive for killing Governor Warrington, what would you say it is?"

That sent one of Werner's eyebrow skyward in concentration. "It's politics. And assassination is hardly a new concept in Louisiana politics, though you probably don't know anything about that." And he was back to smirking.

"Boys," I said, staring at him evenly, "I believe he's calling me dumb."

"Not dumb." His teeth were even, and still on full display.

"Just ignorant. And maybe uneducated, at least with regard to local history."

"Yes, my education is hardly the stuff of legends," I said, "but I am familiar with Huey Long." I met the slight flicker of surprise in his eyes with a grin of my own. "Even an uneducated idiot like me can learn a lot on Wikipedia. And I'm sure all of it's true, too."

Werner let out a pained chuckle, trying to keep his smile in place. "Be that as it may, I wouldn't care to speculate on reasons why some lunatic might want to kill Governor Warrington."

"What about his school bill?" I asked, and at this point I was just plunging him like a toilet to see what would come up. Or to irritate him, since he seemed to be getting thin on patience. It wasn't like I had anything else to be doing. "That seems to have ginned up some opposition."

"It's a financial life preserver for the underprivileged," Werner said, and I caught the first hint of exasperation from him. "That's a hardly a reason for killing a man."

I let my eyes play over the wall behind him, looking at the framed pictures. There seemed to be one missing, I realized, sandwiched between a couple of others that seemed to lean just slightly, as though they'd been pushed closer together to hide the fact that one had been removed. "Say." I pointed at the gap between the angled photos. "Who was in the picture that used to hang there?"

"I'm sure I don't know what you're talking about," Werner said, tightening up immediately a few notches. Now the smile was gone. I sure did seem to have that effect on people a lot. And he'd been trying so very hard to keep smiling, too.

"Pretty sure you do," I said without missing a beat.

Werner blinked a couple times, showing hints of ire at my calling out his bullshit. "Hey—where's the other guy that was with you?"

"Right here," Holloway said, and he stepped up to the door frame next to me. I'd heard him coming back this way, but quietly. Apparently, his search was complete.

Werner didn't seem to find his sudden appearance satisfying. "Look, I've got a lot of work to do. I've tried to be helpful—

is there anything else I can answer for you?"

"Besides the picture question?" I pointed behind his head again. "And the motive question?"

"Yes," he said, "besides those, which I have already answered with 'There is no missing picture' and 'I have no idea,' respectively."

"I have one," Holloway said, and I made way for him to stand in the doorway so he could face Werner down as he asked. "Who pays you?"

"This is a business," Werner said, and boy, did he stiffen up at that one.

"I thought it was a PAC," I said.

"Two of them, actually," Werner said. "But I also have my companies here—"

"That's a lot of different operations in one office," I said. "Do they all pay you?"

Now he seemed to be locked into an uncomfortable position, shoulders stiff and tight. "Yes, of course."

"What kind of work do you do for them?" I asked.

"Management, messaging, janitorial." Werner shrugged, all traces of the smile long gone. "Whatever needs to be done."

"Who are your clients?" I asked. "Your donors?" I was asking Holloway's question again, but a little more directly.

"That's privileged," he said, and rose, signaling our interview was at an end. "Now if you don't mind—"

"I mind," I said. "I'm not done yet."

"Well, I am," Werner said, "and I'm going to have to ask you to leave. If you want to continue this conversation beyond this point, I'm afraid I'm going to have to refer you to my lawyer to set an appointment."

Burkitt, Holloway and I traded a look with each other, a very similar one that was also practically taught at Quantico. "Why do you want us to talk to your lawyer?" I asked, taking the lead again. "Are you guilty of something?"

Now he smiled again. "No. But I'm an expert on messaging, and I'm well aware of what happens when an unpleasant narrative takes hold. I know my rights, and I'm not talking to you again without my lawyer."

"I don't think you know as much about your rights as you

think you do," I said, pushing off the door frame, "but we'll just leave it here for now. I'm sure we'll see you again, Mitchell Werner. Can I call you Mitch?"

"Please don't," he said, jaw tight.

"How about 'Mitch the Bitch'?" I asked. "Is that right out?"

"Yes, it's right out," Mitchell said, pointing at the door. "Where you should be. Thank you. Good day."

"What do you think he's thanking us for?" I asked as I headed out the door. "Not putting him in jail?"

"You're hilarious, Ms. Nealon," Werner said.

"'Tis often said." I nodded sagely as we made our way out the front door. "Usually by people who aren't all that funny themselves, like you. I can only assume they recognize talent when they see it."

He didn't bother replying, instead just locking the door once we were all out with a heavy click that echoed down the shoddy hallway of the office building.

"Well, that went fantastically," Holloway said with all due sarcasm.

"Yeah, it did," I said. "Did you notice how touchy he got about that missing picture?"

"I'm not so sure there was a picture missing there," Holloway said. "I didn't notice much of a gap."

"Color me shocked that you didn't notice a decorating faux pas, Mr. Straight Eye for the Scotch Guy," I said. "Did you see it, Burkitt?"

Burkitt shook his head. "Ah, no."

"Men," I said, as a kind of muttered curse. "Trust me, it was there. The two pictures on either side had been pushed in and were crooked from being off balance on their hangers."

"Okay, so there's a picture missing," Holloway said as we made our way back into the building lobby. "So what?"

"Was there any major Louisiana politician you didn't see in a picture in that office, Burkitt?" I asked.

Burkitt thought about it a second. "I don't know them all, but…no. It was pretty well covered, I'd say. Two senators, several US house members, a lot of Louisiana legislators."

"So he's got a veritable who's who of Louisiana politicians on his wall," I said, a little gleam of triumph in my eye as I hit the exit door back into the sweaty, steamy outside air, "with one very noticeable exception, and he just so happens to have a curious gap right in the middle of his wall just behind his head—the place of honor, you could call it, even." I looked right at Burkitt and he nodded, getting it, then to Holloway, whose face was curiously neutral. "Anyone care to take a guess at which slimy politician of our mutual acquaintance—the one politician that any loser slug who prides themselves on their local political connections would definitely want everyone to know, without doubt, that they were connected to?"

The answer, of course, was so obvious that even Holloway got it, hungover as he was.

Warrington.

35.

My phone rang as I was about to get into the SUV just outside Mitchell Werner's office. It was a Louisiana number, so I answered without thinking too much about it. "Hello?"

"Hey, Ms. Sienna," a peppy, female voice that sounded oh-so-familiar greeted me. "It's Michelle Cheong. How are you?"

"I woke up this morning and my feet still hurt," I said, waving Holloway and Burkitt back toward the SUV so I could talk. "How's my least favorite yoga pants mom/Triad boss?"

"I'm doing just fine, thanks for asking," she said, way too brightly. "Got a busy schedule ahead of me today. Yoga classes, you know. Maybe bump some guy off later."

"I can't tell whether you're joking or not," I said.

"I'm totally joking. Probably. Listen," she said, "I was wondering—am I going to see you at the library dedication later?"

That one caused me to tweak an eye muscle, I raised the People's eyebrow so fast. "Uh, wasn't planning on it. Civic engagement is all well and good, but I'm not really from here, so a library dedication isn't really something that's a great use of my time. Kind of like running barefoot along Bourbon Street after someone whose cell phone number you had."

"Totally slipped my mind," Michelle said, completely chipper. "I just figured you'd be at the library dedication since, y'know, the governor's going to be there. But if you're too busy—"

"Sonofa," I muttered under my breath.

"Sorry, didn't quite get that," Michelle said, and by her glee, I could tell she'd damned well heard me. "Anyway, gotta go. Yoga class starts in fifteen. Laters, as the kids say!" And she hung up.

"What was the local Triad boss calling you about?" Holloway asked, hanging out at the passenger door as I wandered back toward the SUV, lost in thought. "Trying to get you to participate in a barefoot 10k?"

"Hah, no," I said. "Tipping me off that Governor Warrington is doing a library dedication later today." I shook my head as Holloway opened the door and I climbed up into the back of the SUV. "Sounds like another opportunity for our assassin to do her work."

36.

Olivia

I woke to the dual sounds of a lovely buzzing of my phone and a thumping on my door. The second stimulus solved the first because my phone shot out of my hand like it had been launched when the first thump landed.

"Who is it?" I asked, scrambling out of bed. I was still fully dressed, because I hadn't quite trusted the housekeeping in this motel. The air conditioner was humming like it was on its last legs, a repetitive *thunk!* noise coming between steady rattles out of the window unit. I positioned myself next to the door, back against the wall, realizing that if they answered in a hostile manner, I had no solution or action to take.

"It's your mother," came Veronika's heavy voice from the other side. "Seriously, Brackett. This is a new town and you're such a shut-in as to make Howard Hughes look like a social butterfly by comparison. Who do you think it is?"

I opened the door and found Veronika staring at me dourly, the usual sparkle of mischief gone from her eyes. A white bandage was taped on her forehead. She looked past me at the room before letting loose a little shudder. "It's everything I feared it would be, and you actually stayed here."

"It's what Reed paid for," I said, looking at the room as though I'd expected it to change into something out of the Taj Mahal during the space of our conversation. "You want to come in?"

"Hell no," she said, shaking her head for extra emphasis, the dry, hot air flowing in around her. It was already bright out there. "What happened after I passed out? Did you get the hostile?"

"Sort of," I said. "I, uhm, launched them into the desert, but when we went to the scene, they were already gone."

"Wow. I don't remember that." Her dark eyebrows knitted together in concentration. "How far did you launch them?"

"A few miles," I said. "They landed in the desert outside Summerlin South."

Veronika nodded in grudging respect. "Not bad. Did they leave anything behind?"

"A mangled ID," I said. "I gave it over to the Vegas PD. They're running it for a match."

She was quiet for a minute, lost in thought. "You launched this speedster for miles, and they walked away from it?" She eyed my room again. "I'd ask to sit down, but there's no way in hell I'm sitting in there. Consider me floored enough to require seating, but not desperate enough to take it from this place."

I looked over the motel room again. "It's not that bad, I don't think."

"Sweetie," Veronika said, oh-so-patronizingly, "you should be on birth control before sitting anywhere in that place. Men seeking a ten-minute rental for a quickie with the corner hooker would take a pass at this motel."

My eyes got wide. "Wait—you think there are hookers working here?" That would explain the noises I'd heard from a few doors down during the night.

She shook her head. "Even meth heads would take one look at this place and be like, 'Naw, dawg, we're better than this.'" She started to put her hands on my shoulders, but apparently thought the better of it, stopping them about ten inches away. "Olivia. Get the hell out of here before it's too late."

"It's really not that bad," I said, and the sunlight glinted against something about three feet from the open door. I reached down and picked it up; it was my phone's heavy Otterbox case. The screen had a small crack in it from its most recent launch. "Oh, darn."

Veronika stared at the phone in my hand. "Is that what I heard hit the wall after I knocked…?" She shook her head. "Never mind the trivialities. Okay, fine. You won't move? Let's track down this speedster son of a bitch and deal with him so we can get you out of this place and into somewhere that won't result in you becoming a mother just because you accidentally cuddled with the blanket during the night."

I ignored that comment, instead focusing on something more important to me. "Uhm, when we find them, how do you want to…deal with them?"

Veronika peered at me with an utter lack of amusement. "Well, I'd rather not get launched through a hotel facade again, if that's what you're insinuating."

"I don't want that for you, either," I said. "I'd rather not have to deal with this guy or gal or genderless blur by myself."

She stared at me, almost inscrutable, like she was trying to decide something. "Come on," she said, jerking her head toward the vast, empty desert space across the street. Then she slowly backed a couple steps from the door before turning to walk away.

"Wait—uh, where?" I asked.

"Breakfast," she said. "And we need to talk about your…well, everything." She made a hand wave gesture that seemed to incorporate my entire body.

"Oh. Okay. I need to get dr—" I looked down out of habit, then back up at Veronika. She was staring at me with complete pity. "I guess I'm ready to go right now."

"Good," she said, and headed across the parking lot without waiting for me to say anything else. I scrambled to grab my room key and followed after her, trying not to trip over my own feet or zip a car across the parking lot as I did so.

37.

Sienna

"Why would the governor do a public event today?" Holloway asked, channeling the thought we were all having. "And for a library dedication of all things?"

"Clearly the man is deeply concerned about childhood literacy to the exclusion of worrying about his own life," I said, my jaw tense.

Burkitt let out a low chortle from behind the wheel. Sun-dappled trees were blazing past in a blur of green as we headed back to the New Orleans FBI field office on the freeway. "But seriously," he said, "why is the local Triad boss tipping you off about the governor's schedule?"

"I have a theory," I said, "based entirely on logic and speculation and short of any evidence at all: the governor is corrupt and in business with the Triads in some way, and she's protecting her investment."

"That's cold," Burkitt said, "and big, accusing the governor of corruption without any evidence. Not without some precedent in politics, but still…big. I wouldn't breathe a word of that in public."

"Don't worry, Chalke has me off the interview circuit until…well, forever," I said. "But back to the point—all I'm seeing so far is a giant mishmash of data points. Speaking as professional investigators, gents—how is one supposed to stitch these together into a cogent criminal narrative which we can use to, oh, I don't know—crucify Governor Warrington?"

"Not the job," Holloway said, almost grunting.

"You want to be a little careful about that one," Burkitt said, and for the first time, I caught some hesitation off of him. "Ivan Warrington…he's got some power behind him."

"So do I," I said. "But yes, I take your point since the FBI Director called me herself this morning to let me know that saving his life was up there in the President's priorities list, probably between his crayon coloring session and before his paste-eating midmorning snack."

"Gondry was a college professor before he became President," Holloway said, sounding a little outraged on the man's behalf. "He went to Stanford, for crying out loud. He's not a moron."

"Keep telling yourself that," I said, rolling my eyes, "and someday maybe a magical fairy will come and teach you the difference between education and horse sense. I'm not knocking his IQ, just what he applies his immense intelligence to. And since he's nearly killed me on several occasions, I feel like I've earned the right to call him an idiot even absent the First Amendment, which says I can talk shit about anyone I damned well please, President or not."

"Back to the point at hand," Burkitt said, probably trying to defuse Holloway's building response, since his face was now blood red and his mouth a twisted line. "Your inference about Warrington being bent? It could be true, but we haven't heard a whisper of it locally. And that's not the sort of thing that tends to stay secret."

"He's a politician," I said. "They're all corrupt to some greater or lesser extent, at least at the national level. It's just a question of whether he's corrupt within the bounds of the law or not."

"Okay, we get the point," Holloway said, and I quit, because he basically exploded. "You hate politics and the government. Which is a strange position to be in, since you work for it."

"I don't hate the government," I said, keeping my calm while he seemed to be ready to light off like a firecracker. "It's just like Churchill said; to bastardize his quote, it's the worst there is—except for all the other governments. I'm not a big fan of the things they do, but if I'm unhappy with it, it's because I count on them to keep order. I'm a big fan of order, probably because I've tasted enough chaos in my life to know that the alternative sucks. But I'm also keenly aware that the more corrupt or unjust the system gets, the more you invite someone to come along and kick it over, justly pointing out how corrupt it is. And those situations almost never result in a more just system being put in its place, so…"

"So, you're a passionate advocate for anti-corruption," Burkitt said, and it seemed to me he was trying to keep things from escalating between me and Holloway, who was just steaming beside him. I found it a particularly delicious point of irony that Mr. Gropey was such an ardent Lord of Order.

"Thanks for bullet-pointing that for me, Burkitt," I said. "I do so like bullets."

"No problem," Burkitt said. "Now—how do we find out where this library dedication is?"

"I suggest we go right to the source," I said, pulling out a business card I'd pocketed yesterday and then dialing my phone. "Jenna Corcoran strikes me as the horse's mouth."

"Go for Corcoran," came the answer at the other end.

"Really?" I asked, pretty sure my face was as scrunched up as I could have made it. "That's how you answer your phone? 'Go for Corcoran'?"

"Ms. Nealon," she said, so clipped. She must have been pleased to hear from me. I have that effect on people. "What can I do for you?"

"Yes, I'm calling about booking tickets for the governor's dedication ceremony this morning," I said. "I'm very interested in literacy and civic events, and I'd like to be right in the thick of the crowd if possible."

"Really?" Earnest hope. I needed to crush that.

"No, you junior league Sidney Blumenthal," I said, lowering the boom, "not really. Why did you schedule a damned library dedication today? Or keep it on the schedule if it was already there? Are you trying to get Warrington killed?"

"Of course I'm not," Corcoran said, getting huffy. "The event was originally on the schedule, and while we decided to cancel immediately in the wake of yesterday's incident, after some discussion it was determined that upholding the integrity of the governor's office by keeping to our commitments—"

"Save the long-form messaging bologna for the tourists," I said. "I'm a full-blown cynic, and I buy it not at all."

"We consulted with the Louisiana State Police and they said they can protect the governor at this event," Corcoran said.

"I don't know who's in charge over there," I said, "but I'm not sure I believe the conversation was that simple."

"Regardless—" she started.

"Regardless, get your head out of your ass and cancel this thing," I said. "You're giving this assassin a perfect chance to kill your guy."

She was quiet a second. "Well, I'm sure you'll stop her."

"I'm not," I said. "Many and varied are my skill sets. Stopping ice bullets from hitting other people? Not among them. I need more time to investigate, to track this assassin down. It's been twenty-four hours—"

"Are you closing in on the killer?" she asked.

Now it was my turn to pause, and it was pained. "Well, we have some leads. A description, for one, that ties the assassin to a dead body found in Plaquemines Parish a couple years ago."

"You found a prior victim?"

"I don't think so," I said. "Maybe an identical twin, though." Holloway cringed, his eyebrow twitching.

"A…twin?" Corcoran's skepticism bled over the line.

"Yeah, maybe," I said. "And speaking of leads, you know Mitchell Werner, right?"

This produced a long pause. "In passing. Why?"

"Because he's sleazy and in politics so I assumed you would," I said, and savored what I imagined her face looked like on the other end of the conversation. It was really good, eyes kind of half-slitted with annoyance. "I had a conversation with him this morning because he paid for the burial of the dead girl—"

"I don't see what this has to do with the matter at hand."

"Because we're trying to track her 'sister' down, duh," I said. "And I need more time. Which means I need the governor to not put himself into a position to get killed. Kindly cancel the library event." I looked out the window to see the New Orleans skyline.

"No," Corcoran said. "You're here to support us and investigate. If you have concerns about the event, you're welcome to show up and provide security, but the show must go on. The governor's re-election campaign is already in full swing—"

"It's two years until his next election." I'd checked the internet and it had told me so.

"—and we have serious ground to cover."

"This is everything I hate about American politics these days. I read history. I know election campaigns didn't used to last this long. Pretty soon we're going to have gubernatorial and presidential campaigns that start the day after the last one wrapped up, and I kind of wish I had my fire powers back just so I could spontaneously combust in protest without dying."

"Are you coming to the event to help or not?" Corcoran's patience appeared to have reached its end. "Because I have things to do."

"If he dies at this, it's on your head," I said.

"No," she said, not a drib of emotion coming through the connection, "it's on yours. You're in charge of security. The event's downtown, near the World War II museum. I'll make sure the Louisiana State Police know you're coming to take over security."

"The hell I am—" But I heard a click at the other end that signified our conversation was over. "Shit."

"Did we just get roped into security detail?" Burkitt asked, shooting me a sympathetic look. We were sitting at a traffic light that had turned red, sun pounding in through the windows from a blue and open sky.

"We did." I let my phone sag down, staring at the screen that informed me the bitch had hung up on me. "Looks like we're out of the investigating business for a little while, guys." I shook my head and stared out the window. There wasn't a lot of foot traffic out there this morning. Hopefully it'd mean sparse attendance at the dedication, too. "Let's go save this idiot from himself."

38.

The library in question wasn't terribly far from the hotel. I watched the tracking dot on my phone GPS and compared it to where I was staying, and it looked to be within ten blocks. A little down Magazine Street, a little off the Pontchartrain Expressway, and not too far from a giant, circular road called Lee Circle.

"There's a museum dedicated to World War II over there," Burkitt said, pointing in the direction of Magazine Street. "Foremost in the US. Pretty impressive, really. You should check it out if you're really into history."

"It was my favorite subject other than all the combat-related ones," I said.

"Where did you go to school?" Holloway asked. "Hunger Games Academy?"

"I was homeschooled," I said. "I thought everyone knew that."

"Oh, right, the whole basement and box thing," Holloway said, nodding along. "I forgot. You seem so normal. Relatively."

"That's not something I hear very often," I said. "Thanks. I think."

Holloway just grunted. Burkitt rolled us through a traffic light and into a surface lot where a half-dozen Louisiana State Police cars were parked. He flashed his ID to the officer guarding the lot and was waved in, backing up to park us tail-in to the spot for a quick and easy escape.

"This is crazy," Holloway said, pulling his gun out of the holster and gently racking the slide back to confirm he had a round in the chamber. "What kind of moron dedicates a library on the day after he's been shot at?"

"I get the general sentiment on Warrington's part," I said, feeling no need to perform the same exercise; there was always a bullet in my gun's chamber. "He's trying to provide a continuity of leadership. Reagan did something similar after being shot in the 80s. Ford was out and about after the Squeaky Fromm attempt, too. You have to show your face, fly the flag, to tell people you're not afraid."

"That's just stupid," Holloway said, re-holstering his piece. "Warrington should be afraid. That ice queen almost got him. Would have, if not for pure luck."

"I agree with all that," I said, throwing open my door. No child locks today; Burkitt must have remembered. "But I see why he's doing it, even if I, too, think he's being under-cautious."

The sun felt like it was beating down, and I hadn't realized quite how much Burkitt had turned down the AC in the car. The rays seemed to catch my dark suit the second I hit the sidewalk, heating the entire surface area to a hundred degrees plus, even though there was a slightly cool breeze wafting down the city streets.

"This feels like DC," Holloway griped.

"Lot of humidity," I agreed. "That's going to work against us if this lady really is an ice meta."

"How so?" Burkitt fell into line behind me as I headed toward the library, which, by my GPS, was two blocks from here.

"Water or ice metas need moisture to work with," I said. "Even my bud Scott, a top-of-scale Poseidon-type, would really struggle to make anything happen in the middle of, say, the Sahara. With all this humidity, though, our ice queen is going to be able to do just about anything she wants. Make an ice slide, create ice bullets—the sky's the limit."

"Great—I love when it my suspects have lots of weapons to work with," Holloway said. "It really keeps the job interesting."

"Agreed," I said, a little more muted as we turned the corner. The library was ahead, a massive white-grey concrete structure with steps and a colonnade that took up the center third of the facade. There was a picket line of cops and tape at the base of the steps, which looked to be about twenty, thirty feet high. The governor's podium was set up directly under the colonnade's shadow, at the top of the stairs, so he could look over the whole crowd. There were probably fifty, sixty Louisiana State Police troopers posted up and down the street, and when I looked at the rooftops, I saw more of them there, some with long rifles in hand, ready for a sniper.

"Louisiana State Police look to be taking this seriously," Holloway said, a little admiring beneath his usual gruff demeanor. "This is Secret-Service-level protection."

"Well, Warrington did almost catch a bullet yesterday," I said. "That's bound to escalate the threat level. I imagine the LSP aren't looking to let something like that go down on their watch."

One of the LSP troopers waved us through the cordon after we flashed ID. There was no crowd at the library yet—they were being held back a few blocks by the cops—but one was clearly building, and my hopes that this event would go ill-attended were plainly way off base. I wiped my sleeve against my forehead, perspiration already starting to gather there.

We made our way over to the man in charge of the scene. He was pretty obvious, standing in the middle of a few troopers, a head taller than any of them, his dark, ebon skin sweating away in the sun. He doffed his hat to us as we approached, and greeted us with, "Ms. Nealon. I'm Captain Boudreaux."

"Nice to meet you," I said, taking his offered hand for a second. He pumped mine gently and let go after one time. I liked big guys like Boudreaux; they never tried to show off by crushing my hand, they always seemed secure and gentlemanly enough to be brief and on about the business rather than make a thing of it. "You've done a fine job setting up, given what you've got to deal with here."

"The sight lines are bad," Boudreaux said with a touch of Creole or something, a very local accent, pointing down the street. "It's not as clear a shot as she had at the ferry, but it's not airtight for us."

"Looks like you posted counter-snipers everywhere you could," Holloway said, giving the whole area another eyeballing. "It's a good setup."

Boudreaux nodded his appreciation. "Where do y'all want to be for this?"

"Where I can do the most good," I said, looking around.

He gave me a quick once-over. "How are you with a rifle?"

"Fair," I said. "Better than most, but not a pro. I'm best at 200 yards or less." That had been about the range when last I'd had cause to use a scoped rifle, back at a quarry in Maple Grove, Minnesota. I don't think anyone had ever told me the final body count there, but it had to be north of a hundred, because I was fairly merciless in my shot choice, and when the ambulances showed up there weren't nearly enough of them to go around.

"Maybe you should go on top of this roof here, then," Boudreaux said, pointing at the one directly across the street from the library. "It's central, and if you keep your head down and wear one of our hats, the shooter might not pick you out of the crowd of us."

"Yeah, I like the idea of making my presence here a surprise to her," I said, mulling it for about a second. "And it gives me a good vantage for almost everywhere she could manage a shot. Let's do it."

"Where do you want me?" Burkitt asked, drawing a scowl from Holloway. I suspected it was because by putting himself at my disposal, Burkitt had opened Holloway up to being ordered around by me. It faded in a moment, though, as Holloway maybe reconciled himself to being bossed around.

"By the governor," I said. "I'll keep overwatch, and if I see anything, I'll radio to you and you sprint-drag his ass out of here." I adopted the most diplomatic tone I had, and turned to Holloway. "Where do you want to be?" I had no problem being in charge without actually being in charge; unless he offered up something absolutely dumb as a suggestion, I'd go with whatever Holloway said.

"How about I make it easy and go with Burkitt?" Holloway

said, and I just nodded.

That decided, Boudreaux gave me a friendly smile and said, "If you'll follow me, I'll get you up on that rooftop."

"Got a trooper uniform that would fit me?" I asked, falling in behind him. I stripped off my jacket as we went and brushed my hand down my back, taking note of the sweat spots all along there. They were myriad.

He looked me over once. "I doubt it, but we could try. Might be better to just put on one of our jackets."

"Great," I muttered, trying to keep it low enough he couldn't hear me. I'd seen those windbreakers, and they were not going to help with the sweat problem. "Let's do it."

39.

Brianna

Brianna had driven to the scene last night, just to make sure it was viable. The police presence then had been minimal, and she'd parked a few blocks away and commandeered a shopping cart, filling it with garbage on her approach. Once in the zone, she'd muttered to herself and just generally tried to sound like a crazy homeless lady.

The cops had, unsurprisingly, left her alone. The makeup and outfit had done their job, which had been fortunate.

She'd chosen a spot three blocks away, a building with a tilted, A-frame-like roof that had a clear sight line to the library steps. There was at least one flat-roofed building behind her that would surely be laden with Louisiana State Police, though, and some of them had to be dealt with before she could set up.

So that was what she was doing—taking care of business.

There were five troopers walking the perimeter building next to the A-framed one. It had a flat roof, and likely a few snipers atop it in addition to the guards patrolling around it. Three of the plainclothes officers were stationed in the narrow alleys on the sides and rear of the building. Two were posted out front.

She came into the alley on a long-hooking approach from behind the building next door, ditching her rifle bag behind a dumpster half a block out. She had a pistol if she needed it, but she doubted she would. She needed to keep this quiet.

Deadly quiet.

Her hands were slick with sweat, drawing the humidity out of the air and using it to rise, building a slide that her feet adhered to as the ice pushed her along to the rooftop, above the sentries below. As she climbed, she dissolved the slide behind her so as not to leave a sign. Some of the excess dripped down to the alley floor below, but most of it was absorbed back into the air.

She came up onto the roof in the shadow of the protruding stairwell entry to the rooftop, a six-foot-tall structure that rose up above everything and blocked her from the snipers, one of whom was at the corner to her right, the other ahead and to the left, stationed at opposite corners.

She slipped in behind the trooper to her left, tiptoeing quietly up behind him and delivering the coup de grace to the back of his head. He slumped over, unconscious, and she bound his hands and feet in ice, then froze his mouth closed so he couldn't shout if he woke up. She repeated the process at the opposite corner of the building, knocking the next sentry out and then moving to the edge of the rooftop.

The next one was clear, and she'd just eliminated the only watchers that would be behind her. The A-frame, rising roof on the next building would shield her from view of the library until it was time.

She leapt over the alley at a run, and her fingers found purchase on the edge of the roof. Brianna pulled herself up, gasping, trying to keep it quiet. Once she'd made it up, she looked back down into the alley below.

No troopers watching. She was in the clear.

She slid the case off her back and put the rifle together. She could have done it blindfolded, but she did it blazingly quickly instead, finishing by attaching the weapon's sling and loading the magazine. Once she was done, she started a careful climb up the steep grade of the roof to the point. It was a perfect barrier between her and the library and she peeked over the top carefully, and just for a second so as not to expose herself for long.

There they were: the library steps. She was a few hundred yards out with a clear shot. There was nothing happening—

yet. The crowds were still being held back by the Louisiana State Police past a cordon line about 150 yards from her position. They'd let them loose soon, though, and not long after that the governor would show up.

Brianna took a breath and squatted on the slope, checking her watch. In five minutes, she'd check again. No point in exposing herself any earlier than she had to. Not for this. At the right time, she'd bring out the rifle. From drawing a bearing on him to shooting, she wouldn't have to have her head up and exposed for more than ten seconds.

And then it would be done.

40.

Sienna

"How likely do we think the assassin is to change their MO?" I asked, peering through a pair of binoculars. My rifle leaned beside me against the side of the rooftop. I'd been assured it was sighted out to two hundred yards, though I would have preferred to check for myself. I was speaking through the headset radio the troopers had set me up with, on the alternate channel they'd designated for my little FBI group. "Because I'm looking at the setup here and thinking a pro would take one look at this and pass. There are easier ways to kill Warrington."

"Such as?" Holloway's rough voice trembled a little, like he got hit with the full effect of his hangover when he spoke, and it made him cringe.

"One of the ice-slinging types I know of is Captain Frost," I said. "Up in New York, you know? Also, a huge tool, by the by, but he can create an ice slide that carries him through the air."

"Oh," Burkitt cut in. "Like Frozone."

I blinked a couple times. "Yes. Like Frozone from *The Incredibles*. Exactly. Or almost exactly. So, with that ability, this snow queen—if she does indeed have powers—could come sliding in to attack from overhead if she were of a mind to. Or she could slip into Warrington's mansion from overhead, freeze her way through the roof, drop down and kill him while he's sleeping, or on the can—anytime but now, when he's surrounded by security in a public setting."

"That's a good point," Holloway said with a grunt. "And for me, this goes to motive. If she's a cold-hearted assassin looking at it like a job, she's likely to peel off from this particular occasion and look for an easier time to execute. Assuming she's not on any particular deadline. If she decides to give it a go anyway…"

"Then it's a personal motive," I said, nodding along as I surveyed the nearby rooftops in a slow sweep of the binoculars. "You're right. I think that does tell us something if she makes a move today."

"Unless it really is a timer thing," Burkitt said. "You guys ever read John Grisham's *The Pelican Brief*?"

"I must have missed that one," Holloway said drily.

"I think I read it back in the aughts," I said, frowning. "That's the one where someone pays a hitman to assassinate two Supreme Court justices so they can have them replaced to issue a favorable ruling on a court case, right? On drilling in a wildlife habit in Louisiana or something?"

"Bookworms," Holloway snorted.

"You should try reading," I shot back. "Studies show it helps decrease your troglodyte characteristics by 15% or so, and if anyone needs that, it's you, Scotch-boy."

"Anyway, point was," Burkitt said, the soul of patience, "that was done for time-sensitive reasons. What if there's some piece of legislation Warrington is shepherding or about to sign that's going to go through—or not go through—if he's in office?"

"Holloway, did you forward that legislative summary from Corcoran to Shaw?" I asked.

"What am I, your secretary?" Holloway asked. "No, I didn't. I thought you had Corcoran email it directly back to the office."

I felt a sudden compulsion to check in with Shaw back at home office. "I have this hunch that even if we manage to pull Warrington's fat out of the fire in any sort of incident today—" I scanned the many, many rooftops and hoped someone was watching the streets well "—he's going to do this again tomorrow and the day after."

"You think he's got a death wish?" Holloway asked.

"No, I think he's a flaming narcissist with a messiah complex," I said, running the binoculars over a building with an A-like arch at its top. It stuck out against the more common, older French colonial style of architecture. It was a few blocks out from my position, but still well within range with a solid rifle. "He doesn't *want* to do this speech—he *needs* to."

"Well, if anyone in this crew knew something about messianic narcissism, it'd be you," Holloway said, "*Slay Queen*."

I rolled my eyes, which made looking through the binocs impossible. "I didn't pick the nickname, Grabby Hands." I pondered the options available, and stared off at the New Orleans skyline to the north. "Distance is this lady's safety. Getting up close increases her risk of capture and exposure." I was just talking out loud. "So...whether she changes her MO and comes up at him hinges on how bad she wants him, I think."

"That makes a lot of sense," Burkitt said. "I think—"

An explosive round of applause put the brakes on whatever Burkitt thought, and I looked over the edge of the building to see that the police had released the crowds and they were now congealed in a light mass in front of the library. Up front at the police line it was reasonably dense, but getting back about twenty, thirty feet it tapered off so there were five, ten feet between each spectator. I gauged the crowd to be two hundred or so people, two-fifty max.

"One of you guys want to scan the crowd for long blond hair?" I asked. Our assassin might use a wig again, but maybe not.

"No sign of her yet," Holloway said tensely as the crowd launched into another round of spontaneous applause. "Did we ever come up with a codename for Warrington?"

"No," I said. "Go with *Dirtbag*."

There was a long pause, and I could almost picture Burkitt's wide eyes, Holloway's face pinched in horror as they stood down there under the colonnade. "*Dirtbag* is moving,"

Holloway said at last, as if he just didn't want to fight me on this one. Which was good, because I was pretty set on this.

"Let's get this party started," I said, and started peering through my binoculars again, scanning, as I waited for the assassin to make her move.

41.

Brianna

The crowd noise was the giveaway. Brianna squatted behind the A-frame of the roof clutching her rifle, listening to the dull roar of the city in the background, that steady hum and occasional horn honk that filled the New Orleans air. It wasn't a subtle change, the crowd thrum going to a low roar in an instant.

Warrington had arrived.

She knew he was popular, but wondered how much of that was a genuine product of the people of Louisiana loving their governor and how much of it was the local media being enraptured with a man who harmonized with their ideals about the direction change should take. Either way, the crowd was clearly supportive of Warrington. She supposed perhaps there might be a small quartile dedicated to protesting him, but it surely numbered in the single digits.

Brianna slipped the bolt of her rifle partway down, checking the chamber. One round was in there, waiting, though she only saw the cartridge case, then slapped it closed again so as not to allow the spring to eject it.

She was about to need it, after all.

Brianna counted out the seconds, the minutes. She wanted to let enough time elapse that Warrington was sure to be in place. She'd sighted the podium, knew where he'd be when he actually spoke. In this case, hearing his voice would be the key.

As soon as he started to speak, it'd mean he was at the podium. And that would mean it was time for him to die.

42.

Sienna

"Guys," I said, a slow horror dawning on me, "I just figured out a major flaw in our plan." The steady heat of the swampy air was oppressive, and I was sweating like crazy, salty beads running down my face.

"What?" Burkitt's voice held hints of alarm, like he was ready to push the panic button.

"If the assassin doesn't strike," I said, as deadpan as I could, "we have to sit here and listen to Warrington's speech." I paused to let that sink in. "The whole damned thing."

43.

Brianna

Yes, this was it. The crowd's hum was dying away. Warrington had to be close to the podium, close to opening his mouth so that the lies, the endless spew of lies, could start spraying forth. She gripped the rifle and held it tight, waiting for him to start speaking.

She'd wait a few seconds beyond to make sure he was in place. It wouldn't do to rush. Not for this.

This time…she needed to get it right.

44.

Sienna

"I hate my new life," I said, Warrington droning on, firing off meaningless platitudes about the greatness of New Orleans and the people of the State of Louisiana. I was willing to accept that all of those things he was saying were completely true, and in fact, I believed them, being a fan of the city thus far. But the fact they were belching forth from his lips meant I trusted them about as far as I could throw the building I was presently squatting on. "Things were easier when I was on the run. I found bad guys, I crushed them, we moved on."

"You could always go back to being on the run, Nealon," Holloway piped up. I could see him standing next to one of the columns below, didn't even need my binoculars for it. "I think we'd all be happier going back to that status quo, personally."

"The tent in your trousers last night suggested you'd miss me," I said, putting the binoculars back to my eyes and scanning the rooftops again. "Maybe make that argument to your crotch. If it's recovered from the argument I made to it with my knee."

A few blocks out the roofline was interrupted by that building with the A-frame, eaves blowing the line of sight to the governor wonderfully. That meant I only had to look as far as that rooftop and no farther, because anyone farther out wouldn't have a clear shot.

Burkitt chuckled softly over the line. "You see anything? Either of you?"

"I see a whole mess of the chattering classes down those steps," Holloway said, his voice a little more muted. I guessed he was covering his mouth in fear that someone might read his sneering, arrogant lips. "And not a lot else."

I rolled my eyes. "Try taking a look in a mirror; you could add 'dickhead elitist' to your findings." I glanced down at the rifle leaned against the roof edge next to me. "Should we change our comms channel to the one the troopers are using? Might be good to hear what they're seeing. Also, maybe Holloway will suppress his inner dickishness with a local audience."

"They're on channel eight," Burkitt said. "You want to switch over?"

"Let's do it," I said, and lifted my radio to do just that. It took a few seconds, then I plastered my binoculars back to my eyes, trying to assess the clearest angles for a sniper to get a shot at Warrington, who was still blathering on across the street below me.

45.

Brianna

He'd been talking for a while now. She could have heard every word if she'd really wanted to, but she didn't want to. They were all lies, spilling from vile lips, dripping from a poison tongue. If Brianna'd had her druthers, she would have gotten him alone somehow, and ripped that damnable appendage from his mouth, freezing the wound closed behind when she was done. The look on his face—it'd have been priceless.

But that would have required her to get close to him, and that was not something she was willing to do.

She'd waited long enough. Grasping the rifle, she checked the round in the chamber one last time and applied her finger to the bullet. It had started to melt in the Louisiana heat, and her powers worked quickly, smoothing the running drips and moving them right back into place, solidifying it.

It was perfect, frozen solid. Ready to whistle through the air soundlessly ahead of the rifle's crack, the sound that would herald Ivan Warrington's doom following milliseconds behind the frozen instrument of wrath that would kill him.

It was time. Brianna took one last breath and exhaled. The moisture steamed in the hot air, wafting out frozen. She liked the cool feeling that came over her just before she shot. Her breath steamed again, and she turned, slowly, to stand and acquire her target.

46.

Sienna

There were really only two clear lines of sight to the governor. One ran down the street to my left, and was very limited. Anyone who wanted to shoot from that direction was going to have to do so within three blocks, lest they lose sight of Warrington under the colonnade. It was good positioning by the Louisiana State Troopers, the best you could manage with so public a place. I was scanning that avenue every thirty seconds or so, but it was a brief look, because there were only two rooftops from which you could make a shot, and about a dozen windows, none of which I could see. Watching them was someone else's job. Several someone elses', actually.

That left the long road to my right, down which we'd parked, down which there was a clear view of the library for some six blocks, ending on my side of the road in a block or so due to my building being in the way, and on the other side of the road in six blocks thanks to that A-frame roof jutting up like Holloway's trousers last night. This direction was where I was spending the lion's share of my time scanning.

The farther out you got from the library, the higher our potential assassin would need to be in order to get a clear shot at Warrington. Fourth floor or higher, I figured, three blocks out, and it just climbed after that. I was scanning those windows, taking in those rooftops, almost all of which had Louisiana State Police posted on them. Double checking, you might say. Or triple. Quadruple, maybe.

If Warrington was going to die, I didn't want it to be because of my negligence. I wanted it to be because after I left, he stumbled down the stairs while eating a crawfish, and the damned thing accidentally burst out of the back of his head like some sort of alien. Whoops. It'd be a fitting end for that scuzzbucket. But I wanted no part of it.

I just wanted to do my job, get to the bottom of this case, chalk up a win for the system, and go back to New York. I'd say "go home," but New York was not home, and it seemed unlikely I'd be visiting Minnesota anytime soon.

"Clear," I said, for about the thousandth time, into the police radio. I started my quick sweep of the right-hand road again. It took less than five seconds to scan the windows, the rooftops.

Nothing.

I brought the binoculars back around to the long road on the right. What was it called? Hell if I could remember. I started at that A-frame rooftop, started moving them down to the next—

Wait.

I stopped. Moved the binoculars back to the A-frame—

Froze.

"GUN!" I shouted into the mic as I snatched up my rifle. It was in my hands in less than a second, the safety snapped off in a breath.

I honed in on my target and didn't even bother with the scope. I looked straight down the side of the barrel and eyeballed it as the crowd exploded to murmurs behind me. With a careful squeeze of the trigger, the gun barked as fire exploded out the edge of the barrel and leapt in my hand from the shot.

47.

Brianna

The bullet snapped into the roof some six inches below her, making an awful noise as it crashed into the tin and ripped out the other side about an inch to the left of her hip.

Brianna dropped immediately behind the cover of the rooftop, ears ringing from the distant thunderclap that was now echoing down the street toward her.

Someone had shot at her.

She blinked, looking at the hole in the roof. And they'd almost hit her, too.

Her breath surged back into her lungs as though it had been forced in by a strong gust, and her eyes went wide. She lunged to the side, realizing she hadn't moved nearly far enough from the site of the last bullet's impact.

The roof exploded behind her, another hole opening up as a bullet ripped through into the spot where she'd been squatting only a moment before.

Brianna cursed. Now the shooter was putting pressure on her. Hell if Brianna was going to stick her head up now. She cursed again; they'd have moved Warrington inside at the first report of gunfire.

Her blood was surging through her veins, but Brianna was still cool enough to know that this round was a failure.

Again.

But there was nothing to be done, and so she slipped the

rifle onto her back, leaving the case behind. It was generic, and would tell them nothing. She leapt off the side of the roof, pulling moisture out of the air to make an ice slide that would carry her away to safety.

48.

Sienna

"Warrington is in the library!" Burkitt's breathless voice piped into my ear. "Repeat, Warrington is safe and locked down!"

"Unless the assassin placed a bomb in there," I said, rifle in hands. I hurtled over the divide between my building and the next, eyes fixed on the A-frame roof line where I'd seen the gun—and a familiar sparkle of blond hair.

"This is Boudreaux." The Captain's voice cut into the transmission. "Starting a sweep of the library now. Move the governor to the southern exit. We'll have transit waiting."

I could hear the distant squeal of tires as I peered over the barrel of the gun, leaping the short gap to the next rooftop. I'd started moving after I'd fired the second time, putting a bullet hole into the roof where I'd seen the assassin huddling. Now I was moving forward, ready to put pressure on her by firing as many times as necessary. I doubted it would be necessary, though, which was a key reason I was heading toward her position.

"*Pelican* is moving!" a state trooper's voice cut in with what I could only assume was Warrington's code name. *Dirtbag* was so much more fitting, though. "Headed to southern exit."

"Transport standing by."

"I am in pursuit of the shooter," I said into the radio. The rifle was weighty in my hands as I leaped another alley, coming to a brisk landing on the next roof. "Last sighted position was on top of that A-frame roof on—hell if I remember the street name. It's the one that leads straight out from the library's colonnade."

I was having to advance slower than I would have preferred due to the rifle in my hands. It's not easy to run when you have a long gun tucked against your shoulder. Any second, I felt like I was going to trip on something and go down, barrel-first, and shellack my face against the scope.

Now I was only two rooftops away from being even with the A-frame rooftop, and if the assassin was still there, I'd have a clear shot.

"This is Hagman!" a shout cut through my ear. "We've got two troopers down but still alive on the rooftop beyond where the shooter was positioned!"

"Do you have eyes on the shooter?" I asked, bracing the rifle harder against my shoulder. I was already sweating before I'd started running and jumping buildings; now I was positively drenched, the clothing under my jacket as wet as if I'd taken a sauna bath.

"Negative," Hagman's voice came after a second. "No sign of the shooter on the rooftop. But…" There was a pause as the trooper drew a breath. "There's an ice trail leading off down the side!"

"Shit!" I safetied the rifle and slung it over my back as I looked for my exit. Running to the edge of the roof that overlooked the street provided it; just like all over this town, ten feet below me, there was a balcony.

I leapt down, bouncing off the balcony and catching myself on one of the railings. Swinging with my momentum, I dropped to the second layer of the balcony, this one some ten feet below the first. With only enough time for a quick turnaround, I charged the balcony edge and hurled myself down to the street below, where I narrowly missed landing on a woman screaming about the world ending.

Needless to say, my near collision with her didn't quiet her down at all. I didn't waste time apologizing, I just sprinted across the wide street, keeping my eyes on that A-frame rooftop.

"I am in the street, in pursuit of the shooter," I said, hitting the radio mic button as I kicked it up into a dead run. The assassin had a very good lead, and might even be gliding through the air practically like she was flying, but dammit, I was Sienna Nealon, and I could run faster than almost anyone on the planet.

I applied that skill now, hitting the alley that led behind the A-frame building seconds later and plunging into the relative darkness of the shaded alleyway, unzipping my jacket as I did so. Running with the rifle in my hands wasn't an option, so I pulled my Glock as I sped along the dripping brick alley. I dodged a dumpster, and caught a glimpse of the already-melting ice trail that hung overhead.

It was solid, a few inches thick, and suspended in air off the side of the building. I couldn't tell whether it was attached or not, but my understanding of these ice powers hinged on the idea that this assassin could essentially control the movement of ice in the world, even keeping it levitating in midair via a kind of telekinesis that was limited to ice and ice alone.

"Nice of her to leave me a trail," I muttered, beginning to huff a little as I poured on the speed, turning a corner.

The ice trail snaked off around the corner to the left, heading north. At the next block it hung a right, heading east, and I frowned. It looked like it was descending a little, but the height of the buildings was doing the same.

"The shooter has breached the perimeter!" one of the troopers bellowed into the earpiece. I thought I was going to experience sudden explosive decompression of the eardrum he was so loud. "She's crossing Magazine Street now! Just north of the World War II museum!"

"Where the hell is that in relation to me?" I muttered, still sprinting underneath the ice trail. I'd lost all track of where I was, geographically, and was now consigned to dodging the occasional trash can or cardboard box in this snaking web of alleyways as I followed the ice trail, blurring by a block every few seconds.

I got my answer as I took the next corner, following the ice trail as it reached, suddenly, over Magazine Street. I paused as the alley spilled out onto the booming street, the architecture of this block like a strange tableau out of a bygone era. I'd entered a space of preserved architecture and it took me aback for a second, like I'd run so fast I'd gone back in time. Uh, again. The modern cars were the only giveaway.

That and the guy on the modern bike pedaling by, lackadaisically pedaling, his jaw slightly open in a vague smile, bald head shining in the sunlight. "You look lost, Slay Queen," he said, going slower than I could jog.

I blinked at him a couple times. "I need your bike."

He skidded to a stop, smile vanishing as he put his feet down to catch him. "You serious?"

"I am an FBI agent in pursuit of a suspected assassin," I said, breathing heavy. I readjusted the rifle on my shoulder so he couldn't miss it, holstered the Glock rather obviously, then pointed at the ice trail overhead. "I need your bike to catch her."

He blinked a couple times as he thought about it, looked like he wanted to argue, then thought the better of it, almost leaping clear of it. "Hey, yeah, take it. Just, maybe mention my name if you catch her using my bike? On TV?"

"Sure," I said, grabbing the handle bars as he surrendered them. "What's your name?"

"Richard Dixson," he said, thin smile spreading back over his face.

I tried not to guffaw, but failed. "Thanks for not being a penis about this, Dick Dixson."

His smile melted immediately. "You just had to go there, didn't you?"

"They don't call me Slay Queen because I pass up the obvious—but still funny—jokes," I said, mounting the bike and speeding up over twenty, thirty miles an hour immediately. Someone honked as I blew across Magazine Street into the opposite alley, gaining speed all the while. "I am heading…east, I think? In pursuit of the suspect. Just crossed Magazine Street."

"The Mississippi and the cruise terminals are a few blocks ahead," Burkitt cut in. I thought I could hear a car engine revving in the background, but the air was whipping around me as I blew down the alley and onto the next street so quickly, I could barely hear anything on my side of the conversation.

The ice trail turned north and crossed a major avenue in a slow diagonal. It seemed to go on for a couple blocks, then cut to the right again, disappearing down a side street.

"Understood," I said. "Where's she heading? Speculatively?"

"The river, generally," Burkitt said. "Based on her direction."

"Shit," I said. "She hits the river, we lose her. She can cross at will, land anywhere on the other side. The likelihood we pick her up after that..."

I didn't have to say it. We all knew.

If she made it to the river...she'd get away.

49.

Brianna

All she needed to do was make it to the river.

Brianna had a good lead, no sign of pursuit, and she was cranking along on an ice slide at top speed. No cops in sight since she'd blown through their perimeter back at Magazine Street. There was plenty of humidity in the air even before she reached the Mississippi, enough that she could have built ice structures almost indefinitely.

And no one was shooting at her.

The attempt might not have gone as planned, but she'd made it out alive. She might need to give it a rest after this, let the heat die down, but she was walking away from this.

Warrington would wait. He wasn't going anywhere, after all.

All she had to do was make it to the river. She had a car parked on the other side in Algiers. Just shake this trouble and find her way to it, and off she'd go, back to the planning stages again, but safe and sound.

And Ivan Warrington would still die.

It'd just take her a little longer than she wanted.

50.

Sienna

I couldn't let her get away. Everything hinged on this.

If she got away, she could dive into a deep hole and pull the ground up over her. Which was a practical way of saying she could hide out for months or years if she was disciplined enough, leave town and put some distance between her and her crimes, then come back when she was ready to try again, after the Louisiana State Police had relaxed their increased security precautions. They couldn't watch Warrington every minute of the day forever, after all.

So, I had to catch her now, because if I didn't…who knew how long she'd be out there, hanging like a guillotine over Warrington's head?

The ice trail was about twenty feet off the ground on a slow decline over the street, like an icy, alternate lane built for some crazy Evil Knievel type who just couldn't help but be eco-friendly but also suicidally dangerous at the same time. For all I knew, it was now a permanent feature and some dumbass would be using it for just that in the weeks to come.

I was going forty, fifty, sixty miles an hour on the bike, acutely aware that I did not have a helmet on. Any sudden crash would send me flying, headfirst, into a crushing impact with either the street or something else, and potentially splattering my brains all over the place. I really, really wanted to avoid that particular fate because I was really attached to my brains.

"Out of the way!" I shouted, bumping the bike as I leapt over the curb on the cross street. I swerved in front of a Mercedes and bounced back up onto the curb across the street. The pedestrians in front of me responded to my shout by bailing out of the way, and I sped along the sidewalk at motorcycle speeds. Fortunately, there weren't many people out at midday. Maybe they were all tied up at the must-attend event of the season, the library dedication. Or running from it, I suppose, several blocks back.

I took the corner into the alley at about thirty miles per hour, veering to avoid a dumpster. The ice trail extended a couple blocks ahead, a sparking spray of white forming at its head—

There she was. I caught a flash of blond hair and the glint of blued metal extending over her shoulder, her rifle slung there like mine, her hands free for building her ice slide.

"Shooter in sight," I called in. "She's a block and a half ahead of me, and I'm closing fast."

"How?" Holloway came back in a burst of fuzzy static. "Are you flying?"

The alley walls were blurring around me. I was pretty sure I was going over sixty miles an hour now, my legs pumping hard and taking advantage of all my cardio training of the last few years. The New York Post had caught a video of me running in Central Park, something I did at least every other day as part of my rather exhaustive training regimen, though I tried to vary the route so photographic evidence didn't appear again. It had caused people to call me the Flash for a day or two. Whether that was better or worse than Slay Queen, I couldn't decide.

The bike only magnified my speed, allowing me to take it up to a crazy level of zipping past buildings and pedestrians at lethal velocity. For them and me, possibly.

"Stop!" I shouted, figuring I'd at least give that a try. Shooting an armed suspect in the back as she was fleeing was maybe permissible, but pretty on the line, in my opinion. And being the only FBI agent presently in pursuit, my opinion counted for a lot. Especially since I was the one who'd have to do the shooting.

Also, shooting someone in the back as they were running away wouldn't exactly fit the new "Violence Lite" ethos I was trying to embrace. Putting a few rounds in them as they were taking aim at a state governor? Totes fine. Busting caps in them as they fled? Muy bad-o, or however you said "terrible" in Spanish. "La Coldplay," perhaps?

The ice queen didn't slow, and I wasn't entirely sure she heard me since I said it right as I was blowing through a cross street, and I nearly sideswiped a Ford Fusion whose driver laid on the horn in a bid to scare the hell out of me. Fortunately, I was made of sterner stuff and also benefited from meta reflexes, swerving and only barely thumping their bumper. My back tire skidded and I dodged around, maintaining control and all the hell in my soul. I did flip them a bird, though, and for the first time, felt a little pang of sympathy for all the bicyclists out there trying to ride the roads. Not much, because they were taking a lightweight implement into the same lanes where the big boys drove their two thousand pound plus cars, but still some.

"Elsa, stop or I'll put you on ice!" I shouted as the shooter glided around the next corner. She turned her head to look at me, and we made eye contact, now only a block apart as she turned north once more. It really was impressive how she moved on those ice bridges, and I wondered how long they'd survive in this heat once she'd left them behind.

At the next intersection I cut the corner hard, almost running over a pedestrian who'd stopped to gawk at the ice queen flying by overhead. "Move, move, move!" I shouted, hitting him in the kneecap with a pedal as I passed. His cry was pure, mewling pain, and I knew I'd shinned him good by the way he clutched himself as he fell. "Sorry!" I tossed back, then turned my attention back to my escaping shooter. "Also, I'm sorry to you for that terrible ice pun." If she heard me, she gave no sign. Not that I could see her on top of her ice slide.

Burkitt's voice cut in on the radio. "Where are you now?"

"On Convention Center Drive," I said. "Crossing Girod Street now." The street sign blurred by. I was now three quarters of a block behind the ice queen, and closing fast on the straightaway. She cut across Lafayette, still heading north.

"You're a block from the river," Burkitt said, tension infusing his words. "Sienna, you're going to need to get her pretty fast."

"Working on it," I said. "You're more than welcome to take over pedaling this bike if you think you can go any faster."

"Did you say 'bike'?" Holloway cut in. "You mean 'motorcycle,' right?"

"My legs wouldn't be this tired if I'd stolen a motorcycle," I said. "Thanks, Dick Dixson."

"Is that supposed to mean something to us?" Burkitt asked.

"No," I said, and cut the next corner tight. I was getting close now, half a block behind the ice queen. I caught her throwing a nervous look behind at me.

"The Riverwalk is ahead of you," Burkitt said. "It's a busy place, Sienna. Quite a distance to any of the nearby bridges across the Mississippi—"

"I'm well aware of the stakes, Burkitt," I said, bouncing the bike sideways and riding horizontally on the wall for a few seconds to cut the next corner even harder. It probably looked pretty cool, and I was definitely at eighty, ninety miles an hour now. The bricks blurred past as I streaked down the sidewalk, letting out random, siren-like shouts to clear the path ahead of me when I saw a pedestrian coming up.

The immense rear entrance of Harrah's loomed ahead, the triangular roof with its strange, lighted design and columnar entry, the colonial dome architecture like a beacon in the middle of the damned street. The sign ahead read *Poydras St.*, and a hotel tower lay just beyond.

The ice queen cut an abrupt angle right onto Poydras, gliding along a chain-link fence surrounding the tower, which kind of gave me the feel it was abandoned. An archway waited ahead composed of what looked like wooden slats, square and boxy, the words OUTLET COLLECTION written over RIVERWALK.

The shooter slid low under the arch, directing her ice down, and darted over the heads of pedestrians heading toward the river on this path.

"Beep beep!" I bellowed at the top of my lungs, searching the handlebars in vain for a bell. No dice. I hit a staircase just beyond the Riverwalk arch, bouncing up a few steps and nearly wrecking. Now we were both under a portico walkway, the shooter just fifty feet ahead, both of us zipping along in this confined space. She shot over the heads of the few pedestrians, and I wondered why she hadn't chosen to go higher, like over the building next door, where there was no way I could have followed her. She kept casting self-conscious looks over her shoulder every few seconds as I closed the distance.

Ahead, the portico opened up to a flat concrete Riverwalk, an old-fashioned steamboat waiting at the docks with red, white and blue circular bunting hung at the railings.

I poured on the speed, now only twenty feet behind her. She was forced to duck lower in order to escape the confined, decorative archway at the end of the portico, and I saw my chance.

And I took it.

I stood, then bounced the bike, turning it sideways and skipping it up a few feet and off the wall to my right. On the rebound I controlled it perfectly, really tapping into my metahuman dexterity, and came down on the ice slide behind her.

It took every bit of strength and agility I had to keep from wiping out as I went from normal ground to the wall to the ice slide, which had approximately zero friction with which I could ground the bike.

But it didn't matter, because I only needed the bike for another second.

I was now only ten feet from the shooter, and she was half-turned, trying to see where I'd gone, but looking down, at the ground—in the way wrong place.

While she was looking, I leapt over the handlebars, ditching the bike as I flung myself across the gap between us.

It was a gamble, trying this. As soon as I'd gotten to the slide, my tires had started slipping, unable to grip on the ice. But I still had momentum, and I was banking on that.

It seemed like a bad bet for a few seconds, like I was going to come up a few feet short. I was headlong flying toward her, seemingly running out of speed, my hands extended. I could feel her pulling away, or at least it seemed like it.

"No no no no—" I muttered. If I could just grab her, grab that rifle, maybe—

I was five feet from her and coming down fast, then four feet, then three, the ice slide rushing up to greet my face—

Suddenly it felt like she slowed, because I was *there*, and the stock of her gun was right in my grip, and then we were both tumbling, crashing off the end of the ice slide and into the open courtyard, bones rattling as we hit the concrete, a tangle of limbs. Pain surged through my body as we crashed back to the earth, rolling until we came to a stop. I lay there on the Riverwalk, stinging agony running through my shoulder and side, the sky shining above me, stunned.

But I got her.

51.

The flash when I'd gone from over 60 miles an hour to zero in roughly a hundred feet, rolling along the concrete, that had been...how to put it? Bad. That was bad.

Worse were the aftershocks, the little nerves firing all up and down my back as I felt the full effect of my hard landing, the stinging, the ringing in my ears, all of the agony just dripping through into me as I stared up into an incomparably blue sky. How could things be so pretty when I hurt so, so much?

"Awright," I muttered, rolling over onto my face and lifting it. My foe was right there, five feet away, bleeding out of her forehead, blond hair marred by the dark crimson leaking from the road rash she'd developed just below the hairline. "Let's just...call a truce for a second..." I tried to push to my feet, but the world around me spun. I'd rolled quite a few times before we'd come to rest, and my inner ear was still trying to sort out which way was up and which was down. For some reason, I had the strangest notion the sky was down.

"I don't think that's how this works," she said, trying to get a breath. She sounded winded, like she'd belly-flopped onto the concrete. She was sucking in breaths and talking fast between the gasps. "But it's my first time...fighting someone like you."

"Let's make it your last," I said, finally figuring out that no, the sky was up, not down. I bobbled, getting to one knee, planting four bloody knuckles onto the pavement to steady myself. "Come on. Just give up."

The cloudiness in her eyes faded immediately. She shook her head, stray blond hairs loosed out of her tight ponytail. I'm sure that was helpful for sniping, keeping the hair out of her face. "No," she said. "Can't."

"Sure you can," I said, finally getting to my feet but not really in any condition to fight. "You just hang here with me, we shoot the breeze until the cops show up, you go with them. No one gets iced, no one gets shot, no one gets pummeled to death by my angry, Slay Queen fists. Doesn't that sound nice?"

She narrowed her eyes at me. "Not for me."

"It's not all about you, okay? What are you, a politician?" I looked for something to lean on, but there was nothing nearby. Even the minimal crowd had fled at our crashing arrival. Now there was nothing but us, the Riverwalk, and the mighty Mississippi about thirty feet away. Wide open spaces for a little ways all around us; no easy cover. On the plus side, her rifle barrel was bent severely, and I didn't see a pistol on her.

Downside: she had ice powers, and I'd lost an arm to those before. They were not fun, not in the infliction stage, nor in the growing-back-a-hand stage.

"You know," I said, eyeing the river to our left, "the Mississippi starts up where I'm from. Itasca State Park. But it's small there. You could jump across it. By the time it gets to Minneapolis…not so much. Maybe I could, on a bet. But not in October. Probably mid-summer I'd be willing to try—"

"You're not going to get me to surrender by talking me to death," she said, her gasps much more under control now. She no longer sounded like a fish out of water. More like a runner who'd just finished a marathon.

"So, you're not afraid of me?" I asked, trying to put a little humor into it. "You might be one of the only people who isn't these days."

"You're scary," she said, measuring her response, eyes carefully watching me. "But I can't be stopped. Not by you. Not by anyone."

"I'm not sure, factually speaking, that's true, since I just, in fact, stopped you." I was keeping my hand over my Glock, ready to pull it at the least sign of trouble. This was the complicated thing about metas; technically they were never unarmed, so I'd be sensibly in my rights to pull the pistol and put her down if she so much as waved a hand at me.

But that was very "old Sienna," and I was trying not to do that Wild West thing anymore. Which was a real pain in the ass.

"I can't be stopped in the sense that…I can't let you stop me," she said, shaking her head. "I have to keep going. I have to do this." Her eyes were hard like a block of ice. I felt like I could argue with her all day and make not an inch of headway.

"Look, I've met Warrington, and he's a grade-A assclown, no argument," I said. "But…" I shook my head. "Look, I want to help you here. What's the connective tissue between your sister and Warrington?"

She stiffened, eyes getting big. "How did you know about my sister?"

"It's a whole thing, a long story," I said, waving a hand. "Doesn't matter." I figured mentioning that I'd dug her up was not going to be the sort of news that would soothe the savage ice queen, so I kept it to myself. "Point is—I'm trying to figure this out, really I am. I've got you on a killing quest and a dead sister. Connect the dots for me." I listened for police sirens, but heard none. Probably because they were over at the library dealing with the aftermath of an assassination attempt.

She looked down, at the ground, for a long moment, and when she spoke again, it was so quiet I strained to hear her. "Do you know what it's like to hate someone so much that you'd give your life if it meant you could destroy them?"

That one hit like a sack of bricks. "Uhm, yes," I said. "Maybe just a tiny little bit…dozens of times over—okay, yes. Of course I do. I didn't get this nickname because I let people cross me without consequence." I realized I was probably sending a terrible message and cleared my throat. "But that is very bad. For…reasons. Obvious reasons."

Her blue eyes looked jaded staring back at me, and I could see she wasn't buying it. "'Reasons.' Sure."

"Okay, cards on the table," I said, keeping my distance from her. "I don't know what Warrington did to you, or to your sister, although I'm kind of getting a flavor for it, given how she ended up." And here I stepped a little closer to her, though there were still ten feet or better between us. "Warrington is going to be pond scum for the rest of his life, no matter how short it is. But you…you don't have to be a murderer for the rest of yours."

"So, you're telling me to let it go?" She took a step back from me.

"No." I shook my head. "Absolutely not. If Warrington did something to your sister, tell me about it. Help me." I thumped a finger into the center of my chest. "I've got a badge and a gun, and the ability to investigate wrongdoing. If he did your sister wrong, help me sniff it out and I promise you—I'll go after his ass. Because that's what I do." My hand fell back to my hip. "I've kinda made a career of going after the powerful. And I don't care how powerful they are—if they've done wrong, I'm all over them like the stink of reefer on a Bob Marley concert."

"What he did was so long ago," she said, shaking her head. "And he owns Louisiana. You'll never get him here."

"I don't work for Louisiana," I said. "Tell me, and we can go from there." I threw up that hand. "Hell, just give me her name. Your name. Give me something to work with."

Her blue eyes sparkled, a little moisture in the corners. "Her name…was Emily Glover."

"And are you from here?" I asked. "New Orleans?"

She shook her head slowly, never taking her eyes off me. "Baton Rouge."

"Okay, we're getting somewhere," I said. In the distance I could hear a faint siren. "What did he do?"

She just stared right at me. "Now that you know who she is, you'll find how she crossed paths with him." Her gaze flitted lower, to the concrete walk. She shook her head, as though breaking out of a dreamlike state. She started to turn.

"Wait," I said, and pulled my pistol, leveling it at her. "Don't do this. Stay." The siren was joined by another, and they were getting closer. The NOPD was responding to the 911 calls of the pedestrians around here, at last.

She stared dully at the gun in my hands. "You going to shoot me?"

"I'd really rather not," I said, keeping it level, pointed at her side. "Not for Warrington. But you keep trying to kill him, and even though I can smell the stink on him, I don't have anything yet. Give me a reason. Give me something, so I can change the direction of this."

She laughed under her breath. "What? So I can just…walk free? When it's over?"

"No." I shook my head. "You've tried to kill a man. Trust me, there are consequences for that. But it doesn't have to be your life or his." I raised the Glock. "Please. Help me do the right thing by your sister."

Her eyes flashed colder, and I knew I'd lost her. "I'm already doing the right thing by my sister."

She sprinted off, and I didn't shoot her in the back. She leaped over the railing, and I thought for a second she'd plunge into the Mississippi, but she didn't.

I followed her to the edge of the Riverwalk, and there I saw her means of escape.

She'd constructed a miniature paddle wheel, just like the steamboat sitting next to the Riverwalk, and she was spinning along at meta speed, just like I'd done with the bicycle. It only took her a couple minutes to cross the Mississippi, and then she was gone.

52.

Olivia

Staring across the breakfast table at Veronika was a nerve-racking process for some reason. We were at a diner a stone's throw from my motel, a shabby place that was about on par with the lodging I was currently enjoying. She stared at me over her coffee cup, steam wafting over her dark eyes. She seemed to be trying to decide something, and when she finally settled on it, she put the coffee cup down, leaned in and whispered, meta-low, "Can we talk?"

"Haven't we been doing that all along?" I asked, dragging the words out slowly because I was pretty sure Veronika had been non-stop in her verbalizations from the moment we'd met up at the baggage claim.

"Real talk, kiddo," she said.

"Oh." I nodded, eyes flitting down to the stained, vinyl yellow tabletop. "This is about my confidence again, isn't it?"

"No," she said. "Well, yes, but not just that."

"Ohhhh…kay?" Now I was confused.

"You do need confidence," Veronika said, putting her palms flat on the table. Her suit was the nicest and probably most expensive thing in the entire place, and the dark green blouse she wore under it really worked. "But it's more than that. What's with the clumsy thing?"

"I…sometimes fumble," I said, trying to avoid stammering.

"You're a meta." Veronika stared at me, and I felt compelled to look away, then caught myself looking away and forced myself to look back at her eyes. It was not easy. "You have strength, dexterity and agility beyond that of a normal human."

"I don't know, I just lack grace," I said, trying as hard as I could not to look away from her eyes. It felt almost painful, like I was challenging her. I finally let out a breath and looked away, unable to take it any longer. "I get nervous. I trip. I—"

"Okay, look," Veronika said, and now her voice was straining. "You are stronger and more capable than you know." She slid a hand across the table at me, slowly, and took mine, lifting it up. I wasn't sure how to take that, but I didn't detect anything amiss in her manner. She gave my hand a squeeze. "I'm not sure how much time I have to make this point, given I was tossed through a building last night, so let me just say it—your problems are all entirely in your head."

"I…well, duh," I said. "That's what I go to Doctor Zollers for. To get the, uhm…twitchy stuff…under control."

"Oh, no." Veronika let go of my hand and buried her face in her own. "You've been seeing the doc? For how long?"

"Months," I said, again unable to look her in the eye but deeming her reaction to be a) not good and b) not favorable to my feelings.

She slumped into her hands, as though she could just drop right into them and disappear as easily as if they held a pensieve. "The foremost psychiatrist in the meta world—and a mind reader—and he can't stop you tripping over yourself and blowing things out of your path?" She pulled her face out of her hands and leaned back against the booth. "Okay. Maybe this isn't a therapy session issue." She nodded, and it felt like she was changing emotional states manually right in front of me, her eyes getting an enthused glaze. "Maybe it's a field issue. How many criminals have you caught?"

"Since I started?" I blinked, trying to think. "I mean, I've been on the job less than a year. So, I've done some training and—"

"How many meta crooks have you cuffed?" Man, it was uncomfortable being under her gaze, those eyes just burning through me. "How many have you killed?"

"Uh, none on the second one," I said, smacking my suddenly-dry lips together. Had the desert gotten to me? My mouth felt parched. It hadn't a moment ago. "And on the first…uh…one…half?"

"How do you cuff half a person?" Veronika's voice exceeded meta-low range and went into the human whisper decibel level for a second. "Did you catch the one-armed man?"

"I don't know who that is, but no," I said. "I helped Augustus catch a criminal meta in Nebraska about two months ago."

"But none on your own?" Why was she staring so hard at me?

"No," I said. I felt like I was sweating, or wanted to, but there wasn't enough humidity in the air to allow it.

"This is a no-smoking establishment, isn't it?" She looked around like a cigarette was going to drop out of nowhere onto the table. "I don't even smoke anymore, but I mean—I feel like I need to, right now. Did Nevada legalize weed? Because I need a hit of that." She darted a gaze at me. "Actually, you do, too. Desperately."

"I do?" I asked. "Uh, why?"

"Because this is no longer about you being uptight or lacking confidence, Olivia," Veronika said, "although both of those things are most definitely a problem. You need to get drunk, stoned, laid—maybe even hit something stronger."

"I don't know what you mean." Now it felt hot in here. Hot and confined, like she'd pushed the table closer to me. Had she? I felt pinned in.

"Have you ever been drunk?" she asked, leaning in again.

"Maybe," I said. "I had two margaritas at Applebee's one time?"

"Ever been stoned?" She wouldn't stop staring. Why wouldn't she stop staring at me?

"No." I stared at the grungy yellow tabletop.

"Have you ever had sex?"

"That's totally inappropriate and not the point of…anything," I said, and God, was I burning up.

"You haven't, have you?" She sounded…not gleeful, but her

voice was higher, even at the meta-low range she was speaking in.

"I—I—"

"Hey, dudette, it's okay; you had an unconventional childhood." She tried to pat my hand, but hers ricocheted off. She took this in stride, getting control of it after a brief flight in which it looked like she was raising it to ask a question in class. "Why don't we do this? Let's eat, settle the check, touch base with the Vegas PD, and if they don't have anything for us, we go cruising for dudes—if you're into that. I'm not much for it myself, but I promise you I am the best wingwoman you will ever have, and there are like a billion groomsmen in this town looking to hit something, if you know what I mean. Even at this hour, I promise we can find some action on the Strip. We'll get you cleaned up, buy you something nice, and hit a target-rich environment. I can promise you, in this town, you will come up absolute aces in the dude department. I can get you in bed with a ten, if you want—"

"I don't want—"

"I'm just saying you need some drilling done. It would make a world of difference, really work the kinks out, maybe loosen some of that tension you carry."

"No, I don't—"

"Add in some weed, you'd be feeling good in no time."

"No." My eyes were squeezed tight. "No, Veronika, I don't want—"

"If you're worried about losing your virginity to a random dude, trust me," she said, voice getting closer as she leaned in. "It's way easier than doing it with someone you care about. Random dudes are a dime a dozen. People you can actually fall in love with? Well, they're rarer. Not diamonds-rare, because diamonds aren't actually that rare, but—"

My face was buried in my hands. "I'm not a virgin, Veronika," I said, from the depths of my sweaty fingers. I didn't dare so much as crack them to let any light in. "I was raised in…I mean…where I was raised…Tracy's dad, he…he and Tracy…" My throat caught, and I couldn't say anything else.

There was a long, long silence, and I felt a gentle hand

brushing mine. "Yeah," Veronika whispered, and I cracked my fingers apart enough to see now she was the one looking at the table. "I had a feeling about that." She glanced up at me, and the quality about her eyes was different now. "I'm sorry I pushed."

"You…already knew?" There was a sick feeling in my gut, and I would have sprinted out the door, maybe without even opening it first, if not for my legs feeling like lead, and with all the blood sapped out of them.

"I suspected," Veronika said, and now her eyes left the tabletop again, but her finger traced a strange pattern around it. She wore a funny smile, one that curled the corner of her mouth. "The way you act, some of the things you do…they seem a little familiar. Because for me it was this guy I worked with when I first got out of college. I knew I didn't feel anything for him, but I didn't have any friends in the area at the time. So I went out with him for a beer after work. I just thought we were drinking, having a good time. But his definition of a good time and mine…worlds apart." She spread her hands from each other like two birds taking flight in opposite directions.

I tried to say something but my dry mouth just flapped uselessly. "I'm…sorry."

"Yeah, well, so was he, after I figured out what he did the next morning," she said, nodding. "We didn't know what a 'roofie' was back then. You kids are way more on the ball these days."

"Roger," I said, barely able to meet her eyes, and only through extraordinary effort. "That was Tracy's dad. He…" Why wouldn't my mouth produce moisture? It felt like I'd been the one to land in the desert last night, and face-first at that, mouth wide open, swallowing every grain of sand in the process. "Of all the people he had under his control in the cloister—"

"Cult," Veronika said. "Or prison camp, if you prefer. I saw it." She shook her head. "It wasn't a village."

"Whatever it was," I said, "I was his favorite. It's why he sent Tracy and the others to bring me back after I'd escaped." I brushed my hands over my face, felt the smooth skin around my lips, wished I had a wet napkin to brush them with, to wet them—and to just clean off because I felt dirty. Again.

"One of those kinds," Veronika said, nodding along. "I love killing those kinds of guys. It's so refreshing."

"I did kill him, technically," I said. "Though Reed helped." My eyes were dry, too, and that was good, if a little surprising. Usually thinking about Roger had the opposite effect. But I was in public, and Veronika was here, and for some reason it didn't feel like it usually did. It didn't feel good either, but...

Something about her telling her own story? It took some of the jagged glass out of that wound. I couldn't have explained why it did, not even if I had to, but it did make me feel just the tiniest bit better.

"Good for you," Veronika said, and she cracked a slow smile.

I nodded, then looked away. "It didn't help." I stared out the wide, front panel windows at the parking lot. An old grey van was pulling out, a middle-aged couple in the front seat arguing. "I still wake up sometimes at night, screaming, launching things every which way..." I looked back at her. "Because I wake up thinking, 'He's got me.' Again."

"It gets easier," she said. "Over time. Not ever 'easy', I would say, but...it does get 'easier'. Not sure life is ever 'easy', in all its pain and suffering and whatnot, but...it fades."

I nodded. "Yeah."

"I want you to know two things," Veronika said, looking over my shoulder. The server was on her way over with our breakfasts, tray laden with food. "One—you're not alone in this, okay?" She patted my hand.

"Okay." I glanced over my shoulder again, not really sure how to take that, so I just sort of brushed it off. The server was almost here. "What's the other?"

Veronika just smiled, staring right at me. "If you can use that stuff you've got burning inside of you—control it, harness it, make it your bitch instead of letting it make you its?" She sort of lightly shrugged, like all the heavy conversation was just sloughing off her shoulders. "You're gonna be a damned powerhouse, Olivia Brackett. You'll knock 'em all dead."

I didn't know what to say to that, and it didn't matter,

because Veronika turned to the server and smiled, and bantered, as the lady delivered our food. I didn't hear a word of what they said, though, because I was still thinking about what the hell she'd meant by that last thing.

53.

Sienna

I stood on the banks of the mighty Mississippi, hot sun glaring down on me, wet to the skin under my FBI suit, thinking if I'd just pulled the trigger when the assassin turned her back to me, this would all be over now.

New Orleans PD and Louisiana State Police troopers swarmed around me, doing—well, I didn't know what they were doing. I stared across the river, wondering what I should be doing now that I'd let the shooter escape.

"What was that name again?" Burkitt's voice cut across my thoughts, knocking me out of a fixation with the rippling, brown surface of the Mississippi. He was a few steps behind me, messing around with his phone.

"Emily Glover," I said, blinking a couple of times as I looked to the hazy, far side of the river. No sign of the shooter over there. "Of Baton Rouge."

"That's what I thought you said." He shook his head. "I'm not finding anything in a general search. I called it in. We'll see what the office guys come up with."

"The shooter's her sister," I said, turning my back on the river and folding my arms around me. My shirt was dripping sweat, and I caught a glimpse of my hotel less than a half mile away, the tower sticking up beyond the buildings that hemmed the Riverwalk in from the city at large. "And I'm detecting a real, 'I Spit On Your Grave,' Warrington-done-her-wrong quality to this lady's motive."

Burkitt made a face. "You think that's a literal thing? Like Warrington hit this girl's cabin—"

"Not literal, no," I said, rolling my eyes at Burkitt's failure to keep up. "There's just…I don't know, a creepy kind of sexual vibe to it. Maybe I'm just reading that into it myself."

Burkitt seemed to pause and think before answering. "You could well be right. Warrington's, what? Mid-forties? And how old was this shooter?"

"Under thirty. I'd peg her closer to mid-twenties, but some of that could be that metahumans don't age like normal people."

"And they're twins?"

"They sure look alike, comparing her to the composite they made from the body." I shook my head. "I bet that'll give Holloway fits, if they actually are twins."

Burkitt's facial expression did not improve; it turned into a deeper cringe. "That's an uncomfortable age difference between that body we dug up and the governor." I hadn't noticed, but he'd lowered his voice sometime in our conversation, probably owing to all the troopers and local PD around us.

"Plus, Warrington has been married for like twenty years and has a family," I said, keeping my own voice low. "In case we needed to add some more cringe factor to this."

Holloway came sliding out of the sea of trooper hats. "Warrington's out of danger now," he said, lip curled in disgust, though whether that sprang from the current situation or some deep dislike of the city of Baton Rouge, I didn't know.

"Not at the local chicken joint?" I asked. "Because I could really go for a fried drummy right now." Holloway and Burkitt both guffawed under their breath. "You think he can keep his glory-seeking head down for a day or two now while we piece things together and wrap this up?"

Holloway was clearly amused. "You really think we're going to wrap this up that quick now that you let the shooter get away?"

"I don't think we're allowed to shoot fleeing people in the back," I said, completely deadpan. "I mean, I can check the

FBI manual, but I'm pretty sure a suspect has to present an imminent, reasonable threat of death or physical harm to another person in order to justify the use of lethal force."

"A metahuman always presents that threat," Holloway said.

"She never once used her ice powers in an offensive manner, never reached for her rifle," I said. "Sorry. I can't square that."

Holloway shook his head. "If you'd taken your chance here and gunned her down, this would be over." He ran his sleeve over his brow, wiping away the moisture gathering there. It had to be in the mid to high 80s now. In freaking October. "And speaking just for myself, I'm ready to get the hell out of this town. It's like America's crotch down here."

"Then you, being a giant taint, should feel right at home," I said. "Though I think, on behalf of the people of New Orleans, they'd find you completely unpalatable. Also, it was twins." Ignoring his aggravated look, I turned my attention to Burkitt, just as a slight breeze came in off the river. "Did you check the missing persons database for that Emily Glover name?"

Burkitt nodded. "Nobody reported her missing, either to federal or local authorities."

I closed my eyes, thinking it over. "Now the big question—did Warrington have something to do with her actual death? Or did he do something to her that led her down the path she went, which culminated in her death?"

"What the hell, Nealon?" Holloway seemed to burst. "You can't accuse a sitting governor of that kind of thing just because some dumb blonde takes a potshot at him and spins some sob story about her sister to get you to holster your gun!"

"Look, I got the measure of this other Glover sister when I was standing across from her," I said. "She's disciplined, focused, angry as hell, and—this is going to sound like a pun—cold about it. Like every angry action is dulled by a ten-foot-deep sheet of ice. She's not acting hastily in this." I rested fingers on my chin and mouth, finding plenty of moisture to try and wipe away on my upper lip. "Which is worrisome."

"Cold and calculating is a hell of a lot less fun to deal with than hot and crazy," Burkitt said, nodding along. "The dumb ones are always too amped up to think, too ready to make a move to plan it through all the way." He shrugged. "If she's that smart, the best move would be to submerge for six months and wait for things to cool off before making another play."

"Agreed," I said. "We can't give her that time, though. I should have asked her why she's so dedicated to killing Warrington from a distance. It's so different from most of these revenge motives, you know?"

Holloway nodded. "Most of them want to be up close and personal. Give a nice account of how they were done wrong." He looked down at his hands. "See the blood on their fingers or something."

"After this clusterfutz," Burkitt said, "she should be looking at every future opportunity to hit Warrington like the heavens are going to open up and hell's going to rain down. If she's got half a brain."

"I can confirm she's got more than half a brain," I said. "And also that she's thinking—mostly." I looked back over the Mississippi again. "But she is angry. And maybe getting a little desperate to finish this."

"You think now that she's got the scent of her prey in her nostrils," Holloway said, "she ain't going to give him up that easy? Dog with a bone?"

"Something like that," I said. I looked at Holloway. "Have you talked to Shaw?"

He seemed to slump instantly, eyes rolling in pure annoyance. "You want me to call the office for you and tell the boss man why you didn't end this before it could turn into an actual assassination?"

"Would you? Because that'd be great." I patted him on the shoulder, my arm at maximum extension so I wouldn't have to come any closer to him or have him misinterpret my gesture for more than it was—which was me being massively condescending. And maybe a little emotionally extortionate, given that I still had last night to hold over his dumb ass.

Holloway grunted, teeth clamped together. "Fine," he managed to grind out, and he slunk away into the crowd.

Burkitt watched him go. "I can't decide if he feels guilty for what he tried to pull on you last night, or he just worries about his employment. Either way, it's like a personality transplant every time it comes up."

"His personality needs a transplant," I said. "It's been growing in the rich soil of arrogant douchebaggery for entirely too long. It needs to take root in humility and gentlemanly behavior for a while." My phone buzzed, and when I looked at it, it was a local number. "Hello?" I answered it.

"Sienna!" Michelle Cheong's sunny voice came blaring out of the other end of the line. "How are you doing? Weather treating you all right?"

"I'm a little pissed off and a little peckish," I said, "and not in much of a mood to deal with your horseshit right now, lady. What do the Triads want from me today?"

"Why, I don't want anything from you at all," she said, sounding mock-offended. "But I did think, 'Wouldn't it be nice if we had a chance to talk?' Maybe share a meal, take the edge off your hunger."

I stiffened, my brow turning into a furrowed line. "What would we talk about?" Burkitt was staring just as intently at me.

"Oh, I don't know," Michelle said, not fooling anyone for a minute with her innocent act. "Little things. Yoga, maybe? You look like you could use something to de-stress."

"I don't have time for this—" I started to say.

"Wait, I know what we could talk about." Her delivery was note perfect, hooking me right as I was about to hang up, her voice treading the line between innocence and sincerity. "How about…Emily Glover?"

I froze, the air sticking in my lungs. "Okay," I said, once I got my thoughts back around me.

"Great," she said. "I'm parked just outside the police perimeter on Poydras. Why don't you come join me and we'll get a little something to eat and…" I could almost hear the joy she was wringing out of every word, and especially the last one: "…talk."

54.

The Bon Ton Cafe was an unassuming, three-story brick building only a few blocks from where everything had gone down on the Riverwalk. Michelle drove us herself, at the wheel of a well-worn minivan, the Triad queen rocking her usual yoga pants and not saying a damned word as we went. She pulled up into a parking lot beside the restaurant and led the way inside, silent as a mouse until we'd been seated and had a couple waters in front of us.

Mine didn't last more than ten seconds.

"Thirsty?" Michelle asked, eyeing my glass, empty to the ice at the bottom.

"Chasing people across the city by foot and bike takes it out of me," I said. My strategy for this meeting was simple: say as little as possible while trying to get her to say as much as possible. So far, based on the ride over, my strategy was not working very well. "Why'd you pick this place?"

"Bon Ton?" She looked around; the décor was very basic, red and white checkered tablecloths, simple wooden chairs, the occasional pillar right in the middle of the dining room and a ceiling that was aged wood slats and the odd chandelier or fan interspersed. It was basic, incredibly basic, down to the brick walls and perfunctory paintings on the walls. "In a city full of great restaurants," Michelle said, grinning, "Bon Ton stands out."

"Hm." There was a smell of food radiating from the kitchen in the back of the place that was already making my mouth water. "So…am I going to walk out of here with all my articles of clothing this time?" I stared Michelle down, and shameless as she was, she didn't even have the grace to blush. "Do I need to keep an eye on my pants?"

"I have no interest in getting you out of anything you're wearing," Michelle said, "unless you've got an interest in converting to the cult of the yoga pants? Because let me tell you something, Nealon—they would free you up in all the best ways, especially as much as you move."

"Given that I often kick above my head," I said, "I'm not sure yoga pants are the best choice for me. Also, probably not in the FBI approved list for standard wear."

"How often have you ripped the seat of your pants while fighting?" Michelle asked.

"Ripped them?" I snorted. "Hell, I used to go through entire wardrobes of clothes back when I could light my whole body on fire. Rips were the least of my problems."

"Interesting," she said, then piped down as the server came over to take our drink order. She listened politely to the spiel for a second, then cut in: "I'm not having anything, and my companion doesn't drink."

Our server wasn't much deterred, promising to return in a few minutes so we could order. I didn't argue, because I was still trying to figure out what was what with the menu. "How'd you know that?" I asked as soon as the server was out of earshot.

"Know what?" Michelle asked oh-so-playfully.

"That I didn't want anything to drink."

"Oh, come on now," she said, making a big show of perusing the menu. "Surely you aren't tempted to break that longstanding sobriety streak just because you've had a couple rough days since you got here. Though I suppose New Orleans is a tempting city for that sort of thing…"

I felt my blood run cold. "How did you know about my sobriety?" I tried to remember if I'd mentioned it to anyone at any point over the last few days where she or anyone on her payroll might have heard it. I couldn't remember saying anything about it in any forum since arriving in New Orleans.

"I read a speculative article about it on Flashforce," she said, looking up. "Do you know how much mystery there is surrounding you?"

I flushed, my cheeks feeling hotter than flames. "Yes. But it's not like I have time to sift through every stupid clickbait article written by all the wankers who just churn out hot takes by the metric ton so they can afford their apartments in Williamsburg and San Fran."

"Is there a reason you don't do any interviews?" she asked, head cocked a little, clearly curious. "You know, so you could clean up some of those misperceptions?"

I blinked. "The FBI doesn't let me. Presently."

Michelle almost snorted her water. "The FBI may not *let* you, but you know that half the FBI agents in the major cities leak like sieves to every journalist under the sun, right?"

I stiffened. "I'm not in that half."

"Good for you," she said, still looking at the menu, "having principles and such. How's that going for you so far?"

"Does how I answer affect whether I get stuck with the tab for lunch?"

She laughed. "No, I think I can handle this one." She quieted again as the server came back, ordering us a Bayou Jambalaya appetizer each, then a Fried Soft-Shell crab entree for herself. I ordered the Crawfish Etouffee, and our server disappeared toward the back of the restaurant after validating our choices as good.

"So…" I said. "Were you just tired of the social scene here in NOLA when you asked me to lunch, or…?"

"I am a little tired of the social scene here, come to think of it." She looked like she was thinking about it. "May I ask you a personal question?"

"We've already discussed my unwillingness to wear yoga pants. If it's more personal than that, I'm drawing the line."

Michelle smiled tightly, then leaned in. "I want to talk about violence."

My entire body seemed to twang to that topic of conversation, a little offense radiating out from the gut level to clench all my muscles. "So, of course you come to the Slay Queen," I said.

"That's a terrible nickname," she said, making a light

retching noise. "But I do have an honest query for you—you seem to be keeping a good handle on it these days. What's your secret?"

"Well, I did a little three-day stretch in the meta prison up in Minneapolis a few months ago," I said, trying to defuse her question with jokes, as one does when questioned about the murdering and such they've perpetrated, "and I think that really cured me, as far as ever wanting to go back. I feel like it totally cured me of the need to bust heads."

"That's not a serious answer." Her eyes were on mine, shining, but direct.

"No, but it's a somewhat accurate one," I said. "You go do a stretch like that and see if it doesn't change your mind about reflexively killing people."

"That's disappointing," she said, sitting back in her seat. The jambalaya arrived, and it, fortunately, was not disappointing. In fact, it might have been among the best things I'd ever eaten, and not just because I was starving. I scarfed it down, and if the server had been hanging around the table, I'd have ordered more on the spot.

Michelle kept quiet as she delicately went after her own jambalaya, employing patience and table manners where I'd dispensed with both. Consequently, she managed to string out her food and her silence until the salad arrived, whereupon I tucked in and devoured mine in seconds and she again took her time.

"It's good that they course things here rather than just bringing them out when I'm ready," I said, finally having had enough of watching her eat in silence. "Otherwise I'd already be out of here and you'd be sitting by yourself, with no one to talk to."

"That would be a real tragedy," she said, completely inscrutable. "Like wasting any of that jambalaya. Did I see you lick your plate?"

"If I thought it was acceptable, I damned sure would have."

"Don't go stopping yourself on my account. Table manners are overrated when the food's this good."

"Agreed; the food is amazing so far," I said. "And worth the trip, don't get me wrong. But am I going to get an answer about what you brought me here for? Other than 'violence'?"

She pushed a piece of lettuce around with her fork before spearing it and delicately popping it into her mouth, chewing completely, and swallowing. This whole process took well in excess of a minute, and I'd just about given up on actually getting an answer to my question when she said, "Well, if you're wanting to have a discussion about violence, it makes sense to seek out an authority, doesn't it?"

I smiled slyly as she went back to her salad. "Tell me—do the Triads in New Orleans employ violence very often?"

She showed zero surprise—or any reaction at all—at my query, but she answered it much quicker than my last question. "Violence is a part of life in any society. In civilized societies, we reserve the largest part of it for the state, granting them the effective legal monopoly on it, and for its agents. But there are laws, and then there are cultural norms, subcultures...the Triads are a subculture, one that exists below the bounds of societal organization." She kept her eyes on her salad the entire time she spoke. "When you're raised a certain way, it is hard to depart from that. Don't you think?"

"Not sure what you're getting at there."

"In times of stress do you ever find yourself drawn to tight quarters, confined places?" Her eyes shone as she looked at me, and I wondered, for perhaps the first time, if I was dealing with a telepath. Again. "Some artifact of your upbringing, perhaps?"

"Why do you ask?" I kept the focus on her, didn't dare to give her an ounce of reaction to work with. I kept my palms in my lap, kept down the flush that would normally have flooded my cheeks. I didn't deal with customers as cool as Michelle Cheong very often, and it required more control than I could recall producing, maybe in my life, including in my new job, where I'd been on my very best behavior. This was also one of the more circuitous conversations I'd ever been in, with so much parrying and whirling it might as well have been a fan dance. Or a sword fight.

"Maybe I was thinking about the holistic picture of your life," Michelle said. "You were introduced to the theoretical tradition of violence early. That is a feeling I'm well acquainted with. In theory, of course." She paused, fork halfway to her mouth. "No. Strike that. Not in theory. My father was a very violent man. He maintained his hold on his empire with bold strokes of violence. Anyone who stepped out of line faced brutal reprisal. There was no elegance to it, only the certainty of pain and death."

I tried to take in what had just happened. It seemed like Michelle had just broken down a wall between us with that admission. Our whole conversation had been stone walls on both our sides up until now, no exchange of anything other than surface-level pleasantries. For some reason, she'd decided to finally add some actual substance to our talk. "He preceded you in the family business?" I asked.

She didn't answer that, of course. "China has traditionally been a much more patriarchal society. Having a woman take up particular roles, such as leader..." She shook her head. "It was not easily done."

"I probably don't want to know what that comprises," I said. "Even though we're talking about violence."

She looked right at me, smiling slightly. "I'm sure it'd be like a light afternoon for you."

"Ouch," I said, watching our server thread her way through the tables toward us with a couple more plates. "Lucky for me the food's almost here, so I can mitigate the pain of your words with crawfish etouffee."

"You'll love it," Michelle predicted as the server delivered our food, asked if we needed anything, and then disappeared once more, thankfully.

I dug in, and yes, I loved it. The etouffee was so buttery and delicious, the rice beautifully cooked in a way that my rice at home never was. It was smooth and tasty, the roux giving it a richness of flavor that overcame my normal dislike for rice.

Once again, my food vanished in moments, and Michelle's was still 75% intact by the time I was done, no words exchanged as I vaporized mine with meta speed. She showed no sign of impatience with my quick disposal of lunch, and since she'd said it was fine, yes, I licked the plate. That roux was A+++.

"Told you you'd love it," Michelle said, taking in a piece of softshell crab and carefully chewing it up.

"Well, you weren't wrong," I said. "About anything, really."

She arched her eyebrows at this, as though, duh, she knew that already, lending credence to my suspicions about her telepathy.

I decided to fish. "So…if someone is disloyal to you, do you know it immediately?"

She raised one eyebrow. "I can generally figure it out, given a little time. Their patterns of behavior change. It's very tough to betray someone while looking them in the eye. It takes an especially cold character to pull that one off."

"Colder than a killer, you think?" I watched for her reaction.

She nodded. "In a way, killing can be easy. With a gun, I mean. You could almost close your eyes and pretend it didn't happen, if you lined everything up right. Conversing with someone as you're thinking about betraying them—there are levels of emotion that need to be present for that—ambition, greed, anger or a sense of betrayal for yourself. Motive to do the thing, if you're betraying someone you serve."

"That's interesting," I said. "I never thought about it that way."

"Humans are social creatures," she said. "We give off social cues constantly. Like you, with your arms folded across your chest, suggesting you really don't want to give anything away. So guarded."

"It's almost as if I was already run around by you once," I said. "And lost the soles of my feet in the process."

At this, she smiled. "Well, come on…I have to have a little fun in my life. And if I can do it at the expense of the FBI, that only enhances my reputation in my particular subculture. Especially when speaking to you otherwise might be seen as stigmatic, as though I'm giving away the keys to the metaphorical kingdom."

"I guess I can understand that," I said. "Though my feet are less understanding, and looking for an ass to kick in reprisal."

"Perhaps I can suggest one," she said, and now she was back to guarded herself.

"Please say Mitchell Werner," I said. "Pretty, pretty please."

At this, she smiled. "I wouldn't know about Werner and his

strange and tangled web. I was thinking about a larger target, one certainly in Werner's orbit, as much as he might try and hide it from you."

Another strike in the telepath column. How else could she have known about the removed photo? Or my suspicions about who was in that photo? "That's a big target," I said, trying to play as coy as she was.

"Yes," she said, and signaled the server for the check by waving her credit card, once. When the server came to collect it, Michelle took only a cursory glance at the bill before handing her card over. The server dutifully went away yet again, and Michelle looked me right in the eyes. "That particular target deserves a full accounting, for he has so many, many outstanding debts." She took the receipt and scrawled something on it, sliding it across the table to me. I glanced at it, but it was nothing more than a name and phone number:

Whit Falkner

New Orleans Herald-Tribune

504-555-8364

"If you do manage to place something upon his head—" and Michelle stood, all trace of emotion gone from her face save for a very, very small flicker in her eyes—anger, an emotion I was entirely too familiar with "—perhaps you should consider his payment placed upon the account of Emily Glover." And with that, she walked away, leaving me with my jaw on the floor because of what I'd seen her in her eyes at the mention of Emily Glover's name.

Hate.

She hated Ivan Warrington—and that me wonder again what he'd done to Emily, and how Michelle was tied up in all this.

55.

Olivia

When we finished breakfast, we headed over to the Metro PD headquarters on Veronika's hunch that we should "drop by" and see what was up. She ignored my near silent protests of maybe just going back to the hotel and waiting to hear from someone. Or maybe just ignored them.

The Las Vegas Metro PD headquarters was a gleaming glass and white concrete building just off the freeway. The desert sun was beating down on us, no sign of wind in the air today. It felt hot for October, at least compared to Minnesota, where the high today was 65 degrees. I'd checked my weather app while Veronika fidgeted in the Uber.

"See, you can't rely on people to call you back in this world," Veronika said as we walked into the building like we owned the place. The desk sergeant hit the buzzer when Veronika waved at him, and she headed straight into the back, leaving behind the assorted waiting pedestrians like we were people who belonged here. With the real cops. "You have to take the initiative, kiddo. Seize life by the cajones." She made a face. "So to speak. Sorry. Bad choice of words."

"It's a pretty common phrase," I said. "I don't break at words, Veronika."

"Just trying to be sensitive, sweetie," Veronika said. "Not everyone's as...what's the word? Anti-fragile...as you are, maybe. And I try to respect people who might be struggling."

I wondered where that respect had been when she'd smoked my personal story out of me this morning with a whole lot of talk about finding me a random guy to get, uh…frisky…with.

"Yo, Detective Norton," Veronika said, breezing into the bullpen. "What's up, you sexy thing?"

"If it isn't my new favorite metahuman lady," Detective Norton said, her eyes lighting up at the sight of Veronika.

Veronika made pouty lips. It didn't look hard for her; she seemed like she'd had lots of practice doing this. "'New' favorite? Who was your old favorite?"

Norton shrugged. "I got a little crush on the Slay Queen, to be honest." Her eyes lit up a little. "She's your girl, isn't she?" Somehow, by her wandering gaze, she included me in this.

"She's, uh, no, I'm—I don't even really know Sienna," I managed to stammer out.

"She's not my girl, no," Veronika said, sighing a little. "She's Harry's, damn him and his rugged, manly good looks and dripping heterosexual appeal."

It was Detective Norton's turn to make a face. "Who's Harry?"

"Doesn't matter," Veronika said. "We're here about that little incident on Fremont last night. My partner here turned in a piece of ID that you guys were going to try and get a match on. Any word on that?"

"Let me take a peek at the file," Norton said and plopped down on her chair, tapping away at the keyboard a few seconds later. "I swear they haven't updated our computers since the late 1900s."

"You still running Windows 97?" Veronika deadpanned. "Because in some ways, I think that might be better than 10."

Norton stared at her a little blankly. "You some kind of tech nerd?"

"I'm a woman of many interests," Veronika said. "But right now, I'm mostly interested in finding your perp and beating their speedy little ass with a sock filled with quarters. And my plasma-burning fists, though that might be too quick and merciful."

"Must be nice being exempt from 'excessive force' citations," Norton mumbled as she stared at her computer screen. "Okay, I have something here."

"Talk to me," Veronika said. "Hell, sing for me if it involves an address."

"Two possibilities," Norton said, scrawling something on a Post-It pad. She tore it off a second later, strolling over to us and offering it Veronika. Not me, because obviously I was a fly on the wall in all this. "Didn't I give you my number, Acheron?"

"You did, and I would have used it last night—" Veronika waved at the bandage on her forehead, smiling impishly "—but I spent the evening in the hospital. Not sure if you heard that."

"I didn't," Norton said, looking her over. "You okay?"

"Doing better now," Veronika said, smirking at her. She waved the Post-It. "Call ya later."

"You better." Norton was smiling too.

Veronika didn't say anything until we hit the main steps, already out of the station. "And that's how it's done."

It took my brain a few seconds to decipher what she meant by that. "Uh...did you just admit you're flirting with the local cops to get help?"

"Well, I'm actually interested in Norton, too," Veronika said, rolling her eyes as she descended the sun-bleached stairs. "But yeah, I don't have a problem using every available avenue to do my job."

Part of me wanted to ask exactly how far that ethos went, but it was a very small part of me and easily drowned out by the more sensible rest of me who screamed DON'T ASK DON'T ASK DON'T ASK until the temptation passed. "Guess we need another car," I started to say.

Veronika just waved her phone at me. "Already on the way, with the first destination already set." She waved the Post-It with the addresses. "Let's check them out, shall we?"

56.

Brianna

"Why did I tell her that?" Brianna drummed her fingers against the steering wheel. She was westbound, northbound on I-10 heading toward Baton Rouge. New Orleans was in the rearview, and the temptation was to not even look back. She wasn't yielding to that temptation, though, brushing the strands of brown wig hair out of her eyes and glancing into the rearview every few minutes to make sure there weren't blinking police lights behind her.

She'd been beating herself up asking the same question over and over for the last hour. She'd hit up a small safe house she kept in Algiers, grabbed the beat-up 2008 Kia she'd bought for pennies, and hauled ass out of town. Brianna felt lucky to have made it out of her confrontation with Sienna Nealon alive—if you could call it that.

Had she just been starstruck? Hell, Sienna Nealon was the reason she'd started down this road anyway. Reading about her attitude toward taking revenge, back in the early days, when no one had known her? It had inspired Brianna. Sienna Nealon hadn't taken the death of her first boyfriend lying down; there was a trail of bodies that had proven she wouldn't put up with that shit.

And Brianna had known those feelings, and had felt the same. She'd gone through the cycle after Emily's death—disbelief it could be her, at first, after seeing her on the news.

That didn't last long. She'd known almost immediately, of course. The fury came next, the unbelievable anger that this could have happened, even though it had been long in coming. There was no escaping it, though, no matter how much she wished it could be different, or how low she got.

Eventually, it just came down to realizing…Emily was dead. And though it was probably her own fault, in the immediate sense, it really wasn't, in the wider worldview.

It was his.

Ivan Warrington was responsible.

Now that son of a bitch was governor of Louisiana, and Emily had been found in a spillway down in Plaquemines Parish, arms probably full of track marks and her veins filled with that poison she couldn't keep herself off of.

If that wasn't the kind of injustice that stuck in your craw, Brianna didn't know what was. And it had certainly stuck in hers. She didn't know any way to get past it other than one—

Destroy the damned obstruction.

So that's what she'd set out to do with Ivan Warrington. She wished now that she'd done it a year ago, when Sienna Nealon was still out of the picture, but…

She didn't have the powers a year ago. She hadn't read about Sienna Nealon's own revenge plan a year ago. She'd only found all that out after the Revelen incident, when she'd been poking around.

And now she'd come face to face with Sienna Nealon herself, and…damn. It had all just sort of come out.

Okay, not all, but enough. And hadn't Sienna said Warrington had felt dirty to her? Wasn't that something?

But still…why would Brianna have said what she did? She'd as much as identified herself to Nealon, and after keeping her mouth shut for years about Emily. After all this planning, she'd hoped to be able to walk away once Warrington was dead. She hadn't even bothered claiming Emily's body, another calculated decision to let her carry through with the plan.

Brianna's head whirled, moving back and forth between hope at Sienna Nealon's words about Warrington being scum and her actions, which had been to put two bullets into the rooftop Brianna had been hiding behind. If it came down to a real, honest to goodness fight between her and Sienna, she did not like her chances. At all. In fact, she probably needed to think on how to make sure she didn't come out the immediate loser in that fight.

Either way, it was time to disappear for a while. Warrington could wait, and Sienna Nealon wouldn't hang around New Orleans forever. Neither would Warrington, really. He'd head back to Baton Rouge soon enough, and Brianna would head to her next safe house and encamp for a while. Not show her face anywhere, take grocery deliveries, really bury herself for a spell. And eventually Nealon would leave—if she didn't get the son of a bitch for Brianna—and Warrington would go back to doing his usual thing.

Then, if all else had failed, she'd kill Ivan Warrington then. And hopefully still walk away.

57.

Sienna

The New Orleans Herald-Tribune offices felt about like I'd have expected any local newspaper office to be—crowded, noisy, too many people packed into too little space, but probably about a fifth as many as there'd been twenty years ago, before the newspaper industry started getting their teeth kicked in by the internet.

The receptionist had barely raised an eyebrow at my request to see Whit Falkner, following up on Michelle Cheong's tip. She just called ahead then motioned me through into a bullpen. If it was a little quieter, that was probably because people were typing less than they were talking, skimming the internet less than they were making phone calls, though all those things were happening. I counted thirty desks and twenty-eight people on my way to Whit Falkner's cubicle, and I wondered if that was usual for a newspaper office these days, or if I'd caught them at an off time.

I'd checked in, albeit briefly, with Burkitt, before heading to the Herald-Tribune offices. He was still tied up at the scene, and probably would be for some time. I didn't bother to ask about Holloway and he didn't mention him, presumably guessing I wanted Holloway to tag along for this about as much as I wanted to run my bare chest across an industrial-scale cheese grater before plunging into a vat of lemon juice. It was a good guess on his part, if it was intended. He could have just as easily forgotten about the douchebag. I certainly wish I had.

There was a brass nameplate on Whit Falkner's cubicle bearing her name, and a stately black lady with chocolate skin and a nearly shaved head waited for me there, leaning back out of her cube to watch my approach. She nodded along as I took the last few steps, like my footsteps were in synch with a beat in her head. She slid out to meet me, not bothering to get up. "It really is you," she said, staring me down. "I thought maybe Rachel had got it wrong."

"It really is me," I said, "and honestly, I've gotta wonder what kind of nutbag would think impersonating me was a good idea. If they did, I could only hope one half of one percent of the hell I've caught the last few years landed on them."

She kept nodding along, gesturing me toward a conference room that ringed the bullpen. "Come on. Let's talk in private."

I eyed the other reporters, all of whom were watching me now, except for one lone guy still talking on the phone, utterly oblivious. "Yeah," I said. "Wouldn't want you to get scooped or something."

We headed into a plain conference room and she shut the door behind me. She was probably only a couple inches taller than me, but with broader shoulders and similar hips. She gave me the up and down, and I knew what she was thinking because I'd heard it a million times before from people with less of a filter: "I thought you'd be taller." Damned TV, giving people stupid expectations about my height. She didn't say it, though.

"To what do I owe the pleasure?" she asked. "You finally sit down with a reporter for an exclusive interview and chose me?"

I shook my head. "No chance in hell the FBI lets me do an interview with anyone. They won't even let me have a Twitter account."

She paused, thinking for a second. "I hear you have a mouth like a trucker and a propensity to spout off during conflict." Her teeth showed in a slow grin. "They're probably doing you a favor on that Twitter thing."

"Probably," I conceded. "I'm here because a little birdie—"

"Who?"

I sighed. "I thought reporters respected the sacredness of keeping their sources confidential?"

"We do," she said, "and if that's what it is, I'm down with—"

"I'm just giving you crap. It's Michelle Cheong."

Her eyes widened. "The Triad Queen-pin? She sent you my way?"

"Yeah," I said, "with regard to Emily Glover and Ivan Warrington." Whit got quiet, and her head bowed enough for me to know I'd hit something. "I see you have a story here."

"No, I don't, actually," she said, stirring out of her quiet. "I *tried* to get a story out of it. Tried hard, in fact. But I could never get a second source to confirm, and Emily herself—who gave me the whole sordid tale—never went on the record." She glanced up at me. "You know what happened to her?"

"Dug her corpse up myself last night," I said. "It surprises me that a bold and intrepid reporter like you wouldn't have said anything about her being the Jane Doe of the Caernarvon Spillway."

Whit flinched. "She had a sister, you know? Up in Baton Rouge? I know the word reached her there—"

"Name?"

Whit didn't even have to think about it. "Brianna. Brianna Glover. You should look her up; she's famous in her own way." Whit nodded along again, putting something together that she didn't share. "Anyway, I know she heard about it. But she kept quiet. I didn't have to think too hard about why that might be, especially when I did a little digging and found out the cause of death. Emily was chasing when I talked to her. Girl couldn't hardly sit still."

"What did she tell you about Ivan Warrington?" I asked.

"This isn't a story I can tell—" Whit started.

"Brianna Glover is the one trying to kill Warrington," I said, and Whit didn't react. "I just confronted her at the Riverwalk after chasing her down, and she inferred the motive was personal, but she wouldn't say what it was. Now, I've got suspicions, obviously, all the dark parts of my mind active and piecing together terrible ideas about what men of power do with girls half their age—"

"It's…just about what you'd think," Whit said, getting very still. "The Glovers were an old family in Baton Rouge. Good name, big money. But the daddy, he didn't want to tread on that like the other parents. Tried not to spoil his daughters. Brianna was on a competitive shooting team—"

"That explains a lot."

"—and he made both girls get jobs, work for their money, as teens," Whit said. "Tried to keep 'em grounded so they didn't become spoiled brats. Unfortunately, Emily chose babysitting as her first moneymaking career. Started at thirteen. For the Warrington family."

"Oh, shit," I said, cringing.

"Yeah," Whit said, nodding again. "It went about like you probably see it in your head. Fine the first couple times, then suddenly Ivan Warrington stops being the perfect, charming gentleman when he drives her home afterward. He starts showing her a different side of himself. Oh, it started innocently enough." Whit's face was twisting the longer she talked, fury starting to drip out. "'Ever had whiskey? Have a little sip. Ever seen a nudie mag? Take a look at this. Ever done'—" She quivered in disgust. "Well. It went like that from there. She says she didn't want to, but it didn't matter. She was thirteen, he was in his thirties. It happened. Again and again. For years."

"Dammit," I said, my eyes squeezed closed.

"This is the part of the story I could get. Her grades fell off a cliff," Whit said. "She went from being one of the hardest-working and brightest in her class to being surly, uncooperative. She'd get up when she was forced to, go to school all day, go to bed when she got home, and not get up again until they made her. Her parents thought she was just being a teenager." Whit pursed her lips tight. "She didn't say a word about anything. Hell, she wouldn't talk to me about it until she was high, which was another reason I couldn't go to print with it. A single source who was lit up every time I talked to her? Attacking a man who—at the time—was just a legislator with a bright future?"

"Those kind of attack pieces run every day," I said. "And

they usually have less basis in truth than what you're working with."

"Look," Whit said, holding up a hand, "I may know it's all true, in my gut, but it doesn't change the fact that Warrington, when asked for comment, denied it all. See, I went to journalism school long enough ago that they were still teaching me that you can't accuse people of a felony in print without evidence. There was none, no witnesses to back up anything. Emily's parents are both long dead, and she says they would have denied it, too, even if they had known about—which they didn't. Family image, you know?"

I chewed my lip, my hands clenched tightly into fists. "What about Brianna?"

"Don't know," Whit said. "Emily never told me she had a twin sister. I had to find that one out myself. The girls couldn't have been more different, at least from what I could see. Brianna went to the Olympics on the competitive rifle team. Won the Silver for Team USA down in Rio de Janeiro. Emily ended up in the gutter, and dead in a swamp spillway. I don't know that they had much contact after each went their own separate ways." She shook her head. "You sure it's her taking shots at Warrington?"

I nodded. "She's really pissed at him. And now I know why."

Whit nodded. "He might not have done it directly, but Warrington as good as killed that girl. The problem is, you'll never prove it. Emily never talked about it to anyone contemporaneously. Warrington had her scared witless. The best I could do for corroboration was talk to a couple of her teachers and get them to confirm a behavior shift. But it was weak tea; their recollections were fuzzy at best; we're talking about people who teach hundreds of kids a year, and Emily wasn't the worst they dealt with by far. She just went from being among the best to quietly crashing and burning. It wasn't like she turned violent and beat the ass off every girl in school. She just…" Whit shrugged.

"Faded away." I stared at the industrial grey carpeting.

"Yep." Whit nodded. It seemed to be her signature. "Some of the teachers I talked to didn't even remember her. Like she never even existed. And how she ended up, buried in an anonymous grave? It really is like her life counted for nothing."

"The guy who paid for that burial plot?" I tapped my fingers against my pants leg, feeling the soft, slightly damp cotton beneath my fingertips. "He's a political operator. Some sleazeball named Mitchell Werner."

"Pffft," Whit scoffed. "I know that trash. He and Warrington are connected at the hip. You think…?"

"That Werner operated as a proxy for Warrington in picking up the tab for Emily's burial?" I stared at her, fury boiling in my mind. "The thought crossed my mind. Warrington does have that whole 'I am so compassionate my heart bleeds tears of sadness for you' thing going on." I folded my arms back across my chest. "It wouldn't surprise me if he felt a little guilt about the human debris he left in his wake and decided to do the 'gentlemanly' thing about it. But, you know, in the chickenshit manner of not actually doing it himself."

"Doing it himself might have raised a couple questions," Whit said. "I could have reported on that. As it was…" She shook her head. "Once I knew it was Emily, I thought it was over. The story, I mean."

"Can you publish it now?" I asked. "Treat her interview with you as a dying declaration or something?"

Whit looked pained, but shook her head again. "Look…I'm a reporter of the old school, okay? I know this new breed is cool with rushing to publish when they've got one anonymous source, but I came in the tradition where you get at least two sources, and on the record, if possible. I could have gone along with Emily being anonymous. She'd been through a lot in her life—hell, her life came apart before she even went through puberty, thanks to Ivan Warrington." She shuddered. "But I needed someone to stand up and say, 'Yeah, I was around it when it was going on, and here's why I think this did happen.'" She put her head down in one hand. "This is why the old newspaper hounds drank hard. Because reporting is a hard job when you have to go out there and really fight to nail down your stories. Nowadays politics reporting is all going with whatever your 'sources'—and I use that word loosely—hand you, all wrapped up and ready to print."

"Huh?" I asked.

She looked up at me. "Nothing. Never mind. It's a messy business, that's all. But to answer your question—no, I can't print the story now, even though she's dead. Professional ethics still mean something to me. Without another source or some proof, this is still just a messy, illicit, disturbing 'he-said, she-said.'"

"Would Brianna Glover work as another source?" I asked, feeling a little flutter in my heart.

Whit just stared at me. "Someone like Brianna Glover might be able to confirm it enough for me to run it, yeah."

Now it was my turn to nod. "Then that's what I'm going to do. I have to chase down Brianna anyway. I'll get her to go on the record, and you can blow this thing wide open. Take down Warrington—"

Whit snorted. "I'm sorry. I just—you think one story will take down Ivan Warrington?"

"It's a dirty story," I said. "Screwing your thirteen-year-old babysitter? While married and playing the good, upright family man?"

"I'm not saying it won't hurt him," Whit said, "I just don't think it'll finish him. Warrington is strong, locally. Man won the governorship with 65% of the vote. If anything, he's gotten more popular in the last couple years since he took office. His approval rating runs in the mid-seventies. A sex scandal, even one as tawdry as this, isn't going to kill him." She stroked her chin. "But it might hobble him some."

"You don't think Warrington was a good and decent man until this lone thirteen-year-old crossed his path, do you?" I asked, a slithering feeling in my belly. "And then he just snapped and became a pedophile sex fiend?" I shook my head. "There have to be others."

"Not that I've found," Whit said, shaking her head. "And believe me, I've looked. I haven't even found any evidence of infidelity on his part. Nowhere except in the recollections of a junkie. That's why this one is so hard to nail down. Usually a predator shows a pattern of behavior. But if he's got a pattern, it's well hidden."

"So was Harvey Weinstein's," I said, "until someone came

along and put a crack in the wall. Then it all started flooding out. That's what we need to do here—put a crack in the wall and see what comes out."

"All right, then," Whit said, back to nodding. "How do I reach you?"

I handed her my card. "Any time, day or night. Day is appreciated, though, because I love my sleep."

She looked it over, then slipped it into the pocket of her red blazer. "I'll keep that in mind. One other question, though, unless you want to do that interview...?"

I shook my head. "Not a chance. I'll see if I can help you with this exclusive, but that's as far as I'll go."

"That ain't bad, as far as consolation prizes go," Whit said. "But...why do you think Michelle Cheong sent you my way?"

"I don't know. She's a mystery in all this," I said. "But...I'm going to figure it out, eventually. One way or another, I have this tendency to make sure that the truth comes out, and that everyone who deserves justice..." I set my jaw. "...gets justice. And it seems like, in this case...there is a lot of justice that needs to be passed around."

58.

Olivia

"This is it, right?" I asked, standing out in the gravel-laden front yard of a small house in Henderson, Nevada. The lack of a lawn felt disconcerting for someone raised in swampy greenery. There were quite a few yards like this in Vegas, I'd noted on our drive over here, a desert conservation effort of some sort of water saving program in effect. "This has to be it."

"No, it doesn't," Veronika said, eyes hidden behind her sunglasses, which were over-sized and sort of reminded me of a bug's compound eyes. Maybe a queen bee's? "Little rule of investigating—it never has to be *it*. Especially when you think you've got it, it's not it."

"There was an awful lot of 'it' in that sentence," I said, trying to sort out what she'd said. "Enough for a whole clown horror movie."

"Did you see *It*?" Veronika asked, giving me a sideways look.

"No." I shook my head. "I don't do horror films. I have enough nightmares as it is, thank you very much."

"What the hell are we wasting time talking about this for if you don't have a proper frame of reference?" She tossed her hair over her shoulder and headed up the walk like I'd somehow spurned her by not watching horror. "Seriously, though, you should get over that fear thing. There's some great horror out there that'll make you feel alive just watching it. Try *It Follows*, since we're talking about movies with 'it' in the name. Arguably not as scary as actual *It*, but really gripping. I loved…well, it." She depressed the doorbell button as we stood under the shadow of the house's eave, then leaned back at me and whispered, meta-low, "What was the name on this one, again?"

"Ricky Crumley," I said, looking at the list Detective Norton had given us. "Not Richard, not Rick, actually 'Ricky.'"

"That's a little odd, I guess." Veronika shook her head, then turned back to the door just as it opened. There was a skinny, middle-aged woman standing there, smoking a cigarette. I immediately suppressed a cough, because it seemed to flare and sneak into my nose, like an unwelcome intruder. "Hi," Veronika said brightly. "I'm Veronika Acheron and this is Olivia Brackett. We're here about Ricky. Are you his mom?"

The lady in the doorway didn't look impressed. "I'm Sylvia Blanton. Ricky rents a room from me. Kid's a bum. What'd he do?"

Veronika blinked a couple times, taking in that veritable firehose blast of info. "Not sure he's done anything, but we're looking for a suspect responsible for the incident on Fremont Street last evening?"

The lady took a long drag on her cigarette. "Yeah, he wasn't around when that was going on. I watched it on the news. He's in the room down the hall, and his door was open the whole time that was going on. It's only open when he's gone or in the kitchen. So, he must have been gone, cuz I didn't see him in the kitchen."

Veronika looked at me, I looked back. She was inscrutable, but I didn't know what to think. She turned back to Sylvia and asked, still so sweetly, "Mind if we come in and take a look at his room? If he's not here?"

"You can take a look at anything you want," she said, stepping back from the door. "I'd evict the lowlife if I had half a reason, but he keeps paying his rent, so I keep taking his money." She blew out a cloud of grey smoke and I nearly choked to death. "See if you can find you something to arrest him for; maybe that'll get rid of him for me."

"What does he do that you don't like?" I asked, stepping into the house. Every surface reeked of smoke, and again I had to suppress the instinct to gag.

"He's got judgy eyes," she decided after a few seconds of thought. "Always faking coughing around me. Like he's too good for me and my brand of cigarettes." She took another smooth puff and I held in the urge to die, even though my lungs were about to explode. "And he won't watch *Dancing with the Stars* with me, either."

"Oh," Veronika said, making room for me in the entry, then shutting the door behind us both. "Well, that certainly seems like—"

"And he's always mocking my Kardashians," she said, and boy, did she seem to be building a full head of steam now. "He shakes his head when he sees me watching my Hallmark films—"

"Hey, you know, if you could," Veronika said, "maybe write all this down for us? So we can take a full listing with us after we check out his room. We like to gather witness statements, get a real feel for our suspects, and obviously this guy—" she nodded down the long, dark hallway to our right "—has got a lot of suspicious issues going." She sounded perfectly serious, even empathetic, though I was pretty sure she was faking that. "The more you can give us to go on, the more we can fit it to a psychological profile the FBI has given us."

The lady stared at her for a second, and I was sure she was about to see through Veronika's charade. "That makes sense," she said at last, nodded, and headed into the small kitchen, which opened via passthrough into the living area just past the entry. Stuff was piled everywhere, on every surface, and I imagined she'd be looking for a pen and paper for a while.

"And he's just down the hall here?" Veronika asked, pointing into the shadowy corridor.

"First door on the left," the lady said, and I could hear her rummaging. I had a feeling her "statement" was going to very, very complete and detailed. "You don't even have to knock; just go on in. He sleeps like the dead. I go in there all the time while he's out. Never even stirs."

"Great, thanks," Veronika said, and beckoned me forward. "You go first, since you can bounce our suspect if he tries anything."

"Wait," I said, "you're using me as a human shield?"

"Duh," Veronika said, gesturing to me to go. "We're playing to strengths here, Brackett. Get with the program. I'll cover you from back here."

"Oh-kay," I said, lurching into motion. I walked down the hallway slowly, almost robotically, the world bobbing from side to side as I forced myself forward. I half expected the door to come bursting open any second, the black-clothed speedster ready to do battle with me—

But it didn't happen. I made it down the quiet, dark hallway to the door, and not a sound could be heard save for the homeowner scratching furiously with a pencil as she aired her grievances to the pad in the kitchen. I heard her tear off a sheet and keep going.

"Let's do this," Veronika said, a couple steps behind me, as her hands burned to life, casting the hall in a blue glow. "Lay on, McDuff."

I looked back at her, befuddled. "McWho?"

"Just go," she said, and gave me a gentle shove. I felt a little surge of pride that I didn't send her hand ricocheting back at her face. Yay for small victories.

Then I opened the door, pushing it wide. It squeaked a little, and I entered the darkened room.

If Sylvia's part of the house had been a disaster of mess just short of an episode of *Hoarders*, Ricky's was the opposite. Nothing sat on any surface I could see, either dresser or end table. The room looked immaculate save for the lump on the bed beneath twisted bedding.

Veronika lifted her plasma hand up over my head, radiating heat down the back of my collar. I tugged at my shirt, wishing I could get a little more airflow in there, because it was warm before she'd done that, but now that her hand was burning, it was positively stifling. The light it cast was helpful, though, because the room was shrouded in darkness held in place by blackout curtains tacked into the wall at the bottoms and clipped tightly by clothespins at the middle. Black plastic trash bags were also draped at the top of the curtains, blotting out that little extra bit of light that seeped in up there.

"Someone is very serious about their beauty sleep," Veronika breathed behind me. "And their neatly organized gothness."

There was a shadowed lump on the bed, clad in absolute black clothing. There was a black mask sitting on the bedside table, too, and it looked remarkably like what I imagined the speedster's mask looked like, had it been slowed down. A prescription bottle sat next to the mask, the only bright spot on the table its white cap.

"Hey," Veronika said, gently pushing me again. "See if he's really out."

I almost made a meeping noise, but managed to keep it in. I took a long breath instead, and then a long step that nearly made me stumble. I caught myself just in time, tripping into the room but ending up on my feet after a brief moment of stomach-dropping fear that I'd land on the gently snoring figure on the bed.

Veronika made a meta-low sound of pained disapproval, and I flashed her a thumbs-up, hoping she couldn't see the flush of my cheeks in the darkness. I didn't dwell long in that hope, though, because nothing much seemed to get by Veronika.

I took a couple more steps toward the bed, looking down at the sleeping figure on it. He was snoring very quietly, a gentle in-and-out of breath that wouldn't have been audible as anything other than breath to a normal person, but was loudly obvious to me, especially in this quiet. Another step and I was right beside him, looking down at the man in black, and here I noticed something a little funny.

He was covered in grains of dirt. Fine grains, like he'd been playing in a sandbox or something.

I pointed at one of the heavier concentrations, which stained his black shirt slightly brown, the dust having sunk in.

Veronika nodded and whispered: "From the landing. In the desert." She reached down to her belt and pulled something out of a leather case hanging on there. It glinted in the light of her plasma hand, and she stretched it out to me.

Handcuffs.

I took them, my eyes feeling like they were as big as monster truck hubcaps. I stared at them, then at Veronika, as she nodded to the figure on the bed. "Mask. Desert dirt. Black outfit." She was waving her now-empty hand at the sleeping man. "That spells 'probable cause.' Cuff him. This is your chance to go from one half of an arrest to one and a half."

Looking from the cuffs in my hand to the figure on the bed, I realized that yes, she meant for me to do this, and no, there probably wasn't a way I could get out of this, much as my stomach was writhing at the job in front of me. I gulped, swallowing down those fears, because I didn't want to look like a complete loser in front of her. Summoning my courage, I reached down and clicked the cuff around one of the man's hands. He didn't even stir.

"This is our guy," Veronika said. I looked back to find her with a wallet in her hands. It was covered in desert dirt, and she waved it at me. "No driver's license, and the credit card says 'Ricky Crumley.'" She flashed me a thumbs-up, and suddenly I didn't feel quite so stupid for having done the same to her moments before.

I looked down, trying to figure out where in the shadowy murk on the bed Ricky Crumley's other hand was. I mean, presumably this was Ricky Crumley. I stooped down some, searching for his other hand, and caught a glimpse of the prescription bottle. It had his name on it, too, which was strike two against this guy. It was possible, I theorized, a little wildly, that Ricky Crumley had put another person in his bed and left his ID strewn around just to throw us off, but…

There was the hand. He was sleeping with it clutched under his body. Acutely aware of how much damage a speedster could do at this distance, and how fast they could escape, I realized I needed to hurry this up. He was still snoring, but the landlady's encouragements that he was a sound sleeper didn't assuage my many and varied fears at this point. I imagined him exploding awake, doing ungodly amounts of damage that we'd be responsible for, and it made me gulp. Again.

I needed to finish this quickly. Using great care, I controlled myself as I reached out to him again. Rolling him onto his belly, I held my breath. He grunted, shifted position, and suddenly his free hand popped loose on the other side of his body.

Snapping the cuffs on behind his back, I breathed half a sigh of relief. I still had his feet to deal with, after all.

"I'm going to hogtie him," I said, gesturing at the sheets that were all lumped up at the foot of his bed.

Veronika was still sifting through the surface of his dresser by glowing blue plasma light. "You know how to hogtie someone with sheets?" She gave me a nod that seemed to be admiration. "Good for you, Brackett."

"We had actual hogs back at the camp where I grew up," I said, trying to take the ugh out of what she was thinking. "And cows, at times. We raised our own food."

"Should have kept that part to yourself." Veronika just shook her head. "It ruins the mystique you almost had going there."

I sighed, and pulled the wad of sandy sheets out of their pile at the foot of the bed. I twisted them up and snugged them around Ricky's ankles over and over until I could bind them into a tight knot, one I felt fairly confident he wasn't going to be able to just rip out of.

"Now this," Veronika said, and I turned to see her holding out a syringe. Another pouch was open on her belt, and I wondered what the hell was in the rest of them.

I took the syringe from her carefully, staring at the liquid moving around inside. "Suppressant?" I asked.

"No, it's liquid cocaine with a little methamphetamine mixed in," she said. "Because I want to see what happens when a hopped-up speedster launches off of you. I'm guessing it'll be hilarious."

I blinked, calculating whether she was joking or not. She put me out of my misery a few seconds later. "Yes, it's suppressant." Which was fortunate, because I really was struggling with whether I should ask for clarification on whether she was trying to make that particular crazy reaction happen. I was about 90/10 on it, figuring she probably wouldn't do that, but who knew for sure?

Taking another deep breath, I eased up to Ricky Crumley's butt, which was now facing up, thanks to my rolling maneuver. After a moment of positioning him, I slowly lowered the needle to his rear. I hesitated a little just before I reached the back of his shirt, and lifted it so I could angle the needle into his buttock.

"Go on," Veronika hissed. "Don't be a baby, shoot him in the ass! He'd do it to you, given half a chance."

I did, slipping the needle into his butt cheek and then injecting it. He only grunted in reaction, then settled back into his snoring undeterred the moment I pulled the syringe out.

The moment it was done, Veronika snapped on the lights, her phone already in hand and dialing. "Hey, Norton," she said, smirking at me. "Got a pickup for you in Henderson." She paused, and I heard Norton saying something on the other end, though I couldn't tell what it was.

Even with the lights on, Crumley still didn't stir. Looking at his face, I saw a guy in his twenties, cheek mashed into the pillow, a little drool seeping out. Man, he'd really done a number on himself. He was covered in the desert sand, and I wondered if he was just sleeping off the damage to his body, or if this was mostly the product of the prescription by his bed. Either way…he was out.

"Yeah," Veronika said, sounding triumphant. "We got him. Come on out here and pick up your prize. We'll keep an eye on him until then." She hung up the phone and looked at me. "And that's how it's done, kiddo. Let's finish up and head home."

59.

Sienna

I was just boiling when I left the Herald-Tribune offices, seething with a deep-seated fury that bubbled in my guts like I still had Gavrikov powers and had somehow turned them inward. My back-to-back meetings with Michelle Cheong and Whit Falkner had left me with shaking hands, and my short ride back downtown had my Uber driver take one look at me and decide trying to talk was a bad idea.

The Uber dropped me out front of my hotel, and I walked through the rotating glass doors in a blind fog of rage. My phone buzzed and I looked down at it before answering. "What is it, Burkitt?"

"Hey, where are you?" Burkitt's normally even tone came out in a low whisper. There was background noise on his end, like a small party was going on behind him.

"Just made it back to the hotel," I said. "Why?"

"We're here, too," Burkitt said, raising a question of who comprised "we," which he promptly answered. "The governor took over the entire 16th floor. The state police are trying to move him back to Baton Rouge under heavy escort, but he's refusing to go."

"Why?" I asked, a little savagely. "Does he have a girlfriend in town that he needs to see tonight?" *Once her middle school lets out for the day*, I barely kept in.

"Uh, he's married," Burkitt said. "Are you coming up?

Because if so, I'd keep that kind of sentiment in. This place is already at a high boil."

"Gotcha," I said. "I don't think you need me right now. Why don't you finish up whatever you're doing, and we can regroup later?"

"Is that Nealon?" Holloway's voice pierced the conversation on the other end. "Lemme talk to her." There was a rustle, and I figured he was swiping the phone, because a second later he was on, and loud. "Nealon! What are you doing? Playing grabass with the locals? Doing another barefoot 10k? Get your ass back here."

"I am 'back here,'" I said, barely keeping it in as I walked across the lobby, drawing a lot of eyes, because I wasn't quiet, and let's face it, I was famous in the worst way. If the news hadn't reported my presence in town, I might have gotten less scrutiny, but alas, it was not to be so. "But trust me, you don't want me up there. Not right now."

"Hey, listen, I know you're new to the bureau—" Holloway's voice turned serious and stern "—and you probably don't want to hear this from me, but we've got a standard of professionalism to maintain. The governor is asking about you."

"I'm so very flattered," I said, entering the elevator alcove and spearing the buttons for my floor.

"You should be. He wants to thank you for saving his life." Holloway lowered his voice. "So get up here. And afterward, we can plan our next move."

Then the son of a bitch hung up on me.

"Oh ho ho," I said, laughing maliciously and low, a cold rage now radiating out of me. Without thinking about it, I stabbed my fingers into the buttons for floor 16, aware that I was probably doing something I shouldn't be, and unable to stop it nonetheless.

Somehow, I'd entered that state where I knew, in my gut, that I was around the bend, well past emotional stability. The smart move would have been to ride the elevator up to my room, take a long, hot shower, get my blazing feels under control by shutting myself in the closet or engaging in some primal scream therapy, then maybe contemplate facing the governor of Louisiana, who I now knew in my gut was a damned pedophile and a rapist, to say nothing of being an avowed liar.

The elevator arrived with a ding, and I stepped in, hands still shaking. I felt warm, almost clammy, fists clenched as I rode the elevator up. It whirred softly, the machinery moving behind the metal walls, and I closed my eyes. It dinged, presumably at floor 16, and I resolved myself to ride on, to just stay in the box until it closed and started moving again—

"Ms. Nealon?" I opened my eyes to find an LSP trooper with his hand extended over the door mechanism to keep it from closing. "The governor is expecting you."

"How?" I asked, then sighed. "You had someone in the lobby watching." I hadn't even noticed them, I was so damned off kilter and angry.

"We had a dozen troopers in the lobby, ma'am," he said with an almost apologetic smile, as though it was somehow his fault that I was so steaming pissed my situational awareness was down to tunnel vision.

"I need to go to my room and clean up before I see the governor," I said, gesturing at my hair, which was, I realized at last, completely frizzed from the humidity and the run.

"Hey, Nealon!" Holloway rounded the corner and the end of the hall, waving his hand at me. "Come on. Everyone's waiting on you."

The trooper smiled again, apologetically, and I stepped past him. I didn't even catch his name, not that it mattered. The hallway in front of me stretched like in a movie, seeming to elongate before my very eyes. Rage bubbled in my veins as I walked toward Holloway. He turned the corner when I was about ten feet away, and when I came around it, I saw that he'd gone ahead to a door where several troopers were gathered, standing guard.

"Let's go," Holloway said, beckoning me forward. "Warrington wants to talk to you."

"This is not a good time for me to talk to him," I said, dimly aware that I shouldn't do this, not now.

"I doubt he cares what you want," Holloway said, face stiff. "He's the governor; he wants to thank you…now come on.

Get in here." And he opened the door.

The world around me seemed to pitch with every step I took, as though it were swaying, every movement my body made exaggerated. I followed Holloway into the governor's suite, feeling dimly like I was walking into my doom.

60.

The governor's suite was fairly impressive, in that there was not a single hotel bed in sight when I walked in. The room was busy, but not overcrowded, with Warrington over in the far corner sitting huddled over a table with Jenna Corcoran, standing stiffly, her bright green eyes on me.

"There she is," Warrington said, rising as I came in. He brought his hands together in an explosive clap, and Corcoran and the couple troopers in the room joined in. It set my ears to ringing, pushing my kilter even more off. I closed my right eye, cringing at the sound, which, for some reason, pained me more than gunfire usually did.

"I caught her dawdling on the elevator," Holloway said, doing some clapping of his own. He was grinning broadly, perfect teeth just asking to be knocked out. "You didn't think you could get away from this without getting an 'attagirl' for saving the governor, did you?"

I didn't say anything, because all the things I wanted to say were like using a fire truck to spray acid on a parade crowd: savage, brutal, and ill-advised if you weren't a villain.

"You saved my life back there," Warrington said, stepping forward, his suit jacket shed, his tie loosened and shirt unbuttoned a couple in the front. His broad grin was deep and sincere, and he, too, seemed to be asking to lose some teeth by virtue of showing me so many. He slipped his hand out and took hold of mine, unasked, and my eye twitched again. "If not for you and your quick shooting," Warrington said, "I'd be dead right now."

"Which would be a terrible shame," I said, so straight-laced that even I couldn't tell if it was sarcasm.

Burkitt stood a few steps behind Warrington, and his brow furrowed as he stared at me. Maybe he'd picked up on the undercurrent of emotion flooding through me. I couldn't tell for sure.

Warrington didn't, though. "Your dedication to duty and quick reflexes demand recognition, Ms. Nealon." He was still smiling. Did he really not care if he kept those teeth? One punch, I bet I could have taken ten of them, watching them launch out of his perfect smile like buckshot out of a shotgun cartridge. It would be beautiful.

And deserved. So well deserved.

I still said nothing, though, just nodded and mumbled something under my breath, hell if I knew what.

Warrington either didn't hear what I said or didn't care, because he just nodded along. "I'll admit, I was beginning to worry you were just wasting your time on this. Ms. Corcoran informed me that you had a suspicion the assassin would try again, and—sure enough. I was so sure he wouldn't—"

"It's a she," I said. This, I got out with perfect clarity.

Warrington blinked his surprise a couple times. "Is it?" He glanced at Corcoran. "Did you know this?" Then to Holloway, who nodded, and finally back to me. "A female assassin? That's a bit unusual, isn't it?"

"A little," I said, and then my simmer came to a boil, "but less so when you consider that the woman who's trying to kill you is Brianna Glover, and she's super pissed that you raped her sister Emily back when she babysat for you."

I couldn't have brought the room down into silence any faster if I'd dropped a grenade with the pin pulled. Absolute quiet filled the air for seconds that felt like they dragged on for minutes. Burkitt, just over Warrington's shoulder, looked like he'd swallowed a porcupine and was trying to shit it out. Holloway was just open-mouthed, as though waiting to be fed his own porcupine (and God, would he have deserved it). Jenna Corcoran looked like I'd slapped her in the face with said porcupine after Burkitt and Holloway had finished passing it.

The only one in the room who kept his composure was Ivan Warrington. The bastard never even blinked, and all he said, after a brief flicker of surprise that lasted maybe a millisecond, was, "Who?"

"Bree-onn-uh Gluh-vur," I said, emphasizing her name and staring Warrington right in the face. "Good God, man, don't tell me you forgot her sister after nailing her. I mean, the girl was all of thirteen when you started with her. You'd think that'd be the sort of thing that'd stick in the old memory, but maybe it got lost with your moral compass and marital fidelity."

"Jesus, Nealon," Holloway whispered. It seemed like the only thing that he could come up with.

"This is—simply outrageous," Jenna Corcoran finally sputtered, back to life. "How dare you come in here and accuse—"

"It's all right, Ms. Corcoran," Warrington said, holding up a hand to stop her. "Ms. Nealon saved my life today. I reckon she's earned the right to say a little…uh…something. No matter how false it might be."

"I really only have one question," I said, and now my words were just flowing out, like I'd had enough scotch to render Holloway unconscious, plenty enough to remove my good sense, and uncork all my inhibitions. I was burning, and I had to get it all out. "Did you have your bud Mitchell Werner claim Emily's body for burial? And if so, was it because you were being 'gentlemanly'? Or because you just wanted to be sure the body was disposed of?"

"I have absolutely no idea what you're talking about, Ms. Nealon," Warrington said, and he had an almost sad, paternal aura about him. "If Emily Glover is dead, I'm afraid this is the first I've heard of it."

"Maybe the first you've heard of it today," I said, staring him straight in the eyes. He didn't bat one, didn't flinch. Most people standing toe to toe with me, knowing what I was capable of, seeing me in a spitting rage—they would have balked.

Ivan Warrington was one cool damned customer. And I

hated him all the more for the fact he could be so cavalier about the life of a woman that he'd destroyed.

"Uh, Sienna, maybe we should get you out of here," Burkitt said, finally surging back into motion. He was at my side in a couple seconds, a hand gently upon my upper arm.

"How damned cold do you have to be to stick it in a thirteen-year-old, Warrington?" I asked, wanting to see something, anything, in his eyes to explain his behavior. Guilt. Remorse. Amusement, even.

But there was nothing there. No shame. No doubt. Not even a hint of anger at my accusation, which would have been a normal reaction from an innocent man.

Then again, Ivan Warrington was probably well-conditioned from a life in politics of hearing the most appalling sort of insults directed his way. He'd taken mine like a champ.

And I couldn't have gotten angrier if he'd admitted to slamming Emily Glover a hundred times with a grin and then spit in my face.

"You smug son of a bitch," I said, and Burkitt's grip tightened on my upper arm. I could have thrown him through a window in a hot second, of course, and been up to my elbow in Warrington's skull before he'd even cleared the shattering glass.

"Nealon..." Holloway said, and he looked grey in the face, like ash. He nodded behind me, and I looked toward the door.

The Louisiana State Police were behind me, weapons drawn and pointed at me. They'd branched out in either direction so I was at the center of a crossfire between them; X marked the spot where I stood, and the only treasure I'd dig up if I kept going would be the precious metal of lead, injected straight into my body at high velocity.

"We should go," Holloway said, and he sounded...choked.

"That'd be wise," Warrington said quietly. "Gentlemen... please lower your weapons." He nodded at the troopers.

They didn't lower their guns. I wouldn't have either, if I'd been them. I'd presented myself as a clear and present danger to the governor, who they were in charge of protecting. They'd be criminally negligent if they holstered their firearms now, and in spite of the rage that had bloomed around me, suffocating my brain of reason, I knew that, and respected them all the more for it. Their hands were steady, even though I could see the uncertainty in their eyes.

"You're just doing your jobs," I said, loud enough they could hear me. I put my hands up, nodded once, and headed for the door. They looked a little conflicted, glanced past me at Warrington for direction.

"Ms. Nealon saved my life today, gentlemen," Warrington said, slowly. "Kindly let her pass without incident."

That, they obeyed, probably glad to be rid of me.

"She just needs a little time to cool off," Burkitt said, looking apologetically back at Warrington. "It's been a stressful day, you understand."

"I understand entirely," Warrington said, still cool as one of Brianna's ice slides. "Do take a moment to breathe, Ms. Nealon. Relax, perhaps. Maybe see some of the local sights here. Take in Bourbon Street, get a more peaceful view of our fair city than you've had thus far."

"I'll get right on that," I said, passing between the troopers and out into the hall. Burkitt followed after, Holloway a step behind. One last look back showed me Jenna Corcoran, face still blazing with rage at what I'd said, and Warrington—

Well.

Warrington just stood in the middle of the room, towering like I hadn't just accused him of pedophilia and threatened his life and political career. He watched me go, not a sign of turmoil under that implacable exterior, save for maybe a glint of something—triumph? Anger? Sadness?—in his eyes as the door closed behind us.

61.

Olivia

Veronika had launched into a chorus of "We Are the Champions" by Queen after her fifth drink, which seemed a little excessive, given our environs, which were a little bar tucked away in the back of the Venetian casino complex. It was kind of quiet in here, and fortunately her voice wasn't too bad.

"This is the job," Veronika said, slurring a little, slapping her drink down on the bar and waving the bartender back over. "The pure joy of it. Capture done, we get to go back to the fun part of our lives. It's like roughnecking, but without the extended periods of working terrible hours. Most of the time." The bartender poured another round of tequila for her, and she lifted it in front of her. "Here's to our criminals always being dumb, leaving their ID behind and drugging themselves into oblivion before we show up."

"Does…does it happen that way often?" I asked.

"Oh, yeah," she said, the cup paused just before her lips. The bar had a wood-paneled look that made it seem like an old library. "I know it's popular in TV and books to have the criminal be like a super genius, but most people with super high intellects don't go into the field of crime. It's mostly idiots to middling intellects. People with a brain realize there are easier and less risky ways to earn money than doing shit that will get you thrown in prison or killed."

"Hmm," I said, taking that in. I was still on my first drink, which was a very fruity Mai Tai. It was okay, but I could still taste the alcohol, and consequently, I'd taken all of two sips thus far. I think I was already feeling it, too. "Have you ever met any of the brainy ones, then?"

"Oh, yeah." Veronika nodded. "The first mission I met Sienna on? The villain was this super genius evil doctor who wanted to wipe out all the metahumans on the planet with a tailored bioplague." She took down the whole shot in one good gulp. "But guys like him are the outliers. We deal with ten or twenty or fifty morons who accidentally trip over their own genitals during a bank heist or a convenience store robbery before we encounter one who's got a plan, some discipline, and is a real investigative challenge." She frowned, shaking her head. "I hate those assholes. They always gotta be making things tough on me. I just want things to go nice and easy, so I can head home and do some reading, check in on my mom…" She looked for a second like she was going to nod off right on the chair.

"So…" I said, still trying to solidify the thoughts I had, "this thing where we found the bad guy and he was sleeping…that happens a lot?"

Veronika's eyes were starting to get unfocused. "No. Not really. Even the dumb ones aren't usually that bad." She raised her glass, newly filled by the bartender, the tequila sloshing over the edge. "Here's to him, making our lives easier, because without him being a moron, this celebration would not be possible!" And she drank again.

I lifted my Mai Tai to my lips and took a very, very small sip. My stomach was rumbling unpleasantly for some reason. "So, it doesn't bother you that it was easy?"

Veronika stared right at me. "Girl…you gotta take a moment when it's easy to appreciate it. Because often it's not. Right?"

"I don't know," I said. "I guess. I think Reed's been sending me on the easy ones, because I haven't really had any of the ones that you could classify as super difficult."

"You think he's holding out on you," Veronika said, nodding along. "Taking it easy on you, because…what? He feels sorry for you? For what you went through in the past?"

"Maybe?" I tipped back the Mai Tai and almost choked because I took in way, way too much. "I mean, it's not because I'm a girl, right?"

She shook her head. "Hell no. You should see some of the hard cases he sends me after. But he knows I can handle it, right? He's probably easing you in." She lifted her filled shot glass again in a toast. "And bless you for it, my child, because hey, I needed an easy win right now." She tipped back the tequila again, then shook her head. "Brrrrr. Wow."

"I guess that's a good thing," I said, staring at my Mai Tai. "That Reed's looking out for me."

"Maybe, baby bird," Veronika said. "Or maybe it's time for you to ask for more. Step up. Really challenge yourself by going after a superpowered serial killer or a chaotic monster ready to destroy a city. Up your game." She lifted her empty glass to flag the bartender back down, but he was at the other end of the bar, filling someone else's cup.

Something about what she'd said bothered me. "Chaos...the speedster was talking about it on Fremont Street." I frowned, trying to put together a piece I felt like I'd missed. It felt...important.

"Yeah." Veronika nodded. "Sometimes you get those kinds, y'know? They don't want to rob the convenience store, they want to tear it up for fun. They don't care about busting into the casino vault, they just want to make a mess." She shrugged. "The psychobabble explanation is that they hate the system or hierarchy or whatever and want to rip it down."

I blinked, trying to remember something I'd heard about that on a podcast, and it just sort of fell into place. "Right," I said. "So...if the speedster was a 'lord of chaos'..." I paused, putting down my Mai Tai. "You saw his room, right? Not a thing out of place?"

"Yeah...?" Veronika just stared at me, almost inscrutable, like the wheels were turning. "Huh. Yeah. That's an interesting point. Personality-wise, you'd think someone who was into chaos would have a living space that was a little more...chaotic."

"I would have thought so," I said, then shook it off.

"But," Veronika said, sitting up a little straighter on her stool, "maybe that was the driver for their desire for chaos. They hated that everything outside their control was not quite right, so better to knock it all over and start fresh."

I shook my head. "Sometimes I feel so out of place in this job. I don't have a degree, I don't have any prior training—I was a receptionist at a dental office, for crying out loud. There's all this psychology and training and people skills and fighting and guns and whatnot…" I stared at my Mai Tai, not really sure I wanted to take another drink. "Maybe Reed's holding me out of those tougher jobs because he knows…I'm not ready."

"Well, kiddo, there's a learning curve," Veronika said. "And if you're not ready a year in…maybe it's because you haven't been doing the work. How much effort have you put in outside office hours? How many books have you read on criminology? How many times have you been to the range? How much practice are you putting in on controlling your powers?" She held up a hand, flat-palmed, the empty shot glass in the other. "Because me? I've done it all. Like learning to administer suppressant. There was a whole course on it I took from the cops in SF. On my own time, with my own money, so I could be better at my job, since that pays my bills." She leaned in. "Do you do any of that stuff when you're off the clock? Or do you kinda sit around and wonder why things aren't getting better?"

I felt a little like she'd thrown her shot glass right in my face, hitting me dead between the eyes. "Well, no. I just sort of—"

"Ugly little secret that's out there, but not spoken about much?" Veronika leaned back, the authority just oozing out of her. "Sienna Nealon is widely considered the baddest-assed meta on the planet, and she has basically your same upbringing. Confinement, abuse, no traditional high school, no college. But she's brought down more meta criminals than anyone who has degrees in all that stuff because she trains like a mofo." Veronika shuddered. "One of the first times I fought her, she beat the shit out of me, and not one of her powers really lent itself all that well to clashing with mine. She used her flame abilities to create glass boxing gloves out of dirt and proceeded to whoop on me until I embraced the better part of valor and fled." The bartender finally came along and filled her shot glass. "That wasn't anything but her frigging grit and effort coming out." She took down the shot and slammed it back down on the bar just loud enough to get the bartender to turn back around and come fill it again. "The question you've gotta ask yourself, Olivia…do you really want to do this? And are you putting in the work? And there's no shame if the answer is no on question one. The only shame is if the answer is 'yes,' and you keep the answer to question two a forever 'no.' Because that just means you're delusional, and you'll never get better." She lifted the shot glass again. "Capische?"

I felt like I'd had a long guzzle from a fire hose, or been smacked around, or some combo of both those things. "Yeah. Yeah, that makes sense. And I feel stupid that I didn't ever put that together before, that I thought I could just sit back and things would get better."

"Yeah, it's a weird and prevalent thing in our society," Veronika said, "like we believe we'll just get awesomer at what we do by osmosis. Strange disconnect. But whatever—now you know. And knowing is—"

Whatever she was going to say to finish the thought, she never got a chance to get out. A black blur shot by and hit her so hard that she was there one second, gone the next, disappearing in a shattering of glass bottles and wooden shelves, vanishing through the wall so quickly I almost thought I'd missed her getting up and leaving.

But she didn't leave, and the crashing, shattering, screaming noises proved it.

I stood, looking around for the source of the trouble. I found it a moment later, that same black shape that had been present the last few days, that I'd talked to on Fremont Street.

They were back.

We'd arrested the wrong person.

62.

Sienna

"You know, I think that went really well," I said as the three of us—me, Burkitt and Holloway—entered the elevator down the hall from Governor Warrington's suite. The Louisiana State Police troopers were still eyeing me like I was going to fly off the handle, charge down the hall, and murder Warrington, and so every one of them had their hand on their holsters.

"What the hell was that?" Burkitt blew up, throwing his arms wide as the elevator doors closed. "You just accused the governor of Louisiana of raping a teenager!"

"Yeah, I did," I said, nodding along, "and I gotta tell you—it felt real great. Righteous, really—"

"Are you out of your ever-loving mind?" Burkitt's voice strained, and he looked to Holloway for support. "Say something."

Holloway took a second and cleared his throat, looking down. "Well, if true, it's damned near impossible to prove. And way outside the FBI's purview."

Burkitt's eyes burned. "This is your comment? She burns the damned house down around us while we're trying to protect an assassination target, and this is what you have to say about it?"

Holloway's expression seemed torn, like he was really searching for something to say. Which was strange, because

Holloway certainly hadn't been reticent to say…well, anything at all during my association with him. "Yeah, it could have gone better," he finally managed.

"The man raped and abused a teenage girl that worked for him," I said, surprisingly calm. "I'm not going to just sit back and let that slide past because he's gotten himself elected to high office since."

"You don't know that he did that!" Burkitt lost it again. "There is zero evidence. Literally zero!" He threw his hands up. "Or do you have something? Because it'd be great if you did before tossing that accusation and wrecking everything for us."

In spite of the fact that I'd just blasted Ivan Warrington with moral certainty, Burkitt's statement hit me hard, right in the face. "You have an annoying point. What I have is a statement from the victim prior to death via a local newspaper reporter and an inference of the same from her sister—"

"A twice-attempted assassin," Holloway said evenly.

"—and a gut feeling that Warrington is so dirty that his laundry requires extra bleach in every load," I said.

"For the sake of—" Burkitt bowed his head, eyes closed. "Didn't you just tell me that you wanted to believe in the system? Wasn't that the crux of what we talked about at breakfast this morning?"

"Hey, you guys went to breakfast without me?" Holloway asked.

"I figured you were sleeping it off," I said, "and also, I wanted a grope-free breakfast." That shut him up. "And yeah, I said that." I looked right at Burkitt, but he still had his head bowed and had now added massaging his temples to his repertoire. "I do want to believe in the system. But I also want to believe that a man can't rape a thirteen-year-old girl and have it go completely unreported by anyone until she dies of an OD and her sister begins a quest for vengeance. Yet here we are."

"There are proper procedures for these sorts of things—" Burkitt started.

"Not on our end, there aren't," Holloway said. "I'm sorry, but unless he brought her over state lines, this is a Louisiana case through and through, and completely outside our purview unless they call us in for an assist. Likelihood they do when their chief executive is the accused: is there anything lower than zero? Because I'm thinking it'd be around there."

"Which means there's no damned justice for Emily Glover," I said. "Look, I came here to save Warrington from the assassin, and I'm all about that. But justice isn't just keeping him from being assassinated. It's getting to the core motive of why Brianna Glover is trying to kill him in the first place. I can't just ignore what caused all this. I'm not wired to let rapists skate, regardless of jurisdictional crap and no matter how high they've climbed in government."

"But the system is not wired for you to rip it apart going after a man like Warrington when there are no witnesses—I'm assuming—to prove this happened!" Burkitt blew again. "How the hell is the man supposed to prove he didn't rape a girl who's now dead?" Burkitt thrust his index finger at me. "You—prove you didn't kill twelve people yesterday and then violate Holloway after he passed out."

I exchanged a look with Holloway. "See how he's still able to stand upright? That's proof on the latter." I wiggled the fingers of my right hand at him. "Because if I violated him, I wouldn't stop until he became a full-on puppet. We're talking Kermit the Jackass FBI Agent here—"

"You keep those hands away from me," Holloway said, bumping into the elevator wall.

"Same goes, bub," I shot back.

"You can't prove a negative," Burkitt said, lapsing back into massaging his skull as the elevator dinged to herald our arrival at my floor. "That's my point. Our system is set up around proving guilt. Someone doesn't have to prove their damned innocence. That's the cornerstone of our entire judicial philosophy, the idea that a thousand guilty men should walk free before we imprison a single innocent one. Isn't that what you were talking about buying into? So that what happened to you can't happen to someone else?"

I burned a little, mostly because of how right he was. "Yes, okay, I did say that. But I didn't mean someone as loathsome and seemingly guilty as Warrington. Did you see his face when

I accused him? Nothing. No righteous indignation about how I'd wrongly burned him. Dude is guilty."

"Says you," Burkitt said, holding the elevator as it tried to close, face grey. "But if the system doesn't work to defend someone you find loathsome, like Warrington, then it won't protect you, either. Because until the Revelen thing went down, a lot of people found you loathsome, too."

"Low blow," I said, stepping out of the elevator. "How dare you speak to me with truth and honor and shit like that? I just wanted you to validate my hateful feelings toward acts of obvious evil like raping a thirteen-year-old. Curse you, sir, curse you."

"I think we can all agree that, if it's true, Warrington deserves what you just said you'd do to Holloway," Burkitt said.

"Pretty sure that falls under 'cruel and unusual,'" Holloway muttered, sauntering out of the elevator but careful to place himself as far from me as he could, back to the wall.

"But how the hell do we prove that?" Burkitt asked. "After this much time. I mean, ideally, law enforcement would have been informed immediately after the bastard had done it. They could have gotten forensics. Witness statements. Maybe even caught Warrington in the act with a sting." He shook his head. "I don't like this any more than you do. And I don't want to cover for the bastard if he did it. But it's totally separate from what we're here to do, which is stop Brianna Glover from taking the law into her own hands and avenging this perceived wrong."

"If it was your sister, I bet you'd perceive it as wrong, too," I said quietly.

"I would," Burkitt said. "You're damned right I would. And I'd want to saw the son of a bitch in half with a shotgun. But…" He shook his head. "What I want doesn't equal what's *right.*"

"Damn," I said under my breath. "Why couldn't we have had this conversation before I went in there full blow with Warrington?" The answer occurred a moment later. "Oh, right. Because I got dragged into that meeting when I really didn't want to do it yet." I looked pointedly at Holloway.

Holloway raised his hands in surrender. "Hey, I was just

doing what Warrington told me to—getting you up there so he could thank you. I didn't know you'd had a hearty drink of hate-whiskey for lunch and decided our protectee was the most convenient target at hand for all the rage you've been building up in your life."

"It's gotta go somewhere," I said. "Shit. What do we do now?"

"Uh, stay away from Warrington," Burkitt said. "Wait for things to fall out. If I had to guess? You're going to get a very, very angry call from your superiors extremely soon. Take the ass chewing with grace, and tell them you were wrong."

I made a face. "See, I'm not sure I was 'wrong,' per se. I just maybe could have handled it better."

"How could you have handled it worse?" Holloway asked. "Hypothetically?"

"You think that ass-puppet thing is 'better'?" I asked. "Also, you should see what I can do to a man's face with one good punch."

"I don't need to see any of that," Holloway said. "I swear I thought there was steam coming out of your ears at one point during your talk with him. Like, literal steam."

"Just let it cool down on its own," Burkitt said, withdrawing his arm from the elevator door. "We'll see where we stand." He shook his head. "Man. I thought maybe we were going to stumble on Warrington sticking himself into political corruption after this morning. Not this."

"Yeah," Holloway said. "Makes you wonder what else is going to come bursting out of his closet by this time tomorrow. We'll probably get the coroner's report back from that corpse we dug up and find evidence of necrophilia or something."

"And on that note," I said, shuddering, "I'm going to go take a very, very long shower to get the hate of the day and also that comment off of me."

"Do I even have to say 'Stay out of trouble'?" Burkitt called after me.

I waved him off. "I'll stay away from Warrington. He'll live to walk like a normal person for at least another day."

Holloway swore under his breath but followed along behind

me, at a considerably slower pace, owing at least to the fact he appeared to be walking with his butt cheeks clenched tightly together. "You really are hell on wheels, Nealon. I bet Warrington's never had anyone get all up in his junk like that before."

"Yes, I'm a holy terror," I said, as my phone started buzzing in my pocket. I looked at it, and the caller ID said it was from Washington, DC. "Speaking of." I showed him the screen. "I should probably take this so I can get the 'ass chewing' portion of today over with."

"You rock on with your bad self," Holloway said, reaching his room and opening it with a key. "Just remember if it gets too hot, you can always claim you're in a 'bad service area' and disconnect for a while."

"Thanks for the tip," I said as he disappeared into his room and I thumbed the screen to answer. "Hello?"

"Ms. Nealon," came a slightly familiar, male voice from the other end of the line. "My name's Russ Bilson. Maybe you've heard of me?"

All the fine work that Burkitt had done cooling me down instantly faded as my personal thermometer raced right into the red. "Yeah," I said, "it'd be hard to forget you since up until a couple months ago, it was impossible to turn on a cable news channel without hearing you trash talk my name to everyone on the planet."

63.

Olivia

"Ummm," I said, staring at the black blur. A scream echoed over the wood-paneled barroom, this slice of old-fashioned, old world English sophistication suddenly the site of a metahuman showdown between little old me and a blurring, faster-than-the-eye-could-follow speedster.

The hole in the wall where Veronika had flown was filled with motes of dust where she'd gone crashing in, disappearing under the power of the speedster's attack. It looked deep, my ability to see into it vanishing after six or seven walls. It receded into the structure of the Venetian, the wood paneling of the bar giving way to more decorative Italian themes through the hotel and finally to behind-the-scenes employee service corridors that lacked any of the resort's charm.

I wheeled on the speedster, who regarded me with… indifference? Anger? It was impossible to say under that vibrating black mask. It could have been sneering contempt or unbridled lust for all I knew. I couldn't even see the eyes, the blurring effect making it look as though the speedster didn't even have them.

"What do you want?" I asked, glancing back at the hole in the wall, wondering if Veronika was going to come crawling back through at some point. The last time this had happened, she'd been wrecked. That suggested she wasn't going to come, cavalry-like, to my rescue. At least not any time soon.

"Chaos," the speedster said.

I looked back at the hole. "Well, you're doing fine, then."

"*More* chaos," the speedster said, that voice sounding like they'd swallowed a gallon of broken glass before speaking, like a swarm of bees was at war in their throat.

"I...can't let you do that," I said, trying to decide what my next move was.

The speedster took a flashing step toward me, cutting the distance between us in half. "You...what?"

"I can't let you do that," I said, trying to make my voice sound strong, like Veronika would. I stood my ground, not daring to look weak, forcing myself to look the speedster in the—well, where their eyes should have been.

"How are you going to stop me...mouse?" The speedster's voice carried the unmistakable hint of a grin, though I couldn't see it through the black mask.

I just stared. That was not a bad point. I tried to come up with a response, and what came out was, "Like I did on Fremont Street. That's how."

The speedster regarded me, head cocked, like I was some curiosity. Almost faster than I could see, they picked up a glass from the bar and threw it at me, blurry.

The glass flashed as it almost cracked into my skull. I flinched away right as it entered my personal bubble and it rocketed away, shattering against the nearby wall. Gin dripped down the wood paneling as I pried my eyes open to look back at the speedster.

"Hm," the speedster said. "You still can't stop me. Chaos comes whether you want it or not." Some animating urge broke through the bizarre effect around their voice. "It's the natural state of the world. We fight it, try to build walls to keep it out, try to set our world neatly in order, to the detriment of all. Everything we do is to try and keep the world out of its natural state. We fight nature, but the moment you realize you're on the wrong side of that fight...suddenly, you're free." The speedster spread their arms, as though trying to encompass everything around them. "There is no holding back the chaos. Why try? Join it. Embrace chaos."

"I'm not much of a hugger, so, I think not," I said. I took a deep breath. "All right. I have to stop you now."

The speedster's head blurred and shook. "You can't. Even if you want to. Chaos is coming. And you can't hold back its tide, mouse."

With that, the speedster lurched into motion, and the bar exploded as they struck it with incredible speed that translated into force. It almost seemed to shatter, shards of wood flying in all direction. I flinched away, but the pieces reached my personal bubble and bounced in the opposite directions.

A scream cut off behind me, and I looked over my shoulder. One of the bar's other patrons had fallen off her chair and her eyes were wide, crimson sliding down her cheek from a dozen wounds on her face.

It took me a second, and then I realized—

The speedster had used my bubble to accelerate the chaos he'd created, sending the splinters of the bar away from me at high speed…

Right into that lady, who now probably had splinters buried in the bones of her face.

"What are you doing?" My question came out as a cry. The lady was spasming, and I wondered how deep those splinters had gone. Had one lodged in her brain?

"Making chaos happen," the speedster said, over my shoulder, as I slid down to the wounded woman's side.

"She's innocent!" I stared down at her. Her eyes were already unfocused, and her movement was stilling.

"Chaos cannot be controlled," the speedster said. "It falls on the innocent and the guilty."

"Easy thing to say when you're killing people and framing innocent men for your deeds," I said, my knees aching from my slide.

"I'll kill more—if you get in my way," the speedster said. "You won't stop the chaos."

And with that the speedster zipped away. I stared down at the bleeding woman as she rasped, her breaths shallowing. I was helpless, no action I could take coming to mind. The speedster crashed in the distance, more screams echoed through the casino resort, but there was little I could do but sit there and hold this wounded woman as she bled.

Nothing I could do, really, without making things worse, so I just sat there and hoped someone would come and save us all.

64.

Sienna

"Hey, it was nothing personal," Russ Bilson said, and I could almost see his smarmy, shit-talking smile even though we were only on the phone. I unlocked my hotel room and slipped inside, the air conditioner humming to keep the New Orleans heat at bay.

"Let me break some news for you, Mr. News Commentator Guy: it feels really, intensely personal when someone you don't even know shits all over your character on television for the whole world to see." The running AC did not, unfortunately, do anything for the heat that seemed to be building under my skin. "And just as an aside—what is this, asshole day? I feel like the scum of the universe is beating a path to my door right now."

"Hah!" Bilson sounded like he laughed for real, and I rolled my eyes. Of course the TV crap-talker would take me calling him scum as some sort of perverse compliment. "I heard you stumbled into a political consultancy down in Louisiana this morning and didn't know quite what to make of it."

"Oh?" My blood was pumping, hot. What kind of asshat would have told this douchebag what I was up to? "Is that so? Who said?"

"Director Chalke," Bilson said. Of course. "She's monitoring your investigation very, very closely, and mentioned you hit on something involving a Louisiana group headed by Rouge

Future, LLC? Said you were having a little trouble figuring out what was going on with it?"

My eyes flitted around my hotel room as I tried to calculate the odds he was lying to get some sort of scoop. "I can neither confirm nor deny—"

"You don't have to say anything," Bilson said, chuckling on the other end. I would have punched his voice, if I could somehow manage to solidify the sound waves. Ripping out the voice box probably would have been more my style, though. "Like I said, I'm already clear on it. I just figured I'd offer some insight, because this Rouge Future thing? It's right up my alley."

"It did feel like the guy who ran it, Mitchell Werner, was a total and complete d-bag," I said, "so maybe you're right."

He ignored my last snipe. "From what I hear, Rouge Future is housed in the same office as several other LLCs and PACs controlled by the same person?"

"Yeah, they all share office space," I said. "Which is confusing, because—"

"It's only confusing because it's meant to be," Bilson said, apparently deciding the conversing part of our conversation was annoying, and that engaging in a monologue would be better. "This Mitchell Werner? He's a political consultant, and all those groups are just tools in his toolbox to do different things in the political sphere. The LLC is so he can accept donations and transfer payments from donors without having to report them, the way a PAC—that's political action committee—would have to. Because of their tax-exempt status, PACs have to account for their spending, including any salaries they pay. I'm guessing any of the PACs he runs pay him a modest salary. Likely as not, he gets most of his money from management fees the PACs pay to his LLC—"

"Oh, for crying out loud," I said, shaking my head. "It's a shell game."

"Well, of course," Bilson said, and I could still hear the smile in his voice. "Donations go into the various organizations from big and small money donors, and content comes out—content that influences politics in the direction Werner chooses."

"How perfectly scuzzy," I said, pretty sure my voice dropped the temperature in my room by several degrees. I didn't feel it myself, but hopefully Bilson did, over the line.

"Admittedly it's not the cleanest process, but you know what the alternative is?" Bilson's voice-grin had faded as he moved into a more serious mode of explanation. "Accepting restrictions on free speech. Quashing people's ability to speak."

I frowned. "It seems to me that the major people speaking through this swampy mess are people who could afford to get their own damned megaphone if they wanted."

"Not all of them, though," Bilson said. "And maybe not as many as you think. Given some of the issues it looks like Werner agitates for—protecting coastal swamps from drilling, more money into education—he probably has a decent number of small money donors, if he's doing any kind of grass roots—that's lower-level—organizing. This is all local politics, so by extension, it's going to be smaller dollars than Washington deals with."

I blinked. "Wait. This happens in Washington? This weird network of groups thing? Where money gets passed back and forth between companies?"

"Oh, absolutely," Bilson said. "Let me give you an example of how it works. Say Bilson wants to do an ad campaign on protecting wetlands, and he wants to engage on all fronts. One of his businesses looks like it focuses entirely on the internet, another on messaging. What he'd do is have his lead organization issue a press release and use his contacts to make sure it was covered to the best of his ability to spread it far and wide. The web side would create sites and social media profiles, maybe even try and use some sock puppet accounts they have—"

"Do I even want to know what a 'sock puppet' is?"

"It's just a fake social media account," Bilson said. "Anyway, they'd rally these accounts together and follow the new social media presence of this group. Let's just call it 'Save the Wetlands.' Which is too vague to be an actual campaign, but you get the idea. It sounds good, has a feel-good sort of moral air about it—what kind of monster would want to destroy the wetlands, after all?"

"If some of my enemies were clustered together in one, I'd bomb the hell out of it."

Bilson chuckled. "You're special, then, Ms. Nealon, because most people would be horrified to be thought of as being against saving the wetlands. See, that's the beauty of an operation like the one I'm talking about—even calling it what I am defines the moral terms, immediately casting the other side as evil, because what sort of monster would want to do such a horrible, horrible thing?"

I rolled my eyes again. "Yes, congrats to you, Orwell Jr, and all your minions, for defining political reality in such stark terms. Thanks for making any discussion an immediate 'us versus them' proposition. I'm sure that won't have a deleterious effect on our societal interactions at all."

"Anyhow," Bilson said, "money is moved back and forth between the organizations to produce things like advertising campaigns—print, radio, TV, online—and getting their social media presence engaged—"

"I thought you said all they did on social media was get their suck Muppets moving?"

"Sock puppets," Bilson said. "But the sock puppets are just a placeholder to get people to see social proof that others care about the movement so that they feel more comfortable jumping in to the cause. It just warms the water up for others, see?"

"Like peeing in a pool, sure."

"Hah," Bilson said, not actually laughing. "It's just psychology. It also gives them outsized reach if a legislator looks at their movement's profile page and sees six thousand followers versus five people."

"That's really cynical and gross."

"It's politics," Bilson said. "And it's called 'Astroturfing'. Kind of a play on 'grass roots' movements—"

"Hilarious. Or at least it's funny, but not in the humorous way."

"Anyway," Bilson said, "these are the methods of the modern political operator. They use every means at their disposal—advertising, research papers, internet operations, traditional media sources—to influence public opinion to get a movement going. It looks to me like this Mitchell Werner has five, six pet causes he's working—again, mostly state issues—and this is how he's set up his structure to maximize his effectiveness and, well," Bilson chuckled, "what he gets paid, too."

"Wow," I said. "Thanks for the crash course in political skullduggery. That was eye-opening. I really feel like I need a shower after all that."

"Why?" Bilson asked. "It's not at all illegal, and it's totally normal."

"No wonder people hate Washington," I said, "because this crap is cynical, gross, and scuzzy AF. You're talking about people using the internet to inflate the perceived interest in their cause—"

"That does happen," Bilson said, "but it's also a valuable way to get messaging out, to train media operatives like myself in the basic dictums of the issue—called talking points—so we can go on TV and discuss them without being uninformed."

"You train those numbskulls that go on cable news to parrot the same bullshit?" I asked. "This is why I turn on a news panel for five minutes and get these cookie cutter morons that say the same thing over and over again like a robot with its wires crossed?"

"Like I said, talking points. And yes, it's important for messaging that operators don't stray too far from the topic at hand. Or stay 'on message,' rather."

I shook my head, flopping back on the bed with a new, angrier appreciation for the way things were going in politics. "Let me ask you something that I think I already know the answer to—if you had someone, say a famous someone, political candidate, and they got on the wrong side of someone like this Mitchell Werner...how would one of these political networks go after them?"

"With everything they have," Bilson said. "It happens all the time. Private detectives are hired to do background—called 'oppo,' for oppositional—research. The people we have that are better on the web are deployed to trawl their social media and internet footprint for anything they've ever said. We send operatives to their political rallies and film, looking for controversial statements, comb through their past seeking anything we can use against them, let loose an army of commentators to rip them apart in every media appearance—"

"That's kind of what I figured," I said, nodding along. It sounded familiar because it was—everything he was describing had been done to me.

By him.

Bilson seemed to get it a couple seconds later. "Like I said, it's not personal when something like this happens to you. Sometimes it's not even coordinated, it's just the result of the person being in the zeitgeist and on the side of an unfavorable issue."

"Yes, I'm sure that the digital mobs that roam the dystopian internet wastelands are entirely undirected by anyone," I said, feeling the soft bed beneath me. "Thanks for the primer on modern political dickery. I guess the only other question I have is about the way these guys make money. You say it's all legal?"

"Sure," Bilson said. "Unless the politician is directly coordinating with the PAC or there's some sort of favor being exchanged with an actual politician that you can prove, it's all legal. And even those things do happen; it's all in what you can prove."

"So much scuzzy," I said. "I'm going to go get some bleach and take that shower now. Try not to smear anyone else today, hmm?"

"Well," Bilson said, chuckling again. So many punchable faces today. "I'll try. But keep in mind—it's the job."

"Your job is gross," I said, and hung up on him without any further pretense toward politeness. Then I shuddered and went to take that shower, wondering if I could get the water temperature hot enough to scourge off a full layer of skin, because I felt like after today, I desperately needed it.

65.

My phone was buzzing continuously by the time I got out of the shower. I'd partaken of the heat, the steam running over my skin, soaking it in until the mirror was completely fogged over. For all I knew, that might happen in New Orleans just by leaving the window open, but I'd probably taken it up a notch by putting the water heat at a setting that would have made Aleksandr Gavrikov take a step back and go, "Wow, that's hot."

Wrapped in a towel, soaked hair turned black by the wetness and slung over my shoulder, I regarded my buzzing phone on the bed with a wary eye. I'd finally gotten my calm back, and the name on the Caller ID said, "Heather Chalke."

This was probably not going to help my calm. But it was the job, so I swallowed my reservations about picking up and just did it. "Hello?"

"What the hell were you thinking?" Chalke set the tone for the entire conversation with that opening salvo, but I cringed and resolved not to answer in kind. Yet.

"I was thinking, 'Man I could use another round of good jambalaya,'" I said. "Is that so wrong?"

"You know damned well what I'm talking about," Chalke said, the heat fading and her tone turning lashingly cold. "Warrington."

"Oh, him? Yeah, about him I was thinking, 'What a pervy creep and rapist, forcing himself on a thirteen-year-old.' Unfortunately, I could not keep these thoughts to myself, so..." I shrugged, which she couldn't see. Hopefully.

"You've really screwed the pooch," she said, moving more into the domain of cold fury. Which was fine; I was more comfortable there, anyway. "I just got off the phone with Warrington's chief of staff."

"Corcoran?" I asked. "Is it my imagination or is there something really wrong with her? She's stiff as I imagine Warrington would be after no thirteen-year-olds for a while."

"You just can't let off, can you?" Chalke asked.

"I had a bad feeling about this guy from the beginning," I said. "So maybe I jumped on the 'rapey pedophile' explanation for that gut feeling too easily, let myself get carried away—"

"The Louisiana State Police had to draw guns on you. Yes, I'd say you got carried away."

"In my defense, it's not easy to look a guy you believe guilty of that in the eye and do nothing about it, like murder them in the face." I paused, thought about it a second. "At least it's not easy for me. Working in Washington, maybe you have a different take on it. Maybe you have to be able to do that or you'd be murdering people in the face all the time—"

"You cannot do these things," Chalke said, level and still angry at this point. "You cannot accuse a major political figure like Warrington of this sort of atrocity—"

"But...we're good to go on the 'little people,' right? Like I can pick any unconnected rando off the street and make those accusations against them and it's fine, right?"

Chalke paused. "Of course. What the hell does that have to do with anything?"

"That's so wrong," I said. "You can accuse anybody of anything without evidence as long as they're not somebody 'important.'"

"What the hell do you want?" Chalke asked. "An outlet for your frustrations? What are we talking about here?"

"Two systems of justice," I said. "One where a guy like Warrington, who's powerful and well-connected, can't be accused of something, but anyone else who's not those things can. I messed up with Warrington, I'll admit. Burkitt, our local agent, pointed it out—no matter how much my gut told me Warrington was dirty, he deserves due process. So...my bad.

But the fact that he gets that consideration, but I could turn loose that kind of life-destroying accusation on someone else who doesn't have his sway…yikes."

"You want to fight the system, do it on your own time," Chalke said. "Your job here is just that—a job. You were supposed to protect the governor of Louisiana from someone who's trying to kill him. You failed."

"Uh, no I didn't. He's still alive." I blinked. "Or was, last I checked. Did he—"

"Oh, no, he's still alive," Chalke said, and her voice rose to a haughty height. "But it's not your job anymore." She shuffled something paper in the background, and it sounded like a crackle of static in the phone. "You're removed from the case as of right now. Report back to New York. Immediately."

"Wait, hold on," I said. "The assassin is still out there, and I know who it is. I talked with her—"

"Yeah, I read the report you gave to Shaw and the troopers," Chalke said. "You should have shot her."

"She was unarmed," I said. "And retreating."

"Metas are never unarmed," Chalke said. "You know that better than anyone. You could have ended this." Her voice took on a higher quality, and it was the angriest I'd ever heard her. "You failed. Get home. Now."

There was a click, and my chance to argue my case was over.

I took a deep breath, and looked out the window over the city of New Orleans, waiting below. The Mississippi glinted under a hazy sky, dusty water spots stained the window, clouding my view like dirt smeared over the town. The word "failed" kept echoing in my head, over and over as I sat down on the bed, clutching my towel to me, thinking…

Yeah. I really had failed. Big time.

66.

Olivia

"It's a disaster," Reed said, voice crackling in my ear via cell phone. I tried to tune out the ambulance sirens wailing in the near distance. I was standing on the Strip, just inside the police perimeter tape, as the Vegas authorities sorted out the mess.

And boy, was there a mess.

"Yes," I said, because what else was there to be said? If I'd been face to face with him, no way in hell could I have been looking him in the eye. "Yes, it is."

"Just so I have this straight—you arrested the wrong guy?" Reed asked. As though he didn't know. "Then the real villain decked Veronika, used your power against a civilian, putting her in the hospital, then proceeded to wreck the Venetian?"

"The EMTs said they think she'll recover." Maybe.

"Good. How much property damage at the Venetian?" Reed asked. The tension was thick in his voice, strain evident.

"Umm, I don't know." I looked at the facade. It seemed…well, mostly fine. The speedster had run through and done a little more chaos creation on their way out. Knocked a few people over, sending them to the hospital. "It's mostly on the inside."

"Chaos indeed," Reed said, letting a long sigh. "All right, well, why don't you get back to Minneapolis ASAP. There's a flight tomorrow morning you can catch. Until then, stay out of this speedster's way. Let's not make this worse."

"I will," I said.

"Good," Reed said, and he couldn't even hide his disappointment. "I'm sending Jamal and Augustus to take over. Their powers are a little more suited to dealing with a speedster than yours. When is Veronika getting out of the hospital?"

"I don't know," I said. "She was unconscious when they pulled her out, so tomorrow, I guess?"

"Okay," he said. "I'll hold off on booking her travel until we know for sure."

"Why not bring me back tonight?" I asked.

"The morning flight is a lot cheaper," Reed said, and again, the strain evidenced itself in his tone. Why was he worrying about money now? "Keep your head down, and I'll see you tomorrow."

"Thanks, I w—" But the soft click told me he was already gone. I let the phone slip down, and looked back at the Venetian. It sat there, symbol of yet another of my failures, the sirens echoing like laughter in my ears.

67.

Sienna

Ever wallow in your screw-ups like a pig in the mud?

I put on a robe, locked myself in my hotel room and ignored all the knocking from Holloway, the phone calls from Burkitt, and just slipped off into oblivion. I briefly considered going down to the hotel bar and getting wasted, but eventually wrote it off as more trouble than it was worth, since I would have to put on clothes.

To hell with clothes. To hell with people.

To hell with rules and order and society and all this civilization bullshit.

What was the point of a justice system if corrupt, rapey piles like Warrington could just skate right through? That idea warred in my mind with another, the one Burkitt had fleshed out—

How could I be sure that Warrington actually did what Emily Glover—a troubled person, if ever there was one—accused him of doing?

My gut feeling was that Warrington was dirty. But I was hardly infallible in my gut feelings. I'd been totally blindsided by people on a few occasions, betrayed badly enough to nearly die from it: James Fries, Erich Winter, my damned "dog" Owen Traverton, Rose Steward (that bitch), just to name a few. Hell, even Scott, Reed, and Augustus had betrayed me a while back, though it hadn't really been their fault.

As much as the public at large might call me Slay Queen, and as much as I might be enjoying a popularity renaissance coming off my actions in Revelen that magnified my virtues and minimized my vices, it wasn't as though I was infallible. I may have been a metahuman, but "human" was a big part of that, flaws and all. I was no goddess, no all-knowing oracle, no flawless superheroine Slay Queen like some seemed to think I was. Perfect judgment was not among my powers, and I'd messed up enough in my life to realize I misjudged people all the time.

Ivan Warrington could easily be one of them. Two things could be true: Ivan Warrington was dirty and corrupt in concert with Mitchell Werner and whatever corruption he had going on, and he could be innocent of any wrongdoing with Emily Glover.

Or he could be innocent of all of it. Or guilty of all of it.

Without the powers of Gerry Harmon to let me read his mind, or absent a chance to grab his hand and take a deep dive into his memories…who the hell was I to judge?

A screwup. I was an emotionally unstable screwup, which was why I'd been pushed out of the FBI before. I wondered how much longer Chalke would try and make this work when plainly this was not something I was well-disposed to doing.

Night fell outside as I sat in my quiet hotel room, the sounds of a second line band wafting up through the glass window. I thought about my friends, who I'd avoided contacting these last few months, at least via conventional means. I wanted Chalke to think I was out of contact with them, that they were on their own, no connection to me.

When she'd come to me in that room in Washington, I recognized the look in her eyes. Heather Chalke was an operator, a climber, the type of person who would use any leverage she could to get what she wanted. Reading her bio, I knew she'd been doing her thing around the halls of power for quite some time. She knew how the game was played, and the moment she'd stepped into that room with me, I knew she was seeking weaknesses.

I was determined not to give her any that she could exploit in ways I wouldn't like.

So I hadn't called anybody I knew in the months since I'd come back from Revelen.

But that didn't mean I hadn't talked to them.

I drifted off after nine, the lights still on, the smooth sounds of that distant band intruding into my dream as I slipped into a familiar space.

My back pressed against a soft leather couch. A vanilla candle burned in the background, scenting the air. I felt simultaneously taut yet relaxed, like my skin was stretched too tight over my bones. I looked around, my hair rustling against the couch until I heard a familiar voice.

"Hey."

"Hey yourself," I said, sitting up to look at my guest.

Reed was in the chair next to my couch, his long hair loose around his shoulders, bags under his eyes. "Didn't know we were having a talk tonight or I'd have dressed up." He was in old pajamas, ragged around the sleeves.

"Sorry to just drop in," I said. "I needed to talk to someone, and Harry and I got together last night, so…" I shrugged. "Here I am, a couple days early for our check-in. How's life in the Minne-apple?"

"Probably not as exciting as life in the big one," Reed said. His eyelids were low, like he was going to fall asleep again in my dream, if such a thing was possible. He yawned.

"You okay? You're looking a little rougher than usual."

"Just business stuff," he said, shaking his head. "Talked to Ariadne recently. She said to give you her best if I spoke to you, so…" He waved a hand in my general direction. "There you have it. Her best, given."

"Say hey for me if you see her again," I said, and now I knew what was eating him. "How are the finance talks going?"

"Let me worry about it," he said, and I could tell by his demeanor that it wasn't good news.

"I'm sorry I left you holding the agency bag, Reed," I said, leaning against the arm of the couch. "And I'm sorry I've been such a drain the last couple years—"

"It's fine, Sienna. We'll figure it out." He forced a smile. "We always do. How are you doing?"

"Well, I don't know if you've heard in the mighty north," I

said, looking at my feet, which were bare. Actually, I was just wearing my hotel bathrobe, because I hadn't given much thought to clothing before I'd popped in here. "But I got my first real FBI assignment yesterday."

"Oh? I hadn't heard."

"I'm in the Big Easy, not the Big Apple, at the moment."

"So many sleazy jokes I'm holding back right now, little sis."

"Don't hold them back on my account; I'm not exactly innocent, even outside the legal definition." I sighed. "I've already gotten kicked off the case."

Reed blinked a few times. "That's fast work, even for you. Who'd you piss off this time?"

"I kinda accused the Governor of Louisiana of child rape," I said.

Reed's eyebrows shot skyward. "Oh. Yeah. That'd do it." He adjusted in his seat, suddenly a lot more awake. "Do you think he really…?"

"I don't know," I said, letting out a sigh. "In my gut, yeah, but my gut's not exactly reliable. And it's certainly not a viable method of conviction for any court of law I've ever been involved with."

He snorted. "I dunno; I think that Magistrate in the Meta court who tried you used a similar method of determining guilt."

"Yeah, which kind of makes me the villain in this, doesn't it?" I leaned my head against the soft back of the couch. "I mean, how pissed was I when they pulled that crap on me? Convicting me of things I didn't even do in the course of the sham-wowiest of sham trials." I shook my head. "But put me in a position where I sniff out a hint of heinous guilt on a guy, and I do the exact same damned thing I railed against."

"Well, you are human, and human beings are judgy creatures," Reed said. "I mean, really, that's all we do, take in oxygen and spew out judgment. And breed."

"These are some of my favorite things," I said. "Not actually breeding. Practicing it, though—"

"You're crossing a line here," Reed said, eyes narrowing again. "Walk it back. Don't scar me."

I smiled. "Point is, half of the reason I'm doing this FBI

thing is to try and get it right, this time. To buy into this idea you plugged into my head that the law is supposed to be a shield for people. To protect us from those who do wrong, regardless of whether they're criminal or in the seat of power. But…I think I suck at it, Reed."

"Well, yeah," he said, "because you're used to arrogating the power of judge, jury and even executioner unto yourself. To do anything else is to surrender some control." Here he smiled again, though it was more ghostly. "And I think we all know how much Sienna Nealon likes to surrender control."

"Hey, I have no problem surrendering control—over something I don't give a damn about." I slumped against the arm of the couch, felt it pushing against my ribs. "Like the rules of tennis, or whether Cher hires a necromancer to get her through her fifteenth retirement tour. I have no problem having zero control over these things." I squeezed my hand together. "But when it comes to the idea of a really bad person getting away with something…or terrible things happening to good people…" I shook my head. "I have a hard time letting it lie."

"That's the problem, isn't it?" Reed wasn't smiling now. "That's a hero complex, in a nutshell. And the real issue there is that you could be doing something in that vein all the time. Hell, we did, after the war, remember? You and I ran ourselves ragged trying to right every meta wrong we could. Saving people is a full-time job, a life commitment if you wanted it to be. I know you're doing some small-scale stuff in that regard in New York, and—hey, I applaud—"

"Don't say that unless you're actually clapping for me."

He brought his hands together and it was loud. "I applaud your efforts at trying to bring some order to an otherwise chaotic world; to stop some wrongdoers from doing wrong, to keep innocent people from getting hurt. But you're always fighting a battle against people with free will doing potentially terrible things to others. That's a tough beat, because if you do everything within your sizable power to prevent crime and harm, you're kind of a fascist. And if you let everything skate, you're a monster." He shrugged. "And if you can figure out the line between those two, you're a hell of a lot wiser than I am, because I'll be the first to admit I struggle with everything related to this job. Like where to send our people. 'If no one has died yet, is this a serious thing, worthy of our time? If this person looks like they're about to hit a spiral into violence, should I send my people in to stop them before they *really* cross the line?'" He shrugged even deeper. "Hell if I know."

"There's a lady trying to kill this governor," I said. "That's how I got the case. She's trying to assassinate him. Sniper rifle with ice bullets, can you believe it?"

"That's cold," Reed deadpanned, only a little hint of a smile to betray his snideness.

"Well, revenge is a dish best served at that temperature," I said, "to quote—hell if I even know what that's from."

"*Star Trek*, I think?"

I made a scoffing noise low in my throat. "Geek. Then it's your fault I even know it."

His smile grew a bit wider. "I only led you to the font of wisdom. You drank from it, and 'Sokath, his eyes uncovered.'"

"I hate you so much for bringing me down to this level," I said, but then we both laughed. "I'm heading back to New York in the morning."

That raised his eyebrows again. "You're just going to walk away from this case?"

"I guess," I said. "I was ordered to, after all."

He snorted. "And you're such a stickler for following orders, of course, you have no choice but to do so." He adjusted in his seat. "Actually, this comes at an interesting point, because one of my people is going through something similar. Olivia Brackett? You remember her?"

"Blond, kinda tall, quiet, stuff bounces off her?"

"She's got a kinetic bubble around her," he said. "I sent her and Veronika to Vegas to deal with a speedster. Well, Veronika's in the hospital for the second time now, their clashes have trashed a couple places around town, and I pulled 'em back because Olivia has all the confidence of a sweating, seventh-grade Poindexter."

"Ouch for her."

"Yeah, she's got a bad history," Reed said. "I don't think she's going to make it doing this unless something changes in her. She feels…lost, I guess. Scared of her own shadow. But it strikes me that if you're thinking about going rogue and finishing the job in front of you…" He raised his hands and arms in the perfect picture of the shrug emoji. "Maybe you could be a goodish-bad influence on someone who clearly needs that kind of influence from a strong, female, not-her-boss role model?"

"You really just want to go back to dreamless sleep, don't you?"

"Yeah, these evening confabs really take it out of me. Hanging out with you in dreamwalk is cool, but it's like not sleeping at all."

I chuckled. "Fine. I'll talk to your problem child and see if I can steer her right." I paused. "If I can figure out what's right."

"I know you're distrusting of your instincts," Reed said, now pensive, "but look, if you're not colossally arrogant, it's easy to spin yourself around wondering if you're right or wrong on these things. We've both been betrayed by people, so I get it. But when it comes to getting the bad guy, Sienna…" He smiled. "You're the best there is. Go after whoever you think is bad. The right way, of course."

"What if I can't do it the right way, Reed?" I asked, and my genuine nerves were showing now. "I've never really played it that way before, not in the big leagues. Sure, I tried for a while after the war, but I never really had to go all out with anyone, push myself to the limits, while hewing to these rules." I smacked my lips together. "What if I'm not good enough to do it legit?"

He smiled. "You're the Slay Queen. You'll figure it out." And with that, he was gone, leaving me in the darkness of my dreamwalk alone, wondering why the hell he believed so much in me to do the right thing when I couldn't figure out how to do so for myself.

68.

Olivia

I fell asleep hard, after fighting it off, lying on the bed for a while, unsure of what to do, what to say, who to say it to…

Unsure of who the hell I was, honestly. And desperately unsure of what I wanted to do and to be.

When I drifted into the darkness of sleep, finding myself not in darkness was a little bit of a surprise.

Finding Sienna Nealon staring at me?

Not even doubly surprising, that. Infinitely surprising, more like.

"You're Olivia, right?" she asked, dark hair wet like she'd just gotten in out of a good rain. She was pale as ever, pale as death, maybe, but her blue-green eyes reminded me of the Gulf of Mexico off the Florida panhandle on a crystal-clear day.

She had a few freckles, faded but present, and though she'd lost some weight in the last couple years, her proportions would never allow her to squeeze into anything below a size 10. Which was how she seemed to be in every regard—a mold breaker.

"Um," I said, tending toward sputtering. "Um. Hi?"

"You seem unsure whether you're actually saying 'hi,'" she said. "Might want to get definitive on that. It's a little thing. Maybe go ahead and commit and see where it leads you?"

"Hi," I said. "Uhm…what are you doing here?" I looked

around. The place we were was not my terrible motel room on the outskirts of Vegas. It was a calm place, like— "Hey, this kinda looks like Dr. Zollers' office."

Her eyes widened just a hint. "Good catch. Does his current office still have this layout?"

"Sorta," I said, looking around for the fish tank. It wasn't there. "Missing a few things, but it's close."

"I modeled my dreamwalk space after the place where I first met him," she said, looking around, taking it in. "Because I talk to him here, and because early on in my journey, it was the place I felt most comfortable." Her piercing eyes narrowed in on me again. "You see Zollers? As a patient, I mean?"

"When he's available and I am," I said, my heart beating a little faster. "Reed recommended him. Sometimes he travels to do…stuff. You know how that goes, I guess." My voice trailed off the longer I talked, the more I realized I was rambling.

"He's good," she said. "Really good. What do you talk to him about?"

"Stuff…?" I realized that became a question a little late, heat flaring my face because, let's face it, I'd already opened up to Veronika on this trip under pressure, and I really didn't want to do that again, especially not to someone who I respected. Admired.

Okay, kinda idolized at this point.

"Really?" She didn't miss a beat. "Because I talk to him about being raised in captivity, the struggles to control my violent reactions to external stimuli, and trying to maintain normal relationships in spite of my myriad issues." She nodded slowly, eyes up like she was running through them all. "And there are so many."

"Oh. Wow." I blinked a couple times. "Every time I see you, like on TV—hell, even in Scotland—you always seem so put together. Fighting, sure. Under attack, yeah, maybe. But put together."

She laughed out loud. "That's hilarious. I had no idea it looked that way from the outside, because most of the time I'm just running around like a crazy person either attacking or trying to survive the person attacking me. I guess I never gave much thought to how I look while I'm doing it."

"Wow," I said, sitting down on the edge of the chair Dr. Zollers usually used for our sessions. It even looked like his chair, and I almost felt like I was invading it, even in his absence. But I wanted to talk to her, so I ignored that silly bit of discomfort. "All I can think about is how I look to people. How I'm misbehaving. What kind of trouble I'm going to get into for doing bad." I looked around, the slightly shadowed edges of the room darker than the real thing. "I feel like there's people watching me all the time, judging me. For every stupid thing I do. And I do a lot of stupid things."

"Lots of people do stupid things," she said, shrugging.

"It doesn't feel that way," I said.

"Go on YouTube. It's the 2010s," she said. "You'll find no shortage of videos of people taking the 'Being Idiots and Broadcasting It on the Internet Challenge' every day. Anything you do, compared to those morons, well, it's gotta be absolutely brilliant."

I bowed my head. "I don't know about that. I got people hurt today."

"Oh? How?"

"A speedster used my power against bystanders," I said. It was hard to even say it, and once it was out, I didn't dare look up at her, because I knew the condemnation had to be coming. Sienna Nealon didn't truck with people hurting the innocent.

"Once upon a time," she said, low, a little anger creeping into her voice, "a real sonofabitch blew up a town with thousands of people in it to tell me how serious he was about something. A whole damned town. Kaboom. Gone."

I looked up. Her eyes were unfocused, staring into the distance. But I didn't see any condemnation there.

"How did you get over that?" I asked.

"I don't know that I ever have," she said. "And before that, another sonofabitch killed his way through two hundred and fifty people to get me to leave the place I was hiding, to surrender myself to him. Wasn't my idea to hide, but I went along with it, and those people died. So that's on me." She put her hand on her heart. "What happened to you today?"

"I have a bubble around me," I said, waving a hand in front

of my body. "The speedster hit a bar, it broke into splinters, they ricocheted off me at higher speed…into a bystander."

"But she'll be all right?" She was watching me intently now.

"Yes, after some surgery." I nodded, not sure how we'd gotten to this point. "But how do—"

"This speedster," Sienna said, staring me down. "How bad are they?"

I didn't know how to answer that. "Well, they keep talking about chaos, unleashing chaos—"

"Yeah, that's probably not going anywhere good," she said. "So I guess it comes down to a simple choice for you: stand back and let the cavalry sweep in and handle it—"

"What if they can't?" I asked, because the question just bubbled out. "This speedster…they're fast. New to the powers, I think, but fast."

"It's a real danger," Sienna said, nodding along. "Your powers are probably better disposed to dealing with a speedster than anyone I've ever met. And I've met quite a few metas."

"But mine are defensive, only," I said, and I hit a vein of frustration I'd not even realized was there. "Yeah, it's great if someone comes at me, but what about when they're whizzing around, hurting other people? All I can do is stand there and look useless." I bowed my head. "And feel helpless."

"Look, they're your powers, not mine," Sienna said, "but if I may say something, as probably one of, if not *the*, most dangerous metas on the planet." Her lips curled in a very slight smile. "Have you really *explored* your powers? Thought through the permutations for how you can use them in every circumstance?"

"What do you mean?"

"So, for example," she said, standing up, "let's say I had your powers, and I was in a fight. I'd throw myself backward against a wall, an object, whatever, to trip that momentum reflex—"

"But against an immovable object, that'd send me flying," I said, instinctively.

"Exactly."

"But I don't like to go flying," I said. "Most days I really try to avoid it. Except for commercially."

"But it gives you speed and strength if you're going on the offensive," she said, feinting with a lightning-fast punch. "Think about what you could do to this speedster if you got them trapped in a confined space and just started swinging at them. You could basically pummel them into death or surrender without even being that good of a fighter."

I blinked a few times. "Not sure I'm really looking to pummel anyone to death."

"Your powers seem to contain unlimited possibilities," she said, ignoring my clearly stated desire not to kill people. "Like this bubble around you—can you expand it?"

"Expand…it?" I almost choked. "Most of the time I'd prefer to contract it down to zero, not make it grow."

"Or control the vectors of speed manually?" she went on, still ignoring my protests. "Think about that. If you could guide the power rather than just have it trigger randomly when you're beset by a case of the nerves, you could really direct it somewhere. Or at someone, rather. Or even move yourself without having to throw yourself against something. You'd almost be like a mini speedster yourself."

I laughed. "I don't think it works like that. Any of that."

Those piercing blue-green eyes seemed to spear me in place. "How do you know if you've never tried? I'm still discovering powers I didn't know I had until recently. It's not like they come with an instruction manual. And my guess is, given your upbringing, you never had a chance to really 'explore the studio space' with them." She shrugged. "You're in Vegas now. The desert is just out there. You might want to take a little time and really see what you can do."

"But…what if I'm not good enough?" I asked, and boy, did my heart start pouring out. Again. In spite of my desire not to say…well, any of this. "What if people get hurt?"

"When someone's bent on causing 'chaos,'" she said, "people are going to get hurt. What you need to decide is if you're the type of person who is willing to step up and use the power you've got to put an end to the chaos. Because most people? They abdicate that responsibility every day in favor of living their lives. And that's a fine choice, to admit that stepping up and trying to do these things—these dangerous things—is not for you." She pointed a finger at me, and it felt like she really was spearing me with it, even though she was feet away and this was all a dream. "It takes a rare person to be willing to step up and say, 'I'll do it,' knowing there are dangers, knowing that things can go badly, knowing that you could die."

"But…I'm afraid," I whispered. And there it was. The sum total of my past, reaching out to infect my present, all boiled down to one feeling that I couldn't ever seem to shake, no matter how far behind I thought I'd left it.

"Fortunately, doing this doesn't require you to be fearless," Sienna said with a smile. "It just requires you to have courage, and fight through that fear. You can do it—if you want to. But it's a choice *you* have to make." And she started to fade.

"How do I know if I'm the kind of person who can do that?" I asked, a little quiver in my stomach causing a flurry of doubt.

"Anyone can be that type of person," Sienna said, disappearing into the darkness as the walls and furniture faded around us. "You just have to choose to. So decide quickly…" Her voice turned stern, more serious, and it didn't help my nerves. "Because if this speedster is looking to cause chaos? They probably won't wait around for you to find your courage."

69.

Brianna

She awoke in the easy chair that her father used to sit in, the TV flickering in front of her, the ten o'clock news playing. She blinked a few times, trying to re-acclimate to her surroundings.

It was one of the safe houses she'd bought with the family fortune. This one was outside Baton Rouge, in a town called Arnaudville. It was a little off the beaten path, but that was good. This would give Brianna a chance to really hunker down, decide what to do now that her plans had twice failed.

There was an itch in the back of her mind that she hadn't scratched yet. It called to her, this thing she'd bent her whole life toward. It had formed after she'd gotten back from the Olympics the last time.

The Olympics. She'd put her whole life into that, into competition. She was good, too, could have been the best, she felt. Especially after she'd made that little tweak to her genetic code, the kind that no drug test on the planet could read—yet.

Metahuman powers straight out of a bottle. She hadn't done it for the competitive edge, though.

She'd done it after she'd found out what was eating Emily.

She'd done it after she'd vowed revenge.

Brianna hadn't had a clue what went wrong with Emily. It was the mystery of her youth, an unsolvable puzzle that, looking back, should have been so obvious. Their mother said she was just "feeling blue." Their father attributed it to her becoming a teenager. Emily had gone from normal, happy, confident, excited to listless, tired, skittish, and dark in the course of what felt like a moment. Like she'd gone to bed one night her normal self and woken up the next a depressed shadow of her previous self.

She'd limped through her teenage years like that, Brianna wondering, her parents wondering, all of them wondering together what had gone wrong with Emily. Mood swings, depression, a slow drive toward drinking and drugs. They thought the latter had driven the former. Occasionally, she'd seem almost normal for a day or so. Then she'd be back to darkness, back to hell, and none of them could get at her.

Brianna had buried herself in competitive shooting, because what could she do about her sister's burgeoning emotions? She ignored them, got on with her life, went to the Olympics and looked at turning pro.

Then she got the letter.

It had come right after she'd returned from Rio de Janeiro with the silver. Written in Emily's own hand, scrawled from the shaking, the mark of someone trying to fight the need for a fix long enough to excise the demons in her soul.

Brianna read it. And read it again, her own hand shaking like her sister's when she'd poured the wavy scratchings out of her tortured soul and onto the page.

And Brianna got angry.

She hadn't been this mad when she'd failed her shot and ended up with the silver instead of the gold. She hadn't been this mad…well, ever.

Of course they'd all missed it—Emily had gone to bed one night perfectly normal and woken up a hot mess, but before she'd gone to bed that night, she'd been babysitting for the Warringtons.

She hadn't gone to bed normal at all. They just hadn't seen her when she came in, her clothing askew, cheeks flushed, hair all mussed up from Ivan Warrington laying his dirty, lecherous hands on her in the back of his wife's minivan after offering to drive Emily home.

And Brianna had just gone on with her life, oblivious to any of it. Like it was happening to someone the world away instead of the sister who slept in the bunk bed above hers.

There was a conscious snap somewhere in the letter, some flash of red that Brianna couldn't recall ever feeling before. Now that she was done with Olympics, but not set on her next goal, her brain was seeking a purpose. Going pro was an option before her. Competing in 3-gun was interesting. Becoming a shooting instructor was another option. Hell, she could have retired; their mother and father had died just a couple years before Rio, leaving the kids a trust fund that would turn into a full inheritance at thirty. Brianna could have easily soldiered on through that just with her monthly allowance.

But this? Seeing her sister's face on the news less than a month after getting that letter? Knowing that somehow, she'd missed the biggest secret to hit her family ever, while she was off doing her thing, pursuing excellence and Olympic Gold?

Her last family member dying, and after a revelation like that?

Yes, she had snapped. Her new goal had been so quickly decided as to make any previous decisions look slower than cold oil drifting across the Gulf of Mexico.

She'd avenge her sister by killing Ivan Warrington. And maybe, if she used her skills right, she might even get away with it.

The TV was the only light on in the room, and Brianna stared at it blearily, thinking about how she'd gotten to this point. How had she missed Warrington at the ferry? It was a damned disgrace, Rio all over again, and coming back with a lot less than a silver. Sure, it was at a longer distance, but she was better now.

This was losing big, failing to even medal, maybe worse. Today had only compounded it. Now they knew who she was, thanks to Sienna Nealon. Thanks to her own strange desire to open up after so long—so damned long—keeping it all to herself! Why couldn't she have just run and kept her mouth shut?

The news played the weather report. More heat, no cold, making tomorrow look like a light summer day, both in Baton Rouge and New Orleans. Not that out of the ordinary for

October here. Brianna watched without watching, took it in as her mind was on other things.

Then the next story came up, and all the other stuff on her mind? Gone in an instant.

"We're here live in downtown New Orleans at the Hotel Fantaisie," a reporter with olive skin and long dark hair was saying into a microphone. "I'm standing here with Governor Warrington in the aftermath of today's assassination attempt. Governor, how are you feeling?"

"I feel just fine, Jennifer," Warrington said, his smug face taking up the whole frame. "And I want to reassure the fine people of Louisiana that no second-rate assassin is going to throw me off my game. We've got work to do 'round here, and I'm still at it. We're not stopping for anything."

Brianna sat up in her chair. The backdrop was a hotel room, and she could see the city of New Orleans out the window. Behind it was the old, grey United States Customs House building. A few blocks past that, the waterfront was visible.

Was he staying at the same hotel where she'd taken her shot at him only a few days before?

Boy, wouldn't that just be the most Warrington thing he could have done? It made sense, though—why not exploit the hotel's desire to put themselves on the right side of the investigation by handing out some free rooms to him? It wasn't exactly high tourist season, they could probably afford that minor sacrifice, especially since neither the Saints nor the LSU Tigers were playing in town this week.

"What are your plans now?" the reporter asked.

"We just keep doing what we've been doing," Warrington said with that same damned smile. "We've got an exciting slate of legislation coming up before the election, lots of important bills moving through. We have an addendum to the education reform bill, which we're going to try and expedite because it means more money to schools in underprivileged areas…"

Brianna blinked. He was staying at the same damned hotel. The one she'd researched exhaustively before choosing it for taking her shot at him. She knew it inside and out, absent the security precautions they'd probably implemented now that he was in town…but she knew it, backward and forward.

Looking out that window…he had to be on a floor in the middle teens. She snorted; ironic, that. Warrington liked the teens, didn't he?

But that meant…

Brianna smiled in the dark. Without even realizing it, that arrogant son of a bitch had sealed his own fate. A plan was already forming in her mind, and all she had to do was move quickly. She stood, all trace of sleep already gone as she ran through the idea again, then once more, standing there in the dark, TV flickering before her.

Yes, it would work. It'd require doing things differently than she'd originally wanted to, but that was just fine. She was exposed, they knew who she was, they'd be after her. There was no point in holding to the old plan, not anymore.

The new plan…it'd see Ivan Warrington finally get his just desserts.

Brianna smiled. She couldn't wait to get started.

And if she hurried, she could even make it back to New Orleans tonight.

70.

Sienna

I woke in the early morning hours to a city that was sleeping. Riding the elevator to the lobby, I nodded as deferentially as I could to the LSP troopers surrounding the lobby. They kept a wary eye on me, and for good reason, as I exited the hotel onto Canal Street, utterly quiet at this time of morning. It was probably 4:30 or so, and I had a destination in mind.

The massage parlor where I'd first gotten the runaround from Michelle wasn't open, the metal shutter down like most of the other businesses on the street, save a few all-night establishments catering to the Bourbon Street party crowd. I could still hear a little noise coming from Bourbon, and behind me, Harrah's was all lit up. I suspected the party was still ongoing inside, though I couldn't hear anything as I headed toward Bourbon.

The street of legend looked dark at this entry point, neon lighting it farther down. A twenty-four-hour Krystal glowed to my right, and an adult novelty item store waited to my left. Farther down, more bars still writhed, music drifting out.

The smell of over-full trash cans hit me, and I stuck my sleeve up to my nose. I was in my standard FBI jacket, blouse, cotton pants. My primary gun was on my hip, backup on my ankle. It was just a little, single-stack Glock 43 9mm with seven shots, but I was packing I because I felt like walking into this particular encounter, I needed to be ready for anything.

I walked a block down Bourbon Street before I hit a cross street, braving that garbage smell the entire time. I found myself wishing that I had used a laundry detergent with a stronger after-odor by the time I rounded the block, though, because that garbage stink on Bourbon was really potent.

I found what I was looking for about halfway down the block. It was an alley that ran parallel to Bourbon, back toward Canal. I figured there was an alternate entry and exit for employees of the massage parlor and the other service businesses that lined that part of Canal to get to work in the mornings and leave in the evenings. In fact, remembering Michelle sending Liu Min out the door in front of me, I suspected she was doing it entirely for show. That seemed to be all she did—put on some sort of show for me.

Well, I resolved as I walked to the back door of the massage parlor, the show was over. I was done playing games with her, and getting her half-ass help. It was time for Michelle to make a decision, to get off the damned fence one way or another.

I reached the back door of the massage parlor and it was pretty obvious I'd found the correct one, even absent the labeling. The restaurant next door had a massive dumpster right outside theirs; the massage parlor had a smaller one, mostly filled with latex gloves and paper waste. A dozen smashed cigarette butts wafted their stale scent out of a plant pot turned into a jumbo ashtray, adding to the lingering stink of Bourbon Street that clung to me.

The doorknob turned easily, opening into a small break room. There was only one person waiting there, thumbing through a *Style* magazine, her dark eyes looking down at the pages as she flipped them. "Don't you need a warrant to just walk in like that?" Michelle asked, apparently unsurprised that I was here at four in the morning.

"Only if it's locked," I said. "Besides, do I look like I'm doing any searching or seizing?"

"No, you look lost," she said, looking up from the magazine and tossing it aside.

"Same with you," I said. "Shouldn't you be getting ready for yoga class right now?"

"It's not until six." She smiled. "What can I do for you?"

"Oh, I just stopped by to say 'adios,' but however you would say it in Chinese. I've been recalled to New York."

"Yeah," she said, "I heard about that scene you caused in the governor's suite." She shook her head. "Probably not how I would have recommended you handle the situation, but I can't blame you for being upset." Her eyes flashed, showing the most emotion I'd seen from her since we'd met, at least of the non-smug variety. "I know I was when I found out about Emily Glover. At least you kept your violence under control."

"How'd you find out about Emily? What he did to her?" I asked, my voice low and even. Just past the break room, I could see the door cracked open to the massage parlor. There was no one moving out there, which meant she was the only one in the place. Why would New Orleans's Triad boss be sitting in a massage parlor at four a.m., alone?

Her eyes flicked up to me. "You know the business I'm in. Who I am."

"Of course."

She shook her head. "No, you don't. You know what they said, which is what they know, and what they know is my father's business. I've only been in charge for a year. When I came up in my father's ranks, I did not do so as his heir, because he wasn't keen on handing over his empire to a girl. I worked my way up as a common—well, whatever you want to call it." She waved a hand behind her toward the parlor. "I worked here, I worked in other places in his operation. One of them—" and here her eyes flashed again "—was what you could charitably call a flophouse; a hotel that had certain dealings catering to the basest instincts; where a woman could sell herself and then immediately turn over the money she'd made to feed habits she'd accumulated."

"Ew," I said. "A drug house and brothel, all-in-one."

"Vertical integration." Michelle nodded. "I shut it down when I took over. Got out of both of those lines of business." She narrowed her eyes as she thought about it. "But I worked there for a while. Met the girls. Got to know them. Do you know how many weren't addicts? *None*. Hookers who aren't hooked on something? That may happen in the high-class escort ranks, but it doesn't happen on the low end of the business. And that's how I met Emily Glover."

I nodded. "She told you."

"I had to forge a good relationship with the girls working there," she said, and now she was looking back down at the magazine cover, though I doubted she was really seeing it. She seemed very far away. "They don't want to hand over all their money, see? Who would? And the manager's job was to get as much of it as possible, if not all. The previous manager? A pig of a man. He took it by force, classic pimp who felt it was just owed." She looked up at me. "I tried to earn it. To help them. I never took it. I traded for it, provided shelter for it, made sure they had food and—" She shuddered, looking away. "I hated myself every day for all of it, even being there. But Emily…" She shook her head even more violently. "She made me feel the worst I ever felt while I was there."

"What did she tell you?" I asked.

"Everything," Michelle said. "I was just doing my thing; getting close to another girl. You could tell she hadn't had anyone just listen to her, maybe ever. She was high, of course…and she just told me. Everything." She looked up at me, and there was water in her eyes. "She was a really smart girl, too. A little younger than me, and bright—so bright. Could have been anything if she hadn't started using. The way she told her story I felt like I was there in the car the first time it happened. Like it was happening to me. And given who she was, where she lived, it could have been me. It could have been anyone. That's how brazen Warrington was." Her hand was bound tightly into a fist on the table. "I don't think he ever felt an ounce of fear or remorse for what he did to her." Her eyes were glazed with tears in the dim break room light. "And she begged him not to."

"Why not just tell me?" I asked. "Why not just…straight up tell me what was going on with him?"

She laughed lightly. "I don't know you, Nealon. I know your rep—badass avenger, Slay Queen, whatever. But you, actual you?" She shook her head. "Not a clue. You come off this fugitive run into the Revelen war, and suddenly you're more famous than ever. But you take all that goodwill and instead of going back to work for yourself, you join the FBI. Well, I know what the FBI is. They're a known quantity, a thorn in my side, a pain in my ass. You think I'm going to just start confiding the darkest things I know to some FBI agent, then you really did fall off the turnip truck yesterday."

"Yes, I did, but I had boots when I fell off, which is more than I can say for after I met you."

She grinned. "That was fun." The smile faded. "I pulled us out of the prostitution and drug businesses over the last couple years, but that doesn't mean I'm legit. I still have my hands in some pies that the FBI would love to take away." Now she turned stone-faced. "And I have dealings with Warrington, too, that make me—us—a ton of money. I'm not the only going concern in the Triads in New Orleans. Just the biggest."

"So you didn't want to see him take a fall for something that could be traced back to you," I said, nodding along. "Like corruption."

It was her turn to nod. "And he is corrupt. That school bill he's so proud of? A lot of people are benefiting from that who aren't underprivileged kids or teachers. By design. The fix was in. But you'd have a hell of a time proving it."

"I'll have a hell of a time proving that he raped Emily Glover," I said, leaning back against the wall. "Assuming the statute of limitations hasn't run out, there's not a single witness to it still alive other than Warrington."

"You know how this works, Nealon," Michelle said. "Emily cannot be the only one he preyed on over the years."

"Yeah, but if Whit Falkner, local superstar reporter, couldn't find any other victims, what makes you think Sienna Nealon, total stranger, is going to be able to waltz into town and drum some up?"

"Look at other guys this happened with," Michelle said, voice rising with hope. "Bill Cosby. Harvey Weinstein. They got away with it for years until one story broke—and then it was like the floodgates opened."

I shook my head. "Bill Cosby's allegations were out there for decades. The press never covered them, but they were out there. You could find it all on a simple internet search years before the story broke. As for Harvey Weinstein, the press in

New York and LA were bought and paid for by him."

She raised an eyebrow at that. "What do you mean?"

"Reporters in the big markets—and some of the small ones—like to write books on the side," I said. "Weinstein, through his movie company, allegedly kept buying up the rights to all the big reporters' books. That left them invested in him, and he in them, giving them a financial reason to doubt that this guy, doing so much good for them, could possibly be doing bad to others." I thought about Holloway pawing at me in the hotel room the other night, and repressed a shudder. "I don't know. I don't want to judge any of the victims in that situation for not saying anything, because I don't know what pressure they were under. All I know is that the people who were supposed to hold up the magnifying glass to the corrupt—which would be the press—kept their damned mouths shut and let it go on without whispering so much as a peep." I shook my head again. "Warrington is loved by the local press. I can tell after watching two or three fawning reports, seeing a couple pieces in the local paper. He can do no wrong in their eyes. Whit said almost the same, that this scandal, if it came out, wouldn't finish him."

Michelle stared at the wall behind me. "So what are you going to do?"

"I'm not entirely sure," I said, looking at the floor. "Whatever it is, I need to bring him down righteously, within the system."

"I thought you said you were getting sent back to New York?"

"Well, that's what they ordered me to do," I said, and it was my turn to smile. "I'm not the greatest listener. And I've got a little time before I 'accidentally' miss my first flight. Got any suggestions on places to look? You know, for trouble?"

"I wish I did," Michelle said. "I was waiting here for you, you know?"

"I kinda figured when I saw you were here alone, reading a magazine. I doubted the Triad Queen of New Orleans just hangs out here doing that when she could be anywhere in the city."

"It's not very interesting, that's true." She lightly tapped the cover of the magazine. "If I knew a direction I could send you with some assurance you wouldn't blow me up in the process…I would. Even the directions that would blow up parts of my business, I might be willing to make a sacrifice, if I had a clear path for you." She shook her head. "But I don't. Warrington's corruption is arcane and well-managed. A good portion of it isn't even illegal, as such."

"Is that the part where he deals with Mitchell Werner?" I asked.

She gave a quick nod. "Werner and Warrington grew up together. I'd bet you anything that Warrington got his bestest buddy to claim Emily's body, but I'd also bet there's no record of a phone call where it happened. Warrington's good at being dirty, and Werner's the bagman, the one that gets the real dirt on his hands. He doesn't just play that multi-company shell game so he can be an 'independent' attack dog for Warrington. He's getting paid by people who are benefiting from Warrington's tenure as governor, and he's returning that money, cleanly, to Warrington via different channels like campaign contributions and a gubernatorial library fund. I suspect he's even pre-funding a senatorial or presidential run for Warrington with his PAC activity and maybe even preparing an organization for Warrington to step into as CEO with a huge war chest to influence future party activity; turn him into a kingmaker even after he's retired from politics, keep his influence going while bumping up his paychecks and wealth."

"Must be nice to have friends like that," I muttered.

"Yes," Michelle said. "But it leaves us with the same question—what are you going to do about it?"

I pushed the door open, pondering my answer as I stepped back out into the smelly alley, the stink of day-old chicken in the dumpster next door almost gagging me as I went back to braving the humidity outside. "Well," I said, "I don't know. But I'm sure of one thing." And now I looked back to find her watching me, intently, waiting to see what I'd say. "I don't let the bad guys just walk away."

The door closed on her smile as I walked off down the alley, the horizon already starting to lighten.

71.

Olivia

The overnight lady at the front desk of my motel had known a perfect place for me to go practice my skills. I hadn't told her that's what I was doing, of course; I'd just said I was looking for a junkyard where people dumped machinery and garbage in the desert and she'd come up with a place in about two seconds, staring at me over the end of her cigarette as I tried not to cough.

Looking out over the rusted waste of car frames and old appliances and the occasional bag of discarded garbage, I got the feeling that maybe the lady at the desk had dumped a thing or two out here herself.

It didn't smell great, and there wasn't a lot of light when I arrived, my Uber driver skeptically dropping me off with only a 'Not sure what you're thinking, but okay' sort of look as we parted.

There had to be hundreds of appliances laid out in this little gully just off the road, a perfect natural drop in the desert topography. It was like the beginning of a canyon that never got any deeper, and the frames of rusted-out, picked-clean cars interspersed through the mess didn't help with the overall aesthetic. There were even a few old corrugated shipping containers that had rusted out, which must have taken years given the dearth of rain.

"Okay," I said, standing at the edge of the road. The desert air was a little cool at this time of morning, only a slight purpling in the east to give aid to my metahuman-enhanced sight. I could see all right, not great, but it'd have to do for the purposes of this exercise.

"Let's see if you were right, Sienna," I whispered, shedding my cell phone and wallet, and taking a moment to bury them in the sands at the corner of a rusted minivan just a dozen paces off the road's shoulder. I didn't know what was going to happen over the next few minutes, but I didn't want to find out at the expense of losing all my ID and my link to the world.

That done, I shed my jacket and balled it up, setting it just underneath that frame, snug behind a rusted-out axle. I shivered in the cool air, then stood, sandwiched between an old Frigidaire and the hulk of the 90s minivan.

I took a breath, in slow, out slow, and thought about what Sienna had said. I had a personal bubble that could redirect the momentum of others away from me.

So…what happened when I redirected myself?

"I can do this," I said, voice shaking just a little. "I can do it. I can…" Another breath, slow in, slow out. The Frigidaire was only a few feet away. "I can…"

I sagged. "I can stand here all day and not actually do anything." I plopped my face into a hand.

This was the problem, wasn't it? I was so damned tentative, so risk-averse. What if I ran at the refrigerator and something bad happened? I hit it? Okay, I pretty much never hit anything, because of my personal bubble, but what if it failed this time?

Well, I might end up with a bloody nose and a couple bruises. Which was a fair bit better than the lady who'd caught the accelerated splinters from the exploding bar yesterday because of me.

"No more being a coward," I whispered.

And I broke into a run.

Once upon a time, jogging in Orlando, I'd accidentally flung a man. Because he'd gotten too close, and my powers had triggered, and—well, it was a mess.

My fault. I wasn't in control.

I'd never been in control. Not from the day that Roger had gotten his hooks into me.

"I am in control," I whispered as I flung myself into the fridge—

My personal bubble activated against the fridge, knocking it over and sending me—

I rocketed back, flung the dozen paces into the minivan ruin. It shuddered as my personal bubble caught on it, trying to transfer the momentum I'd picked up from the bounce off the fridge.

I was flung, weightless, out of control, jerked in the opposite direction again as I tucked myself into a ball and shot toward a discarded chest of drawers.

It felt like I was going a hundred miles an hour toward it, and I might have been. It flashed toward me and I was there, paused, hung in midair as my bubble worked, momentum being transferred from me to the chest, and—

The chest of drawers launched as though it had a rocket attacked to it, shattering against another rusted-out car frame only a few feet away. It dissolved in a shower of pressed wood fragments, more dust in the desert air.

"Ahhh," I said, gasping after my brief ping-ponging. I touched my chest, my legs, feeling around everywhere for a wound, a pain, something, anything to suggest I hadn't just done something completely insane and gotten away with it injury-free. "Ahh…uhm…"

But I had. There wasn't a spot of dust on me. I'd even managed to land on my feet after balling up into the fetal position during the second bounce.

"Huh," I said. "Hum. Okay. Well, that's one thing…"

The next test was a little more difficult. For it, I strolled up to an abandoned tire from a semi-truck, turned onto its side. I lifted it with my meta strength, testing myself, because I didn't really do the whole 'workout' thing. Turned out I could lift it easily, and I did, pushing it to where one of the corrugated shipping containers sat. This one was in pretty okay shape, the beginnings of corrosion visible down the sides, but mostly hale and hearty, compared to others in the boneyard.

I carried the huge tire in my arms, the top of it several feet above my head, the bottom of the donut arc cradled against my chest. I let the top flop down so that I held it out from my body perfectly horizontal.

"Test two," I said, holding it like that with some effort. It wasn't light, especially extended in this awkward fashion. The shipping container was about twenty feet away, with nothing but small debris between me, the tire, and it. "Let's go."

I thought about the times I'd used my personal bubble to blow dust off my clothing. That was exercising a form of control over it, but it was so small I'd never really thought about it as me doing something dramatically different. But it was—it really was taking control of my powers, using them actively.

Another deep breath, another one out.

Then I pictured myself launching the tire out of my personal bubble, straight ahead. Just like blowing the dust off myself. Except bigger.

Lots bigger.

The tire launched out of my hands as if slung from a catapult, hitting the container with enough force to rattle it, the boom of rubber-to-metal contact echoing for miles across the desert sands. It stuck, dented, and the lack of movability in the container forced the momentum of the tire to reverse on itself—

It flew back at me, big and black and going about a hundred miles an hour right at my face. I made a meeping noise as it came for me, squinting my eyes shut.

I didn't even have to do anything this time. My bubble activated automatically, and the tire shot back the way it came, twice as hard.

It knocked the container back a foot, making a boom that echoed like thunder over the quiet desert.

And I stepped forward as the tire shot back at me, speed double what it had been the first time it came back.

It hit my bubble and wavered for a millisecond, my power turning all its force—and then some—back at the container. Now there was less space between us. I took another step forward as it launched off me, slamming into the container with the force of a runaway train—

The container dented, corrugated side collapsing several feet inward, the container's edge tipping a couple feet off the ground. The tire shot back at me, but by now I was strolling into it, anticipating it coming back at me—

This time it came at me as fast as the speedster, hit my bubble and shook, shivered, and heated up in midair as my power worked to reverse its course yet again. When it left my orbit I swear it felt like I'd just launched a missile.

It homed in on the side of the shipping container and struck, the rubber exploding, the metal shredding—

All that force had to go somewhere, and the somewhere it chose was every damned direction. I looked away by instinct, shielding my eyes, though I knew I didn't have to.

When I looked back…the shipping container was blown open like a bomb had gone off inside. Even the floor was shredded into almost unrecognizable pieces. Fragments of corrugated metal no larger than the tire lay strewn and still settling against the earth and various other pieces of debris in a roughly hundred-yard circle from where they'd started.

Of the tire…there was no trace. At all.

"Holy sugar," I muttered. I was only ten feet from the point of impact when it had gone off. I'd closed the distance in half, finding my courage and walking toward the trouble rather than away. I almost hadn't realized it. "Okay. Okay, that's…that's two. That's…" I broke into a grin. "That's really something."

Because it was. It was kind of amazing, really.

"Last one," I said, and concentrated. I turned around, looking for something to bounce off of, to tie these two lessons together. My ears were still ringing from the explosion of the container, and I rubbed at one of them, hoping it'd go away. It had started high but now had moved to a faint buzzing sound like—

"Oh," I said, and turned around. The minivan where I'd started was only a couple dozen paces away, and I ran for it, finally putting together what that muted sound was. I dove for the rear axle and dug, unearthing my phone as I slung aside sand furiously. I might have been able to do it quicker with my new powers, but the last thing I needed was to launch my phone up into the van wreck.

I pulled it out just as it stopped buzzing. On the screen it informed me that I had ten missed calls.

All from Reed.

"Uh oh," I said, and called him back, hurrying as I pocketed my wallet.

He answered on the first ring. "Where were you? I've been trying to—"

"I'm fine, I'm fine," I said, slinging my jacket on and stumbling back up the hill toward the road. "I was just out in the desert doing—"

"Do you have any idea what's going on in Vegas right now?" The violent urgency with which he spoke jarred me out of my apology and explanation in a second.

"Wh-what?" I asked, reaching the edge of the road and seeing, with my own eyes, what he was talking about.

There was smoke wafting off the Strip, black and heavy, clouding the skies in the distance.

"It's the speedster," Reed said, sounding stricken over the phone. "They're at it again. At least four people are dead. And…" His voice tightened. "Olivia…they're calling you out. Personally."

The phone slipped away from my ear as I seemed to lose strength. The black cloud over the Strip was like a flag of death hanging over the sky.

I lost my voice, felt like I was choking, couldn't get a breath. My mouth was dry, desert dry. My skin tingled, the silence a stark contrast to whatever catastrophic events were happening in Vegas right now.

"Where are you?" Reed asked, tinny and metallic, over the phone.

"Miles away," I whispered, raising it back up to my chin. "I'm…I'm miles—"

"Stay there," Reed said. "Augustus and Jamal will be there in a couple hours, and I'm leaving now; I'll be right behind them. Once we're there, we can—"

I swallowed, and it felt like I was choking on my own fear. "More people will die by then," I whispered.

Reed didn't answer for a second. "Yes. Probably. But—"

I closed my eyes.

This was it.

This was the choice that Sienna had talked about.

I could stand back and let things run their course, let Augustus and Jamal come in on the morning flight and clean things up…

Clean up my mess.

Or I could…

I could…

I balled my hand into a fist. "I'm going to have to call you back."

"Wait, what are y—"

I hung up on him, slipping the phone back into my pocket and then shedding it with my coat.

The desert air, once more, seemed to slip up my sleeves as I stood in the silence for one last second.

"Now or never," I whispered, and I tossed my coat under the ruin of the old minivan and sprinted down the hill toward the boneyard. When I was about ten feet away, my momentum building on the downhill run, I leapt, tucking my feet beneath me and hoping that I could do this—

—I concentrated, thinking about momentum, about speed, about force, about—

—about the old trailer speeding toward my face at a hundred miles an hour—

An inch away from collision, the rusty metal so close I could have stuck out my tongue and tasted it, my bubble activated.

With a vengeance.

I didn't just bounce against the rusted trailer with the force of my downhill run, I blasted off from it with all the directed power I'd willed out with my concentration.

I used my power to launch from the junkyard into the sky, taking flight across the desert, my head forward and arms pulled back like an aerodynamic spear.

Like I was flying.

Like *she* used to do.

"Okay," I said, cool air rushing around me as I flew toward the black skies above the Strip, nervous tingles running across my skin, "let's go do this."

That thought was all I allowed myself to speak, but it wasn't all I let myself think.

Let's go be a hero.

72.

Brianna

She waited until near sunup to make the drive back to New Orleans, figuring it'd be easier to slip in under cover of rush hour. They were looking for her now, after all, and there was no point in making it easy on the cops by giving them a white female suspect driving through New Orleans in the middle of the night. She wouldn't exactly stick out like a sore thumb, and might even get passed by given the right wig, but it was a whole lot easier to slip in concealed in the endless stream of morning traffic on 10.

She listened to Debussy's *Claire de Lune* on repeat the whole way from Arnaudville to downtown New Orleans. The Superdome passed in silent shadow, the rays of the sun barely touching it, orange hues cast along the sides as she turned onto Canal Street.

The city was abuzz. There was the old Charity Hospital, grey and dead, sitting alone in its faded glory. A second line band was starting to assemble at the corner of Villiere, apparently set to march down the street in short order. It seemed early for it, but Brianna just shrugged it off.

She was dressed as a cleaning lady, dark wig and sunglasses paired with a blue uniform of a local hotel back in Baton Rouge. She'd taken steps to gather as many different costumes as she could. She smiled, thinking of the provenance of the idea—Sienna Nealon, again. How many times during Sienna's fugitive years had her cover been blown, and pictures of her in some new and unique style appeared in the newspapers and plastered all over the internet? So many hairstyles, manners of dress. She'd been a one-woman class in hiding, and Brianna had taken notes.

On so very, very many subjects.

The hotel loomed ahead on Canal Street, and she steered for it, pausing at a traffic light. She kept her head down, looking sideways out the window of her beaten-up old Honda Civic at the police officer standing on the corner, scanning the cars. He looked right at her for a few seconds, then kept scanning. Looking for her, it seemed, and he missed her.

Excellent.

The light turned green and she accelerated, not too fast, not too slow, trying to seem utterly normal. Hotel Fantaisie was just ahead, and she surveyed the sidewalk from the light a block back as the tram rang its bells and ran along the center of Canal Street. Shops were starting to open, and pedestrian traffic was picking up.

Still, the five or six uniformed Louisiana State Police troopers stuck out on the hotel block. They stood on the sidewalk, most of them, just watching the approaches, while a couple of the plainclothes officers tried to look casual and failed.

Brianna had to suppress a smile; this wasn't going to be too hard.

She turned into the alley just before the hotel, knowing full well there'd be more cops here, and there were. Five of them along the alleyway, just trying to look like they weren't keeping an eye on everything while they plainly were.

The parking garage behind the hotel would be crawling with them, too. Probably at least a few in the buildings on either side of the hotel, too, for good measure.

That was all right. She'd reached her stop.

She pulled up next to the first officer in the alley and rolled down her window, slowly, carefully, not quick and jerky like a metahuman, and leaned out to talk to him. She put on an accent, tried to make it Eastern European, because those tended to blur together to most ears, and because with her complexion she'd have an easy time passing—at least for long enough.

"Excuse me…what is going on here?" she asked, trying to furrow her brow in worry. She was a maid who was going to be late for work with all this congestion. That was all.

The officer sauntered over to answer without yelling, hands resting on his hips. "Well, ma'am—"

She iced him around the midsection with a quick blast and opened the car door, knocking him over.

"Hey!" The next cop down the alley reached for his gun, immediately seeing what she'd done.

Brianna fired another ice blast down the alley at him and it caught him in the center of the chest. Far from freezing his heart, it splashed around his arms and iced them into place like a hard steel vest.

"Let…me…out!" the cop nearest her said, struggling to get free.

"You'll melt free shortly," she said, striding past him. She aimed down the alley and iced the other two at a hundred and a hundred fifty paces respectively. It was just like shooting, really—steady yourself, let out your breath, aim, and fire. The only difference was that she'd incapacitated rather than killed. "I don't want to hurt you."

This time…she was going to give Warrington the death he deserved up close and personal, with the touch of her own hand.

He'd get the ice in the heart this time…but she'd deliver it personally.

With that, she pointed a hand at the ground and rose on a pillar of ice that grew beneath her feet, rising like an elevator that carried her up to the 16th floor.

73.

Sienna

I was down the street in the Ruby Slipper, enjoying day two of Bananas Foster Pain Perdu French Toast when I heard the screaming. My breakfast wasn't quite filled with enough rum to break my sobriety, but it was good enough that by God, I was working through it like I'd never quit drinking. The sound stopped me, though, because screaming had a tendency to get my attention, even in the middle of the best French toast I'd ever eaten.

After my talk with Michelle, I'd hit a wall that I figured could only be broken by waiting for either inspiration or something to happen. There was no point in waiting on an empty stomach, so I decided to stick close to the hotel and get something.

The screaming was like a gunshot past my ear telling me I'd made the right call. Tossing a couple twenties on the table, I sprinted out the door and in the direction of the sound.

74.

Brianna

The first step was to stop interference. Once she'd reached the 16th floor, Brianna knew exactly what to do to block interference, and it only took a minute or so.

She blasted ice against the side of the hotel, sliding along it in a quick orbit, sealing the entire 16th floor before she smashed in one of the windows, then iced it closed behind her.

Brianna had entered exactly where she meant to, in the middle of the floor. The room was unoccupied, and she hustled through, opening the door to the main hallway.

The beige walls and fluorescent lighting gave the area a dull, calming feel. She took it all in with a glance, then hurled blasts of ice to her right, where two troopers waited outside a door—

The suites. They were just over there.

To her left was the elevator bank, and a clamor as troopers that had been piling out of rooms and preparing a defense realized she'd done an end-run around them. They started to come around the corner as Brianna unleashed her powers in the hall—

And iced it up completely, sealing the state troopers on the other side of the barrier.

She made it heavy, two feet thick, and then, a foot past it, made another just like it, then another: three solid barriers of ice between her and the troopers on this floor.

Her breath came out in white wisps, the cold infusing the air. The exterior windows had been covered over, the governor's escape prevented. She could hear the radios of his remaining troopers crackling through the door to the suite behind her. The two she'd frozen were shouting warnings, howling about the cold that encased them.

She didn't care enough to mute their cries by frosting over their mouths.

Warrington was through that door, along with men with guns.

Drawing a deep breath, she put up another barrier on the other side of the hallway to block access from the emergency stairs. A foot thick, two feet. Once finished, Brianna started to ice the locking mechanism on Warrington's door with one hand while simultaneously forming a shield hard enough to stop bullets with the other…

75.

Olivia

I held in a scream as my momentum started to fade and I came down a few blocks east of the Strip. Bouncing off the wall of a pawn shop, I rocketed backward into a parked bus.

Uh oh.

"Up, up, up!" I shouted, trying to concentrate on pushing my direction back to skyward as I flew toward the bus. Someone was looking at me with wide eyes through the driver's window, but I ignored them, thinking, UP UP UP UP—

I nearly hit it but rocketed off at the last second, flying back in the right direction and over the faux Eiffel Tower of Paris Las Vegas. I missed it by about a foot, reaching out with my bubble to guide me—

It caught and launched me toward the black cloud, which hung over the hotel directly ahead. It was the Bellagio, and the fountains were going, the smoke pouring out of the cylindrical tower at the center of the hotel building.

"Okay, okay," I whispered, coming down again in the center of the fountain. This was going to be a different sort of bounce. I still felt incredibly out of control on every bounce, but it was getting easier. I kept my eyes on the center tower as I came down to the water, wondering how my momentum powers would interact with a non-solid surface like water.

As it turned out, they worked just fine. I bounced off and

shot right toward the tower, targeting one of the windows where the smoke was billowing.

About a second before I hit, I realized…I'd just launched myself into a place where a fire was very likely raging.

Brilliant work, Olivia. Bang up job, there.

I blew through the black cloud of smoke and into the open window before I realized…

I didn't really know how to *stop*.

Blasting into the floor, then the ceiling, I bounced a couple times before I realized that stopping was just a reversal of momentum. I concentrated, and before I rattled off the ceiling at increasing velocity for the eighth(!) time, I managed to somehow blow my momentum out in all directions around me, causing the fire to puff as if hit by a strong wind.

And oh boy, was there fire.

It surrounded me on three sides, roaring up the walls and spreading to the ceiling. Whatever the speedster had intended, chaos was certainly the current effect. Which was probably how they wanted it.

No sooner had I come to a stop than I heard a dull roar over the sound of the crackling flames, and something whiffed behind me. Then again.

I turned in time to see the speedster zip past, through the flames, untouched by them, as the fire spread, madly, to cut me off from the window. A couple of quick motions and the ceiling caught, too, whatever accelerant the speedster had thrown causing the entire room to burn faster.

"Now I've got you exactly where I want you," the speedster said in that quivering voice, "sucker."

Then they disappeared.

Leaving me trapped in the flames.

76.

Sienna

As far as ideas for killing Warrington went, sealing him in an icy tomb after a frontal assault on his hotel seemed downright sensible. Killing him not at all was probably more sensible, but once you got into the whole "cold vengeance" frame of mind, and knew that the police were onto you, coming right at the problem and trapping him in a hotel on the 16th floor seemed pretty reasonable, as plans went. Definitely a fair escalation if your "shoot him in the face at a distance" plans had failed twice.

Unfortunately, it left me in a bit of conundrum.

I saw Brianna slip around the building on her ice slide as she worked to put up a freeze barrier. I had a pretty good inkling of what she was up to, and put together something that I should have long before:

She'd planned to assassinate Warrington from the Hotel Fantaisie for quite some time, and had done so very meticulously, down to her escape route. Of course she'd have examined the hotel blueprints in detail, which meant the Louisiana State Police troopers were effectively guarding Warrington on Brianna's home ground.

I wasn't really one for standing still and doing nothing, though, so I was moving the whole time I saw her doing the same. Going in through the lobby would have been the ideal entry point, but I'd have made a definite mess of my relations with the Louisiana State Police, and who knew if they'd rather have my help or shoot me at this point? I knew I didn't want to find out firsthand.

That left me with an alternate entry if I wanted to save Warrington (and I did).

The construction crane working on the building next door.

I made it up six flights of construction stairs in less than thirty seconds, putting all that fine daily cardio work to good use. As I burst out onto the top completed floor, I saw construction workers who had stopped work to view the ice fort building competition going on next door snap out of it when they saw me burst out onto the scene.

"You!" I shouted up to the crane operator, who stared at me blankly from under a yellow yard hat and sunglasses. I pointed once at his crane, then at the side of the hotel. "Get me up there!"

He opened the side of his control box and said, "You don't have a hard hat on. You can't be up here," like the world's most perfect hall monitor weinie.

"Get me up there or I'll kill you and make that guy do it," I said, and put enough heat on my statement to make sure he was clear that I probably wasn't bluffing. Though I totally was.

He sort of stared at me through his sunglasses, and even over the noise of the machinery and the street crowds below I could almost hear his gulp. He nodded, and the crane started rotating toward the hotel.

"Really need to get around to writing that book," I muttered under my breath as I vaulted onto the crane's arm, which was tilted up at a forty-five-degree angle. He was swinging it around, and its center was a clear path, steel sandwiched between the metal frame, like a miniature running track to my destination. "'How to Win Few Friends but Influence Everybody Who Pisses You Off.'" I think it would be a bestseller for sure. And definitely would have capitalized on my Slay Queen fame.

The run up the crane wasn't that hard. It was a thirty-second sprint, at most, like climbing more stairs, but relying on my steel-toed boots for the hard grip as I surged up, hunched over until I reached those last few steps where the crane opened up, the hotel's 16th floor in all its ice-encased glory just waiting for me there…

Only thirty or so feet from the tip of the crane.

No big deal.

Just a huge jump over open air with a killer fall waiting beneath me if I bounced off.

"Please don't have spent much time on this ice," I muttered as I covered the last few steps. "Please have been so hot to kill Warrington that you didn't bother to really seal it—"

I launched over the gap straight at the ice, hoping that glass was waiting a few inches beneath the layer of ice that wrapped the windows of the entire 16th floor like a frozen hug. Alternatively, I hoped that my momentum in my jump would carry me through if there were more than a few inches of ice.

Shattering through both glass and ice, I crash-landed on an empty bed in an empty hotel room, rolling off and thumping off the wall. I caught myself on my feet and drew my pistol, gasping.

Shards of glass had caught me on the shin and on one of my forearms as I crashed in, and I brushed them out quickly, ignoring the trails of blood that spurted down my clothing as I dodged around the wall and ripped open the hotel room door.

The hallway waited beyond, and I twisted, looking around, getting my bearings. Emergency exit stairs lay to my right, and to my left…

Another wall of ice. And I could see by the lack of light filtering through from beyond it…

This one was a lot heavier than the one I'd just broken through.

77.

Brianna

She smashed through the door and was met with the thunder of gunfire. She wasn't accustomed to hearing it like this yet, no hearing protection, and it was loud and furious. The bullets plinked against the strength of the ice shield she held in her left hand, hardened to far subzero temperatures and thicker than a steel plate.

Brianna let out a broad-based spray of ice at waist level, extending her hand around the shield to manage it. The two state troopers let out noises as it struck them, then a second later she heard a slightly more muted reaction from Warrington and that female aide that was ever present at his side.

With a quick look behind her shield, she confirmed she'd forced the cops to lower their guns just by the sheer instinct of hitting them with the cold blast. Taking advantage of their distraction, she planted a burst on each of them, freezing their hands in place, then binding their feet together. They toppled, one following the other, and she stepped over them, kicking their guns aside as she did so.

And there he was, standing against the iced-over window, blinking swiftly and standing upon trembling knees. "You don't have to do this," he said, in that low and reasonable tone. He licked his lips as he tried to take another step back and bumped against the ice-coated window. His palm left an icy print where he touched it.

"You know who I am?" Brianna asked, advancing slowly on Warrington. She didn't even spare a glance for the female aide, who was sliding away from Warrington, making little gasping noises under her breath as she moved.

Warrington stared at her, and she could see the calculation run across his face, debating how to answer.

Brianna sent a blast of ice that lodged an inch from his head. A spike stuck out where it had landed, and if it had hit him…

He eyed the spike, thinking it through. He came up with the right answer. "You're Emily's sister."

"We met once before, do you recall?" Brianna didn't want to get any closer, but she forced herself to take another step. Now she was twenty feet from him, which felt far too close given that it was *him*. "When I got my car. I stopped by to pick her up from your house after she'd babysat for you one day." Brianna felt the worming, seething anger she'd contained for so long, and it came out now, finally, where it needed to. "I wish I'd known what I was seeing then. I thought she just wanted to get out of there because she was done with work." Brianna shook her head. "She wanted to get away from *you*."

"I didn't do anything with your sister—" Warrington started.

Another ice spike lodged to his other side, six inches out of the window, cracks spiderwebbing out as it joined with the ice pack on the other side of the window. Sweat was already rolling down the glass, and every time Warrington spoke, a puff of white vapor accompanied his words.

"I don't know what you want from me," Warrington said, keeping his eyes locked on her.

"I wanted you to die," Brianna said, that twisting feeling inside her crying to come out, to be done. "At a distance. Because I didn't want to ever be in a room with you, knowing what you are." She stuck out her chin. "What you did. But now? I think I'm okay with watching this happen up close. Hold still. This will only take a minute."

She raised her hand a little higher, taking aiming at his head like it was any other target she'd ever shot at.

78.

Olivia

Fire surrounding me, I stood in the tower of the Bellagio hotel.

Trapped.

Out of luck.

In over my head.

And that damned speedster had run off with no problem.

The smoke was thick and heavy, and I started coughing as it billowed into my face, my lungs, choking me. It was like drowning, but while drinking in the toxic aroma of flames.

My skin wilted under the heat and I doubled over, feeling the burns crawl up my exposed hands and curling my hair like straw beneath a relentless sun.

How had I gotten myself into this?

Oh, right. I charged into a trap set for me by the chaos-loving speedster.

How the hell was I going to get out, though? Surrounded by fire, there was nowhere to go but—

I looked up at the ceiling. It was shrouded in black smoke, but not on fire above me—yet. It was broken open where I'd entered and bounced a few times before landing and dispelling my momentum. And the floor below me…

It wasn't on fire, either.

I thought back to that metal container in the desert where I'd practiced. If I could pound it into exploding by building momentum bouncing a tire…?

Could I do the same with my own body?

"Only one way to find out," I muttered between coughing fits. And with a burst of concentration, I launched from the ground into the ceiling.

It was like being a basketball someone was bouncing, as I ricocheted from the floor to the ceiling and back again five times in two seconds. I was a human Flubber. I thought about all that momentum, my speed increasing with each bounce, the ceiling buckling with every hit—

If I flew out the top of the building, I was going to be up in the clouds in seconds.

But what if I took all the momentum I was building and channeled it out…?

Worth a try.

I did just that next time I bounced down, my reaction imprecise. The effect worked nonetheless.

A blasting impact issued forth from my body, my personal bubble pushing out all that force in a 360-degree arc around me.

The flames snapped out under the blast of air pushed away from my body and out of the room.

I coughed and sputtered and hit my knees as the air rushed back in. Sparks and embers remained, but the fire…

It was gone.

"Oh," I said, rising to my feet. "Yay. Got it."

A blur whizzed past me, a black figure coalescing a few feet beyond my bubble. I heard a soft thudding: golf claps from my opponent.

"Nice," I said, staring them down.

"Knew I'd have to deal with you one way or another," the speedster said, voice grinding like metal on metal. "I guess—"

I used my momentum trigger to launch myself at them, shooting into their personal space and pushing them into my bubble. I saw very surprised eyes for just a second as my powers activated—

And the speedster went launching through the wall the exact same way they'd done to Veronika twice now, disappearing across the Vegas sky and into the distance.

"Whoa," I whispered. The speedster flew in a slow arc

through the air, crashing down somewhere a few blocks past Vegas Boulevard.

What to do? The old me would have counted herself fortunate, having won this round.

But this speedster hadn't yet surrendered, not even after some particularly hard hits.

"Time to be the new me," I whispered, and set my feet. After bracing myself, I released momentum and, in a blur, I shot off in a matching arc—after the speedster.

79.

Sienna

I hit the ice barrier with my shoulder and careened off.

"Damn," I muttered, giving it a push. It didn't move at all.

The hotel corridor was completely blocked with this, and on the other side of it, somewhere…

Warrington waited. Hopefully still alive, though I was a little torn on that.

Gunfire came from down the hall, muffled, and a lot of it. Way more than one person firing. I had a suspicion it was the Louisiana State Police trying to blast their way through another ice wall.

"That's not going to work," I whispered, deciding my course of action. Bullets would just chip at this thing, like slightly larger ice picks going up against a slab. This was thick, several inches of ice hardened to whatever optimal temperature Brianna Glover hit to produce such incredibly solid bullets and walls and whatever the hell else. For all I knew, it didn't even have anything to do with temperature, it might have been more to do with the density of the molecular structure she was manipulating.

Whatever the case, I knew the only way through was to go *through*. No chipping away. No half-assed bumping into it.

I slammed my fist into the ice, launching my punch from the hip. "Should have gone with more protein, fewer carbs for breakfast," I muttered, my knuckles bleeding, a little crack appearing in the center of the ice block. I fired off another punch from the hip, twisting it as I hit for maximum torsion and impact. The crack broadened, a half-inch line right down the middle of the slab. "That French toast was good, though."

My hand ached, and I shook it out. If my punches wouldn't do it as fast as I needed to get through…

"As ol' Clyde would say…'Geronimo.'"

I lifted my leg and let loose an almighty stepping sidekick, my steel-toed boot landing on the heel rather than the steel part of it.

Didn't matter. I busted through that wall anyway.

It came raining down and I was already shoving my way through as the ice rained down on me. The hotel room door in front of me was busted open, and I could see a couple troopers on the floor, iced around the chest and arms like someone had tied them up with a band of hardened snow.

I stormed into the room, hand on my Glock but yet to pull it. Brianna was just ahead, a dozen or so paces from Warrington, who stood against the frozen hotel room windows, sweating as he stared at her, death waiting just feet away.

"I see we've got ourselves a crazy situation forming up here," I said, trying to figure out the combination of words that might calm it down.

If there was a combination of words that could calm this down.

"It's almost over," Brianna said, which was just about the worst thing I imagined she could say.

I pulled my pistol and the click of the barrel leaving the retention holster made her look over her shoulder. "Please don't do this," I said.

"I have to," she said.

"You really don't." I stared at Warrington. "I know he's done some serious wrong—"

"He won't even admit it," Brianna said, her voice sounding far away. "Arrogant, entitled—he thinks he deserved to do that to her, like it was just a divine right afforded him to tear apart a teenage girl." Now her tone hardened. "He deserves to die."

"I—" Warrington started to say.

"I'd keep my mouth shut if I were you," I said. "There's not much you can add to this that's going to make things better."

"How about a confession?" Brianna asked. "And an apology."

"I'm sorry if you feel like I've somehow done you wrong—" Warrington said, before I could stop him.

Brianna fired a blast of ice that embedded itself in the window atop his head, crowning him like a frozen mohawk. Warrington let out a shout and I drew a bead on her. "Stop!" I shouted, putting the front sight on her back where her heart would be. Given the speed with which she could move, trying for a head shot seemed like a bad idea.

"He can't even admit what he did like a normal person," Brianna said, malice and loathing dropping her voice to a whisper. "Listen to that politician doublespeak."

I took another step closer to them, and I don't think she even noticed, so I kept going, albeit slowly. The closer I got to point blank range, the easier it'd be on me if I had to take the shot.

Warrington was dripping blood down his forehead where he'd taken that ice spike. A couple inches down and he'd have caught it in the brain. "Why aren't you doing something?" he asked, looking past her to me.

"You had me removed from the case, remember?" I met his eyes, and there was a very brief flash of panic there. "So, not to go all *Clerks* on you, but I'm not even supposed to be here today."

"You should walk away," Brianna said, not taking her eyes off him. "He deserves this. He's earned it."

"Please don't," Warrington said, and here I caught the first real hint of absolute panic.

"You know what he did," Brianna said, tearing her eyes off him to look at me. "You *know*. You can feel it, can't you, just being around him? He's remorseless, guiltless…he'd do it again tomorrow even knowing what happened to her. Just look at him. He doesn't care about anyone but himself." Her voice dripped loathing.

"That's not true," Warrington said, panic seeping in. "I have a wife. A family. You know this, Brianna—"

"Don't say my name," Brianna snapped, frost dancing around her fingers.

I looked sideways. Jenna Corcoran was practically climbing a table at the edge of the room, trying to avoid making a sound or being seen in all this, but she was here, following all the talk. There was not a chance in hell she could help me, or that she'd find enough courage to so much as speak, but there she was, taking it all in.

"I didn't do what you think I did," Warrington said, shaking his head. "I don't know how I can make you believe me, but I didn't do it."

"You could do it," Brianna said, turning back around to look at me. "I know your powers. You could touch him. Look into his memories." Her lips twisted in disgust. "Prove he did it."

I drew a slow breath, and looked past her at Warrington. "Yes," I said. "I could." I opened my mouth to add a "but" of the size Sir Mix-A-Lot would have found very appetizing for his anaconda, but Warrington broke first.

"Fine," Warrington said, his facade of calm completely gone in an instant. "I did it! You want to hear that?" His eyes were wild, furious, panic stampeding out in a way I'd never seen from him before. "I did it and I'm sorry! I thought she wanted me—"

"Ermagerd." I almost had to look away, my stomach roiled so heavily. "You thought a thirteen-year-old wanted your aged ass? How old were you when this happened? Thirty-five?" I hit a full-body shudder. "That's ancient to a teenager."

"I was sorry it went down the way it did," Warrington said, rooted in place, staring at Brianna. "I didn't know she was hurting so bad. But I didn't make her take drugs. I didn't make her overdose. And when I found out it happened, I had someone I knew give her a proper burial." He dropped to his knees, and his eyes were all on her, watching to see if his begging was having an effect. "I never meant for it to happen. Not to her. Not to sweet Emily."

Brianna let her hand sink from where it was pointed at his face. She seemed to calm, some of the tension coming out of her shoulders. "I understand," she whispered.

Then she fired a blast of ice into his leg, and his scream tore up the room.

"I didn't mean for that to happen either, but I think it wrecked your knee anyway," Brianna said, hand back to pointing at his head. "And you may not have meant to ruin Emily, you might have just meant to use her, but she ended up like she ended up, and it was your fault."

"I didn't make her take heroin!" Warrington shouted, grasping his knee, a six-inch dagger of ice sticking out of the patella. I grimaced; I bet it hurt. He'd walk with a limp for the rest of his life.

"Yes, you did!" Brianna shouted, now firmly at the top of her lungs.

I felt a slow internal tension ratcheting up on me, like someone had taken a screwdriver and was tightening invisible screws in my back. Now they'd gotten them too tight, though, and something felt like it was going to break—and soon.

"Brianna," I said, trying to keep low, be the voice of reason. She hadn't killed him yet, but I had a feeling she was working up to it. Shooting someone through a scope at long distance was a lot less difficult. That was practically point and click, a serious distance in which to discount the humanity of your victim. This, though, up close and personal? It wasn't the easiest thing, looking a human being in the eye and murdering them, but Brianna seemed to be moving that direction fast.

She turned her head to look at me as though remembering I was there. She blinked a couple times, then met my gaze. "Hm?"

"You got him to confess," I said. "Okay? He admitted it. Come on, now." I waved at her with my free hand. "We all heard it. That's enough to get him on. Let the law handle it from here."

Brianna shook her head slowly. "The statute of limitations in Louisiana is ten years starting at the eighteenth birthday of the victim. We're past that now." Her hand was still pointed on target, and her voice didn't waver, back to ice cold. "There is no justice for Emily…except this."

80.

Olivia

I trailed out of the sky, breathing hard, still fighting my natural panic from dropping like a thrown stone, down to where the speedster lay in a crater below. They'd come crashing down on a pawn shop, right through the front and out the side. I angled in that direction, firing off my bubble, and it altered my course, mid-air, by a small amount.

My momentum powers could gain limited traction in air. Huh.

That was kinda neat.

I shot toward the speedster as they stirred, a small groan coming from their lips. It was somewhat deep, too tough to tell whether the voice was male or female, but they started to sit up as I came down—

I collided with them, unleashing another burst of momentum as I came down. It directed all my force down, toward them, thumping them against the bottom of the crater as I launched up.

Centering myself by firing off my powers, I came down again in an ungainly drop, landing and firing off—

The speedster hit the bottom of the crater again, harder, and I launched farther up, bouncing off them.

"You were…a mouse…" the speedster said as I came looping back down. I fired off again as I landed, drumming them into the ground with more force and then popping back to land on my feet a few paces away. Something about their voice sounded…familiar.

"I was," I said, catching my balance on the edge of the crater. I hopped down, hands in front of me, and pictured a boxer as the speedster started to push back to sitting, moving at normal, human speed. "I was scared of everything." I looked at my bare hands, took a deep breath, and then surveyed my foe, bleeding from the mouth but hardly out. "I'm not anymore."

I swung with a clumsy punch and triggered my powers when I got close to the speedster's face. It took all the momentum of my meta-strength swing and multiplied it, launching the speedster's head into the edge of the crater. I heard a crack, and the speedster went limp, body relaxing as they fell into unconsciousness.

God, I hoped it was unconsciousness. Hopefully I hadn't just killed them.

Sirens were blaring behind me as I reached down, pulling off the black ski mask that covered their face. And beneath it…

Was Sylvia, the crabby, complaining, list-making hoarder-wannabe landlady of the guy we'd arrested.

"Oh," I said. So that was how she'd gotten his ID. Heck, she could have framed him while we were walking up to the front door, if she'd been of a mind to.

I rolled her over, pulling her arms up as the cops came screaming up into the parking lot. I waved my hands as one of the LVPD officers came charging out of their car, gun drawn.

"Hey, guys," I said, arms raised, waving at the speedster. They took one look at me and moved on past. One of them had a suppressant needle already in hand. Clearly they knew what they were here for.

"What happened?" the lead officer asked. His nameplate read Morton.

"Well," I said, and a long explanation formed in my head that I immediately dismissed. Besides, there was a much simpler one that encapsulated it all, anyway. I shrugged, and said, "I got her."

81.

Brianna

This was it.

He'd finally copped to it.

He was on his knees, staring up at her, and he'd finally admitted what he'd done.

This was everything Brianna could have asked for.

And it was all thanks to Sienna.

Brianna swallowed, tried not to look him in the face. He wasn't human, after all. Not after what he did.

He was scum. Trash. Subhuman, at best.

And he'd taken everything from her.

"Don't do this," Sienna said, jarring Brianna out of her thoughts.

Brianna turned, her brow deep and furrowed. "What?"

Sienna took a deep breath, closing her eyes for a second. "I said—"

82.

Sienna

"—don't do it." I kept my Glock aimed at Brianna's back. She was partially turned away, her hand aimed right at Warrington's head. "He's not worth it."

Brianna just blinked at me, a few stray blond hairs having found their way into her eyes. "What are you talking about?"

"Warrington is scum," I said, trying to talk her back from the edge. "Listen to me, because I know this—killing him isn't going to solve anything. It won't bring back Emily. It won't even bring her justice." I swallowed. "And what it's going to do to you…it's not worth it."

Brianna laughed under her breath, soft and desperate. "How can you say that?"

"Because I know," I whispered. "This isn't the way. Listen, he's guilty of other things. Guilty as sin. Help me. Help me bring him to justice."

"There is no justice for him," Brianna whispered. "Not for a man like him. He's too powerful, too slippery. No one wants to go after him, not that way." Her hand steadied, and I saw the resolve appear on her face. "This is the only way."

"Please don't do this," I said, keeping my gun steady on her. "If you do this, I have to stop you." I felt a grinding pain inside as I said that.

She froze, staring at him. "Why?"

"Because there are laws for a reason," I said, my hand

sweating on the grip of my pistol. "And they're not just to protect him. We ignore them at our peril. If we just let everyone get their own justice…it starts a spiral where nobody trusts the system, and that way? Chaos lies at the bottom of that ladder. So…please. Don't. Do. This." And I steadied the front sight on her back.

She stayed utterly still for a long moment, and her hand wavered before joining her in stillness, aimed at his head. "I can't do that," she said, and I saw her tense before—

I stroked the trigger automatically, lighting her up with shot after shot. The bullets hit her in the back, peppering her in a three-inch space centered on the middle of her back. I fired ten times before she dropped, a puppet with her strings cut because I'd annihilated her spine with my shooting.

"Thank God," Warrington said into the silence that followed before my ears started to ring like sirens.

Brianna hit the ground face down and I was next to her in an instant. I rolled her over as she gasped, taking her last breaths. I knew the moment I rolled her over that my shooting was way too good, that there was no chance she was walking away from this.

She wasn't going to live more than another thirty seconds.

Her blue eyes found mine as I cradled her in my arms. I didn't say anything, because what could I say other than the vaguely stupid, "Why did you make me do this?" Hell, I knew why she did it. If I'd been her, I would have done it, too.

She looked up at me, and there was a hint of betrayal in her eyes as a thin line of blood slid out of her lips and down her chin. "I just did it the way you would have," she whispered over the ringing in my ears, and it was loud enough it might as well have been a thunderstorm.

I looked her in the eyes and felt like I'd been the one who'd had her heart shot out for a second. Drawing a hard breath, I looked at the betrayal on her face and said, "I know." I nodded. "I know."

Because what else was there to say?

I held her as she died, cursing myself and wondering if maybe, just maybe, I hadn't been here—hadn't been around at all, in fact—Brianna Glover's life might have turned out a lot different. A lot better.

But as I lay her still body down on the floor to the sound of the Louisiana State Police breaking down the ice floe blocking the hall outside, I didn't have any answers.

83.

Sifting through the mess of what happened wasn't a short process. When the state police made it inside and pulled Warrington out, everything started to follow the usual procedure after that: witness statements from me, Corcoran and Warrington (though he was pulled into a different room, probably under the assumption that keeping him away from all threats, including me, was safest).

Once they had those, I didn't even bother asking if I could leave, because I knew I couldn't. I just sat there, watching the morgue techs packing up Brianna Glover's body, wondering if I'd made the right choice.

Burkitt shouldered his way into the hotel room shortly thereafter, Holloway behind him. Burkitt's eyes were lidded with concern, but Holloway was just taking in the mess, scanning the room as they both crossed over to where I stood against the windows, watching the remaining ice slide off as it melted, a little at a time. I could almost see New Orleans through it now.

"Heard you saved the governor," Burkitt said, looking at the black body bag on the gurney. It was already closed and zipped, Brianna Glover's earthly remains probably set for just about the same end as her sister's—if Warrington's pet monkey had the gumption to claim them so the sisters could be buried together when Emily went back into the earth.

"Yep," I said without a single ounce of enthusiasm. It was hard to be excited over killing a would-be assassin who had a pretty good grievance against the person she was trying to kill.

"That's good work, Nealon," Holloway said, and, if possible, he sounded even less excited about it than I did.

"I guess," I said.

"You climbed a crane and jumped into a hotel to save the governor after he'd totally snubbed you," Burkitt said, nodding along. "You saved his life after he'd gotten you kicked off the case. That's dedication. Right, Holloway?"

"Huh? Oh, yeah," Holloway said, still lacking enthusiasm. "You done good."

"Yeah," I said, nodding along, "I killed a woman who hadn't killed anyone and saved the life of a man who confessed to sexually assaulting a thirteen-year-old right in front of me." I puckered my lips, feeling sour. "Yeah, I'm a real hero today. Someone give me a medal for my awesome work, because I totally deserve it."

Burkitt sagged. "I'm sure it doesn't feel that way, but we have a system for a reason. You know what happens when you let injustice answer injustice. I know it sucks, but..." He shrugged. "Maybe we can get Warrington on something else. Legitimately."

I looked over at Jenna Corcoran, who had been sitting on the bed quietly for the last half hour or so, once her statement was wrapped up, and was now looking at me, saying not a damned thing.

"What?" I asked her.

"I heard his confession," Corcoran said, and for the first time since I'd met her, she didn't sound stiff.

She sounded...haunted.

"Yeah," I said, almost whispering. I had a feeling this was going somewhere.

"I *heard*," she said, voice rising, her eyes squinted, some new fire burning in them. "Look, I've worked in politics a long time. I've seen some dirty things. Graft, people enriching themselves. But I've never heard of something like this." She shook her head. "You want him?" She swallowed, throat moving visibly. "I know a way you can get him. I'll give you..." She closed her eyes and shuddered. "I'll give you everything you need to put him away. Just...get me out of here."

I looked at Burkitt, whose eyes were wide, then Holloway, who was just a little cooler about it, then back to Corcoran.

"Okay," I said, rising. I reached in my pocket for my phone. "Come on. Let's find a room and we'll take your statement." I drew a breath as I looked at the black body bag one last time. "We'll get the ball rolling on this." I looked away. "Justice."

84.

Olivia

"Wowee," Augustus Coleman said, sauntering up to me at the scene of the capture, his brother only a couple steps behind him. I'd watched their car show up; the LVPD officer let them cross the police tape. "Looks like somebody had some fun."

I tried to decide if he meant me. "Uhm, no," I said. "There was no fun."

Jamal, quieter, took a look around for himself. "Well, it sure looks like someone got the job done. This was Veronika?"

The old me would have stuttered, would have blushed, would have made some apologetic statement of how I had been the one to actually—

No. Wait.

The old me wouldn't have beaten the bad guy.

"I did it," I said, and it came out somewhere between whispered and proud. "I beat her, uh, ass."

Augustus's eyebrows went up. Way up. "You did? Well done, Olivia."

"Yeah." Veronika's voice came from a little ways behind them as she ducked under police tape held up by another officer. Her face was still bandaged. "I wasn't even here for this, so don't go trying to give me credit." She sauntered past the Coleman brothers and over to me, glancing at the crater before smiling. "Looks like somebody had a coming-out party for her badass self."

I didn't know quite what to say to that. "Uhh…sort of…?"

"I think Veronika just means, in her own, inimitable way," Jamal said, "congrats on leveling up." He glanced at the crater. "Beating a speedster is big-league stuff. They're way up on the power scale." He eyed me. "Then again, I always figured maybe you were, too, if you could channel it right."

"I think I figured out how to do that," I said, flexing a hand. A few motes of desert sand had settled on my sleeve, and I puffed them off with a momentum surge.

The three of them watched, and Augustus nodded. "Well, all right then. Crossing up in my territory, I see how it is."

"Is Reed following you guys?" I asked. They'd already hauled off Sylvia, and I heard Crumley was being released even now, with the apologies of the LVPD. "He said he was on his way when I talked to him before."

"Nah, he turned back," Jamal said, "when he heard everything was wrapped up here. Vegas PD called him themselves to offer their thanks on the big collar. Though they weren't real clear on how it all came down. You probably should have called him yourself to let him know."

"I would have, but I kinda left my cell phone and wallet in the desert," I said, rubbing my shoulders. It wasn't cold anymore, but something about it felt reassuring. I smiled. "I've been kinda busy."

Veronika took another look around. In the distance, toward the Strip, I could see the top of the Bellagio, and its flame-scorched towers. She took it all in with a glance, and did a little nodding of her own. "You really have, kiddo." She smiled. "You really have been."

85.

Sienna

"Is there anything else?" I asked, sitting across from Jenna Corcoran in an empty hotel room, Burkitt and Holloway right over my shoulder. They were acting as witnesses, but we were all recording the whole thing on our phones. Mine was set up to do a streaming upload to the cloud, putting the entire thing on the FBI servers as the story left her lips.

She'd laid it all out for us, the school bill corruption project. It was a tangled web, one that involved construction rackets, contractors bidding on massive projects funded by state and federal money in exchange for kickbacks to Warrington and a dozen others—all under the guise of improving education for the poor.

And the sonofabitch I had just saved was making sure that he and his cronies got twenty percent off the top.

"I think that's everything," Corcoran said. She looked tired, but she'd been strong throughout.

"Good God," Holloway whispered behind me.

It wasn't quite my sentiments, which ran more in the direction of cursing the name of Ivan Warrington, but I didn't object. "This is a good start," I said, clicking off my recorder and pulling it from the table.

"Yeah," Burkitt said, pulling his and Holloway's from the table as well. "This will light a stick of dynamite under Warrington."

I glanced back at him. "You're not stuck here for questioning. Mind getting that back to your office and start the ball rolling on it?"

Burkitt nodded, handing Holloway's phone back to him. "I'll get right on it." He had a glint in his eyes. "It may take a while to unravel all this, but once it does…" He smiled. "Warrington will see the inside of a cell."

"Good," I said. But I didn't meet his gaze.

"I oughta go call Willis and tell him what we just found out," Holloway said, staring down at his phone like he held a bomb. He kind of did, really, with the recording on it. "He'll want to pass it up the chain."

"Yep," I said, stirring to look at him. "You do that. Tell him I'll call him as soon as the troopers clear me to…well, do anything."

He nodded and went out the door, leaving me alone with Jenna Corcoran, who had lapsed into silence, her eyes on the floor in quiet contemplation.

"This isn't going to be enough, is it?" I asked.

She stirred, then shook her head. "Probably not. I mean, the investigators will do their thing, and maybe they'll find enough actual evidence from Mitchell Werner's files, but maybe not. They could flip him, I guess. I don't know how your investigations work—"

"They move slow," I said. "And they'll move slower in this case, because they'll want to gather everything they can before tipping Warrington off that they're after him."

She shook her head. "He's already cleaning up all the messes after your conversation yesterday." She ran fingers through her hair, pulling it back into a ponytail and then realizing she didn't have anything to actually hold it with, so she turned it loose. "They're already moving to cover their tracks."

I closed my eyes. Well done, Sienna. Haste makes waste of investigations, and I had maybe made a waste of this one before it had even started.

That was okay. Or rather, it wasn't, but I had an idea how to blunt its impact as related to Warrington. "Would you be willing to talk to a reporter about everything you just went through with me? And everything you heard in that room when Warrington confessed?"

She looked me right in the eyes, and there was strength there. I didn't know what it was, but something had happened to Jenna Corcoran or someone she loved, something in the vein of Emily Glover's experience, and it had rung a loud bell in her head, one she didn't know how to quiet. "Yes," she said, without doubt.

"You know who Whit Falkner is?" I asked. She nodded. "She was working on the Emily Glover story but could never get a second source to confirm." I leaned in. "You heard the confession."

"So did you," Corcoran said.

I nodded. "But the FBI won't let me talk to reporters. Officially, anyway."

"And you just go along with that?" There was a definite hint of skepticism in how she asked me that question.

"For now," I said. "But you—you could lay all this out for her. Emily Glover. The school scam. Whit could really turn up the heat on Warrington, on Mitchell Werner, get the public eye on them so it'd be a lot harder for him to hide or destroy evidence."

She chuckled. "I don't think that's how it works, but...yeah. Maybe it'd even do some good." She looked down at her hands, kneading them together in her lap. She wiped them against her pant legs. "I'll talk to her."

"Good," I said as my phone buzzed. It was just a text message, a single line from Chalke:

Well done. You are cleared by the Louisiana State Police to leave and booked on the 8 pm to Laguardia. Return to base.

I stared at the simple words, and shook my head. Directive from the boss, and I had to step to it. A trooper appeared at the door, and said, "Ma'am?"

"Yeah," I said, and looked down at Jenna Corcoran. "You got this?"

She looked me dead in the eye. "I got this."

"Good," I said, and followed the trooper out.

86.

"There's a cab waiting for you downstairs," the trooper told me once we got out in the hall. The remains of the ice walls Brianna had made were still melting away in the corridor, their wetness staining the paint and causing the carpet to squish as I stepped through. The air had a strange absence of humidity in here. Which maybe wasn't so strange when I considered that Brianna had drawn it out to make those barriers both in here and outside.

The troopers lining the halls gave me polite nods as I passed. We were on the same side again by their reckoning, and I was forgiven and bygones forgotten. That was fine with me; they were doing their jobs, even if they were stuck protecting a loathsome human tick who fed on society's own blood. That wasn't their fault. It wasn't like Warrington had run on a platform of raping teenagers and stealing from poor kids.

He didn't show his face as I made my way to the elevator, which didn't surprise me. It would have actually shocked me if he had, because I expected I'd never be put in a position to look him in the eye ever again, by his own demand.

Or to touch him, which is what he probably feared more.

The elevator ride down was quiet, and the lobby was full of troopers and no one else. Crowds waited out on the sidewalk surrounding the glass lobby, held back by police tape and human decency, the bounds of a society that was still functioning.

I let that thought comfort me as the trooper led me into the portico, where a cab was waiting, alone, surrounded by local PD and Louisiana State Police cars. Another trooper was waiting with my suitcase, apparently packed for me. Hopefully they hadn't forgotten anything important. He slung it into the back of the cab as I got in, then shut the trunk.

The cabbie kept his back to me and rumbled off, passing a local cop in a yellow vest who waved us out into the back alley and on to Magazine Street. We passed the Ruby Slipper and the Bon Ton Cafe, where he slowed. He hadn't said a word since I'd gotten in, and that was fine by me.

Then he pulled into the curb right next to the Bon Ton, and I frowned. I opened my mouth to ask him what he was doing when someone walked up to the door and opened it, sliding it right next to me as I watched with a jaded eye.

"Hey," I said to Michelle as she wiped a little sheen of sweat off her forehead. "How was yoga class?"

She exhaled swiftly. "Punishing. How was your final confrontation with Warrington?"

I eyed the cabbie, who had yet to turn around or say anything.

Michelle watched me looking at him. "Oh, don't worry. I own the company. He's one of mine."

"And he just happened to pick me up?" I gave her a little side-eye.

"Of course not," she said with a smile. "I volunteered our services to the police in this time of crisis. Anything we can do to help, you know. That's the mark of a community-minded, going-legit company. So here you are, and my question remains—how'd it go?"

"Warrington confessed," I said. "In case you didn't know."

"To Emily?" she asked, breath catching in her throat.

"Yeah," I said. "Jenna Corcoran heard, and it sent her over the edge. She's going to talk to Whit Falkner."

Michelle looked straight ahead, smile fading. "Good. For whatever it's worth…good. At least it'll finally be out there."

"How much of a splash will it make, though?" I asked.

"I don't know," Michelle said, looking out the window. "Depends on how much the local media wants to cover it. They like Warrington."

"Enough to cover up allegations of child rape?"

"I don't know." She looked like she had to fight with that answer. "I hope not."

"What about in the realm of politics?" I asked.

"I think he can count on some stinging condemnation in the legislature," she said. "He has enemies, and they won't hesitate to bludgeon him with the allegations every chance they get. They'll try to make hay of it, but whether it sticks has a lot to do with how much circulation any of Whit's stories get. If she ends up being the lone voice, crying in the wilderness..." Michelle shrugged.

"The story dies in silence," I said, nodding along.

"Is she going to talk about the school bill corruption?" Michelle asked.

I warred with myself before answering, and finally decided saying nothing was maybe the best answer of all.

Michelle just watched me for a second, then nodded. "Just as well."

I gave her another good eyeballing. "'Just as well'? Didn't you tell me you had a piece of that?"

She shrugged. "Like I told you, I'm trying to take this thing legit. It's a process, though. I don't have much of the school thing, mostly on the construction side, and if it goes down, that sucks, but I'll live. I'm not directly involved, and it'll lop off a tentacle of my business I wasn't sure what to do with anyway." She smiled just a little. "And if I get hit, no one will think for a second I gave any of this to you, because why would I be that crazy?"

"Good cover."

"Exactly," she said as the cab slowed just before a freeway onramp. "Well, this is where I leave you, Nealon."

"Thanks, Michelle," I said, mostly sure I meant it. "And about Corcoran—"

"I'll have people keeping an eye on her," Michelle said, opening the door. "But I wouldn't worry about Warrington going after her that way." She stepped out onto the pavement. "It's a lot more likely he's going to come after her reputation, so that these stories have even less impact." She held the door open and leaned down. "He doesn't have to literally kill the messenger in order to silence her, after all. That's Werner's specialty. Character assassination. Muddy her up enough, no one wants to listen to what she has to say. And that…well, it's something the media is more than open to participating in because it's a much more interesting story than some intricate, arcane follow-the-money piece about school corruption."

With a final, melancholy smile, she shut the door and the cab pulled away, and I looked back to see the yoga-pants-wearing Triad boss watching me go and waving.

87.

Holloway caught up to me at the gate about twenty minutes before boarding started. He looked like he'd been run through the ringer, and I was about to ask him what had happened when he answered.

"Willis caught hell from Director Chalke on the corruption thing we turned up," he said, plopping down next to me. Maybe it was a mark of me being weak, but I didn't tell him to move his ass down a chair. Whatever. If he got handsy again, which seemed unlikely at this point, I could always knock his ass into the middle of next week.

"I had a feeling she wasn't going to be pleased about that," I said. "What's the status of the investigation?"

"It's in the hands of Burkitt and the local boys," Holloway said, shaking his head. He ran fingers through his dark hair. "My guess? It'll die quietly. Warrington's too connected in DC."

"I had a feeling you'd say that." I looked down at my phone. It had been silent since Chalke's message to me back at the hotel, so at least she wasn't looking to tear into my ass about this. For whatever reason.

"Look, you did the right thing," Holloway said, lowering his head like a bull as he sat next to me. "If the brass doesn't want to pursue it, well…that's on them."

"I guess," I said. But my actual guess was that Whit Falkner's stories would force them to at least look into it, for as long as whatever heat she generated lasted. Maybe Warrington's opposition in the state would be able to whip up a genuine, long, hard look into his dealings. I doubted there was much hope for it, otherwise, but that was the idea behind a free press—to keep the pressure on the powerful, to keep an eye on them and their dealings.

The sun had set outside the large glass airport windows. I'd killed a whole day talking to cops and interviewing Corcoran, then riding to the airport and sitting around here.

I was feeling it, too, that drag at the eyelids. It had been an early morning, after all, and the day hadn't gotten any easier from there. I let out a yawn, thinking maybe it'd be nice to sleep on the flight home. Or "home," rather, since I was heading to New York.

"We good?" Holloway asked, kind of out of nowhere.

I looked at him like he was an idiot. "We're all right, I guess," I said, not really sure. I didn't hate him anymore, but I didn't exactly like him, either.

"Good," he said, uneasily, settling back in his seat. I don't think he quite bought it, but he settled his gaze on the TV, and nodded at it. "What's up in Vegas?"

I looked up at the TV for the first time since sitting down. The coverage was of some meta disaster on the Strip that had apparently been settled. They flashed to a shot of Olivia Brackett standing behind police tape, looking a little disheveled as she leaned on a cop car, arms folded in front of her. She looked strong, confident—like a different person, really, than the one I'd seen in my dreamwalk only last night.

"That one of your brother's crew?" Holloway asked, watching the TV.

"Hell if I know," I lied. "He and I don't really talk anymore."

Holloway arched his eyebrows at me. "Oh? Why's that?"

"I don't think he much likes that I work for the government," I said, using a well-rehearsed line that was totally true. Thankfully, Holloway didn't ask anything more, just nodded as he watched the TV as we waited for our flight to be called.

88.

Warrington

Ivan Warrington woke in a cold sweat.

They'd moved him to the 17th floor but kept him here, in the Hotel Fantaisie, after it had all shaken out. Brianna Glover was dead, after all; he'd checked her pulse himself once she was wheeled out into the hallway just to be sure.

He hadn't expected he'd be able to fall asleep, not after today, but he had, and now he woke, sweating, slow panic working its way through his limbic system as a calm fell over him.

He'd spoken the truth aloud.

They'd heard him.

Nothing was going to be the same anymore.

Warrington shifted the covers, sliding his legs out from beneath the sheets. The air conditioner hummed in the background, and someone coughed out in the hallway. At least two troopers were on his door, standing just outside, in case someone tried anything.

No one would try anything. Brianna Glover was dead.

She'd failed.

Warrington mopped his brow and bald head with the white covers. He'd been sleeping, but a feeling of creeping panic had followed him out, and one thought had kept him tossing until he woke.

It's all over.

"Shouldn't have said anything," he muttered under his breath, rising on unsteady legs. This room was smaller than the suite; easier for the troopers to storm in if anything went awry. "That was my mistake." He brushed his hand over his smooth, damp forehead, and his eyes settled on the window in front of him, open on a view of New Orleans.

He stood and sauntered over to the windows. Down there was the Algiers Ferry. He stared at it. Had it really only been two days ago when Brianna Glover had taken her first shot at him? And missed?

He thought about it all again, and that same idea kept coming back: *It's all over.*

And maybe, just maybe, it would have been better if she'd gotten him then.

After all, there wouldn't have been any of this running around. None of this foolishness, the pulse-pounding stress of trying to manage his schedule while all this was going on. It would have been easier.

I could have gone out on top, not…like this.

He could see it now. It'd be death by a thousand vulture pecks. They'd take him piece by piece.

The Algiers Ferry was right down there, though. He'd gotten it open again for free. That was something.

Maybe, if he did it this way, instead of letting them draw it out, they'd speak kindly of him, the way one did at funerals, rather than pick at his bones for the next five years the way you did with something that was dying on the side of the road.

It's all over.

Yeah. That was it.

Warrington grabbed the desk chair and ran it into the window. The glass shattered and flew out like a thousand sparkling diamonds into the night. He heard the troopers hit the door as he followed it out, flying off into the night—

Down sixteen floors to the pavement, where the last thought that went through his skull before it ceased being a skull and became a puddle of mush instead, was:

It's all over.

And he was right.

89.

Sienna

I woke to Holloway gently shaking my shoulder, out of a deep grog as the plane rattled on a slow turn. I looked out the window to see runway lights just outside, and smacked my dry lips together. I must have slept through the whole flight.

"Sorry," Holloway said, lighting up his cell phone and turning it off airplane mode. "Didn't figure you'd want to sleep here when you could get off and head home."

I pulled at my neck, which ached slightly from the angle at which I'd had it crammed against the bulkhead. "Good call. I—"

Holloway frowned as his phone buzzed. It looked like fifty text messages rolled in at once, and he opened them immediately. When he did, he paled a couple shades.

"What?" I asked, stretching my neck.

He shook his head. "Looks like Warrington took the easy way out. Did a nosedive out the Hotel Fantaisie's 17th floor window while we were in flight." He let out a low whistle. "They're scraping him off the pavement now." He glanced at me. "Guess they'll be putting him in the morgue right next to Brianna Glover."

"Huh." I wasn't sure how I should respond to that. "I suppose that's justice," was all I could think of to say.

90.

Olivia

I got a little sleep on the plane back to Minneapolis, between Augustus and Jamal bickering about some videogame or another. It was not much of a trial to leave them at the terminal at MSP airport, catching an Uber to the office and arriving so late that I was sure no one would still be there.

I was wrong.

"Hey," Tracy said as I walked into the bullpen. He was huddled over his desk, but looked up at me through squinting eyes, his big frame comically bent as he stared at his computer screen. "You made it back."

"Yeah," I said, pausing before I willed myself to move again. I headed for my desk, cool chill running over my skin, which felt suddenly hot. "Why are you here so late?"

"Boss man's still in, so I'm in," Tracy said, pointing at Reed's door. Sure enough, there Reed was, staring at something on his desk, his head bent over a sheaf of papers, long hair dangling on either side to block his face.

I paused, thinking about it for only a second before I altered my course and headed for the door. I knocked, and a moment later Reed looked up, smiled through the blinds and said, "Come in."

Shutting the door behind me, I stepped up to his desk. "Got it done, boss," I said, feeling like that was more telling than any report I could write. Though I'd still have to write one.

Which is what I'd come here to do.

"I heard," he said, arms folded over his chest, nodding in slow, quiet respect. I hadn't seen the look on his face before, at least not aimed at me. "Jamal and Augustus talked to the local cops. They say you really turned some heads out there, bringing this meta down with minimal collateral damage."

"Minimal?" I blinked. "I thought everyone was mad at me for the Fremont Street mess and the bar in—"

Reed shook his head. "Collateral damage is part of metahuman policing, especially when you're dealing with people who have this much power. Vegas PD are familiar with it, and no matter what their politicians say, they still have a keen memory of what metas out of control can do." He looked pained for a second, adjusting in his chair. "It was only a couple years ago that Sienna got into a rumble with some crooks on the Strip who almost burned down Aria, so I don't think they're much bothered by a small structural fire in the Bellagio and a little damage to the bar at the Venetian. Speedsters can do a lot of damage, and police officers talk across state lines. Vegas PD know they got off light on this one—thanks to you."

"Oh," I said. "Uh. Well. Good. Though…I couldn't have done it without your sister's advice." I hung my head.

"Yeah, so?" Reed asked. "*You* still did it."

I blinked and looked up. "Well, but—"

"You think getting advice invalidates the action?" Reed smirked. "Come on. You did it. She may have pushed you in a certain direction, just like I'm sure Veronika did, but you were the one who stepped up and knocked out that speedster. And it was a good thing you did, by the by." He moved aside the papers he'd been looking at and picked up another page, holding it out across the desk at me. "Check this out. They found it when they raided an alternate property this Sylvia owned."

I took the paper and looked at it. It was a typewritten report with a black and white picture printed at the bottom of what looked like a giant bomb.

"Gulp," I said.

"Yeah," Reed said, taking it back from my limp fingers. "So

I don't think Vegas is going to be complaining about minor damages, since that thing would have leveled about ten blocks."

"Really dodged a bullet there, I guess," I said, blinking myself out of that train of thought. A bomb? A massive bomb, in the hands of a lady who repeatedly proclaimed a desire for chaos?

I felt a little faint and caught myself on the edge of Reed's desk, head lurching down. I shook my head, my eyes alighting on the papers he'd been studying when I came in. The headline caught my attention.

RECOMMENDED LAYOFFS

I read on, into a list.

Friday

Scott Byerly

Chase Blanton

Greg Vansen

Veronika Acheron

Katrina Forrest

Taneshia French

Abigail Garner

Olivia Brackett

I stopped when I saw my own. I met Reed's eyes as I looked up, and saw the guilt burning in his.

"You weren't supposed to see that," Reed said, and he sounded like he'd been caught doing something really dirty. "It's not final—"

"Tracy's name's not here," I said, finishing it to the end. "Who are you keeping?" I looked up. "Are you even keeping anyone?"

"Jamal, Augustus, Angel, myself," Reed said, sounding pained. "Though at a vastly reduced pay rate for all three of us. Scott Byerly's staying on, he's just not getting paid. Same with Kat Forrest. She makes enough through her TV show, and working here generates enough storylines for her that not getting paid doesn't bother her. Everybody else…" He shook his head. "But yeah. I'm keeping Tracy because Tracy works for peanuts."

I didn't know how to take that. The old me would have just

sort of nodded, gone along.

"To hell with that," I said, loud enough that Reed blinked, eyes widening, as I looked up with him. "You know how you came to me before you pulled Tracy out of the cloud? When you were desperate for help to get Sienna out of Scotland? I acted like it was fine. Because I really wanted it to be fine, wanted to be the kind of person that could just put the past behind me and be fine with it—with him."

My mouth felt dry and I shook my head. "I lied. It wasn't fine. I wasn't fine with it at all. I should have told you that then, that it wasn't fine, that it would never be fine working with him, working with the man who—" I closed my eyes, stopping myself in the middle of what was fast turning into an epic rant.

Reed was quiet for a long moment. "I'm sorry."

"It was desperate times, I know," I said. "I should have spoken up when he stayed on afterward. I didn't know how to. So…maybe it's a good thing that he's staying and I'm going—"

"You don't have to go," Reed said quietly.

I glanced up at him. "What?"

"These are recommendations from an outside accounting firm," he said. "Based on the last two years of data. They look at how much we pay versus how many cases people clear. Jamal and Augustus? They churn through them, kicking ass all the way. Same with Angel. Same with Veronika, honestly, but she gets paid more than anyone else. Greg Vansen is way up there, too, so those two were the first to get cut because they're just too expensive. Tracy was at the bottom of the list because he works for almost nothing." Reed looked a little embarrassed. "Because he's still traumatized and brainwashed to follow me like a dog, I assume. But what you did in Vegas…" He picked up the list and waved it. "You changed this. You're a major player now, if you do what you did in Vegas from now on. You could be the future of this agency, so…" He looked right at me. "You can stay, if you want. And Tracy can go."

It was funny how quick I knew my answer. "Okay," I said. "I'll stay."

Reed smiled. "Good. You should probably get some sleep, though, because tomorrow…" He looked at the list in his hand. "Well…this happens tomorrow. So…" His smile turned bittersweet and lost some of its luster. "There's not going to be a lot of rest around here after that."

"That's okay," I said, and meant it. "I feel like I've rested enough this last few months. You took it easy on me to start out with, and…now I'm ready for more. A lot more, I think. So…" I opened his office door. "See you tomorrow, boss."

"Thanks," Reed said, his smile fading. "And, uh…would you mind sending Tracy in when you go? Since he's here?" He looked down at the list again. "No point in circling this any longer than I have to."

I thought about what was going to happen, and I felt a little twinge of pity for Tracy, which surprised me. "Sure," I said, a little hoarsely, as I left his office.

Tracy was looking at me down the cubicle row as I stepped out. He waited for me to get close to my desk and asked, "How'd it go?"

"Good," I said, a little stilted as I looked at him. He was so different from how he'd been when he'd tormented me. He used to be bald, big, like a bodybuilder. His time in Reed's prison had left him scrawny, and there were perpetual dark circles under his eyes, with a hint of twitchiness always in him.

That I could relate to, even if I could barely stand to be around him.

And I really did feel sorry for him.

"The boss wants to see you about something," I said, picking up my suitcase and wheeling it toward the door.

"Oh, okay," Tracy said, hopped right up. "See you tomorrow." And he headed toward Reed's office without waiting to hear me respond.

I watched him go, then turned away as he went in. Reed's head was already down, and I didn't want to see this happen, so I turned and wheeled my suitcase out. The rattle of the wheels covered the sounds of their conversation until I was out of earshot, and I walked out of the office with my head held high, maybe for the first time since I'd started working there.

91.

Sienna

It was the next day, and I found myself sitting in Dr. Kashani's office again, making up for playing hooky and dealing with that bank robbery of a few days prior. I stared at the walls, the windows, the chairs, each in turn, assiduously avoiding Dr. Kashani's eyes on me until I could ignore her no more.

"So…" she said, after I'd covered a brief summary of what had happened in New Orleans, with a heavy emphasis on how I *felt* about it, since that was apparently all she cared about, "what do you believe?"

"What do I believe?" I chewed on the words experimentally as I parroted them back to her, trying to give real, sincere thought to what she was driving at here.

"You went through this whole case protecting a very bad man," Dr. Kashani said. "Do you believe killing this Brianna Glover was the right thing to do?"

"There are gradations of 'right,'" I said tepidly.

"But was what you did 'right'?" she asked. "To any degree?"

"Yes," I said, "I believe it was. To some degree."

"Would you mind explaining your feelings about this—"

I moaned, making a noise that would do a teenager proud, complete with eyeroll. "Fine," I said. "You want it? Here we go. Here's what I believe." I sat up on the couch and stared right at her. "I believe there are evil people in this world. You can define it however you want, slice it however you want—

call it lack of empathy, call it total lack of attunement to the cares and survival of others in favor of your own wants and desire, but whatever you want to call it, it's out there. It's malevolent, it's horrifying, and while there may be less of it these days than could have been found a hundred years ago, what of it there is? It's as strong as ever. I've watched people try and scourge the earth to remove it, try to eliminate free will to get rid of it, to blunt its impact once they got a good taste of it directed at them. And I saw it, this viciousness, looked it right in the eye this week in New Orleans." I sat back in my seat, arms folded over my chest. "In the face of the damned governor, no less."

"That's a power attitudinal driver," Dr. Kashani said, her eyes warm, voice soft. "How does it make you feel, knowing that evil, as you call it, is out there?"

"Like I have a certain amount of job security," I said, flippant to the last.

Dr. Kashani shuffled her papers and smiled. "That's an easy answer."

"It's sort of true, though," I said, looking down at my arms, like a wall in front of me. "You know what the worst part is, though? It's watching someone like Brianna Glover get a taste of evil and react like I did…except not get away with it." I looked up at the doctor. "I killed my Warringtons. Killed the people who took from me. If there'd been a Sienna Nealon in my path…well, hell, I probably would have gotten shot down like a dog, too, because no way was I letting go of that bone." A little wet spot formed in the corner of my eye. "I have a cold hate for people who do evil things. It has built and burned and now it just seethes and radiates and freezes everything it touches."

"Who is it aimed at?" Dr. Kashani asked quietly.

I looked her right in the eye. "Whoever I catch doing wrong that week. And I'm trying to hold it in, like with Warrington, trying to find the way to move within the system so I don't just burn it all down myself. But it's…so hard." I let my anger out in a puff with the last word. "So hard. Because the dark thought I carry with me all the time? I could do it, you know?"

Dr. Kashani stared at me blankly. "Do what?"

"Absorb a hundred metas. A thousand metas, all their powers," I said. "Become a god…dess. Loom large over this world, judging everyone for their wrongs. If I wanted to, I could wipe out this evil I see, everywhere I see it. Become the great arbiter of all things for humanity."

There was a slight edge of worry in her voice. "Why not, then?"

"Because no one is good enough to judge like that," I said, "least of all me. I've done terrible things. Arguably evil things. So I act small. Locally, if you will. Go after the Warringtons of the world where I stumble on them. You want to know what I believe? I want to believe in a system that keeps *anyone* from being that grand judge. Because I'm not a goddess and no one should be. Not one of us is good enough to rule the rest." I shook my head. "All I want to do is fix the little wrongs I see, remove the corruptions, and leave the rest to a system where people can just try and carve out their own happiness, knowing it won't always work out. I want to put a check on power, on the worst offenders, so the system can work without them blocking everything up and making things horrible. Because to try and turn it all over and start anew?" I shook my head. "That way lies misery. Chaos."

She was quiet for a moment, but her last question? Killer.

"What if you can't?" Her voice was almost a whisper. "What if they're too powerful, the forces that try and take over parts of the system for themselves? What if you can't stop them?"

I had to think about that for a while before I came up with an answer. "Well," I said at last, "then I guess maybe I'll have to re-evaluate whether me being the goddess that looms over the world is better or worse than having someone else do it."

I don't think that was the answer she was looking for. And hell, it didn't satisfy me, either.

92.

Jamie Chapman
San Jose, California

It was night, and the 1337 cafe was still buzzing.

Jamie Chapman didn't do much coding himself these days. He had people to do it for him, after all, being the owner of Socialite, the most widely used social network on the planet, but every once in a while…

He really liked to get back to his roots.

So here he was, a Venti Soy mocha at hand, and nothing but code in front of him, doing just that. He'd been at it for almost six hours, eyes blurred from looking at the screen, tiredness creeping in as he tried to solve a very particular problem. He was getting close, he could feel it. He focused all his attention, all his thought on it. Maybe if he…

His phone buzzed.

He ignored it. At first.

Then it went again. Hadn't he disabled notifications?

It went a third time, just as he was narrowing down the problem…

Chapman fished into his cargo shorts and came up with the offending phone. He had muted the notifications, he could see that plainly, but…

The Escapade app had sent one anyway. As it should have.

It's time to play!

Taking a moment to glance to his left, then his right, he

found the seats vacant. The place was busy, but his back was to the wall and he was in as private a situation as he was going to get without leaving, and he'd vowed to stay until he worked out this damned problem. He slid the app and pressed his thumb to the biometric reader.

The phone unlocked and the Escapade app opened, the text bar unrolling right in the middle of a conversation.

HEATHER CHALKE: She saved Warrington's life, but the dirt came out anyway. He jumped out a damned window, so now he's dead.

RUSS BILSON: I contacted her like you suggested, talked her through some of the politics going on there. I didn't think she'd be able to turn it into anything.

HEATHER CHALKE: She didn't exactly spin straw into gold. Warrington gave her plenty to work with, was playing dirty. But he was on our side, and helping advance the "Gondry" agenda in Louisiana, so it's a blow to lose him.

Chapman frowned at all this. He hadn't caught the news today, and he had little care about what happened in Louisiana. Any consideration of saying anything went by the wayside when he realized he didn't have a dog in this fight, certainly not enough of an investment in Louisiana politics to put his valuable and waning mental energy into responding.

MORRIS JOHANNSEN: To my eyes, this looks like a local story. I can't imagine national publications wanted to delve much into this.

HEATHER CHALKE: Good. Warrington's dead; better to just let it go down quietly, and whatever comes out, let it come out in the Louisiana press.

DAVE KORY: That should be simple. Like Johannsen says, it's a local thing. I won't cover it on Flashforce, and none of my reporters will, either. I'll kill any story they try and post.

Let it live and die in the Louisiana swamps, lol.

Chapman had another frown for this. If he'd learned anything from running the largest social network on the planet, it was that things that went big in a locality tended not to necessarily stay in that locality. He was debating how much he should say about all this when someone else spoke up and took the conversation a different direction.

TYRUS FLANAGAN: How much did Nealon have to do with this disaster?

HEATHER CHALKE: She unearthed the dirty parts. The child rape, though that might have come out anyway given the assassin gunning for Warrington was the sister. Any other cop probably would have gunned her down before it could all come out, but maybe not. Nealon got her in the end, though. She also came up with the school corruption business, though how that will play out, especially now that Warrington is dead—again, that's more on you guys than me. We'll investigate it up to a point, but I'm going to try and keep it local business rather than let it leak out onto the national stage.

DAVE KORY: Should be easy to keep it down.

MORRIS JOHANNSEN: I won't cover it in my paper, or give it any signal boost.

Here, Chapman felt he really did have to weigh in. These people were tiptoeing past the graveyard in his view.

JAIME CHAPMAN: I don't care how much you want to sit on this, if the local press covers it well enough, it has the potential to break out from the political opposition covering it and sharing it on social media. You might think you can deny it oxygen, but how many times have you guys thought you could suffocate a story, like, say, Sienna Nealon's innocence video, only to have it go viral and bite us all in the ass? Don't overestimate your ability to kill the truth here. If Warrington's dirty and you think it hurts us somehow, let's get out in front of it. Distance ourselves from him and/or the cause. Have Bilson get his political consultants on it and counter it before it becomes something.

Nobody typed anything for a couple minutes, and Chapman was about ready to put the phone down and get back to coding when someone finally broke the virtual silence.

HEATHER CHALKE: How about you suppress the virality of the thing this time instead of letting it blow up on us?

Chapman's cheeks felt hot, and he composed three replies in anger before settling on a more neutral one.

JAIME CHAPMAN: Look, you can't control the flow of information through the press anymore, if you ever could. And I can have my engineers suppress it, but I'm hardly the only game in town.

BILSON: I've had some preliminary discussions with the guys over at Inquest, the search engine? I think they're good candidates to join us at some point. And they probably have just as much influence over the flow of information as Jaime. Maybe between all of them and some of their other friends out in Silicon Valley, we could start to come up with a solution to problems like that?

Chapman steamed, going between looking at his phone and his laptop. The coding problem called out to him, but these idiots talking on his phone needed answering, too.

HEATHER CHALKE: We have months to deal with this, and it's probably not even that big of a problem. I just want it contained so it doesn't go any farther than Warrington. Let it get buried with him.

Chapman typed his reply slowly, trying to dispense with the white-hot rage he'd felt upon her initial suggestion.

CHAPMAN: Sure. We can talk to Inquest. Between us, we can cover a decent portion of the net. And maybe, yeah, we could rattle some other trees, see what shakes out.

That would be kind of a cool expansion of theoretical power, being able to exercise that much control over so much of the internet.

RUSS BILSON: Great. Let's work on our respective projects and catch up when we have something to report. Later.

Chapman was the first to log off, tossing his phone onto the table in front of him. The lines of code on the screen were blurring, and he couldn't tell if it was because of rage at all the stupid permeating that conversation, or just simple tiredness. Probably both, he conceded, yawning as he put his face in his hand—just for a second.

"Is this seat taken?"

Jaime pulled his face out of his hand, blinking his eyes blearily as someone stood over his shoulder. The voice had been soft, delicate, but to the point, jarring him out of his momentary reverie.

"What?" Jaime looked at the chair next to him. "Oh. No, it's all yours." He glanced back at his screen, still blurring his eyes. He wiped at them, trying to figure out if they were just tired from the day of meetings that started at 6 a.m. Eastern time, or whether they were dry enough to be tearing up. He looked at the clock in the corner of his screen:

12 a.m.

"Damn," he muttered, looking at the person who'd just sat down next to him. "Is it really midnight?" he asked before he'd fully taken her in.

Then…he was a little sorry he'd asked such a stupid, obvious question.

She was a knockout, to say the least. She was tall, willowy. Her glasses were thick-framed and black like her raven-colored hair, which was up in a bun. She was freckled and tall, thin arms slightly tanned. Her blue eyes were bright and intense, and her nose had a tiny piercing in the left nostril.

Plus her focus was entirely on the computer screen in front of her, where a window was open and her hands flew over the keyboard, spilling out lines of code onto the page.

She didn't look up as she answered. "Yeah. I do my best work after midnight."

"Yeah," Jaime said, looking back at his screen. "I used to."

"Used to?" She still didn't look up. "Seems like you're still at it."

"That's true," Jaime said, wiping his eyes again. It didn't help. "But I don't think this is my best work anymore. That might have come a few hours ago. I'm starting to think it's a young person's game."

"Well, you do run a company," she said, a little trace of a smile sneaking out as her fingers flew across the keyboard. She was good; he could see it by how fast she put things together. "Maybe leave the coding to the little people like me?"

Jaime shifted in his seat. "Oh. You know who I am."

"Everybody in Silicon Valley knows who you are," she said, not stopping for a second. Damn, she was good.

"Yeah, but not many people would choose to sit next to me at a coffee house," Jaime said. "At least not without pitching me some VC deal or mobile app they want to build or—"

"There weren't any other seats," she said, waving at the cafe around them.

Jaime blinked. That, he could see clearly, now that he looked. "What's your name?"

"Gwen Summers," she said, pausing for a second like she was suffering for taking the break. She cracked her knuckles.

"Do you work for me?" he asked.

She shook her head. "I used to be at Amazon, but I've been independent for a while…working on my own app, actually." She grinned, and it was…wow. "But I've got all the VC money I need for now, so I don't really need to pitch you, even though this seat was open."

"What's your app do?" he asked.

"You know, if you keep asking me these questions, people are going to keep pitching you every time they see the seat next to you vacant," she said, still with that impish smile.

"They're going to pitch me anyway," he said, matching hers

with one of his own. "It's Silicon Valley."

She laughed. "That's true. I'm kinda new here, so I don't really know all the ins and outs and protocol yet."

"Where'd you move from?" he asked, leaning just a little closer.

"Seattle," she said. "Been there for about five years. But everyone kept saying that Silicon Valley's the place to be for what I was trying to do, so…" She smiled. "Here I am."

"An app developer and new in town, come to pursue her dreams?" Chapman felt himself chuckling. "Wow. That's…"

"A cliché, right?" Gwen laughed. "I know. But here I am anyway."

"Welcome to town," Jaime said, smiling. "I think you'll do just fine here."

"Thanks, Mr. Chapman—" she started.

"Call me Jaime."

That smile turned impish again, and boy, did he like that. "Thanks…Jaime."

93.

Sienna

I came in from my morning run around Central Park just before 6 a.m. and hit the showers. The apartment was quiet, and I was sweating like a fiend even though the air was considerably colder than what I'd been dealing with in Louisiana.

It was back to the routine, back to doing the job—back to preparing myself for trouble, not knowing where the next case would come from or when it would hit.

I'd be ready, though.

I always was.

The hot shower felt like a million bucks, and was made better by the coffee cup I left sitting just outside the curtain. I let the water pour over me for a while, taking infrequent sips and then letting the scorching heat roll over my skin as I sat in this tight space, confined by the white subway tile on one side and the shower curtain on the other, enjoying the pleasant drumming of water against my scalp for about an hour before I turned it off, my coffee long since drained, much like the time I had remaining to get ready before going in to the office.

When I stepped out of the shower, towel wrapped around me, I paused to look at the mirror. It was all fogged up, of course, and a thin scrawl was traced in the fog. I stared at it like I was looking at myself, hoping that if there were any cameras in here—and it was possible there were—they were fogged up, too.

Two words were written in the fog.

Julie Blair

"Who are you?" I asked, meta-low, committing the name to memory. Julie Blair. I said it in my head again as I wiped the mirror.

My face stared back for just a moment before it fogged back over, and all I could see was a smile. Then, so quietly that I knew no one could hear me, with the possible exception of the man watching me, across time and distance, I whispered, meta-low:

"Thank you, Harry."

Then I set about getting ready for my day, wondering, all the while, who Julie Blair was and why she was important to me.

And equally certain that eventually…I was going to find out.

Sienna Nealon will return in

BLOOD TIES

OUT OF THE BOX

Book 25

Coming May 15th, 2019!

Author's Note

Thanks for reading! If you want to know immediately when future books become available, take sixty seconds and sign up for my NEW RELEASE EMAIL ALERTS by visiting my website. I don't sell your information and I only send out emails when I have a new book out. The reason you should sign up for this is because I don't always set release dates, and even if you're following me on Facebook (robertJcrane (Author)) or Twitter (@robertJcrane), it's easy to miss my book announcements because...well, because social media is an imprecise thing.

Come join the discussion on my website:
http://www.robertjcrane.com!

Cheers,
Robert J. Crane

ACKNOWLEDGMENTS

First things first – thanks to Lewis Moore, Jeff Bryan and Nick (https://nickbowman-editing.com) for editing and proofing. Thanks also to Karri Klawiter of artbykarri.com for the wonderful cover, as per usual.

Thanks to Sharyl Atkisson for writing her amazing book, The Smear. Lots of what it elucidates involving politics and the smear machine made its way into this story in simplified form to explain the dealings of Governor Warrington and Mitchell Werner. It's an eye-opener of a book and I highly recommend it.

And finally, thanks to my wife and kids, parents and in-laws, for keeping things running around here. Or just for running around here, in the case of the kids.

Other Works by Robert J. Crane

The Girl in the Box *and* Out of the Box

Contemporary Urban Fantasy

Alone: The Girl in the Box, Book 1
Untouched: The Girl in the Box, Book 2
Soulless: The Girl in the Box, Book 3
Family: The Girl in the Box, Book 4
Omega: The Girl in the Box, Book 5
Broken: The Girl in the Box, Book 6
Enemies: The Girl in the Box, Book 7
Legacy: The Girl in the Box, Book 8
Destiny: The Girl in the Box, Book 9
Power: The Girl in the Box, Book 10

Limitless: Out of the Box, Book 1
In the Wind: Out of the Box, Book 2
Ruthless: Out of the Box, Book 3
Grounded: Out of the Box, Book 4
Tormented: Out of the Box, Book 5
Vengeful: Out of the Box, Book 6
Sea Change: Out of the Box, Book 7
Painkiller: Out of the Box, Book 8
Masks: Out of the Box, Book 9
Prisoners: Out of the Box, Book 10
Unyielding: Out of the Box, Book 11
Hollow: Out of the Box, Book 12
Toxicity: Out of the Box, Book 13
Small Things: Out of the Box, Book 14
Hunters: Out of the Box, Book 15
Badder: Out of the Box, Book 16
Apex: Out of the Box, Book 18
Time: Out of the Box, Book 19
Driven: Out of the Box, Book 20
Remember: Out of the Box, Book 21
Hero: Out of the Box, Book 22
Flashback: Out of the Box, Book 23
Cold: Out of the Box, Book 24
Blood Ties Out of the Box, Book 25* *(Coming May 15, 2019!)*

World of Sanctuary

Epic Fantasy

Defender: The Sanctuary Series, Volume One
Avenger: The Sanctuary Series, Volume Two
Champion: The Sanctuary Series, Volume Three
Crusader: The Sanctuary Series, Volume Four
Sanctuary Tales, Volume One - A Short Story Collection
Thy Father's Shadow: The Sanctuary Series, Volume 4.5
Master: The Sanctuary Series, Volume Five
Fated in Darkness: The Sanctuary Series, Volume 5.5
Warlord: The Sanctuary Series, Volume Six
Heretic: The Sanctuary Series, Volume Seven
Legend: The Sanctuary Series, Volume Eight
Ghosts of Sanctuary: The Sanctuary Series, Volume Nine
Call of the Hero: The Sanctuary Series, Volume Ten* *(Coming in 2019!)*

A Haven in Ash: Ashes of Luukessia, Volume One *(with Michael Winstone)*
A Respite From Storms: Ashes of Luukessia, Volume Two *(with Michael Winstone)*
A Home in the Hills: Ashes of Luukessia, Volume Three *(with Michael Winstone)*

Southern Watch

Contemporary Urban Fantasy

Called: Southern Watch, Book 1
Depths: Southern Watch, Book 2
Corrupted: Southern Watch, Book 3
Unearthed: Southern Watch, Book 4
Legion: Southern Watch, Book 5
Starling: Southern Watch, Book 6
Forsaken: Southern Watch, Book 7
Hallowed: Southern Watch, Book 8* *(Coming in 2020!)*

The Shattered Dome

(with Nicholas J. Ambrose)
Sci-Fi

Voiceless: The Shattered Dome

The Mira Brand Adventures

Contemporary Urban Fantasy

The World Beneath: The Mira Brand Adventures, Book 1
The Tide of Ages: The Mira Brand Adventures, Book 2
The City of Lies: The Mira Brand Adventures, Book 3
The King of the Skies: The Mira Brand Adventures, Book 4
The Best of Us: The Mira Brand Adventures, Book 5
We Aimless Few: The Mira Brand Adventures, Book 6
The Gang of Legend: The Mira Brand Adventures, Book 7
The Antecessor Conundrum: The Mira Brand Adventure, Book 8* *(Coming in Spring 2019!)*

Liars and Vampires

(with Lauren Harper)
Contemporary Urban Fantasy

No One Will Believe You: Liars and Vampires, Book 1
Someone Should Save Her: Liars and Vampires, Book 2
You Can't Go Home Again: Liars and Vampires, Book 3
In The Dark: Liars and Vampires, Book 4
Her Lying Days Are Done: Liars and Vampires, Book 5
Heir of the Dog: Liars and Vampires, Book 6
Hit You Where You Live: Liars and Vampires, Book 7* *(Coming in Spring 2019!)*

* Forthcoming, Subject to Change